LENT

TOR BOOKS BY JO WALTON

LENT

JO WALTON

A TOM DOHERTY ASSOCIATES BOOK NEW YORK

This is a work of fiction. All of the characters, organizations, and events portrayed in this novel are either products of the author's imagination or are used fictitiously.

LENT

Edited by Teresa Nielsen Hayden

A Tor Book
Published by Tom Doherty Associates
175 Fifth Avenue
New York, NY 10010

www.tor-forge.com

Tor® is a registered trademark of Macmillan Publishing Group, LLC.

Library of Congress Cataloging-in-Publication Data

Names: Walton, Jo, author.
Title: Lent / by Jo Walton.
Description: First Edition. | New York : Tor Book, 2019. | "A Tom Doherty Associates Book."
Identifiers: LCCN 2019006678| ISBN 9780765379061 (hardcover) | ISBN 9781466865723 (ebook)
Subjects: | GSAFD: Fantasy fiction.
Classification: LCC PR6073.A448 L46 2019 | DDC 823/.914—dc23
LC record available at https://lccn.loc.gov/2019006678

Our books may be purchased in bulk for promotional, educational, or business use. Please contact your local bookseller or the Macmillan Corporate and Premium Sales Department at 1-800-221-7945, extension 5442, or by email at MacmillanSpecialMarkets@macmillan.com.

First Edition: May 2019

Printed in the United States of America

0 9 8 7 6 5 4 3 2 1

For Suzanna Hersey:
because Goldengrove still isn't bare.

On the other hand, the worst that will happen is that you will die and go to Hell; but so many have died, and there are so many men of quality in Hell—is there any reason why you should be ashamed to join them?

Niccolō Machiavelli, *The Mandrake*, 1518

Every kingdom divided against itself is brought to desolation, and every city or house divided against itself will not stand. If Satan casts out Satan, he is divided against himself. How then will his kingdom stand?

Gospel according to St. Matthew 12.25–26

Prophecy is not an art, nor (when it is taken for Praediction) a constant Vocation, but an extraordinary and temporary Employment from God, most often of Good men, but sometimes also of the Wicked.

Thomas Hobbes, *Leviathan,* 1651

PART ONE

LENT

CHAPTER 1

Thy kingdom come.

Have the Gates of Hell been opened? Shrieking demons are swarming all over the outside walls of the convent of Santa Lucia, everywhere the light of their lanterns reaches. It's unusual to find so many demons gathered in one place. They are grotesque and misshapen, like all the demons Brother Girolamo has ever seen. Stories abound about demons that can take beautiful human forms for the purposes of seduction and deceit, but if there is truth in them, God has never revealed it to him. He sees only the monstrous and misshapen. Some are almost human, others seem twisted out of animal forms. One, swinging from an unlit sconce beside the doorway, has an eagle's head in place of a phallus—both mouth and beak are open, emitting howls of mocking laughter. Others flaunt all-too-human genitals, of both genders. One, perched above the door, is pulling open the lips of its vagina with both hands. Hands, head, and vagina, are huge, while the legs, arms, and body are tiny. Taken together, the demons remind Girolamo of the gargoyles serving as waterspouts on Milan cathedral, except that those are the colour of innocent stone, while these are the colours of all-too-guilty flesh.

He glances at the two monks flanking him. There is an old pun on the word *Dominicani* where, instead of its true meaning, "follower of the rule of St Dominic," the word is split into two in Latin, "Domini cani," the hounds of God. Brother Silvestro, short and swarthy, the greying hair around his tonsure tightly curled, is like an old grizzled guard dog, and Brother Domenico, tall, broad shouldered, with the pink cheeks of youth, is like an overenthusiastic puppy. Brother Girolamo sometimes sees himself, with his long nose and his ability to sniff out demons, as a Pointer in God's service. "Anything?" he asks.

Brother Domenico frowns, holding his own lantern high. The swinging light and shadows ripple over demon wings, scales, and fur. "I think I can hear something—it sounds like distant laughter. It's very unsettling. I can see why the nuns might be disturbed." A demon with stub-wings and a snake's tail hanging from the eaves pulls open its beak with both hands and roars close by Domenico's head. His peaceful countenance remains unchanged. Another, scaled all over, nips at him with its dog's head. Girolamo makes an irritated gesture towards them, and they shrink away. Good, they still fear him.

Brother Silvestro is gazing intently down at one that is fondling itself with one hand as it tweaks at the edge of Silvestro's black robe with the other. "I don't see or hear anything, but I feel an evil presence here," he says.

The convent echoes with the demonic laughter. Girolamo is more inclined to cry. Domenico and Silvestro are the best of his brothers, the most sensitive to such things. The fiends are all around them, visibly, audibly, palpably present, and Domenico could perhaps hear something, while Silvestro could almost feel a presence. No wonder the forces of Hell gain ground so rapidly in the world when they can do so unobserved. He himself had dismissed the rumours from Santa Lucia at first. Hysteria among nuns is much more common in the world than demonic incursions. He is only here now because the First

Sister was so persistent. Why are the forces of Hell unleashed here? Why is this little Dominican convent on the south bank of the Arno of such interest to demons at this time? It's true that the little commonwealth of Florence is home to many sinners, but he has never seen so many demons gathered anywhere. If he banishes them immediately, he will never know. Better to let them rampage just a little longer while he investigates.

"Is there something here?" Silvestro asks.

"Yes. Just as the First Sister told me, it's full of demons," Girolamo says. He rings the bell, which cuts clearly through the renewed demonic bellowing. "God is truly guiding your senses." If feebly, he does not add. Few people seem aware of the presence of demons at all. Silvestro and Domenico at least feel something. He looks at them as encouragingly as he can, his good honest brothers, each with a lantern in one hand and a flask of holy water clutched tight in the other. They look back at Girolamo with identical expressions of expectant trust.

With a grating sound that rises above the clamour of the demons, a nun draws back bars inside and opens the door a crack. "Thanks be to God. Who's there so late?" she asks, and then recognizes him. "Oh, Brother Girolamo!" She opens the door wide. "Please come in, Brothers."

He strides in, passing under the demon over the door, who leers down at him. Inside is a cloister, stone arches supporting a covered walkway running around a central garden square. It must be pleasant enough ordinarily, but right now it is as demon-infested as the rest of the place. He takes a step to the right, stops, and takes a step to the left. The wardress stares.

"What are you doing?" Domenico asks, his voice full of trust in Girolamo. Domenico is intelligent, if young and overenthusiastic. He is also deeply devout. And he has seen enough to make him believe utterly in Girolamo's powers. Domenico's unswerving faith in him can at times exceed his own faith in himself. He looks into that deep reservoir of faith and trust in his brother's eyes and doubts for a moment—is it right for a man to trust anything human that much? Well, he would with God's aid endeavour to be worthy of Domenico's trust.

"I'm hoping they'll try to prevent me going in one direction, so I'll know where they don't want me to go," he explains. "But they don't seem eager to cooperate. We'll just have to search the place." He turns to the wardress. "Can you take us to the First Sister? I don't want to cause a panic among the nuns by going among the cells unheralded."

"Wait here, I'll wake her," the wardress says, bustling off. He can barely hear her answer over the racket the demons are making. There is clearly something here they don't want him to find. Interesting.

Girolamo sits on the wall of the cloister and folds his hands in his sleeves. The clean green scent of medicinal and culinary herbs rises up around him from the garden behind. His brother monks sit down beside him. The sobbing laughs of the demons rise all around, but they keep away now, scuttling from shadow to shadow catching the lantern-light along the edges of his vision. He ignores them as best he can and waits with what patience he can muster. Patience is not one of the gifts God has granted him. Rather the opposite. He has always burned, as long as he can remember. He burned as a child in Ferrara, wanting answers to questions his father and mother could not answer, and his grandfather only sometimes. Then he burned for education, for a girl once, which he does not like to remember, and then for God and the life of dedication and worship his parents refused him. He fled towards God. But even after he became a Dominican he burned, not so much the hard battle with lust, but with ambition. Pride. The everyday reality of the monastery was a disappointment. He burned then for more purity, more severity, more preaching, more rigor. He burned always with a desire to be closer to God.

He breathes deeply, and tries to identify the scents. Rosemary, comfrey, melissa, something sharp—a little bat-eared demon interrupts him by bellowing in his ear, and he banishes it impatiently with a gesture, drawing it through his fingers back into Hell where it belongs.

The wardress comes scurrying back, the First Sister following behind. He stands up. "It is very late, what brings you now?" the First Sister asks grumpily. Her headgear is a little askew. They keep the divine office properly here. She would have gone to bed after the Night Office at midnight, to sleep until Dawn Praise at three.

"You asked me to come across the river to exorcise your demons," he says, trying to make his voice soft and gentle. He knows his Ferrarese accent sounds always harsh to the Florentines, so sometimes they hear his most ordinary speech as roughly intended. "You told me they plagued you after dark. I am here to rid you of them."

"Brother Girolamo can see demons," Silvestro puts in.

"Do you see them here?" the First Sister asks. "You said it was imagination, hysteria, as if I can't tell the difference after all these years."

"I was mistaken, Mother." He bows his head in humility. "I did trust your belief and experience enough to come to see for myself. You're right. You have an infestation of demons. I could hardly avoid seeing them, they are so many." He points at a dog-faced one with spikes on its back that is peering at the First Sister from behind a pillar. It darts away from his pointing finger. "There is one, and there—" A snaking shape, vanishing as he points at it. "And there, and there." His finger stabs at them as they disappear into the shadows. "I am not surprised your sisters heard them, for they are shrieking and yammering so that my ears ring with their jeering. What puzzles me is why they are here, what's drawing them, or who."

"I'm sure all my girls are well behaved," the First Sister says, drawing herself up.

"It needn't be misbehaviour. They sometimes bother the especially holy, because they hate them more," Girolamo says. "Something must be attracting them here. It may be one of your nuns, or something else. Do you have any new sisters?"

"Not very new—we have four novices, but the newest had been here for months before this began."

"I'd like to walk through the convent before I banish the demons, to see if I can learn why they came," he says.

"It's true that you can banish them?" she asks, relief visible in the sudden relaxation of her shoulders. She isn't an old woman, Girolamo realises, perhaps no older than his own forty years. It was anxiety that had lined her face.

"God has given that power to me," he says, stiffly.

"What do you want to do? Sister Clarice said you wanted to search?" She spares half a glance for the wardress. Girolamo does not.

"I want to find what attracts them. Come with me—we will all search together."

"I cannot see the demons," she says, uncertainly.

"No, but you can see that I and my brothers do nothing wrong," he explains. "Show us the place."

She begins to lead the way along the walkway of the cloister. "This is the chapel," she says, at the first doorway. He holds his lantern high and looks inside. There is an altar, with a single wax candle burning before a plain wooden crucifix. On the wall is a fresco he cannot make out in the wavering light. The floor is tiled in red and black, a repeating pattern. The room smells of the candle, with a faint undertone of incense. There are no demons.

"That's one place clear at least," he says.

"I never feared them in the chapel," the First Sister says, and the wardress nods.

"You need not fear now. They will not harm you when I am with you," he says. Earlier the First Sister had told him a tale of overturned inkpots, spoiled bread, spilled soup, and similar little misfortunes. He felt compassion for her, doing her best to keep her little realm together, as he did his at San Marco, but without his resources.

"Some of the girls have been pinched black and blue, and when I came back from visiting you this afternoon, I was told that Sister Vaggia heard a trumpet blow in her ear as she was coming down the stairs, and tumbled," she says.

"I am with you now," he says, calmly. "Was Sister Vaggia badly hurt?"

The First Sister shakes her head. "Bruises and scrapes. But she could have been killed."

"Not likely," he says. "God does not seem to allow demons power to do true harm." She leads on again. "We don't know why God permits them into the world at all." At the end of the cloister is a set of stone stairs leading upwards, probably the stairs down which the sister had fallen. The foot of the stairs is barred with demons, one like a skeleton, another with one long arm and one short one, another covered with multiple breasts everywhere beneath the chin. They scatter as he advances on them. "But their power to harm seems limited, unless they have human help. Then they can be truly dangerous."

"If they possess someone, you mean?" the First Sister inquires as she leads them up the stairs.

"Yes, or if someone enters into a compact with them."

"Surely no one would do such a thing?" she asks, sounding shocked at the idea.

The demons set up their screeching again, perhaps trying to drown out what he is saying. He raises his voice a little, though he knows none of the others can hear the demonic screams and laughter that hang behind his words. "Strange as it is to think, some will risk eternity for Earthly power."

"And can the demons give such power?" she asks. They follow the First Sister down a corridor lined with cells. He can smell tallow candles, though none are lit now. She opens each door as they come to it, and he looks in. Each one holds a handful of demons, darting away from his light, and a single sleeping nun, on a straw mattress beneath a devotional painting. Some of them sleep quietly, others move restlessly in their sleep.

"They promise it, and sometimes it seems they fulfil those promises," he says, quietly, so as not to wake the sleeping sisters. "You only have to look about you at the world and see who has the earthly power to know that such compacts do occur."

"But God—" Silvestro protests.

"God allows us free will, and allows the demons to work in the world. We have to make an active choice to seek God and what is good, and we have to repeat that choice over and over. If the temptations weren't actually tempting, it wouldn't be much of a choice, would it? The vanities of this world are empty, we know that, but we also know how hard it is to fast when a feast is spread before us. God put Adam in a garden where everything was fitting and there was only a single wrong choice, and still he was tempted and fell. Since then, we have lived in a world where we are surrounded by temptations and there are more wrong choices than right. But we can still win through to God, through his own grace and sacrifice."

Silvestro does not answer. He is looking, as far as Girolamo can tell, at the bare arm of a young nun, flung out in her innocent sleep. The First Sister closes the door and they move on. The demons are everywhere, lurking along the edges of the light, but they seem to pay no more attention to one nun than to another.

"Is there nothing we can do against them?" the First Sister asks, as they come to the end of the corridor.

"Prayer," says Domenico, confidently.

"Prayer works if we are firm in our faith and hold tightly to it," Girolamo clarifies. "If we fear, or waver, as is so easy to do, then they can find a way past. But they hate prayer, and the name of our Saviour."

She opens the door to her own rooms. He notes a writing desk, a prie-dieu, her hastily disturbed bed, and the scent of lavender. The next door is to the novice dormitory, where four girls lie sleeping. "That's Sister Vaggia," the First Sister whispers, gesturing to a big-boned girl with a bruise visible down the side of her face. A demon is sitting boldly on her feet. It has a man's face with a pointed beard, but the breasts of a woman. Everything beneath its waist is covered in scales. It shrieks piercingly and then laughs in Girolamo's face as the girl wakes, terrified.

"Begone," Girolamo says to it. The girl screams then, and the others, less sensitive to demons, wake and scream with her.

"Hush, girls, hush," the First Sister says, uselessly.

The demon slides between Vaggia's lips and speaks with her mouth. "Mock monk, false friar, hell sunk, hell fire, so high, fly free, hell's gate, see be, other brother, burn and smother—"

As soon as he sees the demon disappear into the girl, Girolamo hands his lantern to the wardress and steps forward into the room. His shadow falling before him in the light of the three lanterns looks as monstrous in shape as the demons. His flapping sleeves look like bat wings spread out at his sides as he raises his arms to take hold of the nun's shoulders. He is uncomfortably aware of her young body beneath the thin nightgown covering it. She struggles and strikes out at the crucifix around his neck. "Friar Agira!" she shouts. "Friar Gira-affe, Giraffo! Gyra-tion! Friar Agitator!" She strikes him hard in the chest as she deforms his name over and over.

"Come out of her," he says, more for the comfort of the shrieking nuns than because he needs the words. "Begone, and let Vaggia be, in the name of Father, Son, and Holy Spirit." The demon is peeping out from between Vaggia's lips, and he is about to banish it when Domenico throws his holy water, soaking both Girolamo and Vaggia. He shudders at the cold shock, and the girl shudders too, and the demon bursts from her mouth as if she were vomiting it. It cowers away from Girolamo now that it no longer has the protection of the girl's flesh. He lets Vaggia fall back onto her bed and makes a circle between thumb and forefinger of his left hand. "Back you go, in the name of Jesus Christ our Lord," he says. He feels the power of the holy name thrilling through him. He always feels that power, and so he is sparing of its use and never speaks it lightly. The demon is drawn towards him, compelled. It passes through the gap in his fingers and is utterly gone. The other demons flee the room, but he can hear them still rampaging through the monastery.

"Was that it? Was it Vaggia drawing them?" the First Sister asks, her voice shaking as she speaks. He wonders what she saw. The only things visible to worldly eyes would have been him leaning over Vaggia amid her babbling and the screaming of the other girls, and then Domenico throwing the water.

"No. Though she is especially sensitive and holy and should make a fine sister," Girolamo says. He does not know if the sobbing girl can register what he is saying, but he knows the First Sister will, and the other novices, who are all staring at him wide-eyed. "It used her fear and pain, nothing more. There is something else. Let us go on. Domenico, next time wait until I call for the water. There was no need."

Domenico looks abashed. "I feared for you," he says. "And it worked."

"It drove the demon out of her, yes, but I could have done that without a soaking." He takes his lantern back from the wardress. "Let us move on."

"Stay to comfort the novices and get everyone quiet and back in bed, Clarice," the First Sister instructs the wardress. Doors are open all along the corridor and nuns are peering curiously out. It is probably the most exciting thing that has happened in Santa Lucia for years.

The First Sister leads them in the other direction, down a flight of stairs, through the kitchen, where bread is rising with a strong yeasty smell, then through storerooms, laundries, with a faint scent of harsh soap, and finally through the refectory, where the aroma of last night's bean soup lingers. His sandals squelch as he walks. He sees no more demons, but he hears them still.

"Is that everywhere?" he asks, disappointed, as they come back out into the cloister.

"Everywhere but the library," the First Sister says.

"You have a library," Silvestro asks, surprised. Any Dominican monastery should have a library, but many women's houses do not.

"We each read a book every year, as the Rule of St Benedict dictates," she replies. "We recently had a bequest of additional books from the King of Hungary."

"Show me," he says, excited. He has always loved books, though like his namesake saint, Jerome, he has had to teach himself to hunger only for those that were wholesome.

The library is dark now, but he can see by the shapes of the windows that it would be well lit in daylight. It is not a proper scriptorium such as they have in San Marco, but it is a good room. It smells of leather and good wax candles. The demons completely fill all the space in the room, and the sound they make is deafening, louder than the streets of Florence at the end of Carnival. Whatever is drawing them, it is here. "Stay back," he says to the others. "And no more water unless I call for it." He takes a step inside. The demons withdraw reluctantly, making a clear space around him. He moves to where they are thickest, holding the lantern high on one hand and searching with the other hand outstretched until he touches it. He finds himself reluctant to grasp it, though it seems to be just an ordinary brown-covered book. He draws it forward, ignoring the howls of the demons. They can not speak proper words unless they are encased in flesh, but they keep up their endless gibbering and laughter. He turns the book so he can read the title in the lamplight. Pliny. Strange. He was a secular author, a Roman, a nobody. Not the kind of book you'd expect demons to be drawn to. He opens the cover, and sees that the pages have been hollowed out in the centre to make the book almost a box. In the gap is a flat green stone, about the length of his palm, and as thick as his thumb, with a shallow depression in the centre.

"Now I have you," he says, conversationally. He sets the lantern down on the writing table and moves the book to his right hand. With his left, he makes the circle again. "Begone, you legions of Hell, begone all of you foul fiends, in the name of Jesus Christ!" Rapidly, but one by one, the demons stream through the space between his fingers and vanish. The silence that replaces their clamour beats on his ears. "Thank you, Lord," he says, and wipes his empty hand on his robe before taking up the lantern again.

"Are they gone?" Silvestro asks.

"Yes, all gone. Can you tell?" he asks, hopefully.

"I think so," Silvestro answers. "I sensed some change, as if the wind had changed and blown a more wholesome air."

"And it's quiet now, isn't it?" Domenico asks shyly.

"Yes, yes, it's quiet."

CHAPTER 2

Thy will be done.

APRIL 4TH, 1492

April morning sunlight falls on Girolamo's desk as he makes notes for his next sermon. The heady fragrance of blossoming hazel wafts in through the window. He has been chosen to preach the Lenten sermons in San Lorenzo this year—a great honour, and a tribute to his powers of oratory. He has to admit that producing and delivering sermons daily for forty days does put a strain on him. Lent follows Carnival and goes on until Easter. It is the end of winter and the beginning of spring; it always feels like the longest season of the church's year. He smothers a yawn. After the exorcisms he went straight to Dawn Praise, then slept for three hours before First Prayer at six in the morning. Then at nine he was preaching to a packed church in San Lorenzo. Now he needs to write another sermon for tomorrow. He has to force himself to concentrate on his work.

He has been taught how to put a sermon together—it was literally beaten into him at Bologna. Yet time after time God speaks to him in the pulpit and he finds himself extemporising. He knows it is a sin— and yet he wonders. How can it be a sin to speak of the future without premeditation when God shows it to him so clearly? He sometimes wishes God would reveal what is to come at quiet times, when he could better consider when or whether to share the vision. In the pulpit, speaking, it is easy to be carried away by his own emotion, and the emotion of the enthusiastic congregation. It isn't easy to be politic. He has a reprimand on his desk from Brother Vincenzo, First of the Lombard Congregation of Dominicans, his direct superior. It is a letter which he must answer, humbly, once the sermon for tomorrow is written. And tomorrow he should definitely read his sermon as written, and not get into more pulpit dialogues with God. Yet the people like it, and God obviously likes it or He wouldn't encourage it.

Girolamo sighs. He is First Brother of San Marco, in Florence, and Brother Vincenzo, who hates him, is far away in Bologna, up in Lombardy. But someone, probably one of the lazy Dominican brothers at the rival monastery of Santa Maria Novella, is writing to inform Vincenzo of every lapse Girolamo makes. In any case, he shouldn't defy his superiors, however much he feels the matter of his sermons should be between him and his conscience, between him and God. He has taken a vow of obedience. He prays to Saint Mark for help observing it as he dips his quill. He thinks of the demon the night before, speaking from the lips of the poor bruised nun, the twistings of his name, the crude rhymes: "Other brother, burn and smother . . ."

Domenico comes bursting in, red in the face. Girolamo puts down his pen and turns. "Thanks be to God."

"Thanks be to God," Domenico says, hastily, and goes on without pause, "Brother, the Count is here! He insists on seeing you immediately. I told him you were working, but I can't keep him out."

"That's all right, Domenico, I'll see him." He sets his quill down carefully, then stands and stretches. He is glad of the interruption. Is that a sin? He looks guiltily at the unfinished sermon and prays to the Virgin to intercede for him for forgiveness.

"Should I bring him here?" Domenico looks around Girolamo's room. As First Brother, Girolamo has two cells, in addition to the office through which they are reached. His inmost cell is as austere as those of his brothers, but this outer cell has a writing desk and two wooden chairs made by a carpenter to Girolamo's own design. Here he can work in private, or see one of his brothers. There is a fresco on the wall, painted by the late Brother Angelico. It shows St Dominic embracing the foot of the cross. Every cell has one, each different, and used in the right way they are a fine aid to guide each brother to a true understanding of the sacrifice and the redemption. It is one of Girolamo's more pleasant tasks to consider which brother should have which cell, how the painting of the Garden of Gethsemane might help Brother Tomasso lift his mind from the quotidian details of running the monastery, while the fresco of how the crucifixion was experienced by senses other than sight might help calm Domenico's exuberance. He redistributes the cells every year at Pentecost.

"I'll come down and see him in the parlour." He walks through the outer office, where Brother Tomasso and Brother Silvestro have their heads bent over the accounts, then down through the monastery, quiet at this hour. His brothers are working or praying. Some of the cell doors stand open, showing the frescoes on the walls within, others are closed. Brother Benedetto is scrubbing the floor in the corridor, as he does every day at this time, to help him develop a proper humility. Girolamo nods to him as he passes.

The Count is Giovanni Pico della Mirandola, Count of Concordia, scholar and Platonist, presently under city arrest in Florence, far from his own domain. What does he want with Girolamo today? Could the Count have managed to get into trouble again? It isn't much more than a year since Girolamo had to write to Pope Innocent on the Count's behalf, after he'd been arrested in France for heresy. The theses he had written *were* heretical, of course, technically, but Girolamo agrees with the Count that the proper response of the Church was to engage with his arguments critically, not to try to pretend they hadn't been made. The Count's Nine Hundred Theses might indeed be riddled with error and far too much Plato and Origen—but he is a young man and ready to learn. He has amended several of them already, though the Holy Father, Pope Innocent VIII, has been assured by both

Lorenzo de' Medici and Girolamo himself that the Count is doing nothing in Florence but translating Psalms. Girolamo smiles. In this case, what the Holy Father doesn't know won't hurt. There is no harm in the Count. He is vastly learned in both sacred and secular matters. He has read everything. He has even taught himself Arabic and Hebrew the better to inquire into the nature of God. His errors come not from wickedness or ignorance but from moving too fast. And in some cases he is right and the Inquisition was wrong—on apocatastasis, for instance, which doctrine was endorsed by St Gregory of Nyssa. The Count is a good man. They are friends. Girolamo wants him to become a Dominican, and the Count wants Girolamo to become a Platonist, so they often disagree. But how much joy there is in their disagreement, how much meeting of minds! The Count can follow Girolamo's full thought, as so few can. What a Dominican he will make, one day, Girolamo thinks, smiling, as he walks down the stairs.

He finds the Count sitting on the cloister wall, playing with one of the monastery kittens, letting it pounce on the edge of his embroidered sleeve, which he is trailing on the dirt, where the shoots of vegetables are already poking through. The Count is, naturally, dressed as a nobleman with parti-coloured tights and a doublet with a short green riding cloak tossed back over his shoulder. This is quite an unusual sight in Florence, which has no real nobility, and where the rich and the rulers proudly display their merchant origins in guildsmen's red gowns. Cosimo de' Medici once said that three yards of red cloth make a gentleman. Count Pico, however, was born in a castle in Mirandola, between Venice and Milan, and is a hereditary lord. It's very unusual for someone like him to become a scholar and a philosopher. If he becomes a Dominican it will be even more unusual, but then he will wear a habit like all the brothers.

The Count jumps up when he sees Girolamo and stops smiling. "Brother Girolamo, I come to ask you a favour," he says at once.

Girolamo hesitates. "Shall we sit down and take refreshment and talk about it?" he asks, gesturing towards the door to the parlour, where the brothers entertain visitors.

The Count smiles again, brushing dirt off his sleeve. "No more of your Lenten refreshment, thank you. Let's speak here for a moment, and then if you will, we can talk as you accompany me."

"Accompany you?" Girolamo's heart sinks. It will be hard for him to refuse the Count a favour. In addition to the sums of money the Count has often donated to San Marco, he has this last year personally dowered Girolamo's sister Chiara, back in Ferrara, allowing her to make a good marriage. True, the Count owes Girolamo for his letter to the Pope. But in the web of friendship and alliance and worldly ties that bind everyone together, Girolamo stands deep in the Count's debt, and they both know it. Before God, things are different. It is only God, only Girolamo's status as a Dominican and First Brother of San Marco, that allows the two men to be friends at all. The Count is a scholar, yes, but he is also and always a Count, a rich and powerful nobleman, while Girolamo is no more than the son of a Ferrarese doctor. In the normal way of things, he wouldn't be coming to ask Girolamo a favour, he'd be commanding that he attend on him. And if he did that, it would be much easier, because Girolamo would of course refuse such a command. It is not God but reason that tells Girolamo now what the Count has come to ask. "You want me to visit Magnificent Lorenzo?"

"He's dying," the Count says, bluntly. "There's no doubt now, failing a miracle. His father and grandfather died the same way, Ficino says."

"He has his own confessor." Girolamo feels churlish as soon as the words are out.

"He does, and he has seen him and been given the last rites and been absolved. But I want him to see you. I'm asking you, Girolamo. Please come and bring comfort to a dying man. It isn't about currying favour with the master of Florence, I know how you feel about that. This is about the soul of my friend. He wants to see you."

"I can't refuse you," he says, heavyhearted. "I'll come."

"Thank you! I knew you would."

"Are you sure he wants to see me?" he asks, summoning young Brother Leonardo from his weeding with a snap of his fingers.

"Yes, I am sure."

"But he said—" Girolamo breaks off and gives rapid instructions to Brother Leonardo. He makes excuses to God as he does it. He'll be back by Twilight Prayer. Silvestro can oversee things until then. He'll finish the sermon before morning, and the letter to Brother Vincenzo can wait another day. Visiting the dying is a more urgent duty.

"It was you who refused to see Lorenzo," the Count says, as they walk out of San Marco's gates together.

"God is my master."

"Yes. All Lorenzo said was that a stranger had come to live in his house and didn't want to visit him."

"San Marco isn't his house," Girolamo says, angry again at hearing the words. He prays God's forgiveness for the sin of wrath.

"Fifty years ago, Lorenzo's grandfather, Cosimo de' Medici, paid to have San Marco rebuilt, and had the Pope give it to the Dominicans from the order who had it before," the Count says, shrugging. "And he had a cell in San Marco, where he would come to pray."

"Cosimo de' Medici had himself painted as Saint Cosmas in the most overdecorated cell in the monastery," Girolamo says. "And if he paid for the monastery, he also put his balls all over it, like a dog spraying every street corner. And for all his famed piety, he said the city can't be governed by saying Our Father."

The Count glanced up at where they were passing under a Medici crest featuring the eight circular balls that were their symbol. "Well, whatever Cosimo did, all of Florence is Lorenzo's house."

"He thinks it is. Florence is a free commonwealth still, ruled by the Senate, the elected lords. Lorenzo isn't a king or a duke. Florence isn't a tyranny." Girolamo scowls as they come out into the sunlight.

"Lorenzo could have had himself made duke, or king, if he'd wanted to. He didn't because he too values the forms of the commonwealth. But you can't have it both ways. You can't both despise him for being nobility and then throw it in his teeth that he isn't!"

A pair of horses are saddled and waiting, with one of the young boys who hang around the city hoping for work holding their bridles.

He grins at the Count, showing a gap in his teeth. The Count flips him a coin, which he catches deftly before it falls into the dirt of the street, whose usual stink is made worse by the fresh droppings of the horses, not yet trodden in.

"We're riding to Careggi?" Girolamo asks. "It's what, an hour's walk?"

"Don't worry, they're my horses," the Count says. "I know you don't want to take favours from the Medici."

"I don't want to be bought by them," he says, swinging himself up into the saddle of the nearest, a roan mare. The skirts of his black robe ride up his hairy thighs, and he adjusts it hastily. It is a long time since he has ridden. "It's simony."

"Three days after Leo de' Medici celebrated his consecration as cardinal at sixteen isn't a good time for me to pretend the Medici don't know anything about simony." The Count, whose clothes are designed with riding in mind, mounts gracefully, clucks to his horse, and they set off. "But Lorenzo wasn't trying to buy you, or pay for your office. He just wanted to know you. He's not what you think."

"He thinks Florence is his house, and that he owns everyone and everything in it. He has you all jessed with silken chains, but you belong to him all the same. You're a rich man, a titled man, and he captured you with favours—Pope Innocent didn't agree to free you because I wrote to him on your behalf, but because Magnificent Lorenzo did, and guaranteed to keep you safely mewed here." The Count screws up his face in silent protest, but does not speak, so Girolamo goes on. "Your friend Angelo Poliziano he bought more openly, with patronage, a villa, a job as a tutor, money to live on while he writes his poetry. It's true Lorenzo doesn't rule with soldiers like the Bentivoglios in Bologna or the Sforza in Milan—except when he hires their soldiers for his wars, the way he did after the Pazzi Conspiracy. He doesn't rule with laws like Trajan or Solomon, either. He rules with favours and patronage and gold coins—buying a man's freedom here, giving another work there. Writing ribald songs for Carnival and drinking in the streets with the wool workers. Having a Platonic symposium in his villa with the scholars. Paying for the education of an orphan who will be his man when he grows up. Giving donations to monasteries and priests to buy influence in the church. Commissioning work from poets and painters and sculptors and then using the results to reflect his glory and show how magnificent he is until everyone is bound up together in his net."

"You say that as if it's a terrible thing, but what's the alternative? Everyone lonely and lost and alone? No help for me when I cross the Church? Angelo to starve to death when he loses his parents at age ten? The poets and painters to work dying wool or carrying bricks because they have no patron? Yes, Lorenzo looks out for his people, as his father and grandfather did. He rules with a gentle hand. If he wants something in return, all right. If he wants the dedication of my book, or Angelo's, so that it reflects his glory as well as ours, what harm? He is magnificent. He gives so much to the city. He cares about Florence. The city is his house, and we are his family who live in it."

Girolamo is suddenly aware they are talking about a dying man, and that whatever Lorenzo has been and done, he will be doing it no more. "I don't deny that he cares about Florence, but—"

A sudden loud clatter of hammering on stone interrupts him. A church is being rebuilt. Florence is a perpetual building site. People are always pulling down old houses to build new workshops and palaces, restoring churches that have fallen into disrepair, and of course, adding to the cathedral. Brunelleschi's huge dome has been in place for sixty years, but cathedrals are never truly complete. The façade is still rough and unfinished, and of course there is endless decoration to be done. The Office of Works is always commissioning something, or unveiling something. If it isn't the cathedral, there'll be a new chapel or a restoration or a new altarpiece at one of the neighbourhood churches, or the guilds will be setting up a new statue in a niche at the Guild church of Orsanmichele. Girolamo has sometimes questioned the purpose of these ceaseless building works. Are they for the glory of God, or the glory of the donors? When Giovanni Rucellai builds a new palace, it exalts his family, in addition to the practical purpose of giving them somewhere to sleep and work. When he pays to put a new façade on this neighbourhood church, with the family coat of arms prominently displayed, is his purpose the same? Girolamo doesn't know. It's the same with Cosimo's motives in restoring San Marco. William of Ockham wrote that going to church to display yourself and your piety was a sin, while going to church out of love of God was a moral act, but the two are indistinguishable to any Earthly witness. Old Giovanni Rucellai wants to give to God, and to save his usurious soul from Hell, and to make people think well of his family, all at the same time. Only God can judge the complex motives of a human soul.

The beautification of churches certainly does raise souls towards God. Many among Girolamo's flock have told him how a particular picture or statue has touched their hearts, spurring their devotion. As so often, Girolamo wants lines as straight and clean as a birch sapling, where human motives turn out to be as tangled as a bramble thicket. He wants sacred art to be more devotional and less self-aggrandizing. And he wants it to be displayed in churches for the benefit of everyone, there to stir up souls, as his words stir them. But only the rich can afford to pay for it, and he distrusts them and their motives. They put naked goddesses on their walls at home, and Madonnas on the altars. Still, he wants the churches and monasteries restored and beautified, not left to crumble disregarded.

They ride past the building work and are soon at the city gates, which are standing open. The single guard is sitting comfortably eating a bowl of soup. The breeze brings Girolamo the scent of it, leek and barley, good Lenten fare. It makes him hungry, but he is fasting until evening, and will then take only bread. The guard glances up from his meal and waves a hand casually at the Count, barely glancing at Girolamo as they go through and out into the countryside beyond the walls.

Whenever he sees the Tuscan countryside Girolamo is freshly struck by how beautiful and well cultivated it is, compared to Lombardy and Emilia-Romagna. Here vines and olives grow in orderly profusion, with wheat and vegetables and fruits in their proper places. Each little farm has its pigs, sheep graze on the hillsides, cows in the meadows along the river. This is country that has not known war in his lifetime, unlike the lands further north. What wars Florence has fought she has kept away from her own farmland. But war is coming, God has told him so. A cloud passes over the sun, and the shadow of war and cloud together darken his vision.

"Did God speak to you?" the Count asks, turning around and looking into his face.

Girolamo nods, realising he had pulled his mount to a halt without thinking.

"Was it about Lorenzo?"

Girolamo shakes his head and jerks the reins for his horse to catch up. "No. It was the war. War is coming, the Sword of the Lord sweeping over the Alps, soldiers settling like a plague of locusts across this pleasant countryside."

"Soon?" the Count asks.

"Soon, yes, but not immediately."

"In our lifetimes?"

"I will see it, but you—" He nudges his mare to a trot.

"I won't?" The Count's horse keeps up easily.

Girolamo is ten years older than the Count. "I don't know why I said that, but God was speaking through me. You won't see it. But death can lie anywhere, in any chance. Plagues and other sickness, accident, war, riots. It doesn't mean the Pope will burn you."

"An angry husband is what has come closest to killing me so far," the Count says, smiling, though Girolamo can see he is making an effort to keep his voice light. "Lorenzo cleared that up for me too, though she had to go back to the dolt, more's the pity."

"Yes, crossing the rich and powerful, that's a shortcut to the grave." They pass a little church and start to ride uphill, through beech and chestnut trees leafing out in spring green. Under them, the rough ground is sprouting poppies and blue anemones. They have to ride in single file now, the Count ahead.

"You did say soon, though," the Count says, his voice raised to reach Girolamo over the sound the horses make clopping through last year's leaves.

"Soon in God's time. I never know the world's timing of these things, unless they are pressing on me, imminent, like a summer storm. This wasn't imminent. You could have ten years." He means to sound reassuring, but he realises as he speaks that a promise of ten years wasn't much to a man not yet thirty. "You should take the habit now. I would like to call you Brother Giovanni while I can. And—"

"Always back to that." The Count's voice floats back, light. "You can call me Giovanni and brother as much as you choose. I have asked you and asked you, but always you stick to Count, as if you loved titles instead of hating them as you say."

"They all call you Pico," he says, sounding peevish even to himself.

"It's because I'm tall," the Count says, still lightly.

"Do penance, and return to God, become a Dominican and put your talents in God's hand, as I have," Girolamo says, getting back to what is important, not his friend's form of address but the eternal safety of his soul.

"I should finish my book, and we should work together on our project against the astrologers." They ride on in silence for a moment. "One wastes so much time. I must try to sort things out with my family in Mirandola too, get things straightened up there. And there's Isabella. She's a good girl. I know you don't think so, but she is. I'd have to make arrangements for her. I couldn't just abandon her to take vows."

It isn't a promise, but it is the closest he has come. "I don't disapprove at all of you making arrangements for your doxy," Girolamo says, meaning it. "Too many men ruin young girls and then abandon them with nothing to turn to but prostitution. It's one reason why there are so many whores. But what can a poor girl do, when she can't go home and no one will marry her? There are not enough convents for Magdalens. Everyone rails against fallen women, as if they have been sinning on their own. It is the men who lead them astray, and what are they supposed to do afterwards? It would be better if you'd never taken up with her, but since you have, it's much better for you to do something for her."

"Maybe I could set Isabella up with a shop, selling ribbons and cloth," the Count muses. "Maybe she'd enjoy running a business. She's certainly smart enough. But it would take time, and bribes, and she'll cry if she thinks I don't love her anymore."

"We know not the day or the hour," Girolamo reminds him.

"You've told me that—no, you're right, all that was just as true before. And surely if I am to take vows, I should do it for the love of God and because I think it right, not from fear of death?"

"Yes," he says, uncompromisingly. "But you do love God, and we both know it."

The Medici villa comes into in sight now as they come out of the trees. With its white walls, red roof, and large windows, it is very much a villa in the ancient Roman style; not a castle, but it is defensible. There are no windows in the lower floors. Again, he is aware that an army will be coming, a huge army, and after them another army. God is showing him another vision of the future. "The Sword of the Lord," he says. "The New Cyrus will come over the Alps. He will unsheathe the Sword of the Lord. Rome will fall, be sacked, blood will run in the streets. Books will burn and bones of saints be ground underfoot. Florence too—" He stares at the Count, who has reined in beside him. "Florence will be sacked too, unless I can prevent it. So many dead, so many innocents."

"Will God let us change what you see?" the Count asks.

Girolamo slides down from his horse, simply to feel the comfort of the ground beneath his feet. "Yes," he says. The dry leaves crunch under his sandals and the scent of them fills his nostrils. The roan snuffles at his shoulder. "Yes. The future is like a great river sweeping down on us inexorably, but there are eddies. Little things can turn them one way or another. We have free will. There are times where our actions can make a difference. I can save Florence, I know it." He pushes the mare's nose away and takes the reins to lead her on.

"And Rome?" The Count is still mounted, and seems to be looking down from a great height.

"I have never seen Rome. I will try to save it. But I think whatever I do, that sack can only be postponed. I can hear those cries very loudly. All the currents of the river sweep on to that destruction."

The Count dismounts now, and they walk on together, leading the horses. They jostle together, and the stirrups clang. "So could you stop the Sword of the Lord from coming?" the Count asks.

"No. I don't think so. I don't think I could or anyone could. I don't think there's anything I could possibly do that would stop that now. That's the floodtide. But once he comes to purify Italy, I can stop him burning Florence. That's an eddy. Perhaps I can lead Florence to the path of righteousness." Girolamo is trembling with the force of the vision. He can see boys in white processing around the Palazzo della Signoria singing hymns, men and women in plain clothes praying in the familiar streets.

"Who is it that you call the Sword? The Emperor? The King of France?"

Girolamo shakes his head. "I don't know. A king from the north. One barbarian leader is the same as another to prophecy. This is the new Cyrus, sweeping down over the Alps with his forces, all Italy falling down before like ripe wheat to a sickle."

"But you could prevent him destroying Florence, though it lies in his path?"

"Perhaps." He is suddenly aware how rich and tempting Florence is, and how vulnerable to the kind of great army he knows is coming. The city is a valuable prize, one of the richest cities in Europe, but he can protect her. "If enough will listen to me. Perhaps I can lead the city to righteousness. I have seen the city given into my charge."

"Then could you lead Jerusalem to righteousness?" the Count asks.

Girolamo laughs aloud, jolted out of his vision. "You always have the most extravagant ideas!"

"It's a real place in the world. Our crusading ancestors went there. You and I could go to Venice and take ship. I have the money, and I can't imagine a better use for it. We'd be in the city of Jerusalem less than a month from now. You could lead it to righteousness, and the whole world would follow." The Count is so enthusiastic he is almost bouncing on the soles of his feet, scattering dead leaves and bruising the wildflowers.

Girolamo is sorry to have to shake his head. "God has put Florence into my hand. I am First Brother of San Marco. I can't just leave. God wants me here. Here is where I can make a difference. It's so hard for any one man to make a difference. You've found that already. You were young, brilliant, rich, and a count, with solid scholarship and innovative ideas, but what could you do but put your head into a noose?"

The Count sighs and kicks at a white stone, which rolls a few paces and then sticks in the mud. "Could you win back Constantinople from the Turk?"

"I don't know anything about it. I'd be just one more madman raving on a street corner. Here—this is where God wants me, Giovanni." Sure of himself and filled with fervour, he dares to take the Count's free hand. The Count squeezes his hand in return, and lets go.

"Then maybe you will make Florence the New Jerusalem," the Count says.

"Yes," he says, thrilled to hear this deepest dream spoken aloud by another. "Maybe I will. The City of God. There is a way from here to there. I do not know if I have strength to take it."

Then they come into the courtyard and a groom takes the horses. They scrape the mud off their shoes at the door, and another servant bows them inside.

CHAPTER 3

On Earth.

APRIL 4TH, 1492

He had thought of the villa at Careggi as an overgrown farmhouse in the Roman style, but once they are inside, Girolamo realises that it is better thought of as a country palace. The Count leads him through richly furnished rooms smelling of wax candles and cinnamon and rose petals. It isn't as big as San Marco, but San Marco houses a whole community, close to a hundred monks drawn together for the glory of God. This villa is dedicated to nothing beyond the worldly glory of the house of Medici. It is vanity, conceit, vainglorious trumpeting of empty earthly pomp. A marble faun's head leers at him from a polished pedestal. It is harder not to flinch from it than it had been before the demons. The demons feared him. This statue fears nothing.

Girolamo follows close behind the Count, who apparently knows his way around. They see no one but servants, who greet them courteously, until at last they go up a great flight of stairs and turn into a large airy room, frescoed with pagan pastoral scenes. The big rumpled bed is empty, but the rest of the room is full, even after the servant courteously withdraws. A doctor and his assistant are compounding something at a table by the window, grinding with a mortar and pestle that makes a sharp scraping noise and fills the room with the acrid scent of pepper and poppy seeds. A man is writing, bent over a desk. Another is sitting in a chair with an open book on his lap, but making no pretence of reading. A well-dressed young woman is sitting sewing beside the bed. She looks up at them alertly, biting off her thread. Angelo Poliziano is pacing to and fro. He's a tiny man in scholar's robes, a poet famous all over Italy for his translations of Homer and his original poetry in Italian. He works as one of Lorenzo's secretaries, and was once tutor to his children. He turns to the Count as they come in. "Giovanni! You found him!" The Count smiles at him, his face full of fondness.

"Yes, Angelo, I found him."

"I am here," Girolamo says.

"Thanks be to God," Angelo says, taking his hands.

He knows Angelo—the man comes to his sermons and has visited him at San Marco—but they are not such good friends that this could pass for a normal greeting. "Will you take refreshment?" Angelo asks. "Wine? Beer? Some bread and cheese?"

Girolamo shakes his head. "I'm fasting today," he says.

"Water, then?" Angelo offers.

The man in the chair leaps to his feet, paying no heed to the book which falls to the floor. "Another priest?" he says. "What are you doing here? They gave my father absolution yesterday."

So this was Piero, Magnificent Lorenzo's heir. Girolamo doesn't think much of him. His face isn't attractive, and his petulant expression is less attractive still. Petty and spoiled, he thinks. Piero is only twenty years old, but is married already to a Roman aristocrat, an Orsini like his mother. People say he thought himself too good for Florence. When you think you're too good to marry your neighbours, you start expecting them to be your servants. Lorenzo's mother and grandmother had been from Florentine merchant families, but the Medici thought themselves beyond that now. Or so Girolamo has

riches do not help, not now. They can do nothing more for Magnificent Lorenzo. He only hopes they have not damned him already. Angelo and the Count seem concerned in a way he does not quite understand.

They lead him out onto a big upper balcony, large enough to be considered a small room, but open to the air on two sides. Even here, essentially out of doors, the walls are painted with nymphs and shepherds. The roof extends out above them, and there are floor-to-ceiling pillars on the two open sides, perfectly proportioned. Between them he can see the lush farmlands falling away, and the distant hills. He takes it all in at a glance, for it is the dying man that compels his attention. He is lying on a small bed, and another man sits beside him on a stool, reading aloud in gentle tones. The man on the bed glows with a clear blue light, so bright that Girolamo almost wants to shield his eyes against it. The colour is serene, celestial, the deep clear blue of a midsummer evening. The Count and the poet do not appear to notice the glow. The man reading breaks off as they come out. The word he stops on is *Anima,* the Latin word for soul.

"Lorenzo, Marsilio, let me make known to you Brother Girolamo of San Marco," Angelo says formally.

The little man introduced as Marsilio sets down his book carefully, marking his place with a ribbon, then stands and bows. He has silver hair beneath a red hat, and a lined face. Girolamo recognises him at once: he is Marsilio Ficino, a teacher and translator of Plato. Rumour says he is a sodomite. He is another man like Angelo that the Medici have educated and moulded into their creature. Girolamo has seen him before, in church, but they have not spoken. He bows now in return.

"Could you try to talk to Piero? He's very upset," Angelo says to Marsilio. "It's getting harder and harder to keep him away."

Marsilio nods. "I'll do my best," he says, more loudly than he had been reading. "Or should we let him see his father now?"

"I'll speak to him soon," Lorenzo says. "Let me have a little while more in peace."

Marsilio nods and goes in.

Girolamo looks down at the man on the bed. He is ordinary, dark hair streaked with grey, a beaky nose, a face much like his daughter's, but worn with pain. Not old, middle-aged only, but certainly dying. There is nothing unusual about him except the celestial light shining from him. "Stay, Pico," Lorenzo says. "And you stay too, my recording angel."

The Count stands at the foot of the bed. Angelo walks over to the wall of pillars and stands staring out over the countryside. His head only just comes over the balustrade.

"Sit down, First Brother," Lorenzo says, looking up at Girolamo. He starts, realising he had been standing there like an ox, not speaking or moving. "Not what you expected?" Lorenzo asks. His tone is playful, mocking.

"Not at all," he says, and lowers himself to the stool where Marsilio had been sitting beside the bed. This close, he can smell the sickly odour of the dying man's skin, and the jasmine scent they have used to try to cover it. He has read of an odour of sanctity that attends dying saints, but there is no sign of that.

"I just wanted to get a look at you," Lorenzo goes on.

"I came because the Count of Concordia expressed concern for your soul," he says, perching uncomfortably on the stool, drawing in his knees and elbows, forcing his shoulders not to hunch. If he stays here long he will have a backache.

Lorenzo looks serenely up at him. "But now you're not concerned?" he suggests.

"I don't know what to think. There are snares and deceptions in this world." He has seen many dying people, many who had received the last rites, but never anything at all like this. What is it? It isn't a halo, at least not as portrayed in art. And why is it blue? He looks at the Count, who is staring at Lorenzo, and then back down at the glow. "Is this from God?"

"I am from God, you are from God, we are all from God."

"It is not from Hell," he says, feeling sure of it, because the things of Hell shrink from him in fear, and this light continues to shine undimmed from the dying man.

The Count lets out a sigh of relief. "You are speaking of the glow? I can see it, a little, and Marsilio sees it clearly." What a Dominican the Count will make, how useful it will be to have another at his side who can perceive such things, Girolamo thinks. "It is from God. I thought so. The colour—everything. But I feared—the world is full of deceptions. I knew you'd be able to tell. That's why I brought you."

Angelo crosses himself without turning.

Girolamo turns his attention to Lorenzo. "But what are you, banker, merchant, prince, to have this vouchsafed?" This is a miracle even greater than a camel passing through the eye of the needle.

"A man, only a man."

Girolamo bows his head. He wishes now he had come before, to know how long this glow, this miracle, has been shining around Lorenzo. Had his stubborn pride, always his worst sin, kept him from knowing a saint on Earth? He prays to Saint Lucy that his eyes might be opened, and to the Merciful Virgin for forgiveness. "How long have you been like this?" he asks.

"I have been like this on occasion for some time, but continuously only since I have been dying."

"Saints sometimes have a visible glow, in the *Golden Legend*," he says, tentatively.

"And philosophers in Diogenes Laërtius," the Count adds.

"Will you give me your blessing?" Lorenzo asks.

"If you live, you must give up usury and manipulation of the state," he says, as he has been planning to say.

An incipient smile becomes a grimace of pain on the dying man's face. "If I live, I will." They both know he will not live. "Take care of my city, Brother Girolamo."

Girolamo wants to protest, to say, as he had said to the Count, that Florence is God's city. And yet, as Lorenzo lies there dying he is resplendent with the pure light of God's love and favour. The glow shines through him like sunlight through the Virgin's robe in a stained glass window. Who is he to shun a man granted a miracle of this kind? Furthermore, in asking him to care for Florence, Lorenzo is showing that he knows that it will fall to Brother Girolamo's part to look after the city in future, which means God must have given the prophetic gift to him, as He has to Girolamo. Their eyes meet. "I will take care of it."

"And take care of Pico, and Angelo, and my children too, so far as you may."

The Count is openly weeping.

"I wish I had known you," Girolamo says, in all honesty. He has never known anyone else who had any gift of prophecy. They could have had such fascinating conversations.

"Too late, Brother," Lorenzo says, shaking his head a little.

He leans forward, feeling his back twinge at the motion. He moves the book that Marsilio has left lying on the bed. He had thought it was a testament, now he sees that it is a volume of Plato.

"Marsilio read that at Cosimo's deathbed too," the Count says, taking it up gently.

"It's good to give comfort," Lorenzo says, and Girolamo does not know whether he means that hearing Plato was a comfort to him or that reading it was a comfort to Marsilio.

"Plato saw as much of the truth as anyone could by the light of human reason, and it is good to have independent confirmation of these things," Girolamo says, looking from Lorenzo to the Count, who has convinced him of this much in their conversations. "But it is only through divine revelation and the sacrifice of our Lord that we can be saved."

"There is no contradiction," the Count says, very confidently.

Girolamo can't argue, not with the divine light so clear before him. He sighs and sets his hand on Lorenzo's forehead. The light does not change, not even a flicker, nor does he feel anything beyond the natural heat of human flesh. He must have hurt Lorenzo inadvertently though, because the dying man flinches for an instant at the touch, then stills himself and closes his eyes as Girolamo begins to speak the blessing. As Girolamo straightens and makes to rise, Lorenzo's eyes open again. His face looks troubled.

"I will pray for you," Lorenzo says.

"And I for you," Girolamo replies, surprised.

As he begins to stand, he sees there is another bowl of precious stones beside the bed. These are flat, and some of them are carved with words and faces. He stops, half bent, then sits again. Inside his habit he still has the copy of Pliny with the green stone he picked up in Santa Lucia the night before. He has prayed and wondered, but has no indication why the demons were wailing around it, or what he is meant to do with it. "Perhaps God sent something for you," he says. "You know about stones."

"I believe some of them have virtues, yes," Lorenzo says, cautiously. "Marsilio knows more."

"Last night I found something," he says. "I think it may have been meant for you." He stumbles his way through an explanation of the nuns, the demons, and the library. Angelo comes over to join them and listens. Lorenzo smiles through his pain when Girolamo gets to the moment he was soaked with holy water. At last he draws out the book, opens it, and sets the green stone on Lorenzo's glowing palm.

"Oh!" Lorenzo says, closing his fingers on it. "I never thought I should see this."

"What is it?" the Count asks. "Is it the stone of Titurel?"

"It has many names . . . and none of them matter now, I think," Lorenzo says. "Marsilio would like to see it . . . but not now. No. The time may come. This is for you, Brother. It came to you, and you can use it. You should keep it with you and take it when you go. This could—" He stops, and shakes his head a little. "I may not speak. Keep it with you. Remember the harrow, and remember me, and the love of God."

Girolamo isn't likely to forget the last. He takes back the stone and turns it curiously in his fingers. The stone of Titurel? Some Platonic significance that Marsilio Ficino would appreciate? But meant for him? It is translucent, and the central hollow fits his thumb. He slips it back into the book, and the book inside his habit.

CHAPTER 4

As it is.

APRIL 2ND, 1493

Bologna reeks of failure and disappointment, though to others it might seem no more than the usual miasma of tanners and dyers. He has always come here with such high hopes, and every time they have been crushed. He understands now that this is not where he was meant to be, is not the city God has given to him, which was always waiting just over the mountain passes. Yet it is the mother city of the Dominicans, where St Dominic himself preached and taught, and where his sainted body rests.

Girolamo sighs as he makes his way with his brothers through the narrow Bolognese streets between the Dominican mother house and the cathedral. Most of Bologna is built of brick, and all the buildings are built so that the upper stories hang out over the sides of the streets, supported by mismatched columns, making porticoes to protect the citizens from rain and sun. It's an excellent design, and he wishes it would spread elsewhere. But today it does little against a clinging pervasive March drizzle. Very little has changed in Bologna since he first saw it eighteen years ago. It is a city of warm terra-cotta, with surprising faces peering out of the brickwork here and there, reminding him of an infestation of demons.

He supposes he must have grown used to the racket of building in Florence, to the fact that there is always something changing in the streets. Bologna seems sleepy in comparison. Bologna, Ferrara, and Milan have princes who rule them. The princes might choose to build, to glorify themselves, their families, their cities, and perhaps first or perhaps as an afterthought, God. But they do not compete to do so, not within their city. In Florence the Medici run things, yes, but the city has the forms of a commonwealth still. Many families have wealth and dignity. The Medici say who gets to have their names in the purses, but nine names still get drawn out every two months, and those nine men drawn rule the city as the Eight First Men and the Standard-Bearer of Justice; the elected lords, they get to dress in crimson and ermine and live on the top floor of the Senatorial Palace. The honour of governance is shared, if not the real power. Lorenzo ruled, as his son Piero does now, but others share the appearance of ruling—and even do some of the work. There are fifty-four First Men of Florence every year, and they can point at things they have achieved in their times of office. They are for the most part Medici supporters, and they won't do anything the Medici don't want, but they retain pride and a measure of independence, they are not puppets. They think of themselves as only a little lower than the Medici. They compete with the Medici and with each other, and the city and the poor profit by their competition.

In Bologna, on the other hand, there is a Bentivoglio prince, and the rich families are no more than his courtiers. Courtiers might compete to please their prince, they do not compete with him. In cities with princes, church and civic renewal has became an area reserved for princes. Despite three generations of Medici dominance, Florence is still much closer to a free commonwealth, as Rome had been before Julius Caesar. The Serene Republic of Venice is closer still, with its Great Council and elected Doge. Venice impressed Girolamo when he was there last winter. There is much to learn from it.

Grizzled old Brother Silvestro, who has come to Bologna with him, puts a hand on Girolamo's sleeve. He stops. While he'd been off in his own thoughts, their third companion, Brother Antonino, one of the Bolognese community, has paused to gossip with a rosy-cheeked woman selling salt fish. Girolamo gives him a reproving glance, which Antonino ignores. That would not have happened in Florence. Two more weeks and it will be Easter. Once Christ is safely risen for another year, he can go home. It is Florence that is his earthly home now, not the motherhouse in Bologna let alone his own mother's house in Ferrara. Brother Antonino is lazy, and far too easily distracted. If he'd been under Girolamo's discipline at San Marco he'd soon have learned to conquer his faults. Here in Bologna, under Brother Vincenzo's slack arrangements, such things are left uncorrected.

Bologna has always disappointed him. The first time he came, Girolamo walked here from his father's house in Ferrara, leaving before dawn, arriving as the gates were closing at dusk. He felt himself exalted at every step, even as his soft feet blistered. His whole being was filled with longing to be accepted at the monastery St Dominic himself had founded. He had been twenty-two, young enough to imagine taking Dominican vows would be the fulfillment of all his dreams.

It wasn't so much fear of his father's wrath as of his mother's repining and his sisters' tears that caused him to walk away without warning, leaving them a letter of justification. Even now, in her old age and widowhood, his mother remains utterly set on worldly advantage. His father had wanted him to become a doctor, in the family tradition. While that isn't his vocation, it isn't a despicable one. He worked hard at the university of Padua. He learned there that it was souls he wanted to cure, not merely flesh. He tried to explain it in the letter, and perhaps his father understood. His mother never would. She still just wants him to attain rank and riches and everything he most abhors. She doesn't mind how he does it. She wouldn't have objected to him taking orders if he'd become a typical cleric, paying and accepting bribes, rising in wealth and status, wallowing in luxury. She'd have been delighted to have him one of the rich cardinals selling indulgences while promoting his bastards left and right. She can't understand his asceticism, his devotion to God, his loathing of carnality and opulence. If he had become a doctor she'd have wanted him to be one like his grandfather, cynically prescribing warm wine to dyspeptic courtiers for fat fees. He prays to the Virgin for his mother's soul, and trusts in God's mercy.

Certainly it would have been braver to face his family before he left, to explain his vocation to their faces, he admits that. He was a coward. He fled from enduring the interminable reproaches. Letters are hard enough to bear. Even now he flinches when a letter arrives from Ferrara in the familiar accusing script. He can obey the commandment to honour his parents more easily at a distance. He made no farewells when he left to walk to Bologna. He remembers trembling as he knocked on the portal of the Dominican monastery, longing to escape to God, to give his life into God's hands. If only it had been that simple.

He sighs again. His novitiate was a disappointment, lacking in severity, discipline, and the true Christian fellowship he had longed for. Even from the first, he had attempted to reform the Dominicans from within, to bring them back to St Dominic's original strictures. More fasting, more penance, more prayer, more rigor. Many of his brothers want it, but some do not. He has support, especially now at San Marco, but he has also made enemies. There are always people who like to be lazy and comfortable while still thinking well of themselves. First Brother Vincenzo is one of those. Girolamo has discomforted him on all levels, and he refuses to forgive him. And Vincenzo is not just First Brother of the monastery in Bologna, as Girolamo himself is at San Marco. Vincenzo heads the whole Lombard Dominican Congregation. Only Cardinal Carafa, the head of the whole order, stands above Vincenzo, but Vincenzo stands between him and Girolamo.

Brother Antonino comes back, and they begin walking again. "It's wrong for a Dominican brother to even give the appearance of flirting," Girolamo says, reprovingly.

"I wasn't," Antonino protests. "She had some important news."

"Gossip," Silvestro mutters.

"No! The fishwife says that a Genoese captain went out of Aragon and has discovered a new route to the Indies, westward, across the Atlantic!"

"Nonsense," Girolamo says, crisply, walking a little faster. "It's too far. It would take months to sail all that way."

"Well, it did take months, but he got there and came back, she says," Antonino retorts.

"Praise be to God," Brother Silvestro says, and Girolamo echoes him automatically, trying to put such trivialities as new trade routes out of his mind.

Girolamo's second sojourn in Bologna, three years ago, was even worse than his novitiate. Dominicans are the Order of Preachers. St Dominic founded them to preach, to spread the word of God. The brothers are trained and sent out to preach, and those thought capable of it return to Bologna for a year of additional training. Those deemed worthy in that year stay on and earn their degree as Master of Sacred Theology, then teach and continue to learn and preach and rise in the order. The unworthy get sent out again. It is never openly called failure, but they all know what that winnowing means. Despite his dedication and scholarship, despite the fact that his Latin is good enough that he was asked to help teach his brothers from the very first, Girolamo was dismissed with the second rate. Brother Vincenzo was in charge, and in his additional year they had clashed on everything from Aristotle to the penitential use of scourging. Vincenzo's decision was final, and Girolamo was sent away ignominiously. He understands now that it was God's will, part of God's plan for him. But at the time, when Vincenzo said scornfully that he was not fit to be a Master of Sacred Theology, this was not yet clear. He left Bologna that time filled with chagrin, his eyes burning and his heart swollen so it almost filled his throat, so much so that it was difficult for him to swallow. Even now, remembering, and knowing it was God's test, he feels a little of that choking feeling return.

This Lenten season he would have preferred to stay in Florence, in his own priory of San Marco. But as always he is obedient to his superiors in the Order. They called him to Bologna to preach the gruelling schedule of Lenten sermons in the cathedral. His preaching is, thanks be to God, the same as ever. But the Bolognese are different, less attentive, than his flock in Florence. Novelty can be a good thing in a preacher, he understands that. A congregation will listen to a new voice when an old one might have gone stale through familiarity and repetition. That is part of the logic of the Dominican rotation, especially when Dominicans preach to souls whose parish priests might be ignorant or uneducated. But there is also an advantage to staying in one place long enough that thoughts could build—not just in his own mind but in the minds of his listeners. In Florence, he does not have to go back to the beginning every time. Many people come to his sermons often enough that they remember what he had said on a subject before. He only has to remind them. When he preaches on a book of the Bible, moving forward through it, they don't just remember the sermon on yesterday's text, but that of the month before, the month before that, even last year. His superiors understand this in the case of a community of monks, but he is building that kind of rapport with his general congregation. In Florence.

The wind whips at their robes as they walk towards the vestry door.

"Are you prepared for your sermon?" Brother Silvestro asks, as they scrape their sandals free of muck.

Girolamo nods. He makes sure to be very orthodox in his form, here, under the direct eye of his superiors. He believes his preaching is better in Florence, where he can be a little more free. "I hope I can keep their attention today," he says quietly, as they go in.

"They are led astray by their lords," Silvestro says. The vestry smells of incense and wax candles, chasing away the miasma of the streets.

He nods again.

"The Lady Ginevra won't dare to be late this time," Silvestro says, soothingly. "Not after you spoke to her last time."

Antonino curls his lip. "She'll be late if she wants to be. She's always late. She's not afraid of you."

"I've spoken to her twice now," Girolamo says, shrugging. "I hinted the first time, and then last time I went up to her politely after the service and invited her to come on time, because it causes a disturbance. She took no notice the first time, she probably won't take any more notice this time."

"You shouldn't reprove her," Antonino says, clearly still smarting at the reproof Girolamo had given him. "She's the wife of the prince, and the daughter of the Sforza duke of Milan."

"Does that make her higher than God?" Girolamo mocks. "She thinks so, perhaps, but I do not."

"Surely she doesn't think herself high enough to ignore Brother Girolamo's direct reproach," Silvestro says. "I'm sure she'll come early today."

They walk out of the vestry into the crowded cathedral. The monks are singing a psalm. Everyone is packed in, standing close together. Here the scent of damp wool overwhelms the incense. The lord, Johannes Bentivoglio, is in his place, resplendently dressed, but there is no sign of his wife. "Shouldn't we wait for Lady Ginevra?" Antonino asks, anxiously.

"God does not wait," Girolamo whispers in response. "Besides, what if she isn't coming at all? She might be sick, or going to one of the other churches this morning." Bologna has many churches. He is ready now; he wants to begin. He makes for the pulpit eagerly, notes for his sermon in hand.

The congregation are attentive. Even Brother Vincenzo seems to be listening without frowning.

Girolamo is in full flow when Ginevra Bentivoglio sweeps in, surrounded by her ladies and guards. The ladies are all dressed sumptuously, in layers of bright colours, with their faces painted. Ginevra is wearing a rope of pearls with a ruby dangling from it, and she has more rubies in combs in her teased-up hair. The gems advertise the Bentivoglio wealth, and their connections with the rich trading nations, especially Venice and Spain. Pearls are very rare and immensely valuable. As she moves towards her seat beside her husband,

the whole congregation moves about, making room for her, and bowing. The courtiers are fawning, the common people cringing before
her, the destitute trying to abase themselves in the hope of her favour.
Gusts of strong perfume drift in the wake of her party, both floral and
musky. One of her ladies takes her ruby-red cloak, and she seats herself, smiling. A corner of the smile is cast in Girolamo's direction,
and contains a hint of false penitence, over a great deal of smug satis-
faction.

Pride has always been his besetting sin, pride and the hot flash of
temper that defends it. It flares up now as the silly woman simpers
and everyone in the cathedral loses the thread of what Girolamo was
saying. "Is it the devil?" he booms, at the top of his voice, pointing at
her. "Did the devil send you? Did you come to mock God, or to dis-
tract us all from Him? Well, it won't work, we can't be distracted by
any tricks of the devil, we're about God's work here."

A child titters, and is abruptly hushed. Ginevra goes white. The
paint on her face stands out like a carnival mask. She sinks down, almost falling, on the throne that is the special perquisite of the lord's
wife. Her husband puts out his hand and steadies her. He is frowning. Brother Antonino's mouth has dropped open. Girolamo goes on
with his sermon where he had left off, his words falling into a silence
so complete that it feels almost chilling. He can feel Brother Vincenzo's furious eyes fixed on his as he finishes, genuflects to the altar,
and stands with his brothers.

The service continues. The Bentivoglios leave as soon as it is seemly
to do so. The rest of the congregation follow them out as fast as they
can, not speaking as long as they are within the confines of the church
but they can be heard bursting out into conversation like so many jack-
daws as soon as they are out in the air. No one stays to conduct business or gossip the way they normally would. Even the other priests
and monks hurry away, and soon only the four Dominicans are left in
the strangely empty space. "Did you see her face? She'll have you assassinated," Silvestro says, and his voice echoes.

"I wouldn't stop her if she did," Vincenzo says, sweeping up. The sinews of his broad neck stand out as he throws back his head. "What were you thinking, Brother Girolamo?"

"I lost my temper. I will do penance. Forgive me." Girolamo knows he is in the wrong. It makes it worse that he has to abase himself before Brother Vincenzo, who hates him and will take delight in seeing him humbled.

"It wasn't God speaking through you this time?"

"No." Girolamo bows his head and looks down. He is biting his tongue on the urge to retort.

"You seemed to confuse yourself with God, up there in the pulpit."

"No, Brother." He stares down at his sandalled feet on the patterned tiles. There are a few dark hairs on each of his toes.

"She was interrupting you, not God. Is it a sin to interrupt you now, Brother Girolamo?" Vincenzo asks, sarcastically.

"I said 'God's work,'" Girolamo says, eyes still on his feet. He isn't absolutely sure now what he said.

"You called her a devil," Brother Antonino says, in awed tones.

Had he? He darts a quick glance up at Brother Vincenzo, who seems shocked and triumphant at the same time. His fringe of beard wags as he shakes his head.

"Brother Girolamo said the devil sent her," Silvestro says. "And so he did send her, painted up and hung about with jewels that could have fed the poor of the city for a year."

"Thank you, that's enough, Brother Silvestro," Vincenzo says. "Do you have any more to say for yourself, Brother Girolamo?"

He has said nothing in his own defence. "I apologize for my sins of pride and wrath, and I ask your pardon and God's. I will do penance."

"Of course you will. You delight in penance, we all know that. You take enjoyment in pain and fasting like normal people take in pleasure and eating. It brings you fulfillment."

It is an accusation he has heard more than once, most frequently from Brother Vincenzo. "No," he says, as humbly as he can.

"I daresay you'd enjoy it more if I told you to scourge yourself and wear a hair belt than if I sentenced you to go to spend a night with a whore."

"You can't order me to break my vows," Girolamo says, looking up and meeting Vincenzo's angry eyes despite himself. Humility does not come easily to him. He routinely scourges himself and frequently wears a hair belt under his clothes, letting the goat-hairs rub his skin raw. The pain and mortification of the flesh does not arouse his lust as Vincenzo is implying. He needs the reminder to subdue his bodily desires and keep himself focused on God. The hair belt feels right, the constant irritation of the raw flesh under his robe a reminder of the sham of worldly things. "I was wrong to lose my temper and shout at the tyrant's wife, and I will do what penance you choose."

"And if I order you to apologise to Lady Ginevra?"

Brother Silvestro sucks in his breath loudly.

"I will do it," he says.

"You can't order him to commit suicide," Brother Antonino says. "He humiliated her in front of everyone. If he went to apologise, she'd have one of her guards kill him."

"You're right. She would. And unfortunately, that would be bad for the prestige of the Dominicani." Vincenzo sighs. "I'll go to her myself and explain that you're simple in the head. You can keep up your Lenten fast until next Easter. You must keep on preaching, but try some texts about humility. I doubt the lord and lady will come back to hear you, but it will do you good. And the sooner you get back to your sodomitical Florence the better."

"You—" Brother Silvestro begins, and stops. He knows how hard Girolamo has worked over his course of sermons, and how much they make a complete whole.

"And the same goes for you," Vincenzo says, and sweeps out, taking Antonino with him.

Girolamo lets himself breathe, and looks at Silvestro. "Writing new sermons is a fair penance," he says.

"Why are we here?" Silvestro bursts out. "Why are you subject to that lascivious man? Why are we of San Marco, who are reformed and pure and holy, under the control of these Lombard Brothers who fatten and enrich themselves instead of caring for the poor?"

"I did lose my temper," Girolamo points out.

"You were right, the devil sent her to disturb God's work. A whole year of Lenten fasting because you reproved a painted Jezebel from the pulpit! In all my years as a Dominican, I have never seen anything like this."

"I never eat much more than that," Girolamo says.

"We pure houses should separate ourselves from the others," Silvestro says, ignoring him. "We should be our own order. They're always trying to stop us from doing things properly. The way Brother Vincenzo spoke to you was far worse than the way you spoke to Ginevra Bentivoglio."

"We'd have to have an order from His Holiness," Girolamo says. "It wouldn't be a simple matter."

"We should start working towards it," Silvestro says. He is vibrating with indignation, his grey curls shaking. "To speak to you that way. You, Brother, whom God has chosen."

Girolamo puts up a hand in aversion. "I'm only a simple brother."

"But God talks to you. And he has given you the power to banish demons." Silvestro's simple faith is sure and steady. Girolamo feels warmed by it.

"Yes, but that doesn't give me the right to give way to my temper and pride," he says. "I lost my temper up there. It was the sin of pride. Brother Vincenzo was right."

"Even so, he shouldn't have spoken to you like that. Feebleminded! A night with a whore! Is that the way to bring an erring brother back to the light? We should find out how to separate ourselves so you don't have to accept."

"We'll need the support of the Senate of Florence, and the Eight, and of Piero de' Medici, and Cardinal de' Medici, and Cardinal Carafa," Girolamo says, counting them off on his fingers. He feels tired at the thought of it. "And we'd need to have the support of the Chapter and all our brothers in San Marco."

"Write to them!" Silvestro urges.

"I'll write to Cardinal Carafa in Rome. I hear Pope Innocent is sick, but maybe he can feel him out anyway. I'll wait to speak to our brothers and the Senate when we get home. It's not long now before Easter."

"Thanks be to God," Silvestro says, wholeheartedly.

CHAPTER 5

In Heaven.

SEPTEMBER 21ST, 1494

It is the day of St Matthew the Apostle, and Brother Girolamo is preaching in the cathedral on the subject of the Flood. He has made notes, he always does, but once in the pulpit he allows himself to speak as God directs. He has succeeded, this past May, in separating the Tuscan from the Lombard congregation of Dominicans and is subject now to no one but Cardinal Carafa, Pope Innocent, God, and his own conscience. The brothers in some of the other monasteries in Tuscany, in Santa Maria Novella and Fiesole in particular, chafe under his supervision. They do not like to see the rule of St Benedict and St Dominic enforced. The monks had put down rugs on the stone floors of their cells at Santa Maria Novella, and when he reproaches them they dare to object that the stone is cold in winter. Is it a sin to have warm feet? they ask him. It is a sin to put bodily comfort before love of God, he replies, and do they think the tile of San Marco is warmer? Offer your suffering to God. The Dominican nuns in their convents of Santa Lucia and the Annalena tend to become overenthusiastic in their asceticism, often claiming to see visions that may or may not be valid. They are very demanding of his time and attention. It is not easy being father of a wider family.

Now he is no longer under the supervision of Brother Vincenzo, he can preach as he chooses. The removal of restriction on prophecy in the pulpit is a great boon. He preaches today about Noah and the Ark, and hears himself saying Florence is an Ark and the water is rising, the flood tide poised to pour down. The Sword of the Lord is coming from the north, and soon. He calls for repentance, for them to make this city the City of God. The congregation listens, rapt, caught up in his words. Many of them are weeping. He sees the Count among them, transfixed. Afterwards, everyone wants to speak to him, touch him, tell him what a good sermon it was. He is a little bemused. It was a good sermon, yes, but he is surprised by how strong a reaction it has provoked. It seems people want to be purified, to be in the ark he is building.

When he makes his way through the throng, he sees that the Count is waiting for him, standing to the side of the main entrance, under the equestrian fresco of Acuto. He's standing with Girolamo Benivieni, who never misses a sermon. Benivieni is a Florentine guildsman of moderate wealth, in his early forties, though the deeply graven lines between his nose and his chin make him look older. He writes poetry that displays his erudition, and always dresses in severe black, giving a simultaneous impression of austerity and ostentation. He and the Count are both wearing scholar's caps; his is black and the Count's is red. Girolamo sends his brothers on to San Marco and joins them under the fresco. "That was one of your best sermons yet," the Count says. "It made my hair stand on end."

"God spoke through me," he says, as he always does. It is true.

"The French are poised to invade, are they your flood?" Benivieni asks. He has a slight cast in his left eye, which makes it hard to meet his gaze properly, or know exactly where he is looking.

"It will sweep down through Italy," Girolamo says. Rumour says Charles VIII, the King of France, is in Lombardy already.

"You're always wonderful, but today you were on fire," Benivieni says. He keeps on, with fulsome compliments. "Can I walk somewhere with you?" he asks the Count after a while.

"Not today, I wanted a private word with Brother Girolamo, if you don't mind," the Count says. Benivieni excuses himself and hastens off.

"It's strange, as he's entirely sincere, but I wish I could like him as much as he seems to like me," the Count says, as they watch him go.

Girolamo laughs. "I feel exactly the same about him! There's something a little too much—"

The two of them walk back through the bustling streets in the direction of San Marco.

"Your sermon was so powerful it even distracted me from the reason I wanted to speak to you," the Count says, looking as if he has just remembered something terrible. "Angelo's sick, maybe dying. Can you take his confession, and give him the last rites?"

"Angelo? Dying? But I saw him two, three days ago!" My recording angel, Lorenzo had called him. He had written a wonderful poem after Lorenzo's death, you still heard people singing it, *Lightning has struck our laurel tree*. He had become a regular at Brother Girolamo's sermons, rarely missing one. "I need to get the host and the oil from San Marco," he says.

"I'll come with you, and then I can show you the way," the Count says. They walk up the familiar street towards San Marco, through the thronging stalls of the leatherworkers.

"He's not at the Medici Palace?" Girolamo asks.

"He's at my apartment on the Via Porta Rossa. That is, Isabella's apartment. He wasn't well enough to go out to his own house at Careggi, or mine at Fiesole. But all the servants except my man Cristoforo ran away, thinking it was the plague because we were both sick."

"But it's not the plague?" The summer had seen the usual outbreak of plague. Mortality is highest among the young. Brother Girolamo has grown only too familiar with the signs.

The Count shrugs unhappily, frowning and looking down. "It's definitely not plague. No black spots, no swellings. I'm not sure what it is. I think—we both had dinner with Piero, three days ago. He hadn't invited either of us for a long time. Did you know he's instituted hierarchy of seating? At Lorenzo's table anyone sat anywhere, and you could find yourself between a sculptor's apprentice and the Ambassador of Venice, and we'd have the most fascinating conversations. But he's done away with all that. Usually when we eat there now, he puts me beside him, because of my rank, and makes Angelo sit down at the end with the servants. But this time he put Angelo on his other side. I thought it was a sign of reconciliation, or being kind so we could eat together, but now I don't know." He sighs. "Maybe he wanted to make sure we both finished our meals. I only went because I wanted to ask Piero a favour—Elia Pardo, one of my old Hebrew tutors, is being thrown out of Bologna with his family. I wanted Piero to invite him to Florence, maybe get him to give a few Hebrew classes at the University, the way del Medigo did. He agreed to invite him. He seemed affable. He was paying attention to Angelo, even seemed to be listening to his advice for once. Angelo was so pleased. He tries to hide it but he's hurt by the way Piero has been pushing him away. But almost right after, we both fell sick. I got better, though I'm still not quite right. Angelo just got worse and worse. The doctors bled him, but he's getting weaker. He's been so cold we put the bed curtains up already."

"You think you were poisoned?"

The Count pulls a face. "I can't accuse Piero. But—"

"Why not? If anyone can, you can. You're the Count of Concordia, he has no formal status."

"I'm his guest, in his house." He looks sideways at Girolamo. "You remember when we talked about Lorenzo and you said he had us all jessed like hawks? Piero thinks he owns us all, and his hand isn't gentle on the traces. He doesn't like opposition, or advice. Lorenzo would always listen, and make new plans if necessary."

"But to try to kill you! Why?"

The Count shakes his head. "I didn't imagine he would do that. And it might just have been bad octopus."

"I hope it was," Girolamo says, though octopus in mild autumn weather is usually safe. "Did it taste bad?"

"No, not at all. Tasty, done Genoese style. But—well, it could be simply a fever. But Angelo is very bad. And of course I'm twice his size, so if we both had the same dose of poison, that makes sense. But you said I wouldn't see the war," the Count says, lowering his voice and stopping on the corner.

"It has been two years, and you still haven't settled your affairs."

"I'm close. Now I am no longer excommunicate, which was the most difficult thing. But it's so complicated! I've given away all my money, but sorting out the Mirandolan inheritance is taking forever. One of my brothers is in Rome and never replies to letters, and the other argues with everything. His son Gianfrancesco is a good boy, with a philosophical bent to him, but he's spending all his time riding between here and Mirandola carrying messages." The Count raised his hands and eyes to heaven dramatically. "Soon. Any day now, I expect Gianfrancesco to come back with the news that I am free to join you. Though Camilla Rucellai prophecied that I'd become a Dominican in the time of the lilies, so I expect it will take until Spring." He sighs.

Camilla Bartolini Rucellai is a married woman whose prophecies do not seem hysterical, but genuine. Deborah, in the Bible, had been a prophetess, so it is possible for them to exist. He has tried to restrain Mistress Rucellai from spreading her prophecies, even where they overlap with his own. This is because she has seen so many visions of Girolamo guiding the commonwealth. She shouted out her prophecy about the Count and the lilies in the church of Santa Maria Novella, disrupting a service, and it is now widely known in the city.

"How about Isabella?" he asks.

"I've arranged for her to go to Genoa and start a business."

At San Marco, the Count waits in the courtyard while Girolamo runs into the Pilgrim Hall for a bag with the oil and the host. The brothers at San Marco are among the few who will visit those dying of plague, and calls have been so frequent all summer that they keep

everything ready. In some towns the Franciscans would take care of
visiting the dying, but here most of that work falls on San Marco. First
Brother Antoninus began it when the monastery was built a generation ago, and now it is expected. He takes up the bag and turns to go.

Domenico comes up to him, bursting with the thousand things he
needs to ask about, but Girolamo raises a hand. "A dying man needs
me. Nothing can be more urgent. I will be back for Ninth Hour
prayers."

It is like, and unlike, the time the Count took him to Lorenzo. He
follows him through the narrow twisting streets. A cold wind is blowing and it is spitting rain. They pass a tripe-seller's stall, the smell
savoury and heavy with onions. "Why would Piero want to kill you?"
he asks.

"Pique?" the Count suggests. "Or . . ." He hesitates, looking at
Girolamo. "He asked me at dinner if I really meant to take vows, if I
wasn't afraid it gave you too much power, for someone of my status to
join San Marco."

"That's not why I want you," Girolamo says, horrified.

"I know. Of course. But if Piero thinks that—"

"If he thinks that and he poisoned you, it's an attack on me as well
as you. It's an attack on the Dominicans. On the Church." They come
out into the open space by the Baptistery, with the huge dome of the
cathedral looming up above them.

"Lots of people come to your sermons and listen to what you say.
After this afternoon, even more people will come. You're becoming
very influential. Camilla Rucellai tells people God tells her you'll guide
the commonwealth, and she's not the only one to think so. Piero could
well be afraid of your influence. You can't make Florence pure, the
ark, and leave him secure in his position. He's not Lorenzo."

Girolamo shakes his head, wondering again how Lorenzo had attained God's grace, despite wealth and power. He touches the green
stone in his pocket. "I haven't attacked Piero. Never."

"No, but you talk about how people ought to live. And if he's afraid
of that, and if he's afraid my joining you might give you more standing

with the community, then maybe that's why." The Count touches his elbow and they turn into another narrow street.

"Then why did he poison Angelo?" It's amazing to Girolamo that anyone would want to hurt Angelo, who is enthusiastic and friendly, and besides, a poet famous all over Italy.

The Count shakes his head. "He used to be Piero's tutor. Piero hates him because he'll never be grown up in Angelo's eyes. You saw a little bit of that when Lorenzo was dying. Piero's been cold to him. Lucrezia and I have been trying to get Angelo to go to Ferrara or Mantua for this last year. The D'Estes would be only too glad to support a poet of his quality."

"Yes, because it would give them status," Girolamo says. "And Piero thinks you and Angelo are giving me status, and that is taking it away from him."

"Status. Influence. Authority. It's all tangled up together and has nothing to do with God and what's truly important." The Count sighs. "I never thought Piero would stoop to poison. It's such a contemptible ignoble thing to do. If Angelo dies the world will have lost a man worth far more, by any real measure, than Piero. And I will have lost a true friend."

"Don't eat with Piero again," Girolamo says.

"I won't," the Count replies, fervently, as they turn alongside the church of Orsanmichele onto the Via Porta Rossa. "And I hope that soon I can enter San Marco and leave such worldly things behind."

"There is too much of the world in the cloister," Girolamo warns.

"Here we are. Come in."

It is the first time Girolamo has visited the house where the Count lives in sin. The door is grand enough, but it stands between a woodworker's and a silk merchant. Once in the courtyard inside, it's clear from the faded frescoes and pieces of junk lying about that the family who own this palace have fallen on hard times, and the building has been divided. There are stairs leading up around the courtyard, which makes a light well in the middle of the building, up to the fourth floor. "The ground floor is all shops. The family keep the nobile floor, at the top of the first flight of stairs. Our apartments are on the second floor," the Count says, leading the way. "I don't know how many people live up on the third floor."

"How long have you lived here?" It seems a strange place for a man of his status to live.

"Isabella has lived here since I came to Florence. I pay the rent. I don't live here, I live out at Fiesole or at my rooms in the Medici Palace. I came here on and off, you know, to visit her."

When Girolamo first sees her, Isabella is carrying a bucket of strong-smelling vomit down the stairs. He assumes she is one of the people who live on the third floor, until the Count introduces her. She surprises him with her wholesomeness. She doesn't look like a courtesan but like a strong-armed country girl. He recognises her immediately, he has often seen her at his women's sermons, listening intently with her head to one side. She is modestly dressed in brown and white, like the respectable wife of a small guildsman, with no ostentation and her dark hair modestly covered.

"The servants have left, and Cristoforo refuses to carry this," she says, apologetically. She is holding the handle in both hands.

The Count takes the bucket from her. "I'll take this to the cess, and you take Brother Girolamo up to Angelo," he says. Girolamo thinks it is good to see him doing such a thing, but he is also shocked to see how naturally he does it. He's a count, after all! No matter how much he tells himself such things are vanity he can't quite erase his instinctual flinch. Isabella leads the way on up to the narrow gallery with a waist-high wall that runs around the second floor, and then around the corner.

"Angelo wants to make his confession," Isabella says quietly as she opens the door. "I'll leave you alone with him."

Girolamo hardly hears her. The room is dark, all the shutters but one are closed. There is a single immense demon looming over Angelo's huddled figure on the bed, filling the whole space visible between the yellow-and-red curtains. It is a skeleton with a great gravid swollen belly, like a pregnant woman, with long flowing golden hair sprouting from its skull. It holds a scythe and is crouched over the dying man as if sharing his breath. Girolamo doesn't hesitate or wait for Isabella to leave. He forms his fingers into a circle and strides forward. "I banish you in the name of Christ Jesus!" he shouts. The great demon, like all the other demons Girolamo has banished, shrieks, shrinks, and passes through his fingers and back into Hell.

Angelo is looking at him with wide eyes, and behind him the woman Isabella gasps. "What was that?" she asks.

"It was death," Angelo says. "The friar has banished death."

"It was not death, it was only a demon, come to terrify you and, if it could, to draw you with it to Hell in fear and despair," he says confidently. "Death bears no such fearsome shape, but is the gateway to eternal life in the love of God."

Angelo begins to weep. Girolamo turns to Isabella. "Did you see it?"

"I saw a great shadow with a scythe," she says. "Only now, when you were here. Before I felt the pressure of its presence. I too thought it was death in the room with us."

"It only became visible after you left, here under the curtains with me," Angelo says. "I thought—"

"I am here," Girolamo says, drawing back the bed curtains. Even if Angelo is cold, it is surely better for him to be able to breathe. He is not surprised the dying man saw the demon, but he would not have expected the woman to be able to. So few people are aware of the presence of evil. He looks at her. "Go to the Count, while I hear Angelo's confession. I will call you in a little while." Her eyes go to the stinking buckets beside the bed, one of which is half-full, then to the dying man, then back to Girolamo. She nods, picks up the half-full bucket, and goes out without speaking.

Brother Girolamo goes to the window and opens the other shutter, letting in more light. Then he opens the window to the fresh breeze, which cuts through the fetid smell in the room. As he turns, he notices that the room is frescoed with birds and shields in red and blue, not hung with tapestries as the best rooms would be. The bed curtains and covers are rich and heavy brocades in yellow and red, and the bed itself sturdy carved walnut. Angelo Poliziano, never a big man, looks little more than a shrimp huddling under the covers.

On the wall opposite the window are shutters pulled over a painting. He opens them tentatively and sees, to his relief, a sweet-faced Madonna, the Christ child on her lap and young John the Baptist at her knee. He leaves the doors open.

"Now that the atmosphere is more wholesome, let's see," Girolamo says, going to the bed and kneeling beside it. "You may be near death, Angelo, but you are not yet dead." His medical training taught him to observe some signs, but his work with the poor has taught him more. He would judge that Angelo has a day or two more of pain and suffering before God finally takes him. "Certainly you have time to confess your sins and be absolved."

Angelo tries to smile. "I may not have time for all my sins."

Girolamo does not respond but looks at him evenly. It is no time for levity.

"Bless me, Father. I have loved the pagan poets more than the Scriptures," Angelo says, chastened and sincere. His breath has a heavy scent of garlic. "I have used the names of pagan gods in prayer."

"To worship idols, or using them poetically as other names for God?" Girolamo asks, calmly. It is important to make the distinction, but even more important to have the dying man confess his real sins, so he can be truly contrite and have true absolution.

"The latter," Angelo says. "Always the latter."

Girolamo nods, relieved. "That is not a sin." It's not even uncommon, in Florence. There are even men here who do the former. He suspects Marsilio Ficino of being one of them. Since Lorenzo's death, Ficino has avoided him as much as he can, and he suspects that may be why.

Angelo goes on. "Pride. I thought I could revive the ancient world, that everyone who learned Greek could be a friend, that I could reach them all and be the centre of the rebirth of antiquity. I thought my talent for poetry made me important. I thought I could be the new

Petrarch, even the new Virgil." His face looks grey on the pillows, and his heavy hair is soaked with sweat.

"And do you repent this pride?"

"I do." He breathes heavily, then resumes. "Worse. When I was tutor to the Medici boys, I fought with their mother over teaching them Ovid when she wanted them to read psalms."

"Ovid wrote better Latin," Girolamo admits. "But you know you were wrong."

"I cannot repent of loving Homer and Cicero," Angelo says.

"Loving them is not a sin. But they have no power to save you."

"You do." He is looking at Girolamo with desperation.

"God does, and I am his instrument," Girolamo says. He is used to being people's last hope. "What else?"

"Sins of the flesh," Angelo says, looking away, then catching sight of the Madonna over Girolamo's shoulder and looking away from her too. He stares down at his own thin hands on the embroidered bedcover.

"You have sinned with women?" Girolamo asks, gently.

"No, with men," he says.

"With boys?" Girolamo asks, disgusted, but trying not to show it. He hates to see the young boys from poor families sell their bodies down under the Old Bridge. The sodomites seduce them into unchastity, turning their heads with flattery and paying them a little for their favours. If they get caught, it is the boys who suffer, who cannot afford to pay fines. There are young boys there every day. Girolamo wishes he could rescue them, but what could he do with them? There are so many of them, and they are hungry.

"Men. Never boys, not since I was a boy myself." He sees that Angelo is ashamed of this, as if he believes it would be a lesser sin to fornicate with boys than with grown men. "Always men. Friends. Humanists. Plato—"

"Plato wrote *against* sins of the flesh," Girolamo says, firmly, sure of his ground. He won't allow Angelo to use Plato as justification for this.

"Plato says it is second best," Angelo says. "I believe he's right. But second best is still—I have sinned in this way over and over again. I've repented and confessed and done penance, and then sinned again." Yet he saw Lorenzo glowing blue with God's grace, Girolamo thinks. But who knows where he was in his cycle of repentance at the time Lorenzo died?

"Do you truly repent now of these sins?"

"I do." Girolamo hopes he sees truth in Angelo's red-rimmed eyes.

"And if you live, you will strive your hardest to resist such things?"

"If I live, I will come to you at San Marco and take vows like Pico," Angelo says, which he has never said before. "But I will not live, will I?"

"There are miracles," Girolamo says. "Do not doubt God."

"I do not. He sent his Son. He sent Lorenzo. He sent you."

Girolamo bows his head and prays to Saint Jerome for humility. He sees that Angelo is shivering.

"Should I shut the window?"

"Thank you," Angelo says.

Girolamo walks over to the window and closes it, leaving the shutters open for the light. There is a chest under the window with women's clothing spilling out of it. This room, with the beautiful picture of the Madonna, must be where Isabella usually sleeps. She is entirely unlike what he had pictured.

"Do more great sins trouble your soul?" he asks Angelo, as he settles back down beside the bed.

"It's hard to forgive Piero for poisoning me," Angelo says. "I was his tutor. I felt as close to him as if we were family. And I'm only forty, and I had so much left to do. He could have exiled me if he wanted to be rid of me. I'd have missed Florence, but it is loyalty to the Medici that has kept me here. There are lots of places I could have gone. And if he's killed Pico too I don't know that I can possibly forgive that."

Girolamo must speak as a confessor, and cannot say what he thinks of Piero. "Forgiving enemies and turning the other cheek is one of the hardest things our Saviour asks of us. Are you trying to forgive him?"

"Yes," Angelo says, after a pause. "But . . ."

"Consider how much sin you are asking God to forgive you, and try to forgive those who have sinned against you. It's not the same as condoning what they have done."

"I think I can forgive him for killing me, though it's very hard, but not if he has killed Pico," Angelo says.

Girolamo nods. "The Count says he has recovered from his illness."

"I am trying," Angelo says again.

"Christ forgave his torturers. Do you think Piero knew what he was doing, any more than they did?"

"If he didn't then that's my fault. I was his tutor. I should have taught him right from wrong, or at the very least smart from stupid." Angelo screws up his face and looks as if he might weep again.

"Are you confessing to being a bad tutor to Piero de' Medici?" Girolamo asks, smiling to lighten the mood. "Because that's not a sin."

Angelo smiles back, briefly, then his face falls again into grief. "Ficino made Lorenzo into what he was. He and Lorenzo believed I could do the same for his sons."

"Sometimes God doesn't give us the right material," he says. He has found this often with his monks. "Did you do your best?"

Angelo nods, then the motion clearly makes him queasy, and he lurches for the bucket. Girolamo holds it closer to him as he retches agonizingly over it. The vomit stinks so badly that it makes Girolamo a little queasy to be close enough to hold the bucket. He sets it down when Angelo has finished, and takes up a rag to wipe Angelo's face as gently as he can. Afterwards, he offers him water. A brown glazed jug and cup are set on a stool near the bed.

"I think it was the Pazzi Conspiracy," Angelo says, after drinking. "Piero was six. Lucrezia was eight. The others were too young to notice, but it was very hard for those two. They were very close, but always fighting, even before that. But then all of a sudden one day their uncle Giuliano was murdered, Lorenzo was wounded, all of us were constantly moving from villa to villa, in a terrible atmosphere of fear and uncertainty. Their mother was pregnant and uncomfortable. By the time Lorenzo went to Naples, Piero was eight, and for those two years he'd hardly had a day to be a child, to feel safe. He couldn't play outside in the streets, he couldn't make friends with other children, he had to be afraid all the time. It's not surprising he doesn't know how to deal with people, to trust them. That's when he went wrong."

Girolamo isn't at all sure this excuses Piero de' Medici in any way, as it was fifteen years ago, and he's had plenty of time to grow up since. But if it helps Angelo to forgive him now, he is glad. He offers him water again. Forgiving enemies is always difficult.

"Any more great sins on your conscience?" he asks.

Angelo starts to shake his head, then stops, shivering, and huddles down under the covers. "No," he says, taking the water and drinking. "Will there be poetry in Heaven?" he asks, like a child, as he hands back the cup.

"I think there will be something better," Girolamo confides. "Something that poetry reminds us of, and that is why we are drawn to love it. I think loving all earthly beauty is a way to lead us to love Heavenly beauty. So there will not be sunsets or poetry, but there will be something like them but even better."

"I wish I might have time to make that thought into a poem," Angelo says.

"I absolve you in the name of the Father and the Son and the Holy Spirit. You will need to atone in Purgatory, but the door is open, and at last you will see God and know the truth and beauty behind the joys of this world."

Girolamo takes the host and the oil and begins the ceremony of last rites, forgiving each body part for the sins it has committed. Angelo weeps throughout, but that is not at all unusual. The gospels say that to enter the Kingdom of Heaven we must become like little children.

CHAPTER 6

Give us.

NOVEMBER 7TH, 1494

No one will interrupt him at prayer, but as soon as he steps out of the church into the courtyard of San Marco, Brother Tomasso is hovering. It is afternoon. Girolamo had lingered to pray alone for a little while after the service. In the summer there would be hours of daylight yet, but it is November, and chill high clouds are making it seem dusk already a little before four o'clock.

"Thanks be to God," Girolamo says, resignedly, wondering what it was now that couldn't do without him for an hour. Tomasso is a tottering elderly monk who remembers First Brother Antoninus and the painter Brother Angelico. His spine is bent so that his head juts forward, and he has only the thinnest fringe of snow-white hair around his tonsure, but his blue eyes are clear and warm. He has been assistant to the First Brother for too long, so that he thinks of that chore as his real work and fusses over it, instead of concentrating on his devotions. This kind of over-identification is a good reason for regularly rotating offices, but in Brother Tomasso's case it's too late. Girolamo doesn't want to break a good old man's heart by demoting him.

"Piero Capponi is waiting to see you," Tomasso says. "And that woman of the Count's is here. And Brother Benedetto insists on an interview."

Angelo died, after another day of vomiting and agony. They buried him in the church of San Marco. Piero de' Medici hadn't objected, or suggested that he should be in San Lorenzo beside Cosimo and Lorenzo, or that as a great Florentine poet he should be with the city's honoured dead in Santa Croce. To Brother Girolamo, this makes his guilt clear. Marsilio Ficino came to the funeral mass, and all Angelo's friends. The church was packed with every humanist and educated man in Florence. The Count was in the front row, looking pale. Piero wasn't there. Girolamo conducted the mass. He still wanted to confront Piero with his treachery. Angelo was his tutor, his own man, which makes poisoning him a betrayal of such a magnitude he can hardly believe it possible.

The Count has been failing slowly ever since, declining all through October. He came to Girolamo's All Souls' Day sermon, where Girolamo had preached against rich families trying to buy their way into Heaven by art donations to churches that aggrandize the family. Girolamo had seen him there, looking grey and ill, but he hurried away afterwards and did not wait to speak. If Isabella is here, then the Count must need Girolamo. The King of France, with his huge army, is coming close. Piero de' Medici, attempting to repeat his father's legendary action that ended the Pazzi Wars, has gone alone unarmed into Charles's camp. Girolamo thought of Angelo when he heard, blaming all Piero's failings on his experiences during the Pazzi years. Everyone is drawing the comparison now, and hoping the son can do as well as his father. Doubtless Piero is hoping the same. Charles is the Sword of the Lord, and he is coming. Girolamo has prophecied that the Count will not live to see it. And yet, Camilla Rucellai said that the Count would join San Marco at the time of the lilies. She could be wrong, of course, but when he heard it Girolamo felt that certainty that is the mark of true prophecy, as if her words were confirming something he had always known. Lilies, an Easter flower, will not bloom again until spring. He sighs. Prophecy is only sometimes helpful.

"What does Capponi want?" he asks.

Tomasso can no longer shrug, but he makes a gesture with his bent shoulders that serves the same purpose. "I don't know. He's waiting for you in the Pilgrim Hall. I know he's not a pilgrim, but it's very cold today, and there's a fire there." It was indeed cold, one of the days when the wind came straight down from the snows of the mountains. The last of the leaves had been whirled off the trees, and the Tuscan olive harvest was over.

"I'd better see him first and find out." Capponi is a diplomat, one of the crop of talented men picked out by Lorenzo who do the work of running the city for the Medici. "Tell Benedetto I'll see him in my room after Twilight Prayer, right before dinner. And tell Isabella I'll come out to her as soon as I can."

Tomasso tuts and wrinkles his nose at the thought of speaking to the Count's woman.

"Let he who is without sin cast the first stone. Our Lord spent time with sinners. Think of Mary Magdalen. And Isabella has spiritual gifts. She saw a demon. Perhaps she will take vows, after the Count dies."

Tomasso bows his head even further, acknowledging the reproach. "How can she?" he asks. "She's neither virgin nor widow."

"There are Magdalen orders," Girolamo says. "There's the Convertite. But there's not enough of them. We could do with a Magdalen order of Dominicans here." The problem with that is that it wouldn't be popular for endowments. People wouldn't want to send their chaste daughters there. Rich widows wouldn't want to retire to it. A convent can make some income from spinning and fine embroidery, and from copying manuscripts, but if the nuns are to eat, it also needs to own property that brings in money from rents. The Church is too dependent on wealth, but he can't see how to manage without it. The Franciscans, technically an order of beggars, attract huge donations and are now very rich.

"Maybe the Count would endow one," Tomasso suggests.

"The Count has given away all his money, lots of it to us. Maybe we could endow one. Look into the possibility." What he'd need would be a very respectable widow. Any man doing it, even a monk, would be accused of wanting somewhere to send his discarded whores. It is a sadly fallen world.

He makes his way down to the Pilgrim Hall. Over the door is a Brother Angelico fresco of Christ coming as a pilgrim with a staff and being welcomed by two Dominicans. It lifts his heart to see it, as it always does.

Inside, there are a number of indigents huddled around the fire waiting for dinner, and among them Piero Capponi, in his red citizen's cape, looking prosperous and urbane. He is a short man, and plump, so he also looks very much like the capon that his family are named for. He comes forward to greet Girolamo affably, which is a relief. He was half expecting a senatorial reproach for his last sermon.

"Is there somewhere we can talk?" Capponi asks, after politely declining offers of refreshment.

Girolamo considers the parlour, but it will be cold and unwelcoming. He leads him out through the cloister, along the corridor, and up the stairs to the cells. At the bottom of the stairs is a Brother Angelico fresco of the crucifixion. At the top is his *Annunciation*, one of the most beautiful paintings Girolamo has ever seen. Capponi stops a moment at the turn of the stairs, his breath taken away; then he admires it aloud. "Gabriel's wings," he says. "And the Virgin's face, so delicate, so expectant."

"And her house is so plain, as plain as this one," Girolamo says, pointing it out. Like many of Brother Angelico's paintings, it could be taking place right there in San Marco. "Sometimes they show her in a palace, but no, the holy family were simple people."

Capponi nods. Girolamo leads him down the corridor to his own cell. Brother Silvestro is sitting writing in the outer office, his tongue poking out as he concentrates, so Girolamo takes Capponi into the little cell where he composes his sermons. He seldom brings outsiders here, the second wooden chair is usually for his brothers. "Didn't you design this chair?" Capponi asks, sitting down. "I have one at home. Wonderfully comfortable. Very clever, all these curved slats."

He nods. "It's just an improvement on the old version. Carpenters enjoy making them."

Capponi looks at him shrewdly, his head tilted slightly, and suddenly there is nothing of the capon about him at all. "Have you heard the news from the French camp?" he asks.

Girolamo shakes his head. "Only that Piero went out to them."

"Damn fool thing to do. Lorenzo got away with it fifteen years ago in Naples because he was *Lorenzo*—and also we were desperate. Besides, he had allies in Naples, the crown princess was in his pocket. Pope Sixtus wanted Lorenzo to apologize for not being assassinated, but Lorenzo found a way out. This . . ." He sighs. "This isn't at all the same. Militarily, this time, we weren't in a bad position. Sarzana and Senigallia were well-fortified and strongly manned. We could have held them off until Pope Alexander sent troops to help us. Though with this Borgia pope we can't tell what he'll do. We've had a bad run of popes."

Girolamo can't be tempted into speaking out against the Pope, but privately he agrees. Sixtus IV was a terrible pope, Innocent VIII was only a little better, and Alexander Borgia is working out to be the worst yet. Secretly, he suspects Borgia may be the Antichrist. He has legitimized his son Cesare and appointed him cardinal, and openly moved his mistress into the Vatican.

"You're speaking in the past tense. Has the Pope taken action?" he asks.

At that moment, San Marco's bell begins to ring to mark the hour of four, the high bell they call the Wailer. No one knows, when they cast a bell, how it will sound, and this one has a strange high-pitched lingering D tone. They can't hear each other speak until it stops, but Capponi shakes his head in answer.

"We can't fight against the Sword of the Lord," Girolamo says, when it is quiet again.

"Yes, I've heard you saying that. Florence is the Ark, and the Sword of the Lord is coming to sweep everything else away. This isn't the usual kind of war, nothing like it. Did you hear what they did to Fivizzano? Sacked it, killed everyone. Terrible. You think Charles will take Naples, then?"

"I know he will. He will take it with hardly a blow struck."

"Well, that's the case. He's taking us, anyway."

"What has happened?" Girolamo leans forward.

"That fool Piero can't negotiate his way out of an open wine cup. He's given Charles everything; all our fortresses, *Pisa,* and two hundred thousand florins, too."

"That's bad." Girolamo shakes his head. "That's disastrous in fact. Pisa! In exchange for what?"

"Nothing," Capponi says. "We're supposedly allied with him now, and he's got all that—well, except for the money, which Piero hadn't packed along. The Senate won't put up with this."

"You can make them put up with it," Girolamo says.

"And you can make the people put up with it, if you stand up and say it was God's will. We don't want blood in the streets. A sack doesn't help anyone."

"Hasn't Charles promised not to hurt Florence?"

"Not even that." The two men stare at each other for a moment. "First Brother, Piero's not a bad man. He's arrogant, and he's not half the man his father was. And he's young. I'd hoped he'd learn. Poliziano—"

"I believe he poisoned Angelo Poliziano. And Count Pico, too."

"What!" Capponi starts up out of his chair, then settles back into it. "Perhaps he *is* a bad man."

"By what right does he rule Florence? Lorenzo, yes, Lorenzo was first among equals, I'll grant you that. And I've heard the same said about his grandfather, Cosimo. But young Piero? What makes men like you follow him?"

Capponi shakes his head slowly. "Brother Girolamo, I'd be prepared to die for Florence if necessary. For the Medici, even. Lorenzo made me all I am. But not for this piece of foolishness which benefits no one. We're neither of us fools."

"No," he says, cautiously. "Is Piero back?"

"No, the news came ahead of him. Bad news has wings. The Senate wants to send another delegation to Charles, repudiating Piero's terms, making a better deal. Piero had no actual right to negotiate for us, not a scrap."

If Charles granted Piero authority to negotiate, then the authority existed, whether it did on paper or not. The Medici had always ruled from behind the scenes, seldom holding office. "Sending another delegation seems like sound sense in the circumstances."

"I came to ask you, to beg you, to keep the people quiet. The people will listen to you. You don't need an official voice, you're a prophet. It cuts past all of that."

Girolamo doesn't need God to tell him that this is the moment to act. "And now?" he asks.

"Now I'm asking you to join the Senate's delegation to Charles. You can persuade him not to harm the city."

"Yes," Brother Girolamo says.

"Yes?"

"Yes, I can do that. Charles won't harm Florence once I have spoken to him." He is sure, and awed by his own certainty even as God speaks through him. The most unstoppable army Europe has ever seen is sweeping towards defenceless Florence, and he *knows* he can stop them, singlehandedly, with nothing but words. He is sure, as sure as he has ever been of anything. "But it will take all of our strength. We must trust in God, but trust ourselves, too, and be alert."

Capponi nods. "Are you ready to go?"

"I have to speak to someone first," he says.

"I'll assemble the rest of the delegation here. I'll bring a horse for you. We can ride in half an hour." Girolamo considers refusing to ride, but it would be an assertion of pride, not humility, in these circumstances. He nods. Capponi leaves, looking relieved to have his mind made up. Girolamo pauses to kneel before his crucifix for a quick prayer, then follows.

Brother Benedetto is waiting outside his cell. "I want permission to transfer to Bologna," he says, without any preliminaries.

"I said after Twilight Prayers. I don't have time now," Girolamo says. "And I have to go. I'll deal with you when I get back."

"But this won't take long. First Brother Vincenzo has sent for me, and I have a wonderful opportunity for promotion!" Benedetto objects.

"You shouldn't be thinking about any worldly promotion, only the promotion of your soul to Heaven," Girolamo says. Benedetto comes from a wealthy family, and though he is intelligent, he can't seem to let go of being proud and worldly. "Go to the church and repeat the Lord's Prayer thirty times, and then say the rosary, and really think about what you're saying." Girolamo has pity on him. "You can take my big rosary." He reaches to his belt for it.

"I have one," Benedetto says, and shows his own rosary, gold links and garnets, where Girolamo's has black wooden beads on a string. "After I've prayed, can I go to Bologna?"

Girolamo doesn't want to give up on the soul of his brother, but he is in a hurry. The French are coming, and the Count could be dying. "Yes, go," he says, unhappily. Benedetto can be Vincenzo's problem. He hurries out to the gate of San Marco. Isabella is waiting, wrapped in a dark brown cloak. Her face is red with weeping. He can see the edge of her dark hair, slipping uncombed from under her scarf. "Did the Count send you for me?" he asks.

"No. I came myself. I think Giovanni's poisoned, the same as Angelo," she says, low-voiced. "I caught his servant Cristoforo putting a powder in his food. I turned him off, and he went straight to the Palazzo Medici. But Giovanni's worse, and I can't manage to care for him entirely alone. The servants still haven't come back, and if I hire someone new I don't know if they're in Piero's pay. Can you let me have a reliable brother to help?"

He doesn't have time, the whole city, the whole of Italy, is poised on this moment. He can't send a monk back with her, she can't have thought how it would look. "Bring him here," he says, abruptly. "He was almost ready to take vows. The brothers will care for him in the infirmary, as if he were one of us."

"But I—" She stops, and knows what she would have said, that she won't be able to care for him herself, or even see him once he has been taken inside San Marco to the cells. But she is brave, and wants what is best for the Count. She clutches the cloak at her breast. "Yes."

"Some brothers will come with you and carry him here," he says.

Girolamo goes back in and finds Domenico and Silvestro still in the outer office. He gives them rapid orders, concerning both the Count and his own forthcoming absence. Old Tommaso comes up with a clean white under-robe, someone else's, and his own best black robe to go on top of it. "Don't want you to be a disgrace to the Order," he says, in his quavering voice. "There's mud and worse all over the one you have on."

He's right, and the hem is fraying, too. Girolamo takes the clean habit and thanks the old brother. Then he closes the door of his cell, leaving his brothers outside. He prays before his crucifix for a moment, then fumbles in the locked drawer of his desk and draws out the little volume of Pliny he found in Santa Lucia two years ago. He thrusts it into his sleeve.

Then he goes downstairs again, and Capponi is back, with five other men and a spare riding horse, already saddled. He swings himself up, adjusting his robe, and follows Capponi away from San Marco, towards the French and his destiny. The bell is ringing again. The last thing he sees as they ride off is Isabella's tear-stained face.

The day is almost over, and the wind seems edged with ice. When they come to the city gate, it is besieged. As usual, it takes Girolamo a moment to realise that no one else can see the demonic legions that surround the walls. They are demons of all kinds, great and small, animal headed, bat winged, armed with spears and swords and claws, drawn up in a great host that stretches out as far as he can see, covering the hills and fields, with shadowy banners waving about them. They are pressing on the walls, thousands of them, blue, and red, and green, and black, or pink and fleshy, all monstrous, all hideous, and ringing the city. As they see Girolamo they begin to howl. "Stop," he says, in a choked voice, and the other envoys rein in their horses, looking at him curiously. He slides down from his own beast, and tosses the reins to the nearest envoy, without looking.

As he steps forward he realises that, try as they might, the demons cannot pass the wall, and that it is not the physical wall of Florence that repels them, as it might a material army, but the mighty wall of prayer and repentance that has been built up around it and through it. He cannot see the spiritual wall, but he can see the demons flinging themselves against it and recoiling. Florence can hold them off now, she is strong enough. But there is no need to leave her open to their constant assaults, not when he is here. The demons retreat snarling before him as he advances. After a few steps, he fumbles the translucent green stone out of the book and holds it high in his right hand, letting the thin sunlight fall on it. With his left he forms the circle, and he begins to sing, as loudly as he can, the powerful heartening words of Psalm Fifty-one. The demons stream up like a great mist, becoming insubstantial like smoke and flowing through his fingers. When the last of them has gone, he puts the stone back in his sleeve and goes back to his horse.

"Nice to have a prayer for setting off," Capponi says, looking sideways at him as he mounts up again.

He nods. He doesn't want to see demons when other men do not, didn't ask for this power and this responsibility. But since God has given it to him, since he can act to banish them, then he will do so. The city was holding them off without him, he reminds himself. The wall of prayer was resisting. It is the most reassuring sign he has ever had of the effectiveness of his ministry.

CHAPTER 7

This day.

Charles VIII, by the Grace of God King of France, is a short ill-favoured man with a pronounced tremor. Rumour says his sister is so misshapen that there is no chance of her giving birth, and gossip said the same about the king. This was confounded when Charles had a son a year ago, by his wife Anne, the Duchess of Brittany. His next heir, should the baby dauphin Charles Orlando die, is his cousin Louis of Orleans, who is married to the misshapen sister, Jeanne. Girolamo knows this because everyone knows it, but he is shaken when he is ushered ceremoniously into the king's presence and sees in the impressive surroundings this decidedly unimpressive and ungainly man. Can this be the Sword of the Lord, the New Cyrus? Assuredly, God moves in mysterious ways.

Capponi speaks first. He has been Florence's ambassador to France, so Charles knows him. He speaks in French, which Girolamo can usually make out, but not speak with any confidence. Bowing in the French style, while still dressed in red as a Florentine merchant, Capponi looks more like a capon than ever. The folds of his red cloak look just like tailfeathers, and the way he walks, with his head thrust a little forward, is just like a strutting chicken. Girolamo looks around the great embroidered tent, at the swags of brocade holding open the entranceway, at the tapestries showing martial scenes, the gilded throne where Charles sits, and the wooden dais beneath it that raises him up so that his stature isn't as obvious. They have carried all this with them from France, over the high passes of the Alps, to support the king's dignity. The French courtiers are so strongly scented and elegantly dressed that they are hard to take seriously as soldiers. They stand behind the throne muttering to each other.

One of the other Florentines begins to speak, in Tuscan, and Girolamo notices Charles's attention wandering. He is prompted by a forewarning from God. This is his time, the tide is rising and he has to seize his moment, now.

He steps forward, entirely out of the order they had prepared with so much dickering along the way. As the king's eyes rest on him curiously, he blesses Brother Tomasso for making sure he had a clean habit for the occasion. He also thanks God that although he has never been handsome, with his great beaky nose, he is properly formed and straight spined. He does not bow, but stands still, his hands spread and his head back.

"Great King, you will conquer Rome and Naples," he says, in Latin, the language of all educated men.

Charles meets his gaze for the first time, and Girolamo sees that his eyes are sharp and bright.

"And you are?" His Latin has a French accent but is clear enough.

"I am Brother Girolamo Savonarola of Ferrara, First Brother of the Monastery of San Marco in Florence," he says. Florentia, in Latin, the name of the city means flowering, or flowing, or flourishing.

"He is a prophet," says Francesco Valori, another of the Florentine envoys. They are all behind him now, so he cannot see their faces. He doesn't know Valori well, he's another Medici man of Capponi's kind, but he sounds as if he means what he says.

"A p-prophet?" Charles asks, brows raised.

Girolamo doesn't bother to confirm or deny. "God has chosen you as his instrument," he says, passionately, sincerely, meeting the king's gaze with confidence.

Charles waves his hand, dismissing not just the Florentine envoys but everyone else in the tent. Some of the French courtiers and advisors protest, but Charles continues to dismiss them insistently, until friar and king are left alone together.

"I am n-never alone f-from morning to n-night," the king says. "N-now t-tell me," he says.

Girolamo takes a deep breath and begins, leaning on the certainty that he is right. He speaks to the king not as a suppliant but as an equal, because he is sharing a personal message to Charles from God. "God has chosen you as he chose Noah, as he chose Gideon. Italy will be cleansed, and you are the instrument of his will. Rome and Naples will fall into your hand with barely a blow struck."

"N-now you will say, this will happen if I will spare F-florence," Charles says, his voice half-believing, half-scornful.

"No," Girolamo says, full of confidence. "You will spare Florence because you are God's vessel, and just. You are a good man, and a good king, a true king, ruling with God beside you. You come for good, not evil, and though you are ready to fight your enemies, I have no need to beg you to spare your friends. Florence is your friend. We stand together on God's side. You will pass through our streets and go on to your triumph, your destiny."

"N-Naples. I have a very good c-claim to N-Naples," Charles says, hesitantly.

"The Neapolitans will welcome you with flowers," he says, seeing it as he speaks. "You will take it with barely a blow struck."

"And God has t-told you this?"

"He has shown me," Girolamo says, unfalteringly. "You are the Sword of the Lord, the New Cyrus, I have been prophesying your coming for three years now."

"I am n-not worthy," the King of France says to him, Brother Girolamo, son of a doctor from Ferrara, humble Dominican friar. Charles looks hesitant, uncertain, his head cocked a little. He is leaning forward, inclining his misshapen body towards Girolamo.

"None of us are worthy of God's love, His infinite mercy, His trust, but He bestows His grace upon us anyway," he says. "Now we will go back to Florence, and you will follow after, and your army will pass through the city like a rain shower, doing no more harm, and then you will sweep on to cleanse Italy and do God's will."

"Yes," Charles says, leaning back, looking at him curiously. "And P-Piero de' Medici?"

"Florence is done with the Medici now," he says, though this is not something God has revealed to him.

"P-Piero p-promised me money."

"You will have to talk to Capponi about that," he says, making a gesture to dismiss all such petty earthly concerns. "Render unto Caesar. Also, you will need to discuss with him the details for how you will return Pisa to us." The other fortresses are just villages with armed camps, but Pisa was a significant city until Florence conquered it years ago, and important to retain as part of her territories. Florence is inland, but Pisa is a port. Pisa is necessary.

"N-not until the end of the c-campaign," Charles says, more decisively than anything he has yet said. "Then, yes." Charles bites his lip, hesitating. "Is there anything else you can t-tell me?"

"You are in God's hand," he says.

"You can't t-tell me whether my son will thrive or how long I will live?"

"God has not chosen to reveal that to me." He is offended at being treated like some fortune-teller. The most true thing Charles has said is that he is not worthy. But then who is?

Charles calls the others back in, and the tent fills up again with perfumed courtiers. The king informs them all that he will spare Florence, that the army will pass through rapidly and go on to their destiny, and that he will return Pisa and the fortresses at the end of the campaign when he returns to France. He doesn't mention anything about money. The other Florentine envoys are looking at Brother Girolamo incredulously, as if he has performed a miracle.

As they pass back through the camp, they observe the huge cannon, twice the size of any Girolamo has seen before. He thinks how different this army is from the demonic army that had been besieging Florence. There is laughter around the campfires here, but it is not all mocking. Voices are raised in song. A knot of men are gambling with dice, but as he watches he sees the winner, a man missing his two front teeth, divide his takings with the loser and clap him on the back. These are soldiers, not saints, but they are honest human men, mixed good with bad, all of them with souls that can choose the good and come to God. The demons are lost to all hope, reduced to mockery and hate. These men have done terrible things, destroyed towns, killed, raped, looted. But they can repent, can still choose to be kind to one another. It may be necessary for them to do even worse things in order for Italy to be purified. They are still God's children, he thinks, even as two of them get into a scuffle and roll on the ground, pounding at each other.

"Have you ever seen such big artillery pieces?" Valori murmurs to Capponi.

Capponi shakes his head.

They stay that night in a flea-infested travellers' inn a day's ride from Florence. It's not very clean, and it smells of damp rushes and stale sweat, but they are lucky to be in it. They have shelter and food because Capponi is an experienced traveller and sent a servant ahead to reserve them. The bread is under-salted and the soup thin and over-boiled, but they are indoors, with hot food, on a chill night when the rain is setting in hard. The other envoys had been giving Girolamo a wide berth as they rode. Now as they sit to eat, they fall into two groups, with Valori, Capponi, and Girolamo in the first, and the other four in the second, over against the wall on the other side of the fire. They're all in earshot, as are a bunch of other travellers: two portly Franciscan monks, a party of well-dressed merchants from Siena, and a solitary Swiss soldier who is missing half his right hand. The other four Florentine envoys have chosen to sit as far from Girolamo as they can.

"How did you do it?" Capponi asks, as they begin to eat.

"I thought persuading the king is why you wanted me to come," he says, dipping his bread in the soup. He looks questioningly at Capponi, whose red cape is steaming slightly from the heat of the fire.

"It is, man, but I didn't more than half believe it would work!" Capponi says.

"You speak to the people, you speak to kings, is there anyone you can't speak to?" Valori asks, shyly.

"The vainglorious rich," he says. "I speak loud enough, but they can't hear me."

Valori is looking at him with eyes full of hero worship now.

"It is God speaking through me," he goes on, but it doesn't help.

Later Capponi and Valori fall to condemning Piero for his idiocy. "We could have easily held out until they went into winter quarters," Valori says.

Capponi contradicts him. "Now normally, you'd be right. But not this time. I didn't understand this myself until I went to France and lived there for a while. The French army won't go into winter quarters. They're not a professional army. Well, in one sense they are, they certainly know how to fight. They've got those big artillery pieces they made sure we saw when they led us through the camp. Wouldn't like to be on the wrong end of those. We'll need to make our walls stronger, I think. Must talk to the architects and engineers about that. But they're not professional in the other sense, they're not paid, their captains don't have contracts. This is the levy of France. They have to fight because their king tells them to, and they don't get any pay except what they can loot and carry off for themselves. They've been fighting the English on French soil for a hundred years. We're used to contracts, soldiers who get so much a week and extra if there's a battle, have to have a doctor along to patch them up, and no fighting in winter or bad weather. These soldiers aren't like that. They're fighting for their king and country. They're required to, by oath."

"And the captains?" Valori asks, wiping the last of his soup from his bowl with his bread.

"The captains the same, they're knights and lords of France." Capponi shakes his head. "Nobility. We don't have a lot of that in Italy, where every city has its own form of government, and hardly any city-state has rulers who can trace their family back very far."

"Ferrara," Girolamo objects. "The D'Este—"

"Saving your presence, Ferrara's properly a Papal fief, and the D'Este are just lucky to stand where they do, where anyone attacking them risks having a frontier with Venice, so everyone leaves them alone. The D'Este have held on to power for longer than most of the tyrants of Italy, that's all. The Sforza of Milan were nothing but mercenary captains two generations ago, the Montefeltro of Urbino go back one whole generation, the Bentivoglios of Bologna are just another Papal fief. And as for Naples, the so-called kingdom, it's being ruled by a Spanish bastard whose claim, and whose father's claim, isn't worth spit in a rainstorm."

"But what does this have to do with the French not going into winter quarters?" Valori asks.

"They're fighting for honour, not for pay," Capponi says, impatiently.

"Like . . . timarchy," Valori says, tentatively. Timarchy is one of Plato's categories of government, where the rulers put honour ahead of virtue.

"That's about the size of it," Capponi says.

"And what we have in Italy is oligarchy?" Valori asks. Plato describes oligarchy as where the rulers put money first.

"I don't think Plato thought of all the possibilities," Girolamo interjects.

"Have you read Plato?" Capponi asks, surprised. He pauses in the middle of cutting an apple in half with his knife.

"Ficino translated him for everyone," Girolamo says, finishing his soup and pushing away the bowl.

"I thought you were all for Christ!"

"I am. But I've read Plato. You have to if you want to keep up with Count Pico." Girolamo smiles, but he is worrying again about the Count's health. Lilies won't bloom until March, at the earliest. But Charles will be in Florence in a day or two.

"So what do you think Plato missed?" Capponi asks, finishing cutting the apple and offering half to Girolamo. He takes it.

"I don't think he missed anything he could have seen when he was writing, four hundred years before Christ. And I think you're right, France is a timarchy, and Italy is a set of oligarchies, for the most part. But what do you call Venice?"

"A democracy?" Valori asks, moving aside to make way for the Franciscans who have finished eating and are heading for their room. "No, not really."

"It's not a democracy the way Plato talks about, where all the people rule. It has a council of five hundred, and the right to be on it is hereditary. But five hundred is a lot of people, a lot of families. It's almost like the nobility you were saying Italy doesn't have, Capponi, but they elect their leader for life." He takes a bite of the apple, which is sweet and firm.

"Aristocracy?" Valori ventures, resettling himself beside them.

"Everyone says their own system is aristocracy," Capponi says, cynically, crunching the last of his apple.

"And what about us? Wouldn't Plato say we're a democracy, with our elected senate and the names of our First Men pulled out of a purse every two months?" Valori asks.

"It's who puts the names *in* the purse you have to watch," Capponi says. "There's no such thing as a neutral scrutineer. That's how Cosimo took things into his control in the first place, and how the Medici have ruled behind the scenes for the last sixty years."

"And it wasn't a democracy even before, because only guildsmen have ever had their names put in," Girolamo says. "There are close to thirty thousand men in Florence of the right ages, but only two or three thousand of them could even think of being eligible."

"You can't expect a wool-dyer or a barber's apprentice to be competent to run the city!" Capponi protests.

Girolamo can't see why not, if a wool merchant or a master butcher can hold office. He shrugs. "You trust them and even the idle layabouts and thugs when you gather together a great shouting mob outside the Senatorial Palace and call it an assembly," he says. "You don't want to call Florence an oligarchy, but that's what it is now, with a senate of seventy men."

"We have a mixed constitution, as Aristotle recommended. Like the Roman Republic," Capponi says, as if that example settles it. On the other side of the table, a couple of the Sienese merchants seem to be frankly eavesdropping.

"Not really mixed," he says, ignoring them. "You have no nobility. You have to hire younger sons of noble families from elsewhere to work as Power-Bearer and be in charge of policing the city."

"Well, we killed off all our nobility, or banned them from participating in government," Capponi allows. "Sometime. Sometime after the fall of Rome and before the rise of the Medici. We got rid of them because they were Ghibellines, or because they were trouble and started civil wars in the streets. The guilds rule because we're all equal, and all reliable. Or that's the idea."

"But having guild membership be the qualification for government has ruined your guilds," one of the Sienese merchants interrupts.

All the Florentines stare at him, and he shrinks back in his chair.

"I apologise for my friend," says the other Sienese. "He's had too much wine."

"No, let him speak," Girolamo says. "How has it ruined the guilds?"

"Well, because they're political in Florence, they're not proper guilds. They don't do the job of guilds. People join them just for political power, people who don't even practice the trade."

Capponi and Valori nod in unison. "That's true enough," Capponi says.

Encouraged by this acknowledgement, the Sienese goes on. "So the whole system gets loose, and you have stupid things like goldsmiths working in bronze, and painters trespassing on the territory of the sculptor's guild. It's all a mess. Sculptors become architects without the guild of masons complaining. Guild secrets get out, silk weavers learn from linen weavers and the other way around. And the guild leadership doesn't crack down on it, because the guilds are led by politicians who don't care about silk or goldsmithing or whatever."

"It's not as bad as that," Capponi says.

"It will lead to anarchy!" the Sienese says. "There are always new things coming out of Florence. No good will come of it!"

Capponi laughs, and pats the man on the shoulder. "Your friend's right, you've had too much wine," he says. "What does it matter if a sculptor becomes an architect, as long as he's competent?"

Apologising, the Sienese group go off to bed, the drunk one still muttering about the evils of innovation.

"But you were going to tell us what Plato left out?" Valori reminds Girolamo when they've gone.

"Well. Beyond whatever you want to call the Serene Republic of Venice, apart from a good stable example, or an Aristotelean mixed constitution, there's the other possibility Plato couldn't imagine. The City of God. The state that chooses Christ for King, and rules itself that way."

"By the Rule of St Benedict?" Valori asks.

Girolamo shakes his head. "No, because it wouldn't be all monks. St Dominic explains how laypeople can lead a holy life, marrying and having children and living in the world, not withdrawing from the world. We already have communities of monks, sworn brothers and sisters, separate from the world. But we could have a whole city consecrated to God, but that otherwise worked something like Venice."

Capponi nods slowly, and Valori looks at him as if this thought were divine revelation no one has ever thought before. On the other side of the fire, the Swiss soldier has fallen asleep and begun to snore.

"More wine?" Capponi asks.

He shakes his head, and so does Valori. He eats the last bite of his apple.

Capponi drains his own cup. "Well then, we should get some rest. We'll have an early start and a long day tomorrow, and then it might be hard work at the end of it, telling the people, telling the Senate, trying to talk to Piero."

But when they arrive back in Florence the next evening it's to hear that Piero and his brother Leo, the cardinal, have fled. "Florence is ours!" Valori says to him when they hear this news.

"It is God's city," Brother Girolamo agrees.

The next day, preaching to a packed crowd in the cathedral, he puts his hands on the rim of the pulpit and leans forward. "Cosimo de' Medici said cities were not ruled by saying Our Father," he says. "Let's prove him wrong. Our Father—"

The crowd joins in the Lord's Prayer at a bellow that feels as if it could raise the dome. He has never heard anything like the roar that comes from them.

He has built his Ark, and it will float.

CHAPTER 8

Our daily bread.

NOVEMBER 18TH, 1494

He doesn't especially want to leave the Count's sickbed to go to see the French arrive, but everyone assumes he will be there, and it seems churlish to refuse without a good reason. They march into the city with their fleur-de-lys banners flying, with drums and trumpets, with shields and horses and all the panoply of chivalry. They smell of mud, sweat, and badly risen bread. He told the Count that France is Plato's timarchy, and the Count tried to smile. He is in the infirmary of San Marco, on the upper floor, where the brothers care for their own sick. His bed is in front of a fresco of the presentation of Jesus at the temple. *Now let thy servant depart in peace.* San Marco is a relatively new monastery, but he wonders how many of his brothers have departed in sight of that gentle painting. The tapestries have been put up in the infirmary too, covering the lower part of the walls, to keep the cell warmer.

The first of the French to arrive were their quartermasters, to arrange the billeting and provisioning of the troops in the city. Girolamo has heard a quip in the streets that the French have conquered Florence with a stick of chalk, the chalk they used to mark houses where troops can stay. The troops march in now, in splendid style, and Girolamo stands watching them from in front of the Senatorial Palace, standing beside Capponi and Valori and the other men who have taken charge of the city in the sudden absence of the Medici. Girolamo spoke for an amnesty, and against purging Medician supporters. There has been too much of that already. Piero and his brother the young cardinal have fled. Alfonsina Orsini, Piero's wife, has taken refuge in Santa Lucia with her mother and her young son. Let the rest of them alone, as long as they behave, the sisters and their husbands, and the cousins. It's time for the city to pull together, not break apart. They are calling Florence's exiles home, not making more.

The Medici Palace was looted as soon as Piero fled, before Girolamo came back to Florence, but he appealed from the pulpit for the goods to be restored. "They belong to all of us now, not to any of us in particular," he said, and most of them have indeed been quietly returned. Donatello's bronze statue of a nude David, which used to stand in the courtyard of the Medici Palace, has been moved to the Senatorial Palace. David is the symbol of little Florence, alone among the great Goliaths, with God on her side. There are already two statues of David in the Senatorial Palace, a thoroughly dressed marble one by Donatello and a bronze by Verrocchio, but one more doesn't hurt. Now everyone will be able to see Donatello's *David.* His bronze *Judith and Holofernes* has been set up outside the palace, on the dais in the square, next to where Girolamo is standing, shivering, watching endless columns of Frenchmen march through. It's more to his taste than the extravagantly nude *David,* which seems designed to turn thoughts to sins of the flesh. The story of Judith celebrates the overthrow of a tyrant.

The people in the streets are cheering the soldiers, and the soldiers seem in a good mood too. Charles arrives eventually, on a high-striding horse, dressed splendidly in cloth-of-gold robes. Capponi welcomes him to Florence. Charles dismounts, with the aid of one of his men.

He looks as if the glories of Florence have intimidated him already. His route will have taken him past the cathedral of Santa Maria del Fiore, one of the most splendid cathedrals in Christendom, with its huge dome, the largest in the world. His lords and retinue dismount behind him. They go inside, finally, up the steep stairs and out of the wind. The room they are ushered into has a fresco of St Zenobius, the first bishop of Florence. The other walls are blue, and have been rapidly painted with gold fleur des lys, symbol of both Florence and France. Painters have been stencilling them all night, and there is still a slight smell of paint. Refreshments are offered, fruits, salads, and hams, but Girolamo refuses. He is fasting. He goes over to the window, climbing up on the stone step to continue to watch the parade of soldiers pass through the square. How many men has Charles brought? They seem endless. And the flags, lily after lily.

He can't think, later, how he can have been so obtuse about the lilies. Like much prophecy, it is obvious only in retrospect. The time of the lilies. Of course. Tears burn at his eyes. He prays to St Jerome and the Holy Mother for the soul of that good man and good friend Giovanni Pico della Mirandola.

The parade eventually ends. While course follows course and Charles eats lampreys and roast boar with the senators, his troops disperse to their various chalkmarked billets, scattered among the narrow streets of Florence. There they will be fed and rested for a day or two until they move on south. The spectators empty out of the square, looking cold and tired. Girolamo turns to face the room, where Capponi and Charles and the other senators and French noblemen are finishing their meal with pastry delicacies and marzipan shaped like leaves and flowers. Charles and Capponi are both red in the face and scowling at each other. "P-Piero offered me t-twice that much," Charles says, setting down an untouched cream-filled horn.

"We don't have it and can't spare it," Capponi says, leaning forward.

"I could invite P-Piero b-back," Charles threatens.

"Whether the city would accept him back is a different matter," Capponi says, smoothly.

"I could b-blow my trumpets," Charles says.

"Then we could ring our bells," Capponi counters. "You have brought a great army, but now your soldiers are scattered into the streets and alleyways of a city strange to them, where barricades could be thrown up in minutes."

Girolamo does not speak, because he knows he does not need to. For a few minutes Charles continues to glare at Capponi, and then he laughs.

"Oh C-Capponi, you are such a c-capon!" he says. He picks up his cream pastry and bites into it decisively. All the French titter sycophantically, and a shiver of distaste runs through Girolamo. How terrible for human souls to abase themselves that way. Then Charles turns to him, crumbs falling from the corners of his mouth. "What n-news, Friar?"

"Count Giovanni Pico della Mirandola is dying," he says, quite without premeditation.

To his surprise, Charles's face crumples in grief. "Send doctors," he snaps to one of his underlings, who bows and summons an underling of his own. Of course, Pico has a reputation among all educated men. But Girolamo is surprised at this reaction. He remembers that the Count was arrested in France, and Charles did nothing for him then. It was Lorenzo, and Girolamo himself, who had written urgently to the Pope to procure his release.

Two French doctors accompany him back to San Marco. Brother Silvestro meets the three of them at the gate, his face doleful. "Too late," he says, but Girolamo has known it since he understood the riddle of the lilies.

They go upstairs, past the *Annunciation*. Mary's painted face seems to hold all hope and all sorrow. The French doctors exclaim over its beauty, in Latin, and Silvestro tells them in the same language that it was painted by Brother Angelico, of Fiesole, and of this house, and they exclaim again. "Truly he understood the incarnation," one of them says. Girolamo nods, completely agreeing, but does not speak because of the lump in his throat.

They are met at the infirmary door by the Count's nephew and heir, Gianfrancesco and Benivieni, both of them in tears. "Too late," Gianfrancesco says to the doctors. "So kind of King Charles, but there is nothing you could have done." He looks like a younger, plumper, less well-defined version of his uncle, like an apprentice copy of a master's painting. It seems cruel that he still has breath to animate his body when his uncle lies dead.

"He breathed his last as the French entered Florence," Benivieni says, wiping his eyes. "In the time of the lilies, as you prophecied, Brother Girolamo."

Girolamo doesn't bother to deny the origin of the prophecy. He goes into the room and sees the Count on the bed, looking shrunken and smaller in death. His brothers have cleaned him and dressed him in the Dominican habit he did not live to claim. His face is peaceful. Girolamo smoothes the hair from his cold forehead. He thinks of Angelo struggling to forgive Piero, and for the time being can himself forgive neither Piero nor the servant Cristoforo, who gave the Count another dose of poison. He looks at the painting, the baby Jesus in the arms of Simeon, his mother reaching out her arms towards them. Jesus forgave the soldiers who came to arrest him. He reattached the ear of the one Peter attacked. If Girolamo were Piero's confessor he would make him walk barefoot to San Diego de Compostela, and then swim to Jerusalem. He abused hospitality, to poison guests at his table. Girolamo is so angry that if Piero were there he would strike him.

"After the Count was given the last rites, he spoke the name of Lorenzo, almost as if he saw him and recognised him," Silvestro says.

"That's good," Girolamo says, pleased that Lorenzo came from heaven to help his friend's soul at the last. How can God make such a man and let him be lost so soon? How many books would the Count have written, what a harvest of souls would he have brought in, if he had lived? He will be with God, he will understand all the mysteries he always wanted to understand, but the world still needed him.

"Such a loss, such a marvel," Benivieni says, behind him. "Truly he was the Phoenix of our age." It's true, but he resents Benivieni saying it. Now the Count is dead, Benivieni will spend the rest of his life going around telling people how close they were, how he was his best friend. Girolamo sees it so clearly he isn't sure whether it's prophecy or just an observation of human nature.

"He will be with God," Girolamo says, turning to them. His voice is thick with tears. "He will be buried here, in San Marco, with Angelo Poliziano. They both meant to take vows if they lived."

"I know it, it's true," Gianfrancesco says, nodding fervently. "It's better for his bones to be here than back in Mirandola. I will write to my father and my uncle and to all his friends."

Girolamo nods, and then remembers Isabella, who no one will write to, who is not the Count's widow. The doctors bustle about leaving, expressing their regrets. Everyone assures them that King Charles has done all he possibly could. Benivieni leaves, saying he is going to Ficino. He will spread the news through the city, Girolamo sees, with himself in the starring role as chief mourner.

"He will be with God," he says again, to Gianfrancesco, after Benivieni has gone. "After a little while atoning for his sins in Purgatory and being cleansed."

Gianfrancesco sobs, harshly, and falls to his knees on the tiled floor, still sobbing. He is in his early twenties, but he still seems like a boy.

"We will have him taken to the church now, to lie there, with candles," Brother Silvestro says, putting his hand on Gianfrancesco's shoulder. "Would you take your turn watching, with the brothers?"

Girolamo leaves Silvestro to comfort Gianfrancesco and deal with the practical details. There are a thousand things he should be doing. He has sermons to write, letters to answer, problems within the monastery and outside it, and perhaps he should ensure that Capponi and Charles do not need him. There is also the routine of the offices of prayer, which he should not neglect without urgent need. He stares unseeing at the fresco for a little while, then ignores all of his duties and walks straight back out into the chill of the afternoon. He pulls his habit close around him. The workshops and stalls are closed, for the entry of the French. The muck of the streets has barely been trodden since the troops passed through, but there are knots of men clustered outside inns and taverns, talking. Each group falls silent as he passes, one after the next, watching him, and starting up muttering again when he has passed. He overhears his name. There are no women visible at all. He sees the occasional French soldier, swaggering. When he passes the licenced brothel, stinking as always of perfume and sex, he sees it is full of soldiers, with not a Florentine in sight, apart from the girls. At last he comes to the house on the Via Porto Rossa where he had heard Angelo's confession. A child opens the door to him, a dark-eyed boy of eight or nine.

"I'm looking for Isabella," he says.

"I think she's gone," the boy says. "The Count has gone. But go up and look."

The boy disappears into one of the rooms that open off the courtyard on the ground floor, and Girolamo goes up the stairs. On the second floor he taps on the closed door of the room where Angelo died. If she has already gone, he knows he will never be able to find her. He waits, and then hears footsteps, not from inside but from around the portico. Isabella appears, dressed in black, with her hair completely covered, like a widow.

"I didn't expect you to come," she says. She shows him into a different room, one hung with tapestries showing the story of Susanna. It's a little study. On the desk are piles of books, a big silver hourglass, ink pots, a sand-shaker for blotting, and a pile of closely written paper. He sits, awkwardly, in one of the chairs made to his own design, the sleeves of his habit falling forward over his hands.

"I wanted to tell you he was dead," he says. "I knew no one would. I didn't want you to hear it on the street."

"Thank you," she says. "I knew he would die, and yet until now I held on to a tiny shred of hope. Oh why couldn't he have lived! Even if he'd taken vows and I'd never seen him again, the world would not have lost him!"

It is how he feels himself. "He spoke well of you. He wanted to take care of you."

"He has," she says. "I am going to go to Genoa to set up in a little shop as a seller of ribbons. I will say I am a widow. I couldn't do it here, where people know me. It's all arranged. It's what I was going to do when he joined you. I would have gone already, except that it's so hard to leave." She folds the black wool of her sleeve, staring down at it.

Girolamo absently straightens the pile of paper on the table. "Hard to leave Florence?"

She looks up and meets his eyes. "Hard to leave these rooms where we were so happy, where it seems as if he might come bounding in at any moment, saying something I would never have thought of in a century." She tips her head back and takes a slow breath, then straightens up again, holding on to her self control. "Thank you for coming to tell me," she says. "That was kind. I would have heard it on the street, the news of his death will echo around the world. But this is better. And thank you for telling me he'd spoken well of me to you."

"He should have married you," Girolamo blurts out.

"But then he could not have become a Dominican and joined you," she says.

"Well, technically he could, if you'd married and then both taken vows at the same time," Girolamo says.

Isabella tries to smile, and a tear escapes and trickles down her cheek. "He really couldn't marry me. He was a Count. Any marriage he made would have to have been for alliance and position and worldly status. I'm not the right kind at all. My father was a bean seller!" She shakes her head. "No, I knew he could never marry me, but he was fond of me."

"He was," Girolamo agrees. "He said so."

"Well, now that will have to be enough," she says. "You'd better take his papers and give them to his nephew. They're no good to me."

"You can't read?"

She looks at him scornfully. "I can read. But I can't finish his translation of Psalms from Hebrew, or his treatise against the astrologers."

"I'll finish that," Girolamo promises. She gathers up the books and papers and gives them to him, and then when he is standing with the pile in his arms there is nothing to do but go. "Good luck in Genoa," he says, awkwardly. On the top of the pile is a copy of Ficino's translation of Plotinus. His eye keeps falling on it as he walks down the stairs, and as he walks back through the streets. Plotinus was a Platonist. He hasn't read him, but he has heard the Count discuss him. So many conversations they will never have. So many things that he too would never have thought of in a century. Yet he should rejoice for him. All the mysteries are open to him now. He is with God, or soon will be. How he will delight in Heaven! Girolamo feels hot tears spilling from his eyes, and pulls the hood of his robe forward so no one will see.

CHAPTER 9

And forgive us.

Girolamo is working in the library of San Marco when he is interrupted by one of the new novices, Brother Bartolomeo. The novice rooms at San Marco are full, and with Dominicans coming to them from elsewhere there are now two hundred and fifty brothers in the monastery. They have to send new novices to Fiesole and Santa Maria Novella. Fiesole is now happy to live pure, though Santa Maria Novella still chafes under his insistence on living as Dominicans should. The women's monasteries of Santa Lucia and the Annalena are also bursting at the seams. Camilla Rucellai is founding a new third Dominican house in her home for women who can prophecy.

"Thanks be to God. Benivieni is here, he's waiting in the little courtyard with a new poem to show you. And Mistress Salviati has come, and she's in the parlour. And Bonacorsi sent the printed proofs of your sermons for you to check, and here's a letter just arrived from Rome," Bartolomeo says.

Girolamo echoes his thanks to God automatically, wondering whose idea it was to thank God for interruptions. He has so much to do, and Benivieni will waste so much time. He means well, and it had been Girolamo's idea to make sure his poems were orthodox—indeed, he shudders for what Benivieni would come up with in his name if he did not. He prays that God will forgive him for finding the man so constantly irritating. "Thank you Bartolomeo. Take the proofs to my study, and then tell Benivieni I will come down."

In the library, it is cool, with a faint smell of cloves, camphor, and fish glue. The walls of San Marco are thick, and the windows are small, and the shutters have been closed on the sunny side, letting in light to work but not sun to heat the room. The ceiling is high, allowing the heat to rise. Around him, at the two long rows of desks, his brothers are copying sacred texts, illuminating the manuscripts with pictures and gold leaf. As soon as he is outside he knows he will immediately begin to sweat. He rolls his shoulders and stretches. Bartolomeo hands him the letter and scampers off, proofs under his arm. He is very young, and Girolamo envies him his energy. Girolamo has been sick recently, the usual summer fevers, which swept through the monastery felling all before them, and then a bad bout of dysentery. He still feels weak from it, exhausted all the time.

Bartolomeo pauses by one of the copyists, who is dancing his brush over a piece of gold leaf, so that it rises up to the bristles. The expression on the novice's face is awe. He can read and write, perhaps he should be put to work in the Scriptorium soon. There is always plenty of work preparing parchment and grinding paints while learning to be a scribe or an illustrator. Girolamo is excited by possibilities of the new technology of printing, and is working closely with Bonacorsi on his book of sermons, but he doesn't believe it will ever replace hand copying texts to the extent that San Marco won't need to keep training novices to copy manuscripts.

Girolamo turns the letter in his hands. It is addressed "To our dear son, Brother Girolamo of the Order of Preachers of the Observance, living in Florence." That is the seldom-used formal name of the Dominicans. What does Pope Alexander Borgia want now? He closes his book carefully and sets it in its place under the desk. He has been reading Boethius because he is suffering from the sin of pride, and no matter how often he confesses it and how much penance he does, he continues to fall into this one besetting sin. He wears his hair belt and hair vest constantly, even as the summer heat falls on Florence like a solid weight. The band of skin around his waist is chafed to bleeding, but still he cannot rid himself of pride. He prays for hours with his rosary, he barely eats, he sleeps as little as he can. On Maundy Thursday he washed the feet of all his brothers and all the poor who crowded into the pilgrim hall for bread. He has been out and about through the four quarters of Florence, learning the narrow mazes of the streets, giving comfort to the sick and the dying with his own hands, whoever they are. But however much he adopts the outward signs of humility, pride comes creeping back.

He has done it. He has made the Ark, he has saved Florence, and it has actually worked. God put the city into his hand, and now it is, as much as any mortal city can be, the City of God. If it's not quite there yet, it is well on the way. There is a high wall of prayer around it, and demons batter themselves against it but cannot enter.

Valori came and asked him, immediately after the French left Florence and the Count was buried, if he would direct the commonwealth. He refused. "I am a monk, and a stranger from Ferrara. I cannot take power in Florence, it would be wrong."

"But you will advise us?" Valori begged, and Brother Girolamo bowed his head and assented. He preached two sermons on the City of God, and the stable excellent and longstanding institutions of Venice, and then a third on the importance of having a Great Council.

Florence is still ruled by its quasi-democratic system of drawing names out of purses. The Eight, along with the Standard-Bearer of Justice, are shut up in the top of the Senatorial Palace for two months, as always. For that time, they make the decisions that run the state. They are not allowed out, or to see anyone except civil servants. The elected Senate wrangles, and passes bills up to the Eight, and they have the absolute power to say yes or no. At the end of two months, they return to their ordinary lives and are replaced by another nine men whose names have been drawn. Now the names in the purses are not manipulated but the selection left to God and chance.

It seems crazy, and it certainly isn't efficient. But efficiency is not the only merit in government. It is a bulwark against tyranny, and as one Italian city-state after another has succumbed to a powerful tyrant, their odd way seems better and better to the Florentines. It was very good for keeping government weak, and very bad for consistent policy.

In the new system Valori and Capponi have put in place using Girolamo's advice, instead of a senate of seventy packed with Medici men, there is a Great Council of five hundred, just like in Venice. There are no rooms in the Senatorial Palace big enough for five hundred people, so a new great hall is being built. The masons are so happy to be doing it that work is going very fast. Girolamo has agreed to go to consecrate the altar when it is ready.

Many good laws are being passed. Florence now has a law of appeal, where anyone convicted of a serious crime can appeal the conviction before different judges. The rich are helping the poor, using the confraternities to collect money. The confraternities are societies of laymen, not monks or priests, who gather together to do work for the good of their souls. The work is that Jesus commends. Some visit prisoners, especially those condemned to death. Some nurse the sick. Others collect money to feed the poor, or to give dowries to poor girls who could not otherwise afford to marry, or to send poor boys to university so they might have careers. Now that he is so prominent in the commonwealth, rich men keep offering money to San Marco "for the poor," but with the true intention of buying his favour. Girolamo refuses it, telling them where to direct their charity, through the confraternities. San Marco continues as it always has.

There is one new charity project he has taken on. He has rescued the poor boys who sell themselves under the bridges—clothing them in white and feeding them. They come to his services and sing loudly. He has, with Benivieni's help, set new holy words to the tunes they know, which only had filthy words before. He calls them his Angels, and they walk first in the processions he organizes from San Marco to the cathedral or to other churches, on feast days and special occasions. The Angels are open to all boys, and many boys have joined from families rich and poor.

Apart from the demons, who never stop trying to attack the city, everything he has put his hand to has flourished. His Ark is sailing successfully. Florence is a pure city now, a city fit to lead the world, a new Jerusalem. No one is starving, and no one is selling their body as an alternative. If some are still selling their bodies illicitly, when they are caught the men who pay are now being punished as much or more than their victims. When he preaches, everyone comes to listen, and even when his brothers preach, the church will be packed. He preaches special sermons to women sometimes, and they come thronging to hear him. People's minds are on God, on holiness, and no one is smiling at sin anymore.

His only real problem is that he can't stop feeling proud. He knows it is a sin. He confesses it, and swears to do better, then falls straight back into it, like poor Angelo Poliziano with his sodomy. He is no better than Angelo, he is just as much a sinner; worse, for pride is a worse sin than lust.

He opens the Pope's letter, expecting, in his pride, commendation for his work in Florence, or even a request for help and guidance. To his surprise, Pope Alexander Borgia has written demanding that he come at once to Rome.

He knows immediately that if he does, he will die, and all he has achieved in Florence will be lost. Without him to strengthen it, sooner or later the wall of prayer will fall beneath the demonic assault, and Florence will return to sin and death.

He stares at the smoothly written letters, the neat penmanship of the Pope's scribe. The Pope wishes to discuss his revelation, his prophecy. This will end in martyrdom, in fire. He understands that this is God's intention, that whatever happens he will in the end be martyred. But if he goes to Rome, it will be now, and his fragile Ark will founder. He does not want to die. He is not afraid. He trusts God.

He longs for Heaven. But there is still so much to do, and Florence needs him. The wall will grow stronger, with time, and more prayer, but now it is still flimsy. But this is a direct order from the Pope. How can he refuse it? It is not pride that makes him hesitate, this time, it is God's own revelation.

He sighs. Brother Silvestro looks up from the text he's copying. "What's wrong?" he asks, quietly, so as not to disturb the others.

"His Holiness wants me to go to Rome, and God tells me that I will die if I go, but I can't see how to refuse."

"Tell him you've been ill," Silvestro says. "It's nothing but the truth. You're still as weak as a kitten. The journey would be terrible for you, in the heat of summer."

"I could say I have enemies who might attack me, meaning Piero de Medici, who I hear is gathering an army."

"Yes. And say that Florence needs you. That's the truth too."

It is pride, sinful pride, to believe this is true. "God might need my matryrdom as witness," he objects. But he knows Florence needs him to keep the demons away. Surely that is why God has given him the power to see them and to banish them?

"Not yet, surely," says Silvestro. "What's Pope Alexander's problem with you?"

"Probably that I am making him look bad," Girolamo says.

"Well then, he shouldn't do bad things," Silvestro says, bending again to his task, angling his parchment a little into the light.

Girolamo puts the letter in his sleeve. He will deal with Lucrezia and Benivieni first.

In the courtyard the swallows are down at the height of the rooftops, so perhaps it is going to rain and cool things down. He sees their fork-tailed shadows reflected on the wall. He nods to Benivieni, who is sitting reading. "If you're not in a hurry, I have someone to see in the parlour first."

"Go ahead, you know my time is yours," Benivieni says, courteously.

Her attendants are waiting outside in the Refectory, so Lucrezia

de' Medici Salviati sits alone stiffly in the parlour of San Marco with
her hands folded in her sleeves. The room is small, and very hot, and
the air is stuffy, and full of the rose scent of her perfume. There is no
decoration but a crucifix on the wall. It is not a room that is much
used, but the only possible place where he can receive a lady. They have
brought her wine and a dish of golden plums and set them on a little
table at her elbow, he notices, but she has not touched them. She is sitting in one of the chairs made to his design, and looks up alertly as he
comes in. He remembers the directness of her gaze from the other
time he met her, when her father, Lorenzo, was dying. He notices the
swelling under her modest dress; she is pregnant again. "Thank you
for seeing me, First Brother, I know you are very busy," she says.

He inclines his head. He isn't going to deny it. "What can I do for
you?" He opens the window, letting in a breath of breeze, and the
sound of the swallows, suddenly very loud. He sits down opposite her,
and is glad to sit. He hates this feebleness that the dysentery has left
him, so that walking downstairs and opening a window exhausts him.

"My husband is a supporter of yours," she begins.

He nods. Jacopo Salviati has become a fervent disciple, attending
all his sermons and siding reliably with Valori in the Senate.

"And I think you were, at the end, a friend of my father?"

"Yes, though I never met him until he was dying," Girolamo answers cautiously. He remembers her that day, biting off her thread and
reproving Piero.

"And of course our tutor Angelo was your friend, and dear Count
Pico," she says, looking at him assessingly, her head tilted a little to
the side.

"What have you come to ask me in their names?" he asks, cutting
through the flummery.

"Nothing," she protests, then catches herself, shaking her head.
"Yes I do have something to ask. I want to know whether I am safe."

He is surprised. "You know we have exiled none of the Ballsy—
that is, the Medician supporters," he says.

Lucrezia smiles. "We all call them the Ballsy. We always have. I believe my great-grandfather made up the term." It comes from the balls on the Medici shield. She glances up to where one of the ubiquitous stone shields marks the vaulting at the centre of the ceiling.

Girolamo has been sad to see parties developing in the new big Senate. Valori leads a party he calls "Friar's Men" and lots of people call "Wailers" after the bell of San Marco, or because they represent the poor and previously voiceless. The Ballsy, led by Bernardo Neri, oppose Valori and his Wailers and want the Medici back, but Girolamo still thinks he was right to let them stay. There are two other parties. First are the Greys, who are the old oligarchy. They are men of wealthy families used to power, but who have often been in opposition to the Medici. Now they sometimes side with the Ballsy, and more often with Valori. The last party are his outright enemies, the Lukewarm, whom God will spew from his mouth. They don't want the Medici back, unlike the Ballsy; they want to be in charge themselves, or so Girolamo thinks. But they're opposed to him, to God's will, to all positive change. Some people can be shamed into doing good, the Lukewarm need to be shamed out of doing evil.

"And here the Ballsy still are, Medici cousins and supporters and brothers-in-law, voicing their disagreements openly. So why would you fear for your safety?" he asks. It was Girolamo who prevented exiling the Medici allies. There has been too much casting out people who are supposedly enemies of the commonwealth. Most of those Lorenzo and Piero exiled have come back now, including the Strozzi family, who have a huge palace in Florence but have been in exile for decades. It is time to come together as brothers, he said, to heal rifts not deepen divisions. Capponi asked him if he was sure. He told him he had the instincts of a politician, and Capponi preened. But Girolamo is looking at this from the perspective of a man of God. In the nine months since Piero fled, they have exiled no one. They even let Alfonsina Orsini and her baby son go peacefully to Rome to join Piero. Lucrezia should have no reason to fear.

Lucrezia sighs. "I've mentioned the friends we have in common because my brother is your enemy."

"Piero," he says. He is still puzzled.

"Piero. Yes. There's also my other brother, Cardinal Leo, who has gone on a walking tour of Germany and the Low Countries. And my little brother, Giuliano, who is in Rome with Piero and Alfonsina. He's only twelve. My cousin Giulio, who was brought up with us like another brother, is also with them."

"What do you want?" he asks. A bee comes in through the window and buzzes fretfully over the plums.

"I can't stop them writing to me!" she bursts out. "I don't even want to stop them, because I want to hear that they are all right, even Piero. But I'm afraid that if you hear that I have letters from them you'll think I'm plotting with them, and you'll move against me. Jacopo says I shouldn't reply, that I should think of the Salviati and our children as my family now and forget them. But they are my brothers."

"As long as it's family gossip and not subversion, I don't see any problem," he says.

She smiles, and looks very like her father. "The trouble is, with Piero, there isn't any difference. He's plotting to return, and not just to return to Florence but to return to power. He asks me about what's going on in the city, and to feel out the Ballsy and the others to see who would support him if he came back."

"Not many," Girolamo says. Not many of the Greys and few even of the Lukewarm. They want power for themselves, not to knuckle under to Piero, whose heavyhandedness had made them resent him.

"No, not many at all, that's what I told him. You and Valori and Capponi are firmly in control of Florence." She smiles again. "I suppose I'm telling him what you'd want me to tell him, but it's the truth. He's trying to raise an army."

"Would you tell me the details of the plot?" he asks, carefully.

"No. He's my brother. Besides, there are no details, only the most nebulous dreams. But it would be enough to look like treason, in his letters. It *is* treason. Piero's a fool, you know that, I know that, everyone knows it, but he's my brother still." The bee settles on a split plum and falls silent.

He shakes his head. "Write to your brothers, and if Valori or anyone finds out and objects I'll tell them there's no harm in it," he says.

"Thank you." She smoothes the cloth over her great belly. "You have been very kind, and very forthright. While I am here, since it is very difficult for me to meet you, and we are unlikely to have the chance to talk again, could I ask you something for my own curiosity?"

He is intrigued. Benivieni is waiting, but spending time with Benivieni feels like penance. "What do you want to ask?"

"It is about your knowledge of the future."

"God has revealed some things to me," he says, as he always does.

"You predicted that King Charles would invade, and conquer Naples, and he did."

He nods. "God showed me that." Charles conquered Rome and Naples, easily, with barely a blow struck. Pope Alexander Borgia surrendered, and greeted Charles as a brother, which Charles accepted. He took the Pope's son Cesare off with him, and Cem, the brother of the Ottoman Sultan of Constantinople. Cem died of fever in his camp, but Cesare escaped back to Rome, laughing up his sleeve. Popes should not have sons, and if they do they should not make those sons cardinals, nor should their sons be as terrible as Cesare Borgia. People are saying it is Cesare who is the Antichrist, that he sleeps with his own sister, that he delights in brawling in the streets of Rome.

"But how does it work? Has he shown you what will happen next? I hear Charles has misbehaved in Naples, seducing wives and young girls and letting his men run wild. I hear he is returning to France."

"It's true he's installed a viceroy in Naples and is returning to France. I went out to meet him last month."

She smiles. The bee rises from the fruit and buzzes towards her. Lucrezia waves it away before it settles on the pink scarf that covers her hair. "To ask him kindly not to come back to Florence?"

"Exactly," he admits. It feels to Girolamo that Charles is retreating to France without having properly cleansed Italy. He isn't sure what's happening there, whether Charles has forfeited the mantle God gave him as the New Cyrus because of his sins in Naples. Charles agreed to go back the other way, but Girolamo caught his dysentery in the French camp, which makes it harder for him to consider the mission a success.

"And will he return Pisa to us?"

"Pisa has revolted and claimed independence from both Florence and France. We are sending an army."

"Yes, under Capponi, my husband told me. What I wanted to know was how much of this you knew beforehand. Did you know the details, or just the outline?"

He has not talked about this to anyone since the Count died. She was taught by Angelo and Lorenzo, he remembers, and she seems genuinely interested. He unfolds a little. "Sometimes I will just know something, and it will be difficult to understand. Sometimes it is very clear. Sometimes it is like remembering. Sometimes it is only the outline, other times only the details. I knew they would welcome Charles to Naples with flowers. Why that detail? I did not know he would go home so soon. I expect he will come back to fulfil the other things I have seen. But that is a guess. I have seen the things, and they are in Italy, and since he is leaving that logically means he must come back. But God has not told me this. And even when I am sure, I don't know how soon it will happen. I know there will be a terrible sack of Rome. Charles was moving towards it with his great army. Logic suggests the sack would come then, but it didn't. So it is still looming in the future. I don't know when. It is uncomfortable. Prophecy is always so partial and gnomic. I am sure of what I know, but have to guess what it means and how it connects. The Count said that this is a way God protects me, to save my human mind from trying to comprehend more than it can bear. I am grateful to God. But sometimes I find it very frustrating."

She nods. "Fascinating. I also heard that you are teaching women to prophecy, is that true?"

"It's half true. Who told you?"

"My little sister Contessina, who had it from one of the Bartolini girls." She shrugs and gives a half smile. "Gossip. I'm just interested. I'm not eager to join them."

He is relieved to hear that. "Camilla Rucellai and her husband have separated and both taken vows. He is in the novitiate here. Camilla is now a Dominican tertiary, at home, living with other nuns who are sensitive to prophecy, or able to sense demons. I am helping them learn to tell true prophecy from false. It can be difficult. Some, no one could doubt. When God told me that the Sword of the Lord was coming it rang through me like a bell, and I resonated to it. But other times it's just a feeling, a certainty, and then it could be imagination. I am trying to teach them to distinguish, and not to share the knowledge until they are sure, and not to announce logical inference from prophecy as if that too was the word of God." The bee zooms towards him, and he freezes in place.

"There are female prophets in the Bible. Deborah . . ."

"Exactly," he says. The bee circles away again, buzzing.

"And is it true that you can see demons?"

He nods. "God has given me the power to see and banish demons." When he came back from Charles's camp, weak with dysentery, Florence had been again under demonic siege. The walls of prayer were bowing under the weight of demons. He banished them all, but because he was sick it exhausted him, and he collapsed in the gateway and had to be carried to San Marco. Since then he has had his Angels and Dominican brothers parade regularly along the walls singing psalms and holy songs, to strengthen them. When he is properly well again, or when autumn comes, he will resume his daily walks of exorcism. He tries to do part of the circuit early each morning, before the heat of the sun grows too fierce.

"What a responsibility," she says.

"Yes," he says, simply, liking and admiring her for understanding that.

"And can you change what you see, what God shows you of the future?"

"Sometimes," he says.

"So it's not all fated? We have free will?" On her words, the bee finds the open window and escapes the room.

"We have free will, but some things have such weight that I do not think they could ever be changed," he says, thinking of the sack of Rome.

"Well, thank you again for taking the time to talk to me, and for reassuring me that I can write to my brothers," she says, rising to leave, her belly very large before her under the rich brown cloth of her dress. "And it's very interesting to hear about the way prophecy works. I shall reflect on that."

He wants them to be able to be friends, for him to hear the results of her reflections, but it isn't possible. There is too much distance between them. Even making this one visit would have been difficult for her. Her life is supposed to be her children, her household, not reflections on metaphysics. "You should have been a man," he says, unpremeditatedly.

She turns and looks at him over her shoulder, not smiling at all now. "If I'd been a man I'd never have lost control of the city and it would be you coming to ask me for favours, Brother Girolamo."

CHAPTER 10

Our trespasses.

MARCH 27TH, 1496

The war of missives with Pope Alexander Borgia heats up throughout the summer and autumn. The Pope tries to rejoin the Tuscan and the Lombard congregations by fiat, and to send some of Girolamo's most fervent followers to Bologna and the discipline of Brother Vincenzo. He lists them by name, showing that he has spies in Florence. Then comes a bribe: Girolamo would be made a cardinal if he came to Rome. It is easy to refuse when he knows it means his death, but it means his death either way. If he accepts the bribe, Pope Alexander would know he could be bribed, and was not truly a man of God. If he does not, then the Pope will try harsher measures. He sees quite clearly the choice before him—he can be martyred soon, in Rome, or later, in Florence. He chooses Florence. He refuses the cardinal's hat, just like his namesake saint, Jerome. Also like Jerome, he writes. He completes the Count's book against astrologers, edits another book of his sermons for printing and the wide distribution that promises, and begins to write a book to encourage the practice of pure Christianity everywhere, which he intends to call *The Triumph of the Cross.* It is full of ideas he discussed with the Count, and he misses him sharply at times when his unguarded mind suggests asking him what he thinks.

Pope Alexander's next letter bans Brother Girolamo from preaching, which command he has obeyed until now. It is the first Lent for years in which he has not undertaken the daily rigour of giving sermons. He attends the sermons others give, and considers it a penance. But today is Palm Sunday, and the Senate have specifically asked him to preach in the cathedral. It is the day of First Communion, when all the seven-year-olds of Florence are dressed in their best and will become members of the Body of Christ. They were baptised as infants, and their godparents took vows for them; now they have attained the age of reason and can know good from evil and truly become Christians. It is a joyful occasion, and the senators want him to preach, and the Pope is far away.

He knows how dangerous it is to think that, when there are enemies in Florence who write to Pope Alexander of every move he makes. The Pope sent one letter condemning him to the Franciscan monks of Santa Croce, who spread it as far as they could, so that everyone has seen that one. His friends, the Wailers, are only strengthened in their faith by reading the Pope's attack, but some others are made very uncomfortable. This request, this Palm Sunday sermon, shows the vast majority of the Senate are on his side, on God's side.

Besides, he wants the Franciscans to support him. St Francis and St Dominic were sent by God at the same time, around the year 1200, to found new orders of monks and heal the world. The Dominicans do it by preaching and spreading the faith, the Franciscans do it by ministering to the poor and humble. Of course Franciscans also preach and Dominicans also get involved with charity, but that just shows that, as Jesus says, the world needs both Mary and Martha. There are paintings showing Francis and Dominic embracing. There need not be enmity between their orders, though all too often there is an unhealthy rivalry.

The Franciscans of the monastery of Santa Croce have proposed a new financial institution, the Bank of Faith, which will replace the usurious lenders who lend money to the poor at huge rates of interest. These moneylenders are often Jews, as the business is forbidden to Christians, but often enough unscrupulous and evil-minded Christians take it up too. They offer money when people desperately need it, at terrible rates of interest. Then they demand vastly more than what they have given out when their victims are finally paid. It keeps poor people poor and struggling in constant debt. The Bank of Faith will make small loans and expect only a small gift in return. It will provide dowries for poor girls whose families can not afford to pay into the dowry fund. It will lend money to newly qualified journeymen who want to set up their own businesses, and to boys who want to become apprentices but don't have the fee. It is a good thing, he approves, and best of all it will be administered by the Franciscans, in the old Medici Palace, and be none of his business after it is set up. Once he has been asked, he can't possibly refuse to preach on its inaugural day.

His health has been slowly restored, though he has never quite found the energy he had before the dysentery. Every morning now, after prayers, he makes a circuit of the city walls and banishes the demons clustered outside. Some days there are only a handful of them, on others they swarm close in legions. However many there are, he gathers them up and returns them to Hell, and no matter how many there are and how hard they press it, none of them ever come through the wall of prayer that Florence has raised. He continues to encourage the regular processions of his Angels to strengthen it.

It is a beautiful spring morning, cold if you stand still but warm enough as long as you keep moving. The astonishing dome Brunelleschi built for the cathedral rises above the houses and palaces, always surprising as you come to it, always a delight, drawing the eye up to God. The sky is a celestial blue, and as he looks up he sees swallows darting high up. All churches are beautiful. San Marco is home, and San Lorenzo is perfectly proportioned, but the cathedral is the heart of Florence, the city's own church. Standing in the pulpit by special invitation, smelling freshly burning incense covering the pervasive underlay of sheep that always haunts the place, he feels blessed and fortunate.

He looks out over the congregation as they sing the psalm. The huge space is packed. There are thousands of children, dressed in white, holding red crosses and crowned with wreathes of olive leaves. In processing here from the four quarters of the city they have carried collecting boxes, which have all been emptied into one chest, standing before the altar now, overflowing with florins. These are the donations to start the Bank of Faith. These men, women, and children standing before him are safe in the Ark he has built. This is a joyful sermon, a wholly positive message. He is not here today to preach God's wrath, but his entry into Jerusalem, the children's first step on God's path, and the next step for the others. His Angels are crowded together at the back, with their banners ready for the procession that will follow the service. Among them stands Brother Bartolomeo, holding up the banner of San Marco which he has had made, a copy of Brother Angelico's painting of Christ crucified.

He looks at the crowd. Among the rich, he sees fewer jewels and less vain decoration than he remembers from past years. Among the poor, he sees fewer rags, and far fewer signs of emaciation. As his eye passes approvingly over the women, in their modest clothing, he notices among them Isabella, wearing a widow's stern black, with a plain veil. He had not known she had come back to the city. He is glad of it.

The service progresses. He does not conduct the mass, he is here only to preach, and his sermon comes at the end of the service. There is a deep hush when it is time, and into that great silence he begins to speak, and at once he knows God is with him.

He talks about the entry into Jerusalem, and what it means, both historically and now, for Florence. He talks about the children, and about what God has done for Florence. He reminds them not to stand about and get cold during the procession afterwards. He talks about the Bank of Faith and how it will free the impoverished from their chains of debt. He talks about the rejoicing of Jerusalem, and how Florence is the new Jerusalem. He quotes the Count, about how man stands between angels and animals and has a special place in the universe. He sees Benivieni nodding smugly, and seeks out Isabella, who is looking at one of the frescoes and smiling to herself. He continues speaking, meaning to explain further about the Bank of Faith, but God speaks to him, and he begins to praise God, quite without premeditation, speaking to the crowd of God's greatness and wonder. At last he hears himself saying, "Florence, this is the King of the Universe! And now He wants to become your especial king! Florence, do you want Him for your king?"

He thinks for a moment that the roar of the crowd will tear the roof off the cathedral and leave them open to the sky and God's grace. It is louder even than the Our Father they bellowed before the French came, for this is a hosannah, a great shout from the heart, echoing up to the dome and back down. He sees tears and laughter and a strong shared passionate assent from all present. Everyone wants God to be Florence's especial king, the only king, for a city that is, in Plato's terms, closer to a democracy than anything else. "Yes," they are shouting, and *"Rex Regnorum, Dominus Dominantium,"* and "Jesus Christ, King of Florence."

He gives the blessing, though the tumult has not died down, and they stream out of the church, still cheering and chanting. "King of Kings, Lord of Lords, *Rex Regnorum, Dominus Dominantium!"* Trumpets blow and drums beat, and the streets are thronged with citizens joining the procession, all calling out "King of Kings, King of Florence, hosannah!" Monks and nuns, tradesmen and workmen, rich and poor, old and young, march united in the spring sunshine. This is perhaps the most disorderly religious procession Florence has ever known, but also the most joyful and heartfelt. Everyone is beaming.

As he joins them, as he follows this procession he has created, seeing his banner bobbing ahead among the other banners, he knows in his heart, where prophecy unfolds to him, that one day they will crown Christ king of Florence, that he will be elected so in a vote, and that this will be recorded in stone. It will not be today, and indeed, he knows he will not live to see it, but in many ways that is better, it means that this frail craft that is his Ark will outlive him, the legacy will live on, what he has done will endure. He feels tears on his own cheeks.

CHAPTER 11

As we forgive those.

OCTOBER 1ST, 1496

Girolamo is on his way back from visiting Benivieni, which he has come to find preferable to having the man visit San Marco, as he can control the timing of the visits and get away more easily. Benivieni is writing songs for his Angels to sing as they walk in procession. He is also translating some of Girolamo's work from Latin to Italian, for publication. He will be glad to have the songs and the translations, but is glad now to be away from the man, with his constant unreciprocated assumption of a deep degree of intimacy. He walks along the Arno. It is a beautiful autumn day. The sun is sliding down towards the hills behind him, stretching his shadow out before him like a long-legged giraffe, and gilding the city. The light has the especial vividness of autumn afternoons when the days are shortening. The trees are turning brown and vivid gold. There are barges on the river, bringing bales of raw wool, blocks of marble, and stacks of timber, and taking away finished goods. There are far fewer of them than there were. The city is feeling the bite of the loss of Pisa.

As he crosses the square outside the Senatorial Palace, Valori comes up to him, looking smaller and paler. "I was coming to see you. Do you have a moment?" Valori asks.

"Of course," he says, although he would prefer to get back to San Marco. Valori is one of the leading men of the commonwealth now, and the leader of the Wailers. "Let's sit in the Loggia."

Valori nods, and they pass up the central steps to where they can sit on one of the stone benches that runs around inside the covered colonnade. There are a few other people there, but the place is not full the way it would be in summer when everyone takes advantage of the shade. A mother and daughter, plainly dressed and with respectably covered heads, sit spinning silk with drop spindles, a small group of merchants are discussing some business, and a group of boys squat on the stone floor playing a game with horse chestnuts. Valori and Girolamo sit on the lower step in the corner, facing towards the palace. The off-centre tower with its twisting stairs at the top looks like one of the confections bakers make out of glazed dough. Valori fusses with his red robe, then finally looks straight at him. "The news has come that Capponi is dead."

"God rest his soul," he says. "Did he manage to retake Pisa?"

Valori shakes his head. "This is a great blow for us, for our party," he says. "And it seems everyone wants to make war on Florence. The Empire is attacking. There is a great navy heading for us."

"The Empire," he repeats. The Emperor, who is nominally Emperor of Rome but in fact rules a bunch of squabbling German principalities, is also a power from over the Alps, a sword from the north. Having declared the King of France was the New Cyrus, he would lose face if he changed his mind now, even if Charles has gone back to France, even if he might have been wrong. He frowns.

"I hate to ask this, but will you preach to protect the city?" Valori asks.

"It will antagonize Pope Alexander. He has sworn me to silence. When I preached on Palm Sunday in spite of his ban he was very angry. He could demand Florence surrender me to him. He can't prove me a heretic, though he has tried, but he could excommunicate me for meddling in politics." No one could prove Girolamo a heretic, he is as orthodox as St Augustine, as St Thomas Aquinas. Like the late Count, he knows more theology than anyone who could possibly challenge him, and unlike the Count he does not transgress the bounds, nor wish to.

Valori twists his robe in his hands, bunching the material. "Without Capponi, without you preaching, it's very hard. The Lukewarm and the Greys gain power. There is talk of a new party rising, who call themselves the Furious. They are all the men who hate us, and hate everything we stand for. But as long as we are in power you needn't worry about Florence surrendering you. That could never happen. We stood by Lorenzo de' Medici when he was excommunicated after the Pazzi Conspiracy. Even when Pope Sixtus put the whole city under interdict, our priests defied him."

He touches the green stone in his pocket, remembering Lorenzo. He has sometimes felt recently that his position and Lorenzo's are strangely similar. There are positions of power in the commonwealth, but they are held by others, others who listen to him and take his advice, but only by their own choice. Valori is one of them now, as he was for Lorenzo. Lorenzo called himself "master of the shop," not king or duke. The position is one of moral authority, not power. He can compel no one, outside the Tuscan congregation of the Dominicans. He doesn't want to antagonize Pope Alexander by preaching after he has been forbidden. But it is very hard for him to resist Valori's appeal.

"I will hold a day of prayer," he says. "We could have the Madonna of Impruneta brought to the city, and have a procession." It is a miracle-working icon, one that is generally hidden and only brought out in time of trouble.

"Yes, people will like that. And will you preach?"

"I don't suppose Brother Domenico would do?" Even as he says it, he knows he wouldn't. Besides, Domenico is still young and impetuous and sometimes speaks before he thinks, and could get them all into worse trouble. He has put him in charge of the Angels, and he is doing a very good job with them. The boys appreciate his enthusiasm. "No, I'll preach. But I won't make a habit of it while I'm still under the ban. We have to get His Holiness to change his mind. I know Cardinal Carafa is trying."

"Borgia's a terrible Pope," Valori mutters.

"I took a vow of obedience, and I didn't make a proviso to say I'd be obedient unless the Pope happens to be a Spanish nepotistic simoniac," he says.

Valori smiles, thinly. "When shall we say will be the day of prayer?"

"Tomorrow's Sunday, and we have to bring the Madonna here from Impruneta, so shall we say Thursday?"

"Yes, yes, that will be good." One of the playing boys gives a shout of triumph and shovels nuts towards himself.

Girolamo hesitates, not aware of any clear feeling of prophecy, but drawn by a feeling as the boys scatter, calling to each other. "No, let's say Friday," he says.

Valori's face lights up. "God is speaking to you!" he says.

Girolamo doesn't deny it, doesn't say what it is, couldn't even define what it was. He misses the Count, who would have helped him understand.

Perhaps because he was thinking about the Count, he isn't surprised to see Isabella crossing the square. She sees him, and changes her direction to come towards him. Valori gets up and goes back into the Senatorial Palace, happy now he has a plan that he thinks others will endorse. Girolamo stays where he is and waits for Isabella, who climbs up and sits a little way from him, close enough to speak but not close enough for scandal. He appreciates her tact. She is wearing dark clothes, and has her head covered, but her smooth dark hair peeps out at both sides, framing her face.

"I want to take vows," she says, when they have exchanged greetings. "I want to be pure in your pure city. I have been listening to your sermons, and reading them too, for a long time. I think it would be what Giovanni would have wanted."

Girolamo nods. "I hoped you might," he says. "You have a spiritual gift. You saw the demon that was trying to hurt Angelo." That was the last demon he saw inside the walls of Florence, he realises with a start.

"Thank you," she says. "Would you speak for me at Santa Lucia?"

He can feel his eyes widen. "I—you—a Magdalen order would be more appropriate. I could find a place for you at the Convertite."

"You would have taken Giovanni at San Marco," she says. "I can assure you I didn't do anything he didn't do, and he did it with others before me, which I did not. If he could confess and be clean of it, surely so can I."

"It isn't the same for men and women," he stammers.

"Why not?" she asks.

Why not, he asks himself. For worldly reasons. Because people wouldn't trust their daughters and widows in a convent that accepted women who were neither virgins nor widows. They would think women like Isabella would be a bad influence. But he could see that she wouldn't, any more than the Count would have been a bad influence at San Marco, or Angelo. He would have taken Angelo, if he had lived. But men were different. His mind skitters away from the question, he has to force himself to face it.

"It's been almost two years since he died," she says, quietly. "I've lived respectably, and without fleshly yearnings. I could have entered a Dominican convent in Genoa or Siena where no one would have known or questioned. But I didn't want to lie. And I wanted to be here, to be in your Ark."

"Not Santa Lucia," he says. He knows what the old First Sister would think. She might accept his word that Isabella is a worthy postulant. But she wouldn't be able to help treating her badly. "There is a new house where your gifts could be more valuable. Sister Camilla Rucellai will take you in Santa Caterina."

"As long as it is in Florence," Isabella says.

He prays to St Dominic and St Catherine. Heaven sends him no guidance, no warnings. He runs his fingers over the green stone again. "Let us go there together now," he says.

Camilla Rucellai lives in a house on the Via Cocomero, not far from San Marco. They walk down past Orsanmichele, around the cathedral, past the baptistery and Giotto's bell tower. All the stone is luminous in the autumn sunlight.

"It's a Dominican tertiary house," he says as they walk. "They call it Santa Caterina because St Catherine of Siena was a Dominican tertiary, and they share the vows she made. Sister Camilla wants to build a dedicated new monastery on the corner across from San Marco, and she's raising money for that, but for now it's just her old house."

"Is she a widow?" Isabella asks. It's a reasonable assumption. Many tertiaries are, and it's even more likely as Camilla Rucellai has her own house. Florence is full of little convents like that.

He shakes his head. "She and her husband dissolved their marriage to take orders."

"Like Abelard and Héloïse," she says, surprising him until he remembers she was the Count's pupil.

"Yes, I suppose so," he says. "But in her case she was the one who wanted it, and had to persuade him. Ridolfo's in the novitiate in San Marco now."

"She must be very strong willed," Isabella says. "She's the one who predicted that Giovanni would become a Dominican in the time of the lilies, isn't she?"

"That's right. And she's certainly very strong willed."

"So she's a prophet?"

"Yes. Her visions are truly from God. But—" He hesitates. "She's not very politic about when she tells everyone. And they tend to be symbolic. For instance, before the papal election she saw a bull destroying a temple. Clearly a reference to Borgia. She prophesied it aloud and now everyone knows it. She's hard to control."

"Talking about her, you sound the way Giovanni said your superiors talked about you," Isabella says.

He laughs, surprised. "There might be truth in that."

They are in front of Santa Caterina. He knocks. Isabella bites her lip, looking suddenly apprehensive.

There is a long pause before the door is opened by Sister Elena, who stares at them in astonishment. It is not his regular day to visit. Girolamo is the only man who ever comes here, except for the occasional workman, and he (or rather Brother Tomasso, who takes care of these details) has to give permission for workmen to enter when a tile blows off the roof or the well needs mending. Women do visit here, friends and relatives of the nuns, but he discourages this and tries to minimize it. Once people enter the religious life, it is better for them to truly devote themselves to God and not be distracted by reminders of the world they chose to leave. "Thanks be to God. I want to see Sister Camilla," he says.

Elena nods, her eyes darting curiously to Isabella. Elena is the widow of a prosperous mason, in her fifties now, with her children grown and settled. She was plump when she came to Santa Caterina, but she has lost flesh fasting, and now the skin of her face looks baggy under her veil. "Come in," she says, opening the door wide.

They follow her down the hall to the courtyard in the middle of the building. There is a little orange tree there, and a beehive, and rosemary and lavender bushes. The lavender is still blooming, and the air is full of its fragrance. Sister Camilla comes down the stone stairs that lead up from the courtyard without being called. She is dressed in black and white, with a plain wooden cross around her neck. Behind her glasses her weak eyes are red rimmed, as usual. "Glory to God. I thought you would come today," she says.

"Did you write it down?" Girolamo asks.

"I did."

"Good."

He turns to Isabella. "All the sisters here have special gifts. Sister Camilla, Sister Bartollomea, and Sister Vaggia prophecy. Sister Elena and Sister Anna see demons, as you do, and Sister Beatrice has prophetic dreams."

"I don't usually see them, I only have an awareness of their presence. Sometimes I see their shadows," Isabella says.

"That's more than any of my brothers at San Marco can do," he says. "Sister Camilla, I want to speak to you."

"Sister Elena, could you bring wine to the parlour?" she asks.

"Water for me," he says.

He sees all three women take breath to speak, probably to urge him to fast less and take better care of himself, then think better of it. He smiles, as he and Isabella follow Camilla into the parlour, a room lined with very fine intarsia wood panels in geometric patterns.

"Oh it's beautiful!" Isabella says.

"Thank you. My husband's parents had it done," Camilla says. "Most of the vanities here we've sold, but these can't be removed without damaging them. And they are beautiful."

They sit on the stools that are all the furnishings the room now has. Elena comes in with wine for the women and water for him, and once they have settled themselves he speaks. "Sister Camilla, I want you to consider taking Isabella here among you."

He has not decided what to tell her about Isabella's past, but Camilla forestalls him. "She lived with Count Pico on the Via Porto Rossa," she objects.

"Did God tell you that?" Isabella asks.

"Half of Florence knows that," Camilla says, dismissively.

Isabella seems to shrink. She looks at Girolamo.

"I accepted the Count at San Marco, and he was guilty no less than Isabella. Confession and penance washes away sin—that's a fundamental sacrament of the Church. Isabella has done that penance. She has spiritual gifts, she can thrive here among you. And she has a dowry to bring."

"A little more than twelve hundred florins," Isabella says, quietly. He had not known the Count had given her so much. A normal dowry for a nun is between one and two hundred, about ten percent of a marital dowry.

Camilla looks horrified. When God speaks to her, she is very sure. She has managed to negotiate the shoals of her life very neatly, to make the marriage alliance her family insisted on, and yet to end up dissolving her marriage and embracing the spiritual life. She is still in her novitiate, but still tacitly acknowledged as First Sister here, and by many people as a prophetess. While she is obedient to Girolamo's authority, often she speaks to him as a colleague and ally, on equal terms. But sometimes, underneath it all you can see the respectable Florentine merchant's daughter peeping out. "But—" She takes off her glasses and rubs her eyes.

"I know I am asking you to make a sacrifice. We might understand that Isabella has chosen purity, but some in the world will gossip, and you will suffer."

"Girolamo, you know if she is here no one will want to send their daughters to me!" Camilla says. "I don't want to be unkind, but I want Santa Caterina to thrive."

"Ask God about that," he says.

She sets down her wine glass, puts her glasses back on, and nods once. Then she closes her eyes. Isabella draws breath to speak, but Girolamo puts his finger to his lips to hush her, and she subsides. She takes a sip of wine. They wait for a moment. Then Camilla laughs, an irrepressible bubbling laugh. "God moves in mysterious ways," she says, opening her eyes and smiling at Isabella. "Who would have thought you would be the sign I have prayed for?"

"What's that?" Isabella asks.

"God and the Holy Virgin will send Santa Caterina a hundred women, before I die, more than a hundred, because of you. In place of girls thrust into religion to be out of the way of their family, we will have women, grown women, coming of their own strong desire to be pure, to live as Wailers, to be closer to God."

"That's what I want," Isabella says.

Camilla is beaming. "I know. And many of them will be like you, penitent. But who shall cast the first stone? After Brother Girolamo dies we will be a refuge, a sanctuary, a repository of his ideals and dreams. We will shelter a child queen. Many of our sisters will not have full dowries, but we will accept them because they bring us full hearts. And the work of the house will be painting and illuminating, and prophecy. We will walk in the footsteps of Brother Angelico and Brother Girolamo. And my house will last for four hundred years!"

Isabella looks at Girolamo, her face a mixture of delight and apprehension. "It's the first I've heard of painting, but I think it's an excellent idea," he says firmly. "It will allow you to do God's work and help you be independent without producing frivolities like silk thread the way so many convents do."

"The Holy Virgin showed it to me just now," Camilla says.

"And you know that it is a true vision?"

"Solid, sure, unquestionable," she quotes him back.

He nods. "Sometimes it's just a wisp, and sometimes it's unshakeable. The details of that sounded reliable to me. And when it's not what you think you want, that also makes it more likely to be from God. Don't forget to write it down."

"A hundred women, more than a hundred!" she repeats. She stands and takes Isabella's hands. "Sister Isabella must be properly clothed in a postulant's habit," she says to Girolamo, reproachfully, as if it were something he had forgotten to see to.

"I'll leave you to arrange the practical details of her reception," he says. "I must get back to San Marco. It's almost time for the Twilight Prayer."

He smiles as he goes. Isabella is where she belongs, and she is breaking a trail for others like her.

On the Friday, he preaches in the cathedral against the Imperial invasion and prays for deliverance for Florence. They parade the Impruneta Madonna under a canopy, amid trickling rain and gusty winds that rise as they parade, tugging at the skirts of his habit. Later news comes that the Imperial navy has been destroyed that night in a storm. Emperor Maximilian goes home, saying he cannot fight against God. Valori is delighted, the Ballsy and the new enemy party of the Furious are, for the time being, abashed.

CHAPTER 12

Who trespass.

"Lorenzo had a giraffe," Brother Silvestro says.

"Well we don't, and we really can't compete with one," Girolamo says, wearily. They are gathered in Chapter, all the senior brothers of San Marco, in the Chapterhouse. It smells of wax polish and wax candles. The wall furthest from the door is taken up with Brother Angelico's huge semicircular fresco of the crucifixion, with the good and bad thief, to remind them to make good decisions. Surrounding the cross, in addition to the people historically present, are many saints, including all the monastic founders. Underneath, linked to one another by a winding serpentine tree, whose ends are held by Saint Dominic, are Dominican saints and aspiring saints. Brother Angelico did the haloes of those who were not officially saints as a set of lines, and someone else has filled in the ones who have completed the process of canonization since, to give them solid haloes. Around the curving edge of the wall that makes a frame to the picture are painted prophets, each holding the tags of his prophecy. One is a woman, the Erithrean Sibyl, and another a philosopher who predicted

God through nature. The Count used to say there were many who did that. At the top is a Pelican in her Piety. Girolamo has spent a lot of time looking at every aspect of this fresco since he came to San Marco.

The room has built-in wooden benches around all the walls, where the senior brothers sit to debate. The wood creaks under their feet as they shift about. The younger ones stand in the middle of the room. The benches are crowded now, since the number of monks has doubled. They meet in Chapter daily in the early evening, to hear a chapter read from the Rule, and afterwards for discussion. Today, they are talking about Carnival.

"I didn't mean we should get a giraffe," Silvestro said. "It was just an example."

"What is a giraffe?" asks Brother Ambrogio, a young brother from Milan.

Everyone falls over themselves to tell him. "It's a very tall animal from Africa, with a h*uuuuu*ge neck," Domenico says, holding his hands apart to demonstrate.

"Yellow, with brown spots, and a bit like a horse," says Brother Pacifico.

"It was very friendly. It would wander around on its own, surprising people by eating herbs from their upper windows," Brother Tomasso says, laughing to himself. "I remember when it arrived, how surprised we all were! Some people were afraid at first, but we soon came to love it."

"What happened to it?" Girolamo asks. "It was dead before I came to Florence."

"Died of the cold one winter, maybe ten years ago now," Tomasso says.

"Broke its neck in a stable, I heard," Domenico says at the same time. No one is sure.

"You can see it in lots of paintings, though," Silvestro goes on. "It's in Ghirlandaio's *Adoration of the Magi* in the Tornabuoni chapel of Santa Maria Novella. And in lots of others. In Noah's Arks and things.

All the artists wanted to sketch it and paint it because it was so funny looking and interesting."

"Where did Lorenzo get it?" Ambrogio asks.

"Present from the Sultan of Egypt," Tomasso says. It's very characteristic of Tomasso that he remembers this kind of thing.

"So we couldn't get one," Ambrogio says, sadly.

"They say Cardinal Sforza has a parrot that can recite the creed," Domenico says. Girolamo frowns at him, and Domenico shrinks down in his seat. "We couldn't get that either, I don't suppose."

"No. But we need to do something, and not the same things as always," Girolamo says, crisply, taking control of the meeting. "Carnival is getting out of hand. Last year there was stone throwing and dung throwing and boys and young men extorting money from passersby. Too many people think it gives them license to do whatever they want. And last year the Angels got into fights, and some of them were badly hurt."

"Lorenzo—" Domenico begins, and then when people groan, "No, I wasn't going to say anything about the giraffe! Lorenzo always wrote plays and songs and sponsored floats and had a fun procession, with free wine and dancing."

"Which is the spirit of Carnival, coming before the renunciation of Lent," Silvestro says. "But there was plenty of violence and extortion of money in Lorenzo's day too."

"And we don't want to encourage vanity and worldly pleasure," Girolamo says.

"In Milan I've seen people grease a boar and then have blindfolded men try to catch it. That's always funny," Ambrogio says.

Girolamo sighs. "I suppose it might come to that. Anything else?"

"How about a play though?" Brother Pacifico suggests. "A comedy with a good moral, but lots of bad people behaving badly and finding their just reward at the end. We could have the devil show up and shoo them all into Hell."

There is a positive murmur. Girolamo shakes his head. "Watching plays can be bad for the soul," he says. "Even if the wicked are punished, it holds them up as models that can corrupt youngsters." He nods at the philosopher on the fresco, because he knows this from Plato rather than Scripture. It is an example of how useful a knowledge of Plato can be. The brothers sigh, but do not dispute.

"It's always fun to see lions fight dogs," Domenico ventures.

"But the dogs always win," Silvestro says. "And since the lions are supposed to represent Florence that's bad."

"If we're going to have animals, how about that thing they did at Carnival maybe ten years ago, where they put a mare in with stallions?" Pacifico suggests.

"Absolutely not," Girolamo says firmly. "It's God's will for them to do it and produce more horses, but nothing but lasciviousness for us to watch and make it a spectacle. Besides, these things lead to betting. And horses are expensive, and some of them always get hurt fighting each other, so we'd have to ask the rich men to bring them, and then the betting becomes worse than gambling, which is bad enough, it becomes factional. Can't we think of any Carnival entertainment where neither people nor animals are injured?"

They fall into silence for a moment.

"You know, years ago there was a Franciscan who held a Bonfire of Vanities," Tomasso says, his thin old voice quavering. "Brother Bernardino, of Siena."

"Wasn't he the one who went around saying we all ought to use the coat of arms of Christ instead of our own coats of arms, because it would bring about eternal peace?" Silvestro asks.

"Yes, that's right," Tomasso says. "He'd make copies of it and give them to people. We have one here somewhere, and the Franciscans have one up on the front of Santa Croce. But this was before that, must be fifty or sixty years ago, back when I was a novice."

"What was?" Girolamo asks, as patiently as he can. He prays to Saint Dominic to be forgiven for the sins of pride and impatience and wrath.

"The Bonfire of the Vanities. He was invited to give the Lenten sermons in the cathedral that year, and he was here for it ahead of time, and he gave a Carnival sermon asking everyone to give up their vanities, their wigs and jewels and fancy clothes and profane pictures and all of that. And people did, and he built them up into a structure and set them on fire, and everyone danced around it."

"In the Piazza in front of the Senatorial Palace?" Girolamo asks, picturing it. "I think that might work. We could get the Angels working on collecting the donations. They'd enjoy that. And it would be more fun than fighting, and more dignified than a greased boar."

"And we could get Battista to knock together a flimsy wooden structure to display them on, and fill the middle of it with kindling, so it would all go up well," Domenico says. "You know we said we'd try to find carpentry work for Battista, even though he isn't very good."

Girolamo nods. "That's an excellent idea." Battista's brother died of the plague the summer before, so now he has two families to support as well as his elderly parents. All of them were fervent Wailers, and work would be better for him than constantly relying on charity.

"Maybe we could put some gunpowder in there too, so it would really go up with a bang, like fireworks," Ambrogio says.

Girolamo nods again. "Good, yes. People always enjoy that, and it's harmless fun."

"Another thing Bernardino did was have everyone spit every time he said the word sodomy," Tomasso says, grinning. "That was fun. The tile floor in Santa Croce would be sodden at the end of a sermon. Maybe we should start that up again, eh?"

"Maybe." He worries that they are not strict enough against sodomy. A rich man was recently condemned for raping a six-year-old boy from a poor family. It was his third conviction, but because of his social status the magistrates wouldn't vote for death, just exile and a fine.

"Oh, one other piece of news," Domenico says. "Remember Brother Benedetto? He's been made bishop of Vasona."

"Where's Vasona?" Girolamo asks. He remembers Benedetto only too well, scurrying off to Bologna looking for a promotion, to be out of Florence before the French arrived.

"Somewhere in the Fourth Circle, isn't it?" Silvestro says.

Everyone laughs. The Fourth Circle of Hell, in Dante, is where the avaricious are sent.

"Well, if that's everything, shall we go?" he suggests.

"I'll start exhorting people about the Bonfire of the Vanities in my sermon tomorrow," Domenico says. Girolamo is still refraining from preaching, under Pope Alexander's ban, and Domenico is taking his place, and doing surprisingly well. The Senate have sent a petition to the Pope asking for Girolamo to be allowed to preach. He was touched at how many people signed it, even some he thought were supporters of the Ballsy, like young Lorenzo Tornabuoni.

"And if we have a proper structure, then we can get the donations up early, so people can see them before they burn," Girolamo says. "It might encourage more people to give things. And it ought to look quite pretty."

He laughs later when he remembers saying this, as the structure for the bonfire becomes more and more elaborate and the Angels get more and more excited about decorating it. Battista outdoes himself, building a great circular pyramid with display niches. The Angels also outdo themselves in the collecting, so that there are great swathes of cloth, wigs and hairpieces, combs, mirrors, and strings of beads, as well as other trumpery jewelry. There are also some musical instruments, a few small lascivious wooden statues, and some books and dirty paintings. He looks over the books anxiously. They are mostly entirely pornographic, in which category he includes the printed copy of Ovid's *Art of Love*. He hesitates over Boccaccio's *Decameron,* and a volume of Angelo's sonnets. He leaves them there, but not without a pang. There are plenty of other copies out there, and someone chose to make the sacrifice. He has no hesitation over the works of astrology and demon summoning that he finds. Much better that they burn than do harm to souls. But he asks the Angels to bring any donated books to him before arranging them on the pyre.

Lorenzo di Credi, a painter and sculptor who is a fervent Wailer, has made a wooden Satan, surrounded by figures of devils, which has been put on top of the whole thing, where it leers down dramatically.

"Don't you mind that being burned?" Girolamo asks him. "We can take it off again before we start the fire."

"No, no. Anything made for Carnival floats was always temporary, and burning will at least give it a good funeral," Credi says. "It's a good advertisement for my work. I'm getting plenty of commissions doing what you said in your sermon, Brother Girolamo, more shepherds and fewer kings!"

Botticelli too has brought some paintings for the pyre. They are small panels of naked women, and very popular with the crowds. He tells Girolamo that he is hard at work now on a crucifixion. Three years ago when the Medici were expelled, Botticelli's painting of the Pazzi Conspirators was whitewashed over on the walls of the People's Palace, and he came storming to the Senatorial Palace demanding compensation. Since then he has grown closer to God, and Girolamo counts him as one of the souls he has saved.

The Angels have arranged everything on the structure, so that nothing of the underlying wood can be seen any longer. It looks as flamboyant as any show at a fair, and much better than the Carnival floats he remembers. There are dozens of boxes of cosmetics, jars of perfume, dolls, playing cards, chessboards and other gaming pieces, all surrounded by bright cloth and tresses of artificial hair. He keeps thinking it must be finished, and then the Angels bring more. They are draping it with sparkling chains made of linked earrings when a man interrupts him as he stands watching. He is wearing a doublet and hose, and there is something definitely foreign about him.

"Excuse me," the man says, in Latin. "They tell me you are in charge of this."

He nods. "I suppose I am."

"My name is Antonio. I am a merchant of Venice. How much would you take for it?"

He doesn't understand for a moment.

"For this structure," Antonio clarifies. "I understand that you mean to burn it."

"It's not for sale. We collected these vanities from men and women who want to be more holy."

"I understand," Antonio says. "I wasn't proposing to give the things back to them, or sell them to them either. I would pay you a good sum, and take them all back home to Venice and sell them there. You could spend the money on feeding the poor and good works."

He is tempted for a moment, but then he hears the piping voices of his Angels raised with excitement and shakes his head. "Everyone would be very disappointed. They are looking forward to seeing them burn tomorrow."

"But it's such a waste!" Antonio says. "The books, the paintings, all this cloth!"

"It's a sacrifice to God," he says.

"Five thousand florins," Antonio says.

"No."

"I thought Dominicans cared for learning. How do you know there aren't valuable unique books being destroyed there?"

"Because we do care for learning and I have checked them all," he says, angry now.

"Ten thousand florins."

"No. It's not for sale."

"What do you care if we look at paintings and statues of naked women far away in Venice?"

"You are all God's children," he says.

The merchant sighs. "I'm robbing my own children, but twenty thousand."

Brother Girolamo hesitates. Twenty thousand florins is enough to make a real difference. A poor working family can live on fifty florins a year. Twenty thousand florins for the Bank of Faith would dower a lot of girls, start a lot of businesses, feed the hungry, clothe the naked, help fulfil God's direct mission in the world. But this is Carnival, and people have given the goods to see them burn. If he sells their bonfire to this merchant, stones, dung, and dead cats will be flying in the streets, like last year. He looks up at the Senatorial Palace, where even now Valori is probably contending with his enemies, who only become fiercer and angrier as time goes on. The woman poured precious oil on Jesus's feet, when the disciples thought she should sell it and give the money to the poor. The poor will always be here, and the Bonfire of Vanities is the answer to a spiritual problem. The whole purpose of this is to build the beautiful structure and destroy it, with singing and trumpets, processing and partying, all to the glory of God.

"No," he says. "Get thee behind me Satan."

"But—" the merchant whines.

"No. Not everything is for sale."

"The art—" He gestures to one of Botticelli's wooden panels, where a naked woman, masked in leaves, is running through autumnal woods.

"Art is not for sale. The artist gave it to us for it to be burned. This is for God, and you can't buy it."

Lorenzo di Credi comes up to him a little later with a sketch he has made of the wheedling merchant. Girolamo lets him put it in the devil's hand on top of the edifice.

CHAPTER 13

Against us.

MAY 1497

"Nothing ever divided the people of Florence as much as the Bonfire of the Vanities," Domenico says.

"That's not true," Pacifico replies. "Years ago there was a giant feud between the Guelphs and the Ghibellines, and the Guelphs won and killed all the Ghibellines and knocked down their houses and made the square in front of the Senatorial Palace where they used to be. Not even their streets were left."

"Why would they all live in one area?" Ambrogio asks. "I don't believe there were ever any Ghibellines in Florence. That's just a story. It's always been for the Pope."

"Read Bruni, you ignorant Milanese," Domenico says.

"Is this a schoolroom where I have to keep peace among silly boys?" Girolamo asks, wearily. "Domenico, apologize to Ambrogio."

"Sorry, Brother," Domenico says. They give each other the kiss of peace.

"And all three of you do an extra hour of prayer tonight in your cells, as penance for irrelevant squabbling," he says. The Chapterhouse falls silent. Girolamo misses the solid reliable presence of old Tomasso, who was carried off by a fever just after Easter, going to God with an assurance of grace.

"It's true that the Bonfire of the Vanities has divided people," Silvestro says. "Families are squabbling over it, and not just older people, younger people too. Some think it was wonderful, others think you should have taken the Venetian's money and done good with it, others again think the Angels went too far in demanding donations, snatching decorations and adornments and even false hair that the owners didn't want to part with."

"Yes," he says. "It has definitely been a mixed success. People's positions for and against Christ have been made firmer, and we have more enemies."

"Or our existing enemies are more outspoken," Silvestro says.

He nods. "There have been a lot of attacks. The usual thing. Poems pinned up, sermons, open letters against me."

"Saying in terrible Latin that you're from the swamps of Ferrara, you're not a true prophet, you want the whole city to live like monks, you have the new French disease of the phallus, and furthermore you don't understand Aristotle properly," Silvestro adds.

The brothers laugh, or groan. Girolamo is a little hurt by the swipe at his understanding of Aristotle.

"The one I saw says, *A wind from Rome will end your game, snuff out your light, blot out your name,* which at least rhymes," Pacifico says.

Girolamo feels a chill at that. "So should I defy Pope Alexander's ban to preach in the cathedral as the Senate have asked?" he asks them all.

Opinion in Chapter is divided, some advising caution but the majority favouring preaching. "It's an honour to be asked, and if we want the City to protect you from the Pope, it's a good idea to do what they want," Domenico sums it up.

"It's not like the time when the Emperor was attacking," Girolamo says. "That time it was clear enough that I didn't even ask your advice. But now it's not clear at all. Piero keeps feinting against Florence with hired troops, but he hasn't actually struck a blow. He's like the demons that keep on trying to attack us, but the wall of prayer is too strong to let them in. They're not asking me to preach against any solid threat this time."

"Insubstantial threats are just as bad," Silvestro says. "The Medicians conspiring within the city makes everyone uncomfortable. All these arrests."

"I have asked the Senate to spare the lives of our friends who have been arrested," Girolamo says, though secretly he knows he did not ask it as fervently as he might have. He feels guilty of being lukewarm in their defence. He does not want them dead, but he doesn't want them conspiring to bring Piero back either. There were difficulties he had not considered in making a choice not to exile enemies. Lucrezia was named by some of the conspirators, but he did speak out strongly in her defence. He had given her permission to correspond with her brothers, and besides she is a woman, and should not be condemned. Many of the accused men are closely connected with her, but her husband continues to stand with Valori.

In the end, Chapter decides in favour, so Girolamo agrees to preach as he has been asked.

The next day is his day for visiting Santa Caterina. Ground has been broken on the new site, beside San Marco, but for now the nuns are still in the house on the Via Cocomero. Elena lets him in. Camilla is waiting in the courtyard in the shade of the orange tree. "Can I speak to you first?" she asks.

He follows her into the intarsia parlour, which smells of wax candles and spring flowers. "Trouble with Ridolfo again?" he asks. Her husband hadn't settled to life as a Dominican, and when the time came for him to make his solemn vows he chose to leave instead. Now he wants Camilla to give up her vows and come back to him. Although he has some legal claim, Girolamo has urged on him the spiritual importance of her vocation. He cannot marry again while she lives, which irks him, but he has agreed to let her alone.

"He wants his money back," she says.

"Ah. That's a new angle of attack. I suppose it is his money."

"I won't give him my dowry!" Camilla insists. "And I wanted to use all the money to build Santa Caterina."

"Don't be greedy or in a hurry. The women of Florence will all give a little, and it will be built," he says. "You saw it, didn't you?"

She nods. "I wish Ridolfo had stayed with you. Not just for the money, for his own sake."

"God wasn't calling him, it was just you and me," Girolamo says. "It's possible to live a good life in the world."

"Yes . . . I'll give him his money, apart from my dowry, which is mine."

"Morally, but not legally. He'd get it all if he took you to court, and he could compel you to go back to him. I don't think any court in Florence would make you, but this would be a very bad time for us to have to try it." Girolamo sighs.

"Will you speak to him?" she asks.

"Yes. Fortunately, he does still respect me, and your vocation. I think he'll agree."

They go upstairs, to long room lit by big windows on both sides. There's a long table in the middle, and sitting around it Sister Isabella, Sister Vaggia, and Sister Bartollomea, each with a small bound notebook in front of her, of the kind merchants use for keeping personal accounts. Camilla's sits on the table at her place. He brings his own out of his sleeve and sets it down as he takes his seat. The sun streams in and falls in squares on the table and the nuns. Bartollomea has moved her chair a little to get it out of her eyes. She is a small fine-boned woman who came to Santa Caterina from a Dominican convent in Pisa. Vaggia has grown up and filled out since he first saw her. He brought her here himself, because the First Sister of Santa Lucia had never quite trusted her after the incident of demonic possession. She is the youngest of the nuns gifted with prophecy, and the most easily influenced. Isabella looks right in her habit, as if she had always been meant to be a Dominican.

"Whose turn to start?" Camilla asks, settling herself.

Isabella opens her notebook, to a page half-covered in her fine clear handwriting. "Friday, April 28th, nothing. Saturday, April 29th, dream, floating secure above the city rocked in God's love. Sunday, April 30th, dream, Brother Girolamo is preaching in the cathedral." She glances at him shyly, then back to the paper. "I don't remember in the dream that he has been forbidden to preach. He is expounding Isaiah, and he pounds on the pulpit the way he does. There are spikes in the pulpit, and when his fists pound, the spikes go through his palms like the nails of Christ. Then he turns into a donkey and there is a wave of blood throughout the cathedral."

The sisters murmur, shocked.

"Anyone else see anything like that?" he asks.

Everyone shakes their heads. "What sort of wave?" Camilla asks.

"Just an ordinary wash of blood, like you get when you cut a chicken's throat, not like a wave on the sea," Isabella clarifies.

"And you were not bleeding?" Camilla asks again. They have found out that the women are more likely to dream or see visions of blood when they have their own monthly blood.

Isabella shakes her head.

"Go on," he says.

"Monday 31st—nothing. Tuesday 1st—same dream as Saturday, floating above the city, and then a huge demonic bull came up out of the south, champing and snorting, and I fell."

Vaggia and Bartollomea raise their hands. "Tuesday night?" he asks.

Vaggia checks her notebook and nods. "Monday and Tuesday," Bartollomea says.

"Well, it's fairly easy to interpret, and probably better not dwelt upon," he says. "Go on, Isabella."

"Wednesday 2nd, dream of temptation. Thursday 3rd, I am living in Venice, in a printing house where I do composition of type. I have three children. One of them is coughing, and I am stewing a cow's foot to make jelly."

"Have you ever done composition of type?" Camilla asks.

"No. I've never been nearer to printing than picking things up from printers for Giovanni years ago. I don't know where that came from. I have made calf's foot jelly, for my little brothers and sisters, years ago."

"It could be symbolic," Vaggia says. "The three children could be the three persons of the Trinity, and the sick one could be the way the world ignored the Holy Spirit. The jelly could be the work we are doing here, and the printing could be Brother Girolamo's book on the Cross."

Isabella looks annoyed. "Well, it could," she says, as if she doesn't believe it.

"Very good." He opens his own book. "I haven't been preaching, but I have promised that I will on Sunday. I'll watch out for spikes and donkeys, or for the metaphorical dangers they might represent. Friday, April 28th—a dream. Someone throws a baby to me from a loud, fast moving carriage. I make a dive, and just manage to catch the baby. Then I am alone, in a field, at night, holding a baby, which is damp and heavy. I feel helpless. I look down at it. It smiles at me."

"Another symbolic dream," Vaggia interrupts. "Clearly the baby is Florence, or maybe the Church."

Girolamo doesn't know. He can still remember the weight of the baby in his arms, and his helplessness. "I'll go on. Saturday 29th, nothing. Sunday 30th, midafternoon, a vision of the face of St Michael the Archangel, very sorrowful, turned towards me in reproach. Monday 31st, early morning, fasting, another vision of the sack of Rome. Tuesday 1st, nothing. Wednesday 2nd, morning, fasting—the son the Queen of France is carrying will be stillborn."

"Another stillbirth, poor lady," Bartollomea says. "How many is that now since the little dauphin died?"

"Let's wait for the prophecy to prove true before sympathising," Girolamo says. "Thursday, nothing. Does anyone else have any of those?"

"I also dreamed of a baby," Vaggia says. This means nothing, she almost always dreams of babies.

Bartollomea is next. Apart from the Borgia bull attacking Florence from the south, she has nothing.

"I don't have much either," Camilla says, opening her book. "Saturday 29th, dream of Brother Girolamo's death, no new details. Monday 31st, when praying at Dawn Praise, very clear vision of a red rose, including the scent, and a strong sense of Christ's love and protection. Tuesday 1st, dream of Bernardo Neri being thrown out of the window of the Senatorial Palace." Bernardo Neri is one of the most prominent of the Ballsy, and right now he is Standard-Bearer of Justice. He is an enemy of Girolamo, but an open and honest one who has never dissembled. He is also an old man now. Could it be true? Perhaps. People had been hung from those windows during the Pazzi Conspiracy. Girolamo doesn't want those days back.

Vaggia puts her hand up. "Let me see," Girolamo says, putting out his hand for her book. She holds on to it protectively.

"I didn't write it down, I'd forgotten it until Camilla spoke, but now it comes back to me."

"If you didn't write it down it doesn't count," Camilla says, crossly. Sometimes Girolamo wishes he'd left Vaggia in Santa Lucia.

"Writing it down is how we confirm," he says. "Sister Camilla, I don't think that's a true one. It's too much like wish fulfillment. But even if it is real, I don't want you to tell anyone. Whether or not it's a true vision, if you spread it, it can do harm. It would seem as if we are attacking Neri. You've written it down, now leave him alone, and if it is a true vision it will come to pass. Things are bad right now, and we don't want to seem as if we're making them worse. We don't want to seem as if we're inciting people to throw him out of the window."

"All right," she says.

"Sometimes we see things we want to be true," he says, gently. "Don't get carried away by that." He looks at Vaggia, who looks down. "What else do you have?"

She has the usual assorted collection of images that could be anything.

"I'll come again next week," he says. "Don't forget, write every-thing down, don't discuss it with each other until I come."

He prays with them briefly before he leaves.

On Sunday, when the procession arrives from San Marco, the ca-thedral is in uproar. A dead donkey has been left in the pulpit, which is covered with blood and dung. It stinks, and the whole thing is buzz-ing with flies. "Demons!" Silvestro says, but Girolamo shakes his head.

"This is the work of men, angry young men. They call themselves Furious, and Mad Dogs, but no animal would do this." He remem-bers Isabella's vision of him turned into a donkey.

He walks towards the pulpit, but the crowd is made of anger now, some angry with him and others angry on his behalf. They are a heart-beat from open violence. When one of the Angels grabs the donkey to drag it out, a huge wash of blood comes spilling out across the tiles, obliterating the Wool Guild's sign of a lamb bearing the flag of Christ. The smell is sickening. A roar goes up. "Peace, this is the House of God!" he says, loudly, but no one is listening. He looks at the wood of the pulpit, where he does often grasp and pound, and sure enough there are dung-smeared spikes driven in with the sharp points up-wards. How can people hate him that much? How can they think he's so stupid? He thanks God for giving Isabella the warning.

"Snivellers!" someone yells.

"Furious bastards," one of his own replies. Something whizzes past his head. The riot has begun. He hurries away, with his brothers around him, pushing their way through the crowd. He sees Ambrogio throw a punch, and winces. He is struck himself by a thrown missal. Then they are showered with dung. Domenico half drags him out into the square, but as they stand on the steps the fighting is spilling out all around them.

"I can't preach today," he says, spitting on the ground, trying to clear his throat of the harsh sweet smell of horse droppings.

"Does that mean God doesn't want you to?" Domenico asks.

"The Furious don't want me to."

"We can't retreat before our enemies!"

"Yes we can," Silvestro says, older and wiser.

"Having a street fight benefits them much more than us," he says. "They have money for weapons, while what our friends have are numbers. So more of us would be hurt in the fighting. God sends us trials to test our faith."

They retreat back to San Marco, pursued all the way. The next week, Pope Alexander Borgia announces Girolamo's excommunication. The Pope cannot claim he is a heretic and does not try; he excommunicates him for disobedience in not going to Rome, and refusing to reunite with the Lombards, of which he is indeed guilty, and meddling in politics, which he can hardly deny. Girolamo responds with letters, private and public, saying that his deeds do not warrant so strong a judgement. He continues to refuse to go to Rome. He does not offer the sacrament, or preach. There are more riots, during which he stays behind the strong walls of San Marco. An assassin runs at him in the street, and a riot erupts around him as people try to defend him. A journeyman barrel-maker gets a cut on his arm. The assassin, under torture, confesses to having been paid by Piero. After that, when Girolamo ventures out, he takes armed guards, provided by Valori and the Power-Bearer.

The siege has begun.

CHAPTER 14

Lead us not.

APRIL 5TH, 1498

"You've agreed to what!" Girolamo can not remember being so angry. He takes deep breaths to calm himself, and prays to the saints once again for patience. Like St Augustine praying for chastity but not yet, Girolamo has always prayed for patience, but right now.

He stands up and takes two steps across his little studio cell and two steps back, then stops very close to Domenico. Domenico is taller than he is, but he shrinks before Girolamo's frown. "I don't have time for this!"

"It was Brother Mariano's idea," Domenico says.

"Brother Mariano is an enemy!" Girolamo says. Mariano is a Franciscan from Santa Croce, who hates Girolamo and all he does or tries to do. Because Girolamo was involved with setting it up, he won't even help with his own monastery's Bank of Faith. He has been attacking Girolamo from the pulpit for a long time now, and done all he can to be obstructive. The Senate refuses to let him preach, but he ignores them, saying that Girolamo had ignored Pope Alexander's injunction, and the Senate has no right to stop him. Girolamo wouldn't mind those attacks, he could give as good as he got if he were allowed to answer back. "Let them try to outpreach me," he said. But now he cannot preach, and being forced to be silent while Brother Mariano says what he wants, when his sermons are full of lies and defamation (and sometimes borderline heresy), is infuriating.

Girolamo has been dealing with this by helping Domenico to write his sermons. Sometimes "helping" has spilled over into actually writing the whole thing. He isn't good at suffering silently. He keeps praying for patience and humility, over and over. As long as it is Domenico in the pulpit delivering the words he isn't actually breaking his vow of obedience even if he wrote them. He turns away from Domenico now and comes face-to-face with his crucifix, wooden, an arm's length tall, in which the Saviour's face, under his crown of thorns, expresses all suffering and all compassion. He has had a large version of it made for the chapel of San Marco. "Oh you who have suffered so much, help me to suffer fools," he prays, silently.

He doesn't need this kind of distraction now. This really is terrible timing. Piero came to the gates with a hired army, and the Medici supporters inside rose up in support. There weren't enough of them to achieve anything, but some of the ones the Power-Bearer's men caught have denounced others, and some of them are the leading men of the commonwealth. Girolamo is opposed to torture, and has written against it, but the Ballsy leaders have been tortured with the Florentine drop, where they are hoisted with rope and dropped so that their shoulders are forcibly dislocated. This is repeated again and again. People walking past the Magisterial Palace have reported hearing screams. He has protested to Valori about the torture, but obviously not strongly enough, because it goes on. He believes most people don't want Piero back, but they also don't want to see popular dignified old men like Bernardo Neri tortured and executed. (No one has thrown him out of the window of the Senatorial Palace, so Sister Camilla was wrong about that.) Young Lorenzo Tornabuoni has been arrested too. So many of them have said Lucrezia is involved that he has come to believe she must have been actively plotting, under the shield of his protection and the knowledge of how his prophecy works. He is surprisingly hurt at this realisation, at learning that she tricked him, but he still will not allow them to arrest her. He has spoken to Valori about Lorenzo Tornabuoni, but Valori won't promise anything. They have set up a special commission to try them.

He turns back to Domenico. "You have accepted Brother Mariano's challenge to walk through fire for your faith?"

"Yes."

He paces away again. While he has his back turned, Domenico says, "You said God could strike you down where you stood if he didn't want you to say what you were saying. You stood ready."

"I said that in the pulpit, and I shouldn't have said it. But even so, that's different from tempting God this way, demanding a miracle."

"There will be a miracle," Domenico says, his voice filled with sincerity and certainty. "Think how many there have been already."

"God isn't showing me a miracle happening in the fire," Girolamo says.

Domenico shrugs. "Then I'll die for my faith," he says. "The Church needs martyrs."

"Witnessing to the Franciscans?" Girolamo asks, sarcastically.

"Brother Mariano will walk into the fire as well," Domenico says. "He says he expects to die."

"You know this is aimed at me?" Girolamo asks.

Domenico nods. "That's why I couldn't refuse," he says.

Girolamo sighs. "I will pray for you."

It's all he can do. He prays all night. God does not speak to him.

The next day the trial is set to begin at noon. The brothers of San Marco, led by the Angels in their white shirts, process from the monastery to the square in front of the Senatorial Palace. The fragrance of cut boughs fills the square. Half the Senate seem to be gathered in the Loggia, and more than half the city in the square itself. A walkway has been set up and filled with brushwood, green and full of sap. When it is lit, the two monks will walk over fire through the crowd.

Girolamo sneezes, and blows his nose on his sleeve. Half the brothers of San Marco have spring colds, and now he seems to have caught one too.

The women following their procession and the Angels are stopped at the entrance to the square by the Power-Bearer's guards. "Men only," one of them says. They are afraid of a riot, and if there is one he will be glad the women and children are safe. He blesses the Angels and sends them away. As they go into the square, he sees that all the windows of the buildings above them are full of spectators, many of them women. A trial by fire is an odd kind of spectacle. He sighs.

He hopes that Brother Mariano will not come, but the monks of Santa Croce arrive, in their donkey-coloured robes, belted with lengths of rope. They are carrying an elaborate carved crucifix, said to be one that works miracles. Domenico has a simple wooden cross. Domenico is also carrying the green stone Girolamo found in the copy of Pliny years before. He has never really understood what it is for, or why it came to him. Lorenzo said it was for him, but he doesn't seem to need it, or know what to do with it. He usually keeps it with him, or locked in his desk in San Marco, for fear it will attract demons again. It occurred to him in the deep of the night that Domenico was with him that night in Santa Lucia, and that this might be the stone's purpose, to protect his brother in the fire. Domenico will use the stone, which is about the size of his palm, and slightly hollowed, to carry one blessed and sacred Host, the Body of Christ. So protected, Girolamo hopes and prays that God will help. He did send the storm to destroy the Emperor's fleet. But Girolamo keeps thinking of the Devil in the wilderness, the temptations of Our Lord. Domenico has been tempted and at the first of the devil's suggestions agreed cheerfully to step off the rock in the confident hope that angels will bear him up.

"He is guilty of nothing but naïvety, Lord," he prays silently. "Domenico is a good man and truly loves you. Brother Mariano is attacking me through him, hoping to shake my moral authority, to make it harder to make this your city, your Ark, your New Jerusalem. Have mercy upon Domenico. Bear him up in this trial." At least he can be sure demons will not be involved. He blows his nose again, loudly. Brother Mariano scowls at him.

There is no answer from God, no prophetic knowledge of what is coming, nothing at all but the gathering of phlegm in his head.

All the prayers are done. The two monks, Mariano in grey-brown and Domenico in black and white, are ready to begin. The fire is set. There is a hush throughout the square. Even the Furious and Ballsy among the crowd are silent. Domenico looks exalted. He begins to move forward.

"Wait," says Mariano.

"What now?" Girolamo asks.

"Domenico is wearing magical robes, robes filled with demonic power. He shouldn't wear them into the fire, they will protect him."

"Nonsense!" he protests, but the Franciscans insist, and the senators present seem to be worried about it. After a moment Domenico laughs.

"You can't shake my faith this way," he says. "I'll exchange with my brother." He goes to the back of the Loggia and changes clothes with Brother Ambrogio, who is closest to his size. While he is changing, Girolamo challenges the Franciscan miracle-working crucifix, and Brother Mariano agrees to leave it behind. Domenico comes back, ready again, if less neat. The tip of Ambrogio's nose is red. The prayers are repeated.

"All right now?" Domenico asks Mariano, as another ripple of expectation runs through the vast crowd. People are leaning out of windows all around the square, even from the Senatorial Palace. Everyone wants to see what happens.

"No. It's blasphemy for him to carry the Host into the fire. It's tempting God."

"This whole exercise, which was your idea, is tempting God," Girolamo flashes, angrily. "Either do it or do not."

There is a clap of thunder.

"I'll go without the Host," Domenico says. "My faith is armour enough." He hands the green stone and the Host carefully to Girolamo. "Are you ready now?"

"One more prayer," says Brother Mariano. Domenico waits politely. The fire is burning brightly. But as the long Franciscan prayer drags out, the heavens open. Rain drenches the crowd and the square, running down from the lion-spout gutters on the palace, a heavy sudden spring downpour. Girolamo scowls. The rain dowses the fire, sending up clouds of fragrant steam. If Domenico had been walking through the fire when this happened, they would have called it a miracle, and probably made him a saint on the spot. As it is, the event has clearly fizzled. Girolamo feels they have lost prestige. Brother Mariano has a sardonic smile as he leads the other Franciscans back to Santa Croce. Girolamo squelches back towards San Marco, sneezing.

As he passes the Medici Palace, where King Charles stayed when he was in Florence, he suddenly knows, in the way that God abruptly gives him knowledge, that at the moment the rain began, Charles died. He will never be coming back to Italy, to cleanse it. Girolamo has lost another valuable ally.

CHAPTER 15

Into temptation.

There is a demon leering in the corner of his cell. It's just a small one, no more than a misshapen head with a pair of hands attached below the neck. Girolamo scowls at it. It opens its mouth wide and sticks out its tongue, which is forked, and longer than its body. He throws his sandal at it and it scuttles away, crablike, on its bent fingers. He walks over and retrieves the sandal, turning it over in his hands, smoothing the creases in the worn leather. The sole is starting to come loose, but he will never again cobble it back together, nor ever again wear out more shoe leather.

There is a powerful comfort in knowing nothing else you do in this world can matter, that everything that can be done has been done and very soon you will be with God.

Girolamo has been tortured, confessed, recanted his confession, tortured again, and confessed again. His shoulders have been dislocated from their sockets and thrust roughly back in eight times. But now he is beyond it all. It is the night before his death, or to put it plainly, as he does in his most secret thought, his martyrdom. It's pride to think that, of course, pride, his besetting sin, now and always. Yet he cannot imagine a more spectacular martyrdom than to be burned in the great Senatorial Square, on the very spot where he raised his own Bonfire of the Vanities. He will die as saints and martyrs die, die like those who provide examples of faith for those who come after them.

He is done with everything, and everything is done now. It is the last night of his life. He is in the prison cell they call the "little inn," halfway up the tower that tops the Senatorial Palace. When the bells are rung to announce the beginning or the end of the day, the whole tower seems to ring, and his head with it. Most prisoners are held in the dungeons of the People's Palace, the fortress prison near the Arno. There their friends and enemies can call to them through the bars. Up here he is entirely out of anyone's reach. From below, this tower top seems delicate and tiny and graceful with its winding stairs twining around it. Though he has spent so much time in this palace, he never had cause to come up so high, before he was forced to it. The tower surprised him in its substantiality. The walls are thick, and made of solid golden stone. The airy lightness is an illusion, caused by a limited point of view, as is so much in this world. The little inn is a sturdy cell, reserved for Florence's most dangerous prisoners. Old Cosimo de' Medici was held here once, and famously bribed his way out with a thousand florins to the guard and three thousand to the captain. He said later they must have been the two stupidest men in Florence, because he would have paid hundreds of thousands of florins, all his fortune, for his life and liberty. Girolamo wonders what his friends have paid to come to visit him. It won't have been money.

The cell has a curved roof, which magnifies and echoes every sound. It has a straw bed, a stool, a cess bucket, and a piece of wood he uses as a writing slope. It is smaller than his cell at San Marco, but not by much. The door is locked and barred on the outside. There is a window in the door which his jailors can open, but he can not. He is surprised how difficult he finds it, being unable to leave. Noise of people in the square rises up to him, but he does not think they can hear him. He sings psalms sometimes, from memory, more as an aid to prayer than in hope of being heard.

His window looks south. He can see the River Arno winding through the city, and two of its bridges. He can see the spire of the church of Santo Spirito, an Augustinian monastery, and he can just make out the canted roof of the convent of Santa Lucia, where he cast out the demons and found the green stone. He can see the top of Capponi's house, and the small houses of many poor Florentines. He watched the sun sinking spectacularly in a blaze of orange and gold. He will never see it set again, and he will see it rise only once more. There will be no sunrises or sunsets in Heaven, but there will be, he is confident, something even better. He believes what he said to Angelo, that part of God's reason for providing Earthly beauty is to remind us of Heavenly beauty, part of loving perishable things here on Earth is so we can learn to love what we will find in Heaven.

They came to arrest him on the eighth of April, fighting their way in at San Marco, and dragging him out of the library. Poor Valori was killed in the fighting. The Wailers rioted, and many of them were killed. The wrong eight names had been drawn out of the bag, names of Furious and the Ballsy, who united together against him. His own supporters have not protested as strongly as they might, now that Capponi and Valori are dead, and he has been weakened and discredited, by the death of Charles, and by his weakness in the face of the attacks, and worst of all by the failure of the firewalking.

He has spent the last weeks imprisoned in this cell feverishly writing, using paper and ink that was smuggled in to him. He wrote as fast as he could, barely stopping to eat and sleep, keeping at it constantly despite the pain from his dislocated shoulders. They tied his wrists together behind his back and hoisted him up by them, then abruptly dropped him, again and again, until he would have said anything, did say anything, to stop the pain. In everything else throughout his life he has felt very powerfully that he is the protagonist, the subject, the focus of attention, active. For years he has known his words are the fulcrum, that he has the power to change the world.

Through torture alone he was made into a passive object. It was done to him, and he found that utter helplessness terrible. He has tried, since, even with so little life left, to get back into control. He does not want to be a thing, acted upon, unable to act. Writing is agony still, even though his shoulders were roughly reinserted into their sockets so he could sign their confession.

He has prayed, loudly, for his jailors and his torturers, and prayed for them also in fervent silence and all sincerity. He would have no man damned on his behalf, not even his enemies. God forgive them, he thinks, and tries hard to find forgiveness in himself. He can quite easily forgive the rough-handed men who held the ropes, even for their laughter and scoffing. It is with the soft-handed men who ordered it that he has to struggle. As for the Pope—he forgives him. Alexander Borgia. Like everyone, Girolamo had thought Sixtus was the worst pope there had ever been or could ever be, until Borgia surprised them all by surpassing him. Perhaps Borgia isn't the Antichrist after all, perhaps there are worse depths yet to come and a trough of evil ahead worse than he can imagine. But no. He shakes his head. He forgives the Borgia pope, or he tries hard to. They have truly been cursed with a terrible run of popes, but with God's help and a tremendous amount of prayer and repentance he believes Christendom can still recover, be healed. Perhaps at the next conclave they will elect a truly holy father. Though the Sword of the Lord will come from across the Alps to destroy Rome, he still knows that, in the uncomfortable manner of prophecy.

He starts up in his chair, then settles back into it carefully, trying not to jar his shoulders. It is too late to warn anyone, even if there were anyone to listen. He has warned them already. He has given his last prophecy, muttering it as he handed over the papers that afternoon. Rome will fall in the time of a pope named Clement. Some things can be changed and some can not, and this has the weight of inevitability. But maybe his pure Dominican brothers and the Wailers will be able to use his knowledge to avoid being caught up in it when it comes.

Since they brought him back after he signed the false confession, in the two weeks they left him alone in his little cell at the top of the tower, with all Florence spreading out beautiful and corrupt below him, what he has been writing frantically is not a true confession, nor the history or autobiography his brothers urged him to write, and probably hoped right up to this moment that he was writing. What would be the use of the story of his life, of the spectacular rise and fall of a man of God? There will be others to write that, if it is to be of use. His own words would only muddy the waters.

Instead, he has written a fervent intense meditation on two of the Psalms. He, who confessed to lies under torture, has considered Peter, who denied Christ three times and yet was still the rock on which Christ built his church. He has thought deeply about the Psalms, written by David, a sinful man.

Girolamo's little book has been completed and smuggled out. It will be printed, and read. His death will make it notorious for a little while, but perhaps it will help bring people to God. He has been so focused on finishing it these last days that he feels empty now. His last book, done, and the last night of his life running out. One more sunrise. He will hear the birds at dawn once more, and the morning bells, passing the time between this tower and the tower of the People's Palace, and then he will hear the great bell, the Leone, ringing for his execution. Burning is a horrible death, and there will be pain, but it will only be for a little while, and then an eternity with God. He believes he is prepared to die. He has long known that his life would not be long.

The demon has crept out again and gives a desperate shriek, startling him. Girolamo is out of all patience with it. He has been too despondent to attempt to banish it, but now he forms a circle between his finger and thumb and speaks the words. The name of Christ thrills through him, as always. Still shrieking, the demon disappears through his fingers, going back to Hell, where it came from. He brushes his hands together briskly, then wipes them on the skirts of his habit. Despite his weakness, his false confession, he is glad to learn that he still has that gift of God's grace, the power over the denizens of Hell.

He kneels to pray. He does not intend to sleep tonight. He means to spend his last night on Earth in prayer and contemplation and examination of his soul, ready for his last confession.

He is surprised a little while later when the comforters arrive. They are members of the Confraternity of Santa Maria della Croce al Tempio, commonly known as "the Blacks." They're wearing black robes and pointed white hoods, with holes cut out for their eyes and mouths. He approves of the purpose of the hoods, which is to eliminate the visible Earthly social distinctions between man and man, and make everyone equal, as they are before God. He finds the sight of them now disconcerting. He doesn't know who the men are under the hoods, whose side they are on. He knows they are unlikely to be allies, his jailors will have been careful about that. They could be enemies, Lukewarms or Furious Ones come to try to trip him up at the last moment. If so, he is confident that his faith is too strong for them. He would have preferred to spend his last night alone, without this kind of uncertainty. He says as much.

"We have come to pray with you," the taller one says, and Girolamo can tell by his voice that he is a little afraid of him, even now.

"Then we will all pray together," he says, making his naturally harsh voice as gentle as he can.

Of course, he can't see their faces under the hoods, but their shoulders relax a little. He has sometimes come into conflict with the confraternities, many of whom remain stubbornly loyal to the exiled Medici and adhere to the Ballsy despite everything. But he has never denied that they have a place in God's city, an essential place. Charitable works are important. Lay holiness is very important. Whoever these men are, and whoever selected them from their brethren to send to him tonight, they have chosen to do this charitable work, for the sake of the city and their own souls. He honours that. Christ told us very specifically to feed the hungry, clothe the naked, heal the sick, and visit the imprisoned. The confraternities do these things. But he wishes he could see their faces, more than just the occasional glint of their eyes through the slits in their hoods. He can't always judge someone's soul from their face, but he has so much less to go on without it. The little cell feels crowded with the three of them in it.

The shorter man has a bag, and he busies himself for a little while emptying it. They have brought books of prayers, and devotional pictures, which he draws out one by one. Last, he pulls out a crucifix which Girolamo recognises at once, it is his own simple wooden crucifix, from his cell in San Marco. Girolamo's heart goes out when he sees it. Some brother at the monastery must have pleaded with these comforters to bring it. He is moved almost to tears by this simple act of charity, of love. He takes up his crucifix—it is the length of his arm, and it has stood in his cell for years. The Saviour looks at him in sorrow and pity, as always. The sight of it here and now does give him genuine comfort. He strokes the figure's cheek gently. *Thy kingdom come. Thy will be done.* That is all he has ever wanted in everything he has done.

He prays with the comforters then, and accepts their assurance of what he already knows, that death is short, eternal life is long, that God will accept a truly contrite heart. They tell him that if he is innocent, then so were the martyrs, and he should, like them, accept death joyously. He knows that one of the purposes of the comforters is to make executions seemly. Public executions are part of civic life, and it does no one any good if they lead to riots or uprisings. That's a very real danger tomorrow. The city is divided on a fine line now between those who love him and those who hate him. He is in full agreement with the Senate. A riot would do nothing but make things worse for his own people. There should be no more violence in his name. There has been too much already. Many of those who love him are poor and unarmed, and there are a great many of them. Of his enemies, many of the Lukewarm and all of the Furious are better off—they have knives and swords and arquebuses. It is his friends who will suffer, needlessly, if there is a riot. The power of the Wailers comes from their numbers and their moral authority—the plain fact that they are doing what everyone says ought to be done, following the Gospels. He has made it hard to speak against these things. He fears the pendulum will swing too far the other way once he is gone. But he also knows, bone deep, with true prophetic certainty, that soon, after his death, but soon, within the lifetime of people living today, Christ will be crowned King of Florence. Camilla and Isabella have seen this too. The work he has done here will flower. The seed will not all fall on stony ground.

The other purpose of the comforters, the important one, is to save souls. These men under their disguises might be of any class but the lowest, but they are laymen. No monks or priests do this work, though there will be a priest later, on his way to the scaffold, who will hear his confession and give him his last communion. He hopes it might be a friend, or at least not an enemy. He made confession that afternoon, so has little to confess but ever-resurgent pride, losing his temper at the demon (if that is a sin), and the difficulty of the struggle to forgive his enemies. It might be hard to summon the humility to confess even these things to an open enemy, at least to do it with a truly contrite heart. He asks the comforters if they know who his confessor will be.

"It is God who hears your confession," the shorter comforter says.

"But it is to the priest I must speak it, and who will absolve me in God's name," Girolamo says. "Do you know who it will be, so I can prepare myself?"

"It will be the bishop of Vasona," the taller one says. The shorter one makes a motion of cutting him short, but he goes on. "Oh what can it hurt for him to know that now instead of tomorrow?"

Of course. Brother Benedetto, the bishop of Vasona. He is the witness sent by Pope Alexander Borgia from Rome to witness Girolamo's torture. The Pope had wanted Girolamo sent to Rome, where the torture would no doubt have been longer and more inventive. Brother Girolamo smiles. Florence let him down, they betrayed him and tortured him. But Florence had not betrayed him so far as to send him into the Pope's clutches, to Rome. Girolamo has never seen Rome. Well, he will not see it now, and he is glad. Brother Benedetto is a bad Dominican and a greedy man, but it could be worse.

"Thank you," he says. "It's good to be prepared."

"But you'll make a good confession," the taller one urges.

"I will do my best," he says, as patiently as he can.

"After you confess, and take communion, you'll go out into the square, and they'll strip you of your habit," he says.

The shorter comforter tuts.

"After," Girolamo echoes. "Thank you." It is good to know, to build up a picture of the order of things.

"Then they'll lead you out to the scaffold, and hang you over the flames."

"The rope will kill you, not the fire," the shorter one adds. "Many fear the flames unnecessarily. You'll be dead before you feel them. Unless you fall the wrong way."

"The wrong way?" Girolamo asks, thinking this must be part of the technical process of hanging, which these men must have witnessed close up many times, and with which he had never concerned himself. In Ferrara they more often used a headsman with an axe, and he watched that done, from prurient curiosity, when he was a boy. He wonders how many executions these men have seen. The work of the confraternity is voluntary, unpaid, earning merit in Heaven. Some men do it for a year or two, others for decades.

"They say after they're dead good men fall forward onto their faces, meaning they're going to Heaven, but bad ones fall on their backs, meaning they're going the other way, where they'll feel the flames all right," the short man says.

"There's no need for that, and it's rank superstition," the taller one reprimands his brother. "If you make a good confession and are truly repentant, God will open his arms to you, even though you are a sinner."

"We are all sinners," Girolamo says. "So I will confess, and then be cast out of the Dominicans, and then walk to the scaffold?"

"After you've been stripped to your white robe, we're to lead you past the rest of the Pope's tribunal, and then past the Standard-Bearer and the Eight, and then out to the scaffold," the tall one says. "But there might be a wait, they'll strip you first and then the other two, and then you will each be excommunicated . . ."

"What?" The word bursts from Girolamo without any volition.

"You know you are excommunicate," the shorter one says, sharply.

Girolamo rolls his eyes. "Yes, yes," he says. "But my brothers? They are to be . . . executed beside me?" He almost slips and says martyred, which doubtless they are all thinking, but it would be wrong to speak it aloud, unmannerly, despite what they have been reading to him from their comforting manual which draws explicit parallels between execution of criminals and martyrdom.

"Silvestro and Domenico will be executed with you," the taller one confirms.

"Then can I see them? Go to them now? Could we all go to them and offer them comfort?" he asks, urgently. It seems the world is not yet quite done with him.

CHAPTER 16

But deliver us from evil.

The comforters turn to each other, the taller one spreading his hands and the shorter one shrugging. "You should inquire," the shorter one says, to the taller one. Girolamo guesses he suspects the taller one of sympathising with the Wailers and doesn't want to leave them alone together.

"When you inquire," Girolamo says, "tell them that if they want an orderly execution, it would be better for me to have the chance to restrain my brothers. Otherwise, either of them might take the opportunity to make a speech and stir up the people, doing their best to start a riot and rob the occasion of all its dignity."

The eyes of the comforters meet again beneath their hoods.

"I'll tell them," the taller one says.

He prays silently for a while, asking St Jerome to intercede for him, and the Blessed Virgin. The remaining comforter does not interrupt or disturb him, except when he lights a new candle from the collapsing tallow of the old one. The new candle is wax and burns with a steady bright light. The scents mingle as the meaty tallow gutters out

and the wax takes flame. The shadows dance for a moment as the comforter sets it down in place of the other. He becomes aware that
Brother Girolamo is watching him and starts, scalding his hand with
a thin stream of wax. "Pray!" he says, sharply, motioning. Brother
Girolamo regards him a moment longer, then bows his head again.

"Did you doubt, when the rain put out the fire?" the comforter
asks, suddenly.

Girolamo looks up at the hooded comforter and shakes his head
slowly. "Did I doubt what? That Domenico was an impetuous fool?
That the officials of the Senate drag their feet on all occasions? That
the Pope hates and fears me? No, I didn't doubt any of those things.
Did I doubt God? Never."

He speaks more bravely than he feels. Since they tortured him he
has doubted himself, doubted his own motives, and doubted not his
prophecy but the use he has made of it.

"You confessed that you did these things for personal gain and
power," the comforter says, as if he can read Girolamo's thoughts.

He shakes his head again. "St Peter denied Christ three times before cockcrow, and they hadn't even dislocated his shoulders. If I'd
wanted power and personal gain I'd have taken the Pope's offer of a
cardinal's hat, accepted bribes, sold offices, and had a palace in Rome.
It would have made my mother very happy."

It's distracting that he still can't see the comforter's face, just eye-
holes in the mask. He doesn't say anything, but after a minute he
comes over, kneels beside Girolamo and begins to recite the psalm "I
Will Lift Up My Eyes unto the Hills." Girolamo joins in.

The other comforter comes back in the middle, and the short comforter starts to his feet. Girolamo continues until he reaches the full
stop of the "amen" before he pauses.

Both comforters are waiting, their hoods facing him.

"Thanks be to God," he says, expectantly, giving them permission
to speak, as he would have if they had been his brothers at San
Marco.

"I have obtained permission. We can all go to them, and you may pray with them," the tall one says, the words full of expression the blank cloth of the hood denies his face.

"Where are they?" he asks.

"In the chapel, below. You can stay with them until morning."

"Thanks be to God," he says again. "And thank you, friend."

The shorter one starts at the word, but says nothing. He wonders again who decided which of the brothers of the confraternity to send to him, and whose compromise it was to send these two. Both comforters begin gathering up their books and pictures and packing them back into the bag they brought. Girolamo takes his crucifix and cradles it in his arm. "I'll carry this," he says. They look at each other, which is very noticeable in the hoods. Neither speaks. The taller one shrugs.

The shorter one takes the bag and the taller one takes the candle. Girolamo looks out through the window as he turns. There is no moon. The stars are very high and bright and far away. He can make out the silhouettes of the hills and the glimmer of the river. He thanks God. A wavering light is moving in the streets below, probably a watchman about his business. He turns again. The comforters are waiting for him. There are two heavily armed guards outside on the stairs. No one wants to chance him escaping, although it hasn't occurred to him until this minute. A guard leads the way, then the taller comforter, lighting the way with the candle, then Girolamo, followed by the shorter comforter, and last the other guard. They make a strange procession as they go down the many many stairs in the dark. Occasionally one of the stones is loose, and the guard in front warns the others to take care. Girolamo clutches the crucifix. He doesn't remember it being this steep and twisty the other times, but it had been daylight then, and windows in the tower gave light.

The chapel is small, because it generally only serves a dozen or so people, the eight First Men and the Standard-Bearer of Justice, and the half-dozen monks who look after the place. The candles on the altar make the gold on the paintings shimmer, and the Virgin seems to be looking down sadly at Girolamo.

Brother Domenico and Brother Silvestro seem to have been as-

signed one hooded comforter each. All four men look around when
the little procession troops in. Both the Dominicans look delighted to
see Girolamo. Domenico rushes forward at once and kneels to kiss
his hand, and Silvestro is only a moment slower. He is pleased to see
them too, more pleased than exasperated. He had not been sure
whether he'd see another friendly face on Earth.

The guards stay at the door. The four masked comforters withdraw
together to the back of the chapel, leaving the three brothers alone,
though they can all hear each other.

First they pray together, and then he talks to them.

"I want to be burned to death," Domenico says. "Because they
would not let me go into the fire before, and that made everything
worse. I don't want to be hanged first, I want to be thrust into the
flames."

"No," he says. "It is for God to say how you will die. Thou shalt
not kill—and killing yourself counts. Deciding for yourself is a sin."

"Suicides do not go to Heaven, but to Circle Seven of Hell, according to Dante," Silvestro says.

Domenico hangs his head. "I will hang," he says, reluctantly. "Forgive me."

Girolamo blesses him, and turns to Silvestro. "You're not planning
to immolate yourself?"

"No." He looks at Girolamo, his eyes full of so much love, trust,
and devotion that Girolamo almost flinches. "Are you going to speak
to the people?"

Girolamo shakes his head. "No. It would do no good. I—"

"Then let me do it for you," Silvestro begs. "If I do badly, it is no
shame to you, and if I do well it is all the more glory."

"What would you say?" Girolamo asks, warily.

"I would explain how we were innocent and that the Pope, the
Antichri—"

Girolamo raises a hand, and Silvestro cuts off mid-word. "No. Our
Saviour on the cross did not excuse himself or speak of his innocence
and his enemies. We should do as he did."

Silvestro crosses himself. "Forgive me," he says, just as Domenico did.

"Will you hear our confession," Domenico asks, urgently. "Will you give us communion?"

"I don't expect they would let me celebrate the mass," he says, though he longs to have that joy and honour one last time. "I will ask. But I can hear your confessions."

Silvestro confesses to anger and fear, and Domenico to pride and envy. He bids them forgive their enemies and pray, and goes to speak to the comforters.

Although he has refused to recognise Pope Alexander's excommunication, he has not celebrated the mass since he was cast out, over a year ago. Now he asks the hooded comforters, and they exchange uneasy glances. "I don't see why not," one of them says, and he does not know whether it is one of the men who was with him or another man.

He takes this permission to the altar, where his brothers are quick to get everything ready. He says the familiar words, goes through the familiar actions. When the miracle occurs, when the bread and wine become the body and blood of the Lord, he finds himself weeping, tears streaming unchecked down his cheeks. He gives the sacrament to his brothers, and offers it to the comforters. Three of them kneel to take it, and then he takes the blessed host himself, for the last time. In the morning, they will burn him, and already the high arched windows of the chapel are beginning to pale with the approach of dawn

PART TWO

RETURNED

CHAPTER 17

And the rope breaks, and he falls into the fire, not forward onto his face, like good people, but on his back, like the damned.

He lands on his back, slamming into Hell with a force that would have knocked out the breath and broken all the bones of a living man. He knows he is not that, nor never has been. There is no saving moment in which he knows nothing, no breathing space, no time in between the expectation of God's mercy and the reality of damnation. There is no moment when he can wonder if this is dream or delirium. This is reality, unquestionably, and this is Hell. You cannot change or breathe or learn in Hell. The knowledge hits him in the instant of landing and strikes harder than his impact. He knows all at once that he is damned, and that this is his torment. He is a demon, beaked and bat-winged and foul; he was sent into the world to live without this knowledge only to make this moment of returning what it is: Hell.

It is not unbearable, for he must bear it.

It is the utmost imaginable anguish. Of course it is, for this is truly

Hell, and torment is Hell's only handicraft. This moment of utter knowledge and despair is his earned and well-deserved punishment for opposing God. For he had been an angel, long ago, spending all his days praising God, in Heaven, in a happiness of which San Marco and the canonical hours were a pale shadow. And from that, he had, through his own will, fallen to this.

Demons are all around him, covering him in their multitudinous vileness, and he is one of them. Their laughter is laceration. Their voices rise in mockery, for here they have true voices, as they do not on Earth, unless they borrow one from the living. "All that time in a fleshly body and all you could do was mortify it!" "What a life, what a life!" He is himself a demon, one of them, he was no more than a demon all his mortal lifetime as Girolamo, a demon, utterly damned since the Fall, his choice made and sealed and beyond possibility of redemption.

A demon with stub wings and a snake's tail sneers in his face: "Oh you thought yourself so high and holy, but here you are back among us again."

He keeps silent, for he has pride still, pride and wrath. Now let his sins be his strength.

He sits up. The taunting demons tumble away, giving him space. They fear him because he is a Duke of Hell, that is why they always feared him, why he had the power to banish them. Even his gift of prophecy, that he thought God-given, and that came upon him so inconveniently, is simply demonic knowledge of the evil that is to come. There is no relief in Hell, and so he cannot weep for his innocence, his lost illusions. Will is power here, and he has his place in the ranks of power. That is all he has. He pulls himself to his feet. Upright, he scowls threateningly at the demons surrounding him. They flee, leaving him alone. There is no fellowship in Hell, the only relationship possible is that of tormenting one another. Spite, Hell's closest approach to joy. They can torment him, or he can torment them, that's all. It makes little difference whether they are there or not. He can be achingly lonely in the presence of enemies. And Hell, unlike the stories they tell of it on Earth, is the abode of demons only, at least as far as he knows. If human souls are condemned, they must be somewhere else. Demons, in all their sordid ugliness, are Hell's only denizens.

He turns slowly, taking stock. Because he cannot breathe or draw breath he feels always at the point of suffocation. He is at the same time chilled and oppressed with heat. His body is filled with pain, and around his waist there is no skin, only a circle of raw flayed flesh. His great hideous useless wings are a constant drag at his shoulders, making agony of every movement. He has three pointed breasts, side by side, all leaking poison, which burns as it runs down, and the pressure of it built up inside burns too. The lower part of his face is a huge hard beak. All touch is pain, all sight is hideousness, all sound is discordant, and there is neither smell nor taste. But all of this is trivial. The true pain is that he cannot pray.

He glares around the courtyard where he has landed, which is a mockery of a monastery cloister, fallen into ruin. He knows he can will the pillars upright, the walls mended. He can will what he would. He can make no new thing, but can will into being any echo of Earth or Heaven. The moment he removes his attention it will begin to decay, as these walls have decayed. He built them on an earlier return. He raised up this hollow mockery of San Marco in Hell, out of his pride, and forced lesser demons to ape monks in its distorted halls. He could summon up his own cell, as he has done before. Only the crucifix at his bedside he cannot summon, or the painted likeness of the Saviour on the wall, or the faces of the Virgin or the saints. He is filled with the emptiness of where those things should be.

He has done it before. He can do it again. Yet it is only now that he realises the full horror of his predicament. He has been lent to Earth again and again, and in endless iteration will go on being lent, be born again and go through that same life of hope and ignorance, only to return again and again to this first appalling moment where he must face the fact that he has forever lost God, and all hope and possibility of God's love.

This is what it means to be damned.

PART THREE

LENT

CHAPTER 18

Thy kingdom come.

"I will pray for you," Lorenzo says.

"And I for you," Girolamo replies, surprised.

As he begins to stand, he sees there is another bowl of precious stones beside the bed. These are flat, and some of them are carved. He stops, half bent, then sits again. Inside his robe he still has the copy of Pliny with the green stone he picked up in Santa Lucia the night before. He has prayed and wondered, but has no indication why the demons were drawn so densely to it, nor what he is meant to do with it. "Perhaps God sent something for you," he says. "You know about stones."

"I believe some of them have virtues, yes," Lorenzo says, cautiously. "Marsilio knows more."

"Last night I found something," he says. "I think it may have been meant for you." He stumbles his way through an explanation of the nuns, the demons, and the library. Angelo comes over to join them and listens. Lorenzo smiles through his pain when Girolamo gets to the moment he was soaked with holy water. At last he draws out the book, opens it, and sets the green stone on Lorenzo's glowing palm.

As soon as he does it, before his fingers lose contact with the stone, while it is still touching both men, he slams into memory, with the full force with which he slammed into Hell. Lorenzo is speaking, saying something. He can't hear what it is, because he is bowed down under the weight of knowledge and memory. He is not human, he never has been. He is a demon, cast out of God's love forever, incapable, unworthy. He is crushed by the knowledge, devastated, as he always is on his returns. But this is new. He is not now in Hell, he does not stand in the regions beyond hope, beyond change. He has lived this mortal life and lived it and lived it, and died and died, awakening in Hell over and over, the same life, endlessly iterated as part of his torment, the lineaments of his damnation. Now he can remember it, all of it. This is not like the glimpses of prophecy he had before, his demonic certainty of fragments of evil soon to come. This is full and complete memory hammering at him, everything he has ever said, everything that has been said to him, every word every motion, every day and moment, over and over, endlessly. He falls to the ground and curls up on his side, unable to support himself against its weight.

"Girolamo? Are you all right?" the Count says, and because he has never said it before, Girolamo can hear it, separate from the roar of iterated past and future that is breaking over him.

"Don't eat with Piero, he will poison you," he says, urgently, desperately, while he can. "You too, Angelo."

They start to protest, and he sees their faces, the Count surprised and curious and Angelo indignant. He has never seen those expressions, not in this room. He has changed it, and the weight of repetition is lifting. He has free will, for the first time since the Fall he is free to act where it matters. He is still thoroughly aware he is that unbearable thing, a demon in temporary mortal form, cast out utterly from all hope of God's love. He can still remember the other iterations of his life. But he no longer staggers before the echoing repeti-

tion. He has changed it. He has lifted the weight a little even by this
tiny change. He knows what they said and did on every other occasion in this room, but not what they will say or do now. He takes a
deep breath, gulping the air as a man might after almost drowning.
Even breathing is a grace God grants, and he wants to thank God for
air in his lungs and the scent of spring on the breeze, then remembers that he can not. He whimpers. Angelo reaches out to him with
both arms, embracing him gently. The simple human warmth of kindly
intended touch brings tears to his eyes.

"Help him up," Lorenzo says, from above him.

"You know," he gasps when he hears his voice, realising that Lorenzo in his state of grace must have recognised him for what he is, and
that must be why he winced when Girolamo first touched him. With
Angelo's help he struggles to get up, and pulls himself awkwardly
onto the stool by the bed. Angelo steps away, and Girolamo resists
the urge to cling to the little poet. "You said you would pray for me,"
he says to Lorenzo.

"Is it the stone of Titurel?" the Count asks.

"It has many names . . . and none of them matter now, I think," Girolamo gabbles, the words Lorenzo said in every other lifetime in
response to the Count's question.

Lorenzo is still glowing blue, still on the edge of life and death,
still regarding him dispassionately. "What has happened?" He speaks
slowly, as if working it out as he speaks. "Did touching the stone when
I was touching it bring you back to yourself? To memory?"

"Yes," he says, delighted that Lorenzo understands. "This time.
Now. Not last time. The stone is different. It makes everything different . . . but I found the stone in my last repetition, my last lifetime.
I never had it before. It didn't change anything then, beyond the tini-
est things. I didn't use it. I didn't know what it was for, or how to use
it. I still don't. But touching it now, yes. Touching you, touching it,
for the second time. It brought back memory. Awareness. And now I
have changed things."

"Has he gone mad?" Angelo asks.

"No, I think he's sane," Lorenzo reassures him. "When he touched me I knew—God vouchsafed to me what he was."

"Then what is he babbling about? Many lives? Is he talking about metempsychosis?" the Count asks, eagerly.

Lorenzo's heavy ugly face, with its beatific celestial glow, is gentle when he smiles up at the Count. "A kind of metempsychosis I think. Call Marsilio. We need him. Then we will explain as best we can."

The Count goes obediently to fetch Marsilio Ficino from the inner room. Part of Girolamo is amazed to see him tamely running Lorenzo's errands.

"What did you mean about Piero?" Angelo asks.

"Wait, Angelo," Lorenzo chides gently.

Girolamo can't wait. "He will invite you to dinner, in September 1494, just before the French invasion. Don't go. He'll poison you, and it will kill you after a few days of agony. He'll poison the Count too, only it won't be enough, and then he'll pay his servant to give him another dose."

"Then I have failed him as a tutor," Angelo says, and Girolamo remembers him saying the same thing, grey-faced and stinking on his deathbed.

"As I have failed him as a father, and failed Florence as steward," Lorenzo says. "I have failed Piero's soul, and the city's soul. What can we do? I'm dying. Leo is a cardinal, and Giuliano is only twelve."

The Count comes back out onto the balcony, Marsilio Ficino beside him, looking puzzled.

"How long do I have?" Lorenzo asks Girolamo. "Exactly?" His face is drawn into a grimace with pain now, but he is ignoring it, so Girolamo does the same.

"I don't know exactly. Two days, no more. I heard early Monday morning that you had died on Sunday night." He can still remember every moment, every thought, but it no longer echoes. He has made a new space of action. He breathes. He feels the nubbled texture of the mauve linen bedcover under his fingers, and the harsh fibres of the wool of his habit against his skin.

"What is this?" Marsilio asks. "I heard he is a prophet, but not like that."

"Do you trust me?" Lorenzo asks.

"Of course," Marsilio says, immediately.

"And you, my Angel? And you, Pico?"

"Of course," they chorus, slightly out of time.

"Girolamo Savonarola is possessed by a demon, but he did not know it. Now he does. But he wills no evil." The three men recoil from him, by instinct, not by act of will.

"Not possessed," he says, desperate to clarify this point. "There isn't any other. This is what I am. In Hell I have a different body." He shudders, remembering it, the weight of the wings dragging at his shoulders, the poison running down from his breasts. "But I could not be cast out of this one, there is no other soul."

"How does that work?" the Count asks, leaning forward, fascinated. "Is—"

"There will be time for all that," Lorenzo says. "Years after I am dead when you can talk about the metaphysics."

"We will miss you so much in those discussions," the Count says.

"We only have time now to deal with what is urgent," Lorenzo says. "I knew he was a demon as soon as he touched me. I would have told you, Marsilio, after he had left. But I knew also that he was ignorant of his nature, and that telling him would be a great cruelty, and that he would do good for Florence."

"And that is why you avoided me after," Girolamo says, looking at silver-haired Marsilio Ficino and realising it as he spoke. "I have done you an injustice."

"Injustices done in futures that have not yet happened and which will not be done again are easily forgiven," Marsilio says, smiling and shaking his head.

"But how can he be both a demon and a prophet of God?" Angelo asks. "And how can he do good if he is a demon?"

"Providence. God can turn evil to good ends," Lorenzo says.

Girolamo shudders. "I could prophecy because demons know some of the future. The bad parts. And it is part of my punishment, my torment, to forget that I am cast out of God's love forever and to live this life, trying to be close to God and to bring Florence to Him, only to wake time after time to learn my true nature and the weight of my loss. It's not just that I am damned but that I have been damned all along." On Earth, tears are possible, and so he weeps, and his nose runs, and the physical relief of wiping it on his sleeve, and of being able to cry at last for his predicament, makes him cry all the more. Even seeing the wet sleeve of his winter habit makes him sob, thinking how unworthy he is to wear it, to claim to be a Dominican, when he is every bit as bad as the demons he was so proud of casting out at Santa Lucia. False friar, the one that entered into Sister Vaggia had called him. It had been right.

"Were you a human soul or a fallen angel?" the Count asks. "Do you remember the War in Heaven?"

Girolamo does remember. He chokes on his tears. "Fallen," he manages to say.

"This is a soul in torment," Marsilio says, putting a hand tentatively on Girolamo's shoulder.

"Yes," Lorenzo says. "He is. That is exactly and precisely correct. I don't know if we can help him, but he can assuredly help us. He does truly know the future now."

"A future. What I remember. But as I act and change it, what I know becomes less useful," Girolamo says, through his sobs.

"You remember the future, but you can change it?" Marsilio asks.

"I have lived this same life, repeated many times. But I forgot, so it was new each time. Only now the stone has made me remember. I never remembered on Earth before, only in Hell."

"So it's not as Plato says, many lives, but indeed one life reiterated?" the Count asks, looking at Marsilio.

"Repeated, but not unchangeable," Marsilio says, nodding as if he had suspected as much all along.

"But . . . metempsychosis of a demon?" the Count asks. He looks at Girolamo, and, a tiny pain against the great pain of damnation, there is no longer friendship or admiration in his curious gaze.

"He said Piero was going to kill me and Pico just before the French invasion," Angelo says, to Marsilio. "But isn't that just the kind of thing you'd expect a demon to say? To try to deceive us and divide us from our friends?"

Girolamo realises there is nothing he can say to make them trust him. He *is* a demon. Demons are known for deceit. And he had broken under torture and admitted to lies, said he had wanted worldly power. He could not claim he would not betray them.

"But he sounded sincere, the way he said it," the Count objects.

"Yes. You said you trusted me, and I believe he is sincere," Lorenzo says. He is still glowing gently, giving his words more power. He reaches out and takes Girolamo's hand, pushing the green stone into it. Girolamo clutches it. It feels cool to the touch, smooth, no different from how it always was. "Further, I believe that even knowing his nature he is benevolent and means well for us and for Florence," Lorenzo concludes.

"How could a demon mean well?" the Count asks. "And even if he does, won't his actions be twisted to harm by his nature?"

"Trust in Providence," Lorenzo says.

Marsilio crouches beside him and looks into his face. "What do we call you? And what do you want?"

"Keep calling me Girolamo," he pleads. Then he looks into Marsilio's kind blue eyes, and considers the rest of the question. Everything he has ever wanted is false, or unattainable, lost, out of reach. He feels slightly queasy from weeping so hard. He takes a deep breath, relishing breathing, relishing even the discomfort in his empty stomach. "What I want is impossible," he says, choking back another sob. "I want God's love. God's mercy. I want to pray!" Such hours he has spent on his knees, praying, contemplating, praying again. But no saints will intercede and God will never hear him. Heaven's gate is closed to him. He is forever damned.

"It is the sin of despair, to believe you are outside God's mercy," Marsilio says.

"But for a demon it is true," he says. "There is no mercy possible for me. I am fallen, and can have no more hope of Heaven."

"Do we know this for sure?" Marsilio asks.

"You're not in Hell now," Lorenzo says. "The stone came to you, and you can use it. You should keep it with you and take it when you go."

"You said that last time, though I didn't understand," Girolamo says, hearing the echo. "Take it with me to Hell? How can I?"

"Where was it when you died?"

"They took it from me when they stripped me of my habit before they burned me," he says.

He has forgotten that they do not know what is to come, that they are all surprised and horrified to learn that he will be burned. Marsilio can't disguise his horror. "What did you— Why did they do that?" Angelo asks.

"Who did it? Did they find out you were a demon?" the Count asks.

"The Pope and the Senate," he says. It's all too complicated to summarise easily. "We lost control of the Senate, and the Pope had excommunicated me for meddling in politics, and they tortured me to get me to admit I had, and then they burned me. I thought it was a martyrdom. How they laughed at me in Hell for imagining until the last moment that I was going to God."

"The Senate? So that was Piero too?" Angelo asks. A light breeze has sprung up and is tugging the ends of his hair and ruffling the pages of the book on the bed, bringing with it the delicate scent of flowering fruit trees.

"No, no, this was years after Piero fled," he says.

"Piero . . . fled?" Angelo repeats, as if the words were in a language he doesn't understand.

"Yes, when the French were coming. He tried to make a deal with the king, like you did at Naples," he says, looking at Lorenzo. "But it all went wrong, and he fled Florence. After that he kept hiring troops and attacking us, but he couldn't get in."

"So who was ruling Florence when they burned you?" Angelo asks, looking confused.

"Well, it was like a democracy," he says. "But people listened to me. I had moral authority. But then the Pope . . . and I had enemies, and everything got out of control."

"So my son will kill my friends and abandon Florence to the French?" Lorenzo asks, his voice rising.

"You knew. You knew I'd have the guidance of the city," Girolamo says, twisting the belt of his habit in his fingers.

"I did know that." Lorenzo gasps with pain, almost a scream. "But I was spared knowing all this. I hoped Piero could learn. He is the same age I was when my father died. But . . ." He lets his breath out slowly. He stops glowing, abruptly, like a snuffed candle. No one says anything for a moment.

Marsilio stands up, and puts his hand gently on Lorenzo's. "What are we going to do?"

"We'll have time to discuss what Girolamo knows of the future and how he might get the stone into Hell, but for now we should trust that he wants God's mercy and means well by us, his friends." Lorenzo says. "Now we should deal with some immediate tasks that will not wait. Angelo, could you find Doctor Leoni and send him out to me?"

Angelo begins to assent, as anyone would to a sick man calling for his doctor, but Marsilio cuts in immediately and decisively.

"No. I won't let you take that on your soul. Not so close to death."

"Filicide is a terrible sin," the Count says, so Girolamo understands with a shock what Lorenzo is contemplating. "You will not damn yourself to save me."

"You, and Angelo, and my city of Florence," Lorenzo says, smiling grimly.

"You will not damn yourself for anything," Girolamo says, insistently, horrified. "You cannot imagine how terrible it is to be beyond

God's grace. Everything here can change. Hell is forever. And Hell is much worse than you can imagine."

"You can't stop me from seeing my doctor," Lorenzo says. "None of you will take the necessary action. I have killed before. The Pazzi conspirators all died."

"But your own son," the Count says.

"Piero," Angelo says, and his voice is full of pain.

"Piero's not that bad," Girolamo says. "And I saved Florence from the French. Everything was all right. Florence was the Ark, the City of God. Now Pico and Angelo know not to eat with Piero. And maybe knowing, I could go to Charles with Piero instead of after, and we could make a better deal, one where he wouldn't flee and we wouldn't lose Pisa. We can manage. You don't have to kill your son and be damned."

"Lose Pisa! I have to get rid of him fast," Lorenzo says.

"Would he leave if we asked him, do you think?" Marsilio asks.

"He's in there now, expecting to inherit Florence," the Count says. "He had a spat with Angelo as we came in, saying Lorenzo would send for him and if he didn't, eventually the time would come when his father wasn't here and Piero would be in charge. He wouldn't leave for anything we could do."

Lorenzo groans. "Call the doctor. Leoni will give me a potion that will make it look like a summer fever come early."

"Piero is good at heart," Angelo protests. "He's just young and a little arrogant and it makes him bluster. He never had a normal childhood, because the Pazzi Conspiracy loomed over us all, and it scarred him."

"And maybe he would leave, if we put it to him right," Marsilio insists.

"Once Lorenzo's gone, no one has any authority to make him do anything. Leo's the only one he listens to at all, but Leo is in Rome," Angelo says, bleakly.

"Do you think if we told him there was a prophecy he would lose

Florence and die, he'd agree to leave?" Marsilio suggests. "Since that's the case. If we told him that right now? If you told him, Lorenzo?"

"Told him history would record him as Piero the Fool," Girolamo adds.

"If I told him so. And I could say it's because he's so young, too young to have such a burden fall on him because of the Medici curse of gout," Lorenzo says, eagerly. "That it's not his fault. And if he were to go on a pilgrimage, a long pilgrimage, he could learn to be a better ruler and come back in five years' time to look after the city. If his problem is that he feels entitled to power, as if he were a duke or a king, instead of master of the shop . . . Yes, I think he can hear that, from me. I will send you all away and speak with him."

"And meanwhile?" Angelo asks. "Who would manage it until then?"

"There should be a small council to advise the Senate. Scala, and the cousins, Lorenzo and Gianni di Pierfrancesco, and Bernardo Neri, and Capponi, and our Leo, even though he is a cardinal, and you, Angelo."

"They won't accept me," Angelo says. "None of them except Leo and Scala."

"They will, because you'll be there to represent the interests of Giuliano and Giulio. And because I'll tell them."

"The cousins will be difficult to deal with," Angelo says. "But that should work. If I represent the young boys, as their tutor."

Lorenzo's breathing is laboured. "Now, right away, write to all those people and ask them to come and see me tomorrow morning. I'll need to speak to them all personally." He looks from Angelo to Marsilio. "You wouldn't serve on a council, I know." Then he turns his head, and winces, looking at Girolamo and beyond him to the Count. "As for you two, you're not Florentines so you can't serve. But I'd expect you to give your advice."

"Wait," the Count says, and Girolamo realises that he hasn't said anything for some time. "Anything we do will change everything.

Before we decide what to do, we should find out what the most important things to change are. If we change this, send Piero away, set up a council, we won't know what's going to happen. Maybe we should make small changes and observe them and see what happens, and then make bigger changes next time."

"Next time?" Angelo asks. "Are you seriously making plans for doing this one way now and differently in our future lives? And who can tell if we will truly all go through our lives again and again? Reincarnation comes from Plato, not from the Bible."

"Well, Plato was right about many things, and here we have confirmation of it," Marsilio says, gesturing to Girolamo.

"I have always believed in the transmigration of souls," the Count says. "As many people do. And going from what Girolamo says, we may have the chance to go through many lives and see what works best to change."

"But only Girolamo will remember from life to life," Marsilio objects.

"How do we know that? If we all touch Lorenzo and the stone, perhaps we will all remember," the Count says. "Give me the stone, Girolamo."

"But Lorenzo's not glowing anymore," Girolamo says, handing the stone to the Count, who turns it curiously in his hands.

"Marsilio?" Lorenzo says.

Marsilio smiles apologetically at the others and begins to glow with the same clear blue light. Girolamo stares at him. Is this man, who he suspected of worshipping pagan gods, instead a living saint?

"Why didn't you two tell us?" Angelo asks.

"Lorenzo couldn't control it," Marsilio says. "And there are many deceptions. I had heard that Brother Girolamo has power over the forces of Hell, and we wanted to be sure it came from God, just as you did."

The Count gives Marsilio the stone, and he touches it to each of them, as if giving a sacrament.

"Now let's try that again with Girolamo as well," the Count says.

Girolamo stands beside Marsilio, and they both put their hands on the stone, and touch it ritually to Angelo, the Count, and Lorenzo.

"I don't know if that will do any good at all," Marsilio says. He makes a gesture and stops glowing. Girolamo's mouth drops open. "It's inconvenient to glow all the time," he explains, modestly.

"All right. So now we should all remember, if that's how it works," the Count says. "So, perhaps we might have many opportunities to change things. But we should try to act each time the best we can, I think. And we need to know what we're doing before we act."

"I have so little time! And what could be worse than Piero betraying you and Florence and losing Pisa?" Lorenzo asks. "What could be worse than Florence being completely out of control, in the hands of the mob?"

"I don't know. But the point is that we don't know, until we find out in detail," the Count says.

"What would you change if you could, Girolamo?" Lorenzo asks.

"I'd have a better Pope than Borgia elected, and try to deal with corruption in the Church," he says at once. "No. I don't know. I don't know how much it's possible to change. Some things seem so inevitable. The things I prophecied, the things I knew with such force."

"But we can change our own lives, our own deaths?" the Count persists. "Is this death by poisoning at Piero's hand the death you foresaw for me earlier today?"

"It is the death I foresaw. And I think we can change our lives, yes. I think by talking to you like this I have already changed things."

"I think I should attempt to deal with Piero, and that we are wasting time," Lorenzo says.

"What's the worst thing coming?" Marsilio asks.

"The French invasion, and then the Imperial invasion. But the very worst is the sack of Rome," he says. "But that happens after my death. In the time of a pope named Clement. That's all I know."

"And when do you die?"

"May 1498," he says.

"Six years," the Count says. "Six years in detail, and intimations of what happens later. We'll have to write it all down, everything." Girolamo is surprised how quickly they have accepted what he has told them and moved past it to making plans.

"I think, that this time," Lorenzo says, stressing those words, "We should try to set up a council and have Piero leave. Will you give your advice, and your moral authority, to such a council, Girolamo?"

"Of course," he murmurs, and then he realises that he had been imagining he would go back to San Marco and carry on as before, as always, as in all his lives. "But I can't," he says, horrified as he realises. "I will have to leave San Marco, renounce my vows. It makes a mockery for me to be a priest."

"Things done by false priests remain done," the Count says. "If they perform a marriage, or ordain another priest. We have examples from the Great Schism. Not of demons, of course, but when there were rival popes."

"In ignorance, maybe, but I am no longer ignorant," he says. "I do not know where I will go or what I will do, but I will not be able to use my authority in Florence to help your Council."

"You could, under our direction," Marsilio says, looking at him, sharp eyed. "You could stay where you are, for the city."

He shakes his head, staring at his hands, that cannot perform the great mystery of the church, the miracle of the priest to change bread and wine to the body and blood of Christ. He clenches them suddenly, digging his nails into his palms. "I cannot."

"You could give up being a priest and remain a Dominican," Marsilio says.

"I am not worthy," he says. "I should leave."

"But if you leave San Marco that is even more change," the Count groans. "We won't really know anything."

"Then we will be where we were this morning," Marsilio says, "and no worse off."

"You're right, of course," the Count says.

"Where can I go, what can I do?" Girolamo asks, despairingly.

"You must stay in Florence, and I will give you a house," Lorenzo says. "Leo is a cardinal now, and he will be able to release you from your vows, both as a priest and a Dominican if that's necessary."

"For now you should say you have been taken ill and stay with us," Angelo suggests.

"We will help you as much as we can," Marsilio says.

He is caught in the Medici net, as he had sworn he never would be. But Lorenzo is not what he had thought. He cannot imagine such a life—without being able to pray, such a life would be a fresh torment. But so would any life, and death would be worse, because death would plunge him back into Hell.

"I will help you," Girolamo says. He wonders if he will ever see San Marco again.

"And none of you must tell anyone else what Girolamo is without great thought," Lorenzo urges.

They nod their agreement.

"Now go," Lorenzo says, "All of you. I will see you tomorrow afternoon if I have the strength. But for now, leave Careggi, even you, Marsilio. Talk about this and make plans among yourselves. But leave Piero to me."

CHAPTER 19

Thy will be done.

MARCH 1493

What is worth having without God? Nothing, if you still have the hope of Heaven. For Girolamo, knowing himself eternally damned, there are some things. Hell is devoid of breath and joy and change. Earth has those things; pale shadows of Heaven as they are, he accepts them, and with them friendship and human love. Girolamo cares about his friends, about Florence, about saving mortal souls from Hell, that now more than ever. He cannot hope for himself, but he hopes for others. Knowing he is damned is constant torment, but there is kindness and humanity and earthly beauty, here he can breathe and smell and taste and touch. Even if he can hope for no more than the good things of Earth, at least he can rejoice in those. He can help these good men, who are trying to help him despite knowing his nature.

He walks the streets of Florence and remembers a different present, a different future, and increasingly as the changes they have made reverberate, a different past. Much of what happens in the wider world is as he remembers it, but already they are reaching out tentatively to make changes there too. They don't want to change things so much they lose their advantage of knowing the future, so they are cautious. They know the French will be invading, and they want to be ready. Bernardo de' Neri and some other members of the Council of Seven are reluctant to believe in the coming French invasion, but they have agreed to renew the defences and hire a mercenary captain anyway. Girolamo's head itches as hair grows to cover his shaven tonsure, and then it stops itching. He has to visit barber's shops to keep his hair short and his face shaved, which he has not done since he was a boy—in the monastery one of the brothers shaves all the others every Saturday.

One day in Lent, a day when in other lives he was in Bologna getting into trouble with the Bentivoglios, Girolamo walks from the cathedral to the Medici Palace with Marsilio. He is surprised to see how much Marsilio is loved by everyone, from the scholars and the rich merchants to the cobblers and the fish sellers. Everyone smiles to see him, and when Girolamo is with Marsilio they no longer seem confused by him as they usually are. They find it hard to understand a man who has left the cloister and yet lives so quietly. Marsilio buys bread, and the woman selling it asks for his blessing, which he gives, smiling. She beams as they walk away. Young Lorenzo Tornabuoni, riding past, pauses to greet him, and they joke together in Latin about the spring rain and the fresh horse. Michelangelo Buonarroti, a young sculptor with curly hair and ears that stick out, stops to say he has begun polishing the marble for the pieta he is making for Lorenzo's tomb. Even in Girolamo's memories of other times when the people loved him, there had been distance in their love, respect indeed, reverence, perhaps a little fear. There was none of that with Marsilio, he seems on comfortable terms with everyone.

When they come to the gates of the Medici palace, Lucrezia Salviati is just leaving, attended by an old woman and a stout young man. She is pregnant again. She too smiles at the sight of Marsilio, and nods politely to Girolamo. "I've been visiting Leo," she says, after they have exchanged greetings. "He brought me books from Rome. Appian's history of Alexander!" She is carrying the volumes herself, and pats them eagerly as she speaks.

"How exciting," Marsilio says. "You must let me read it."

"Oh, it's not philosophy, it's just a chronicle of events," she says, in a gently teasing tone. "I'll pass it on to you when I'm done."

"There's philosophy in everything if you read it the right way."

"Oh, I had a letter from Piero."

"And did it contain philosophy?" Marsilio is smiling.

"No. I know Father wanted him to go on pilgrimage to learn wisdom, but I don't think it's working. He's in Bavaria, hunting chamois with Emperor Maximilian, they have caught three. The Empress wore a dress that copied the style of Alfonsina's. He has visited the hermitage of St Wolfgang of Regensburg and purchased a miniature painting of the saint repelling the devil." She shrugs. "He has also purchased pearls and rubies but he'll wait to have them made up because the goldsmiths in Florence are better."

"I pray he'll learn wisdom yet," Marsilio says. "And how are your babies?"

She beams. "Gio is home, and running everywhere and climbing, his nurse can't keep up with him. And I hear from the country that little Lorenzo is thriving. I think I'll send this one to the same farm."

"It would be better for you to nurse it yourself. And it would keep you from getting pregnant again quite so quickly," Marsilio says, lowering his voice.

She glances at Girolamo uncomfortably, then back at Marsilio. "Oh well, Jacopo wants sons, you know."

"Too many too close together can ruin your health," Marsilio says firmly. "But I'm glad to hear they're doing well, and that you are too. Enjoy the Appian."

"I will," she says.

"There's nothing we can do for Piero except pray," Marsilio says, as they head inside.

In the courtyard, Girolamo is surprised to see a stranger come strutting along, walking past Donatello's provocative statue of David with barely a glance, as if he saw things like that every day. One shoulder is defiantly higher than the other, and he wears black leather armour buckled asymetrically, as if to emphasise his deformity. "It is all or nothing," he is saying to Capponi, who walks beside him, his mouth pursed as if he would very much like to say that then it would be nothing. "The White Boars are a company, we do not hire out in little groups to protect a child's birthday party or a cavalcade. If you want us, you want all of us, artillery included." He speaks fluently, but he has a strange accent twisting his vowels.

"We don't need artillery and the expense—" Capponi begins.

The mercenary captain's eyes rake across Girolamo and Marsilio, dismiss them immediately and move on. "This is a lovely city. A valuable prize for anyone. But you're vulnerable. I saw half a dozen ways to take her as I came in. Florence needs my artillery."

The captain and Capponi pass on into one of the chambers. Marsilio takes another step, but Girolamo stays where he is, staring at the doorway where they have disappeared. Marsilio stops and looks back at him inquiringly. "Is everything all right?"

Girolamo isn't sure. There is something very strange about the mercenary captain, something he doesn't understand. "I think we should talk about this with Pico," Girolamo says. He has finally learned to address the Count as "Pico," as the others do, and even to think of him that way.

The room upstairs where the four of them often meet belongs to Angelo. There is a bed in it, but it is a study, with a desk and a table, both piled with books and papers. Angelo and the Count are sitting on the bed, a book across both of their laps, the size difference between them very visible in that position. "The Aramaic is very much the same as the Greek," Pico says, in greeting, looking up.

"Not surprising, but disappointing," Marsilio says, nodding. "I still think it's indicative of the possibility of salvation."

"Good morning, how are you both?" Angelo says, rolling his eyes.

"Well, thank you," Marsilio replies, smiling. He sets down the basket of bread by the door. It releases a wave of its tempting yeasty scent into the closed air of the room.

Girolamo moves a pile of books from a chair and sets them on the table. He sits down, cautiously, still not quite used to wearing a belted tunic and hose instead of his habit. "Are you still talking about the Gadarene swine?" he asks.

Pico nods.

Girolamo can't find the hope the others seem to in that passage. Jesus cast demons out of a man, and allowed them to go into a herd of pigs, which promptly drowned themselves. It didn't seem to him to mean well for the demons. "The mercenary captain who just arrived. Who is he?" he asks.

"He's the one they call Crookback, cruelly, because he does have a hump," Marsilio says, as he clears another chair. "Angelo, beds are for sleeping, chairs are for sitting, tables are for piling books."

"All flat surfaces are for piling books," Angelo says, but he stands up and comes to clear another chair, glancing at the books as he moves them. "Huh, Valla, good, I was looking for that."

"Who is this Crookback? Do we know any more about him?" Girolamo asks.

They all look at Angelo, the only one of them who pays attention to gossip. He grins as he pulls his newly cleared chair closer to the table and sits down. "He's the head of a company called the White Boars, after the device on their shields. He's Count of Ravenna and the Duke of Glusta, or some odd name like that. He's not really what you might call a humanist, but he's educated, not an enemy of learning. The important thing about him is that he's the uncle of the King of England."

"An Italianized Englishman is a devil," Pico murmurs, from where he is sprawled on the bed. "Oh, sorry Girolamo."

"Who did they say that about?" Marsilio asks.

"Acuto, or Hawkwood, another English mercenary captain a hundred years ago. The one with the equestrian monument painted on the wall of the cathedral," Angelo says. "They bury people in the cathedral when they have saved Florence, which he did in a way because they paid him not to attack Florence and he stayed bought."

"I didn't know he was English," Marsilio says. "What a long way to come merely to fight. Poggio Bracciolini went to England to examine their monastery libraries for lost works of antiquity, but he didn't find anything new."

"There's something very strange about Crookback," Girolamo says, trying hard to pin down the feeling he has about the mercenary captain. "I wonder if he is the devil, or something demonic anyway. I don't mean metaphorically but literally. I never met him before. But when I saw him downstairs—I don't know quite what it is. He isn't possessed, not a man with a demon that could be banished. But he's something."

"You think he's like you?" Angelo asks.

"Or someone who has made a deal with demons?" Marsilio puts in.

"Or possibly a change we didn't cause," Pico suggests. "If you never saw him before?

"Or a change we caused inadvertently," Marsilio says. He has constantly been worried about this. "Maybe, in the world you remember, he stayed home quietly in England being uncle to the king, but something we changed made him come to Italy and take up arms."

"No, he's been here for years," Angelo says, reassuringly. "More than ten years. He came around the time of the Pazzi Conspiracy, I think. He was here by then anyway, because I remember Lorenzo considering hiring him. He was a young man at the time. A while after that he made himself Count of Ravenna, four or five years ago. So if it is a change, it couldn't be anything we've done."

Girolamo is trying to remember everything he can about England. It isn't much. It's too far away. "Is the King of England called Enrico?" he asks.

"Edoardo," Angelo says. "One of those names only Germans and English could love."

"Was there a civil war?" he asks. He has heard it mentioned in life after life, but never paid much attention.

"Yes, a generation ago. The present king's father and another claimant. *He* was called Enrico."

"Probably what you're thinking of," Marsilio says. "Or do you think it's a change?"

"I don't know," he says, annoyed that he can't remember. "We should watch this Crookback."

"Don't wince, Marsilio, he calls himself that," Angelo says.

"If it's a change, it's the only one we've found so far that we didn't cause," Pico says. "And it's not very important. I want to know how big changes can be, how far we can get from what Girolamo remembers."

"After the French invasion," Marsilio says. This is what they have agreed, to try to minimize changes until Florence is safe from the French, and then be free to take more chances to see what happens.

"If Crookback is another demon in mortal form, do you think I should offer him the stone?" Girolamo asks.

"The stone alone wouldn't work. One of us would need to bring our mind to a higher hypostasis," Pico says, looking at Marsilio. Girolamo rolls his eyes at the term, which comes from Plotinus, but he knows what Pico means—the celestial glow that Marsilio can summon at will.

"He seemed a very worldly man, a violent man, intolerant," Marsilio says. "It might be difficult to talk to him about such things, or for me to stay in that state around him."

Pico nods. "Difficult. There's also the moral question, of whether it would be right to bring him to memory, assuming he is a demon. Before you remembered, you were happy sometimes, Girolamo."

"But that only made the realisation worse when I was returned to Hell," he says. "Over and over. It's better now, knowing and being alive."

"It must be part of God's plan, and God is good," Marsilio says, as he has said repeatedly.

"Speaking of Providence, I have some news," Pico says. They all turn to look at him. He is the youngest of them all, Marsilio is in his sixties and Angelo and Girolamo in their forties, while Pico is not yet thirty, hardly more than a boy. Despite this, they all recognise him as the first among them, because of his speed of thought and understanding, not his aristocratic birth. "I've cleared the Mirandolan inheritance, not even tried to sort it out cleanly, since you told me how long it took last time. I've just dropped it all on my nephew Gianfrancesco. So I'm not a Count anymore. And Leo's back from Rome with the great news that my excommunication has been lifted! So there's nothing to stop me taking vows. I saw First Brother Tomasso first thing this morning, and he's very happy to accept me at San Marco, and to accelerate the novitiate for me."

"That's splendid," Girolamo says, and tries to mean it.

"Camilla Rucellai will be pleased if we take vows now, while the lilies are blooming, as she predicted," Angelo says.

"You too?" he asks.

Angelo nods shyly.

Girolamo immediately starts thinking about which cells he'd assign them, which pictures of Brother Angelico's would bring out the best in them. That will be old Tomasso's decison now. He misses San Marco terribly. "I'm happy for you," he says. "I'm also so envious. . . . I shouldn't be. I have so much. I know what I am. I'm not in Hell. I'm helping to make Florence the City of God. I can see the beauty of the world—a weed growing out of a crack, a sunrise, the glory of art." He takes comfort in even the grain of wood in the arms of the chair, the gentle coarseness of the linen weave of his shirt, the dust motes dancing in the beam of sunlight, the smell of Marsilio's fresh bread. He looks up at the gentle smile of a painted Madonna on the wall and blinks away tears.

"It is seeing how much it means to you not to be able to pray, not to be able to thank God, that makes me want to become a Dominican," Angelo says.

"I am very glad to be doing something for you," he says. "I wish there were more."

"There is something you could do for me," Pico says, awkwardly. "You know about Isabella?"

"I have not met her in this life, but I remember her well in the others," he says.

"Really? I introduced you to her? Why?" Pico seems astonished.

"I met her at Angelo's deathbed, and then she came to me to ask for help with you when you were dying. Later I found a place for her in a Dominican convent, at her request," he says. He is used to telling them things like this about the life that he remembers that is so different from this life. He is working hard at writing it all down for them.

"Isabella was at my deathbed?" Angelo asks, seeming charmed at the idea.

"She was carrying a bucket of your vomit when I arrived," Girolamo says, truthfully but dampeningly.

Marsilio chuckles. "Not such a romantic picture."

Pico is shaking his head in amazement. "Isabella took vows?"

"She has spiritual gifts. She can see demons. She became part of Camilla Rucellai's new convent of Santa Caterina," he says.

"She never said she wanted to," Pico says. "Never gave any indication. She's been trying so hard to stop me doing it. I'm frankly amazed. People are endlessly surprising. I thought I knew Isabella well. We've been together for years."

"I think it was the combination of your death and my preaching," Girolamo says. "She hasn't had either in this life, so perhaps she's never turned in that direction."

"Wait until people hear *my* preaching," Pico says, smiling.

"What were you going to ask me about her?" Girolamo asks, cautiously.

"Oh, only whether you could take her to Genoa. I have everything set up there for her to open a little shop. I was going to go with her, but Tomasso says I could take vows right away. And now I can, the sooner I enter the better, to be in position for when the French arrive."

"Yes, I could do that," he says. "I'd be away for a couple of weeks. I'd be home before Easter."

"Yes. Thank you," Pico says.

"About the English mercenary captain," Marsilio says. "I don't think we should risk offering him the stone until after the French invasion."

"All right," Girolamo says, not sorry. The man had made him uneasy. He hadn't been at all afraid of Girolamo, or taken any notice of him at all. If he was one of Hell's creatures and knew it, he must outrank him. But perhaps he didn't know. "We'll try it then, if he's still alive."

"And if not, then next time," Angelo says.

"If we find a way for Girolamo to get the stone into Hell, maybe there won't be a next time," Marsilio says. "I believe God allows these eddies so that our souls can complete their journeys to him. Perhaps we will complete our journeys and find our way towards God."

"May St Jerome and St Augustine help us," Pico says, looking back at the text on his lap. "We were just going through these books to see which to take to San Marco to supplement the library. I hate being without all the books I need."

"What do you think will happen if I do manage to get the stone through?" Girolamo asks.

"Christ harrowed Hell," Marsilio says. "Think about what that means. He broke it by being there, changed the nature of what Hell was. Until that time all human souls went to Hell, from Adam onwards. Hell was the only place for sinners, and we are all sinners. Once Our Lord was there, He led them out, and since then those who have died in his salvation, with their sins forgiven, go to Purgatory to cleanse themselves and then at last to Heaven. You say you don't interact with human souls in Hell, only demons. That doesn't necessarily mean they're in a different part of Hell, as Angelo suggested. I believe it's possible that there are no human souls at all in Hell now. And if you could get the stone there, it might be harrowed again."

"But the souls the Lord led out were good people," Girolamo protests. "I'm a demon."

"I have warned you about despair," Marsilio says. "Demons are damned because they are in Hell, where there can be no change. You're not in Hell now. If demons can leave Hell, perhaps Hell is better thought of as more Purgatory, part of the long road to Redemption."

"Do you remember the Fall of the angels?" Pico asks, looking up from his book.

Girolamo hesitates, trying to remember. "It's like a dream," he says. "I remember being in bliss."

"What was it like?" Angelo asks.

"It was like—" He reaches for similes. "Like when you have been writing all afternoon, doing good work that you know is good, and then you look up and there through the perfect arch of the window, the sky is filled with the sunset, and from far away you hear people singing in harmony." He stops, realising he is picturing his old cell in San Marco. "I don't really remember. Just a glimpse. But it was like that, only going on all the time, unquestionably there, everything was like that in the sustaining presence of God."

"And you were working?" Marsilio asks.

Girolamo nods. "I don't remember what I was doing, but working, yes."

Marsilio sighs happily and flexes his hands, as if he can't wait to get on to the real work waiting for him in Heaven.

"But how could you turn away from it?" Pico asks, leaning forward full of urgency.

Girolamo stares at Count Pico, where he's sitting on Angelo's bed, his beautiful intelligent human face, with his shoulder-length chestnut hair tumbled around it. He shakes his head. He can't possibly explain, especially not to Pico. How could he have turned away from God? He cannot remember defiance. What he remembers is Michael's shocked and terrible face, full of pain. His brother's face. And then Hell, slamming into it, over and over. "I don't know," he says, and it's true. "I can't really remember. Why do people sin, and perform evil acts? God put Adam and Eve in the garden, and they did the one thing that damned them. It was worse for us, we were actually in

Heaven, and we did it. It's not God. We did it to ourselves. We de-
serve our punishment."

"Perhaps this is contrition," Marsilio says. "And perhaps God has
given you the stone because of it."

"I don't remember turning away from God. I don't know how I
can have come to do that. I don't think I understood what it meant,
that it would have been possible to understand that." He frowns,
trying to remember. "I wanted—something. Something about the
world." Michael's face rises up in his mind's eye again, filled with new
wariness, a new pain. Even now there are things Girolamo believes and
things he knows. He knows he is eternally damned.

"Adam ate the apple and was damned, and Christ led Adam out of
Hell," Pico says. "St. Gregory of Nyssa taught the doctrine of apocatastasis, which means everyone is redeemable, that all souls, however
much they have sinned, will eventually be restored and healed and
reconciled to God, that Hell and damnation are part of that process."

Girolamo turns the stone in his hand and looks down on its green
smoothness. Hope hurts.

CHAPTER 20

On Earth.

MARCH 1493

He had thought it would take about a week to walk to Genoa, going to Pisa and then up along the coast between the mountains and the sea. Without thinking about it, he had been imagining himself walking as a solitary friar, being fed at the pilgrim halls of monastic institutions along the way. He had not realised that Isabella would be taking all her possessions and a wagon full of cloth. Having two wagons, and drivers to see to them, and a guard to ensure their safety, means they need to ride, but having horses does not make the journey faster, since most of the time the wagons go more slowly than walking pace. They are constantly getting stuck in the heavy spring mud, or one of the mules throws a shoe in a tiny hamlet with no blacksmith. Isabella is very subdued. Once, when they are moving goods to try to lighten a stuck wagon, she weeps when one of the drivers drops Pico's for chased-silver hourglass in the mud. She wipes it clean and berates him for carelessness, saying that the glass could easily have broken. For the rest of that day she sits cradling it in her arms.

She does not really speak to Girolamo until the third day, when the rain clears midmorning and they stop to eat at midday in an inn perched on the slope of a hill. Girolamo has not had much experience of travellers' inns before this journey, but he already has a very low opinion of them.

The road runs along a ridge in the narrow space between the mountains and the sea. The sea down below is a dark blue, flecked here and there with white as the wind whips it. The mountains above are snowcapped, still, but here on the lower slope the trees are green, pines above and chestnuts and hazel lower down. All around them the grass is thick with crocus and anemones. The well-used road is a ribbon of mud rolling out ahead and behind. The inn is painted white, and has an orange terra-cotta roof. Inside, it stinks of sour wine, scorched porridge, and wet dogs. The fire is smoking. Without discussion, Girolamo and Isabella take their meal outside, sitting on the wooden bench that runs around the outside of the inn. A brisk wind is blowing clean salt-scented air from the sea. They are alone out there. Everyone else has chosen to huddle inside.

He bites into his bread. It's stale. "This is a rotten inn. Even worse than the others."

"I'm glad we're not staying the night. I hope we make good time this afternoon," she says.

This has been the kind of conversation they have had all the way, the petty details of the road, between near strangers. But now she looks at him with her head tilted, in a way he remembers. "I'd venture you haven't thought much about clothes, Master Savonarola?"

"Clothes?" he asks, disconcerted. "No, I haven't."

"That's what I thought," she says. "I've been thinking about them a great deal, since I decided to set up in this business. You see, clothes tell you a lot about a person. They tell you their social status, and very often their profession. Doctors, lawyers, scholars, senators, and of course their wives and daughters. And you can tell a lot from the cut and quality of cloth, too. Did Giovanni give you what you're wearing?"

"Angelo Poliziano did," he admits. He didn't know where Angelo had found the clothes. Angelo had offered them to him the morning after he had realised he couldn't go back to San Marco, and he'd pulled them on, awkwardly, hardly remembering how to fasten them.

"Angelo? I'd have thought he'd have more about him. But it was right after Magnificent Lorenzo died, wasn't it, so he probably didn't have time to think about it too much."

"Why? What's wrong with my clothes?" He looks down at his belted fawn tunic and dark hose.

She is smiling when he looks back at her. "They should have given you a scholar's robes, you'd have found them more comfortable. What you're wearing says that you're some kind of middling guildsman, except your hat is wrong for that, and that makes you look out of place, so everyone looks at you and wonders. Now in Florence that doesn't matter so much, because everyone who looks at you knows you were Brother Girolamo and First Brother of San Marco until you had a revelation at the deathbed of Magnificent Lorenzo and God told you to leave the monastery. But here on the road, where you're not known, it makes people wonder about you."

Girolamo is profoundly embarrassed. "Would you help me find something more appropriate?" he asks.

"I'm sure I can when we get to Genoa," she says. "You are a scholar, now, aren't you, like Angelo, or like Master Benivieni?"

"Not like Benivieni, I hope," he says.

She laughs. "Don't you like him either?"

"Since I left San Marco, he's been at me constantly to tell him why. He behaves as if he's enough of my friend he has the right to know, and he acts hurt when I don't agree."

"He's just the same with Giovanni. And he's gallant with me in a way that assumes that because I was living with Giovanni without being married to him, I must have no morals. I despise him."

Far off in the distance, Girolamo sees the sails of a round ship heading north. "She'll be bound for Genoa," he says, pointing her out.

"I could have gone by sea from Pisa, later in the year," Isabella says.

He nods, eating an olive sour enough to curl his tongue. It's early enough that sailing is risky.

"But Giovanni wanted to pack me off right away. You wanted to get out and he wanted to get in, and neither of you could wait, or tell me what the hurry was. It's not as if I'd have embarrassed him. It's not as if he's getting married."

He looks at Isabella in surprise. The wind is whipping a tendril of her hair across her face. "I thought you were resigned to it," he says.

"Did he tell you that?"

Pico hadn't. He had told Girolamo that she'd been complaining. Girolamo was going on his memories of Isabella the other times, and they were two years later and from another world. "You seem so sensible," he says, feebly.

"Well, in this world we have to make the best of what we have," she says, biting into an onion. "My father was a bean seller. I'm lucky to have had what I have had with Giovanni, these last years, and luckier that he's setting me up with a business now. But it's hard to see him so eager to get away from me when I am so fond of him. Was, that is. I was fond of him. I'll never see him again."

"And he is fond of you. He's making sure you're comfortable."

"Like giving away a dog," she says, pushing away the strand of hair, trying to disguise the fact that there are tears in her eyes.

"He has always spoken well of you," Girolamo says, and his *always* encompasses more than one life.

"It's the onion," she says, now openly wiping her eyes. "It's a strong one, that's all."

"Of course," he says, joining her in her lie. He eats a piece of hard dry cheese. It is a conundrum he doesn't know how to solve. Clearly Pico should be a Dominican, for his own soul. Besides, he needs to become the Dominican preacher Florence needs to become the City of God, now that Girolamo can no longer take that place. And it is sin to fornicate without marriage, and as Isabella told him after Pico's death in his previous life, they could never have married, because of the difference in their social status. The daughter of a bean seller could never marry a Count. "How did you meet him?"

"In the market. He charmed me away from the beans and lentils.

I was sixteen. Five years ago. Many people aren't happy so long." She sighs.

"I suppose not."

Isabella unfastens her headscarf. For the first time he sees all of her hair, a deep brown in the spring sunshine. She fixes the loose strand back, then refastens the scarf firmly. Her hands are deft and accustomed to the task. She sees him looking and blushes. "I'm sorry. I didn't think."

"I've seen it before, my mothers, my sisters."

"It's so difficult on the road. And of course I think of you as a priest. I heard one of your women's sermons. In San Lorenzo. On the Creation. It made me think."

"You wouldn't be able to live with Pico without being able to think," he says. Has he failed this woman's soul by ceasing to preach? Or would God find a way? He urgently wants to talk to the others about this.

She smiles, staring out over the waves. "I thought about taking vows, since he's doing it. The way husbands and wives do, when they both go into the Cloister. But no one would have me but a Magdalen order, and I don't want to spend my days doing endless penance. If I could be a Dominican and use what I've learned from Giovanni, maybe."

He cannot pray, or even thank God, for him to address God would be to attempt to besmirch Him. Not being able to pray is like having an amputated arm that constantly aches despite not being there to ache. He tries over and over to reach out with the missing arm, and grasps only pain. Yet although he cannot thank God, and not being able to thank God is the constant reminder and yoke of his damnation, the wish to thank Him rips through Girolamo the way a strong gale uproots trees.

"You could become a Dominican in Genoa where people will know you as a widow," he says, when he can speak. He notices that he has spilled his plate and the food is on the grass around his feet. "You have spiritual gifts."

"Did God tell you that?" she asks. She picks up a wizened apple and an onion he has dropped and wipes them unselfconsciously on her skirt.

"God—I—indirectly, yes," he says, in consternation, unable to explain. He wonders how she would react if he did explain. He imagines that she would take it well, but he dare not risk it for such slight cause.

"I have done nothing Giovanni didn't do," she says, unaware of the turmoil within Girolamo. "It is so unfair that the world holds different standards for men and women."

"I have often thought so," he says, accepting the apple and the onion back from her. He bites into the apple. It is old, but sweet and good, and the taste of it fills his mouth. He swallows. "There is a house of Dominican nuns in Genoa, the New House of St Dominic." He remembers corresponding with the First Sister there, in other lives.

"I will think about it and pray," Isabella says. "I would not lie before God. Passing as a widow in business is different from saying I am one to take vows. And no nuns would want to live with me if they knew."

He remembers her outfacing him on this subject last time. "As long as you live to love and serve God," he says.

She looks at him oddly. "I don't want to pry like Benivieni, but it seems very strange to me that a man like you would leave the Cloister."

He cannot burden her with the truth, dares not. "It was necessary," he says, and concentrates on eating the rest of his apple slowly, enjoying the fragrance and flavour of it. She watches him, and after a while when he has finished she silently hands him the matching apple that had been on her plate.

CHAPTER 21

As it is in Heaven.

OCTOBER 31ST, 1494

It is the same elaborate tent holding the same unimpressive king, but Girolamo is dressed as a scholar and standing at the side with the perfumed attendants, while Pico stands in Dominican robes with the Florentine delegation, speaking Girolamo's words. Girolamo always feels a strange mixture of emotions when he sees Pico now. It is mostly gratification, as he had always wanted his friend to be a Dominican. But part of it is envy, because he misses San Marco and his old life. Pico has taken his place. His hair is cut short and his tonsure shaven, and he is wearing his Dominican habit, all of which makes him look very different from the handsome aristocrat he always appeared. He seems older and more serious.

"This is too important," Pico had said before they left. "I need to know exactly what you said to convince Charles. Every word, precisely." Girolamo told him.

This time, they are the first and only official delegation from Florence. Piero has been in the Empire, and to the Holy Land, and recently wrote to them from Spain about his plans to visit a shrine in

Sweden. By the vow he took on his father's deathbed, he will return to Florence in 1497, having done his best to learn wisdom. His younger brother, Leo, the cardinal, is spending most of his time in Florence, serving on the Council of Seven Lorenzo set up on his deathbed. There are two Medici cousins on it as well. Florence is still a state under Medici authority, and it is as that that it has sent the delegation out to meet with the French king. But all the same the Count, Pico, Brother Giovanni, is making it into an Ark, a City of God, as Girolamo did.

They are in a better position relative to the French than they were in his memories. The White Boars are defending the fortresses at Sarzana and Senigallia, and the French camp is further north than when he visited it in other lives. Nor was Florence under demonic assault when he left it, unlike the previous time. He needs to talk to the others about that, when he has the chance, as it is a definite change, and not by their deliberate intent. It is a beautiful autumn afternoon, with the mellow sun shining through the cloth of the tent making everything glow with an underwater kind of light.

Pico has completed his novitiate, but not yet been sent out to preach. He is not the First Brother of San Marco, as Girolamo was. But he was already internationally famous before he took his vows, and whenever he preaches the church will be full. It was easy to have him added to the delegation. Angelo, although now also a brother at San Marco, is still on the Council of Seven. Valori is among the delegation, but it is another man, Piero Soderini, who tells Charles that Brother Giovanni is a prophet. Girolamo thinks of Soderini as an opponent and one of the Greys, although there is no such party in this changed life. Soderini hadn't been on Capponi's delegation last time. Valori treats Girolamo as a stranger, which feels odd and uncomfortable, when they had been such close colleagues before. But their friendship began after events which will never happen in this life, and in circumstances which will never occur. They will remain strangers, unless he can find a new way to become his friend. That would be hard. There is a social gulf between them now. Girolamo is a poor scholar, a Medici dependent, and Valori is a wealthy merchant and a power in the commonwealth.

Charles shooes everyone out of the tent so that he can talk to Pico alone. Girolamo looks back as he goes, and notices that everyone else is doing the same, a whole crowd of men walking out through a tent door looking over their shoulders. Some French noble trips, and someone else catches his elbow with a murmured word. Girolamo wonders if that happened last time and he didn't notice, or whether this little interaction will draw the two men closer, or further apart, or have no effect. How could anyone tell, but God? He goes to join Capponi and the other Florentines, who are standing in a very visible clump in their red merchant gowns among the peacock bright French lords and the soldiers in leather-and-metal armour.

"Brother Giovanni will persuade him," Capponi is saying.

"It's a very good thing you hired the White Boars last year," Soderini replies, gesturing to where the French cannon are prominently displayed, as if they should terrify the Florentines. The White Boars have pieces equally good. "We can hold off the French until Pope Alexander's troops arrive."

"Or until the French go into winter quarters," Valori says.

As Capponi begins to explain about the difference between contract armies and armies fighting for honour, Girolamo stops listening. Pico will find his own way to start talking about Florence as the City of God. And with Cardinal Leo de' Medici on their side, it should be easier to evade the wrath of the Pope.

"What do you think Count Pico's talking to the king about?" Valori asks.

"Brother Giovanni will be telling him God's plan, seemingly," Capponi says, stressing Pico's new religious title. "That's what he said he'd do, and I expect he's doing it."

"And do you think this will work?" Soderini asks, sneeringly.

"We haven't lost a thing if it doesn't," Capponi says. "Now you and I have had our differences, but we've known each other since we were boys. I know you love Florence even if you don't have any time for the Medici, and you know I love Florence as well as being a Medici man. I'd die for Florence, if necessary, and I know the same is true for you."

Soderini nods, cautiously.

"We could hold off the French for a while, yes. But we're not a big military power. We never have been. Maybe the Pope will send help and maybe he won't, Borgia's a Spaniard, and not to be trusted. And if he doesn't, eh? We could die for Florence, but then we'd be dead, and Charles would still keep on coming."

"We're not helpless!" Soderini says.

"Not helpless, no, but our troops are like a little dagger compared to a great big spear. You can see how many troops the French have brought. My point is that we need to make Charles think better of attacking us. One way would be to make him our friend. Having the White Boars helps, because you can die from a sharp little dagger in the side as easily as from a spear, and Charles knows that and doesn't want to risk the stab. Having the war chest helps, because maybe we can pay him to go away. That's worked on other enemies before."

"We can go up to eighty thousand florins if we need to," Soderini says.

Capponi nods. "Right. But maybe Brother Giovanni can do it. He says he can. It's worth trying. It doesn't cost anything. And if it doesn't work, there are other things that are worth trying, and they'll work just as well after as before. So it's worthwhile letting him try."

"He's not even a Florentine!" Soderini says.

"He's lived in Florence for years now, and he's given up his countship to take orders in a Florentine monastery. I'd say that makes him one of us, even if he hadn't been a close friend of Lorenzo's."

Soderini looks as if he's bitten into a lemon. "We'll see."

Charles summons them back and they all troop into the tent, the French nobles jostling for position, the Florentines staying together uncomfortably, Girolamo at the back. The tapestries on the walls are almost glowing in the afternoon sun. Girolamo's eyes dart from Charles to Pico, but neither of them is giving anything away. It ought to work. It worked before. But a different day, a different prophet, the king in a different mood, sunshine instead of cloud, anything could have happened.

"We will be signing a treaty of friendship with Florence, and advancing to the east, through Forli and San Merino," Charles announces. "Florence will give us ten thousand florins and a miracle-working crucifix in token of friendship."

The whole Florentine delegation is trying not to grin too widely as the treaty is drawn up. Pico catches Girolamo's eye and nods. "The crucifix is to come from Santa Croce," he explains to Capponi. Girolamo isn't at all sorry to hear that the Franciscans will lose their relic, the same one Brother Mariano was going to carry into the fire. He knows they will be furious and that it might stir up trouble later. But for now, they have an alliance with France and need not fear. And the French will not even pass through Florence this time. This is even better. Even Soderini is smiling.

"Don't forget the Empire will invade later," Girolamo whispers to Pico after they have left the tent and are remounting their horses.

"Sufficent unto the day," Pico says, grinning. "And with your help, my prophecies don't have to be vague at all, but can be very very accurate. This was the hard test, and we've done it."

CHAPTER 22

Give us this day our daily bread.

"You have told the others when they die, but how about me?" Marsilio asks, nothing in his voice but mild curiosity.

Girolamo shakes his head. "I don't know. You were still alive when they burned me."

Marsilio smiles. "I believe I will die in 1499, when I am sixty-six. It would have a pleasingly Platonic symmetry. Living to be ninety-nine would take me to 1532, which isn't such an appropriate pattern. Besides, it might be hard to manage."

"Very few men live to be ninety-nine. And I think there are bad things ahead in 1517 and 1527 which you might prefer to miss," Girolamo says. "I don't know what, but I feel them looming."

"But not 1507? Curious," Marsilio says.

Girolamo finds none of the power the older man sees in numbers. But Marsilio is a kind of living saint, and he is a demon. It would be easy to dismiss numerology as nonsense, but perhaps it is a clarity God reserves for the holy. He sighs. They are alone in one of the rooms Pico once rented for Isabella on the Via Porta Rossa, which is where

Girolamo lives now. It is the little study, where she once gave him the Count's Plotinus. He has heard nothing from her since he left her in Genoa, and Pico has said nothing to indicate that he has had news of her. He wonders whether she has found a monastery to accept her. Genoa, being ruled by Milan, is allied with the French and safe from the invasion. But there are other chances in the world, and other dangers.

He lives in this room, which now has a bed in the corner. It is quite big enough for him, three times the size of his old cell in San Marco. The rest of the apartment is presently occupied by Elia Pardo, Pico's old Hebrew tutor, and his wife and children. He hears them singing in Hebrew sometimes on Friday evenings, and they greet each other courteously when they meet on the stairs or the balcony. Sometimes Girolamo draws up water from the well in the courtyard for Mistress Pardo, and she thanks him gravely. Otherwise they leave each other alone.

It is a very hot day, and both men have taken off their sandals to cool their feet on the tile floor while they work. Flies are circling high up near the ceiling, making a persistent infuriating droning. Outside he can hear the clucking coo of a dove in the eaves, above the usual sounds of the market down the street, where the heat will not stop people buying and selling until the afternoon.

Marsilio is reading through what Girolamo has been working on. He spent the first year after he remembered what he was, writing down everything he remembered of the six years that were to come, for the others, and to make a detailed record. Then he wrote about what else he knew of the further future, little more than hints of disasters to come. What good could it do for anyone to know of the more distant horrors he has seen? Christianity schisming and the two halves slaughtering each other furiously. Engines powered by fire roaring across Europe. Guns that fire rapidly, and men running across the mud towards them and dying. Jews, naked and trembling, old women, children, being pushed into ovens. He hates to remember them, and writes them down, in case. Pico, reading them, asked whether he was sure these were visions of the future and not memories of Hell. They are not, he is sure, because even in the worst of them there are signs of love and hope.

After he was done with that unpleasant task, Marsilio suggested that he reconstruct his sermons and other books. He said Pico would need them, though now that Pico is giving sermons he is going his own way, and mixing in much more Plato than Girolamo ever would have. In his sermons now, only the prophecies are Girolamo's, and the message of the need for purification, to make Florence the City of God. Pico has rescued the Angels and clothed them in white and given them into Domenico's charge. He has altogether taken Girolamo's place. Now Girolamo lives quietly alone, translating, and Marsilio checks his translations and brings him more things to translate. It is useful work and keeps him busy.

"And you, Girolamo? How long do you want to live?" Marsilio asks.

He has never thought about it. He has been sick this summer, along with half of Florence, with the fevers that have swept the city, though Marsilio kept as healthy as ever. But he has not thought he might die. He has not realised that he is no longer bound to die only when he always did, in May of 1498. He touches the stone, which he now wears in a soft leather pouch around his neck, tucked inside his dull blue well-worn scholar's robe. He was always forty-five when he died. He could live twenty-five years beyond that before reaching the biblical measure of fourscore and ten. "As long as possible. Because I dread Hell, and I fear I may not be worthy or capable of taking the stone with me, or of using it there if I can. I may have no power at all in Hell, now. In Hell, will is our strength, and my will has been broken."

"Was it not broken always on your return?"

He shakes his head. "In Hell, my sins were my strength. Only on Earth am I ashamed."

"Can you sin in Hell? If sin is action against God, driving the nails into His flesh, it's hard to see how you could."

"Pride, wrath, tormenting other demons . . ." He shakes his head. "Maybe you're right, it isn't technically sin in the eternal absence."

"Are those your sins?" Marsilio asks, putting the closely written sheets down and looking at him.

He nods. "Yes. And recently gluttony."

Marsilio raises an eyebrow. "Gluttony? That doesn't sound like you."

"It's true. I've been enjoying food, and thinking about it even when I'm not eating it," he admits, ashamed.

"What food?"

"Apples, when I went to Genoa. And the strawberries I've been growing in the courtyard. And pine nuts."

"I don't think that amounts to gluttony so much as appreciating God's good gifts. You're still as thin as a rake."

"Pride has always been the worst," he says, looking down.

"I absolve you of all your sins," Marsilio says.

Girolamo stares up at him, astonished. The flies buzz louder than ever in the silence.

"I am a priest," Marsilio says, smiling, shrugging one shoulder. "I do have the right."

"Not for a demon," he says.

"Where is that written?"

Girolamo shakes his head. He knows it, but the Bible is full of lacunae on the subject of demons and damnation.

"We don't know anything like enough about demons," Marsilio goes on. "God might miss you. Not just you, personally. The absence of all the souls who reject him."

"But God is perfect, God can't lack or have needs," Girolamo says.

"Plato would agree. But we know, as our dear Plato did not, could not, that God sent his only son down to Earth, sent himself down, one of his persons, to suffer and die and free us from sin. This shows that he has a pretty strong desire to save souls. He loves us, even if he does not strictly speaking need us. And I very specifically include you in that *us*. God loves *you,* Girolamo, and all this must have a purpose. Maybe it's Gregory of Nyssa's apocatastasis as Pico suggests. This translating work is good, but I think you should be writing theology, writing about who and what you are, about the things we know for sure now that were only held in faith before. We need to—"

Pico flings the door open at that moment. He doubles over and stands that way for a moment, panting harshly and covered in sweat. Girolamo gets up and goes to the credenza and without asking pours him a cup of watered wine from the two covered jugs he keeps there. Pico takes it and dashes it back without pause, then slides into one of the chairs at the table, still out of breath.

"Have you run all the way from San Marco?" Marsilio asks, concern in his voice.

Pico nods. Girolamo mixes him a second cup that is mostly water, good well water from the courtyard, and he drains that as well. "Another?" Girolamo asks.

Pico shakes his head and kicks off his sandals so that they skitter across the tiles. "Look," he says, dropping a crumpled letter on the table.

Girolamo steps closer and looks at it. *To our well beloved son, Brother Giovanni of the Order of Preachers of the Observance, living in Florence.*

"Ah," he says, taking his own seat. "Pope Alexander is insisting you go to Rome?"

"Exactly the same as what he said to you," Pico says. "Exactly. Despite Leo. Despite my not having attacked him."

"I hadn't attacked him. I didn't attack him until it wasn't worth trying to conciliate him anymore, and even then I just talked about the Antichrist and the Whore of Bablyon and didn't use his name, though it would have been obvious to a child I was talking about him."

"You shouldn't have given Charles the Franciscans' cross, it made them resentful for no reason," Marsilio says.

Pico smiles. "But it was very satisfying."

"Brother Mariano was a very energetic enemy to me," Girolamo says. "But we do have a cardinal on our side now. Maybe Leo could go to Rome and talk to the Pope?"

"That's a good idea. Because I can't go to Rome," Pico says. "They'll kill me. They couldn't possibly condemn you as a heretic, but they can me very, very easily if they want to. The Nine Hundred Theses gives them all the ammunition they could ever want. My synthesis of Plato and Aristotle and the Cabala and the Koran with Christianity isn't heretical, not really, but it's very easy for misguided people to see it that way. I was already excommunicated once because of them. It would take very little for that to be revived."

"No, you shouldn't go to Rome," he agrees.

"But if I don't, Borgia's next move is a letter to Brother Mariano and the Franciscans of Santa Croce forbidding me to preach, right? And how am I to make Florence pure if I can't preach? And if First Brother Vincenzo orders First Brother Tomasso to send me to Bologna, Tomasso might do it. He's very obedient. Or if he ordered him to send me out to preach somewhere? I suppose I could do that. But most importantly, how can I avoid your fate? I don't want to be burned. I really don't." He shudders.

"You can't be burned in Florence unless we lose control of the government," Girolamo says. "Angelo is on the council, Leo is. Even though they're still formally drawing nine names from a purse every two months for First Men and a Standard-Bearer to rule the state, the power rests with the Council of Seven until Piero comes back in two years. You can't lose control the way I did."

"Not until Piero comes back," Pico agrees. "We're assuming he's actually going to discover wisdom. The last letter he sent was all about hunting white foxes in the snow."

"I am praying for him," Marsilio says, quietly, but with such authority that the other two fall silent and look at him. He folds his hands and looks back. "I think we should learn something from what we know from Girolamo. We don't need to be in such a hurry. If our lives eddy and we always have free will, then there should be time."

"But if Girolamo harrows Hell then that may be the end of that," Pico objects. "This might be our only chance."

"I was just saying as you came in how much God loves us," Marsilio says. "Consider Augustus's motto. Hurry more slowly."

It isn't in Pico's nature, or Girolamo's either. They look at each other, acknowledging that, then back at Marsilio.

"Let's try it," Pico says, after a long hesitation. "But I'm not going to Rome."

"No, that would be running your head into the noose," Marsilio agrees.

"Pope Alexander's next move after forbidding you to preach will be to offer you a cardinal's hat," Girolamo says. "If it goes the same way, that is. I refused, like St Jerome. But you could take it. You could build alliances in Rome, across Europe, among the cardinals and bishops. You have the birth and the authority. You could be the next pope after Borgia."

Pico pokes the letter from the Pope with a long finger. "Didn't you think of that?"

"I was afraid for my soul, in Rome," Girolamo says. "Ironically enough. And there were no indications from the future that this was the way things should be. The glimpses I had did not lead in that direction. It was Florence I believed God had given me. I thought it was here that I must begin the renewal of the Church. And I didn't want Pope Alexander to think I could be bought. So I stayed. What mixed motives: pride, fear, and a belief in Providence!"

"If you were pope, you could bring the whole world to God," Marsilio says.

"You're a priest, Marsilio, you could do it," Pico suggests.

"No one is offering to make me a cardinal."

"Oh come on, if you wanted it then Lorenzo would have worked just as hard to get it for you as he did for Leo."

"But I didn't want it," Marsilio said. "And things were different. Now we know something of what's coming."

"If I were pope, I could prevent the sack of Rome, and so much loss," Pico says. "But it would be very hard. And we have had popes who were saints, and they didn't bring the world to God. And it would take a lot of political manoeuvering of the kind Angelo's much better at than I am. And it might well be dangerous for my own soul."

"I have been wondering about that," Marsilio says. "About what happens with free will and our souls across these iterations, if we do different things? Consider Lorenzo. In every life you remember, Girolamo, he died in a state of grace, indeed in the higher hypostasis, the highest state a human soul can reach on Earth, purified, glowing. His soul would have gone straight to God. If in this life we had permitted him to kill Piero to save Florence, we assumed his soul would go to Hell for eternity. As it is, we assume he spent some time in Purgatory being purified before he could again reach the state he was in before. So, given this, we have free will. We can change. Our souls can, and their destination. But how many times is the ultimate fate of our souls in question? Can a soul be saved in one iteration only to be lost in the next? Or the reverse? Are our souls called back every time from bliss and safety once more into peril?"

Both of them look at Girolamo. He spreads his hands. The sound of an altercation over the price of cabbages can be heard faintly from outside. "I don't know. Before this time, there were only tiny variations. People did what they were going to do, because they were who they were. Small things might change between iterations as I remember them, but nothing much. Have I endangered everyone's souls, that were safe?" He feels guilt settle heavily over him.

"God sent the stone," Marsilio says, soothingly.

"We don't know that," Girolamo says. "We can't count on it. The stone was in a volume of Pliny, not a holy book. It was demons who led me to it."

"Providence. God works through all things," Marsilio says.

"But we don't know about the stone," Pico says. "And it's been impossible to find out where it came from before that. The books came from the library of King Matthias Corvinus, from Hungary. Did he know what it was, and want you to have it? Maybe you should go to Hungary to try to find out."

"I think staying here with us is better for Girolamo," Marsilio says.

Girolamo nods agreement. It is a long friendless way to Hungary.

"Besides, I am sure God sent it," Marsilio says.

"What is the stone?" Girolamo asks. "You knew a name for it, the stone of Titurel?"

"It was a way of asking whether it was what the writers of romances and songs call the Holy Grail," Pico says. "It is sometimes described as a green plate, not a cup."

"Or an emerald that Lucifer dropped when he fell," Marsilio says. "Your stone is green, but not an emerald. It's jade, I think."

"The Grail, the Stone of Titurel, is very hard to research because it's all mixed up with nonsense and folklore," Pico says.

Girolamo pulls out the stone. It looks the same as ever, a polished green stone. It fits on the palm of his hand. He tries to remember Lucifer, and the rebellion, but as ever sees only Michael with sword and helmet, looking at him, his face full of fresh pain.

"I've been reading everything I can find about demons, and the rebel angels, and there really isn't much," the Count goes on.

"That's one reason why I think Girolamo should write about what he knows," Marsilio says.

"I've found a lot about how to cast out demons, and much more than I want about how to summon them, but I can't find any reason why they might have surrounded Florence other times but not this time," Pico says.

Girolamo has a theory about this, but he has been reluctant to voice it, because it doesn't reflect well on Pico. "Maybe it's not that they're not here, but because our wall of prayer isn't strong enough to keep them out yet," he says. "I'd been preaching solidly, and you have had to catch up."

"Are there demons in the city now?" Marsilio asks.

"Sometimes yes. I see them hiding in corners. I banish them, but it's more of a struggle than it used to be."

"Are you banishing them in the name of Christ?" Marsilio asks.

"I always did," Girolamo says. "But I was always doing it by the power of Hell, and I still am."

"The power of Beelzebub," Pico says, thoughtfully. "Could you cast out demons by the power of Beelzebub as our Saviour says?"

"Yes," Girolamo says. "Or by my own power."

"Is Beelzebub a person, like you are?" Pico asks.

Girolamo nods, and gets up and goes to the credenza to disguise the fact that his hands are shaking. In this hot room, on this hot day, thinking about Hell makes him feel cold.

"I mean could you, when you are in Hell, go and find him and talk to him, like we're talking now?"

"Not like we're talking now, because all you can do in Hell is torment each other. But I could talk to him. I wouldn't, because he's more powerful than I am. He's a prince of Hell. I'd avoid him if I could." Girolamo turns and takes the covered jugs of water and wine and brings them back to the table.

"You can only torment each other? You really can't just exchange information?" Pico asks.

"No," Girolamo says, looking at the cups as he pours.

"How do you know? Have you tried? Stop fiddling about and look at me!"

Shocked, Girolamo spills a little water and mops it with his sleeve. He looks at Pico. "I have tried," he says. "It's hard to explain, especially to you. It would be easier to explain it to worse people, strange as that seems. Have you ever known someone who annoys you? Or have you ever known someone for a long time, and fallen into a bad pattern with them so that you're always quarrelling? So that no matter how good your intentions are, no matter that you've prayed to do better, when you start to talk to them you hear everything they say as malicious, and they do the same with you, so you can't even say good morning without them saying sarcastically that it might be good for some people? Or if you haven't done that yourself, you might have seen some brothers get like that with each other, in the monastery? The

First Brother will always try to separate them and maybe send one of them elsewhere when that happens, but you might have seen it."

Marsilio shakes his head in wonder, but Pico nods reluctantly. "I do know what you mean. It can be like that with a woman, when love is gone, and the arguments have lasted too long, where it isn't even the words but the tone of voice that reminds you of old spite. And I find myself feeling like that about Benivieni sometimes. I know he means well, but he has irritated me so much with the way he tries to act as if he's closer to me than anyone that now anything he says irritates me, no matter how innocuous. I have prayed for patience and tolerance."

"Well, in Hell it is all and only like that, only worse. Anything you say, anything anyone says, is tinged with malice, and lacerates, intentionally or unintentionally. It isn't like Dante says. He couldn't have had those conversations there with Virgil. They'd have been constantly taking offence at everything each other said, and resenting it." Girolamo shudders, and strokes the smooth glazed clay of his wine cup. He hates thinking about it.

"But Dante wasn't damned," Pico says.

"No. Maybe not then. But for those of us who are, it's like that."

"What if you said *I love you*," Marsilio suggests.

"It would sound false and malicious, and would remind them of all those who did love them and are forever lost, or even that I might have once loved them and now hate them, or am indifferent to them, so that being reminded of lost love is pain."

Marsilio picks up his own cup and takes a long drink.

"Surely you've at least seen married people quarrel where the most innocent thing becomes a weapon," Pico says.

Marsilio shakes his head and puts down his cup. "Is that Hell, then?"

"Hell on Earth," Girolamo says. "And Heaven on Earth is when we do—when people do love each other."

"God loves you, and you are capable of love and being loved, on Earth," Marsilio insists, and puts his hand on Girolamo's arm. Girolamo feels tears start and tips his head back and bites his lip. Even

Marsilio said it in the passive and the abstract. No one could love a demon, not knowing what he was.

"But the twisting of words, the impossibility of saying anything that isn't pain in Hell is because of the nature of the place itself?" Marsilio goes on.

Girolamo isn't sure. He shrugs, still choking back tears. "I think so."

"So kindness, goodwill, is like a steep slope, with Heaven at the top, where unkindness is unimaginable and impossible, and in Hell at the foot, the reverse, and here we're in between?"

"I wonder if on Earth it varies by physical location?" Pico muses. "Impossible to tell, really. But someone could, if they wanted to, gather demons together in Hell and tell them things? I appreciate that it would sound like torment, but would it be possible to do that?"

"Preaching despair," Girolamo says.

"No. But for instance you could tell them about the stone. And maybe someone already has, and that's why they are drawn to it."

"Who?" Marsilio asks.

"Matthias Corvinus," Pico suggests.

"Pico! Corvinus wasn't a demon! He was a humanist!" Marsilio protests.

Pico laughs. "Perhaps Girolamo demonstrates that the two are not quite as easily distinguished as you think? I didn't know him, so it's easy for me to suppose. He had the stone. He had it sent to Santa Lucia in a book. He may be in Hell, and he may have told the demons about the stone."

"I suppose it's possible," Marsilio says, dubiously.

"I tried to preach, once, in Hell," Girolamo says, quietly, so that the other two have to lean closer to hear. "It really was preaching despair. Because it was giving them the news that there was salvation, but not for us, that God loved Earth, but not Hell. It wasn't actually news to anyone, of course, but even being reminded was still agony to hear. And to say, too, of course. It brought us all face-to-face with the fact of our damnation, instead of whatever distractions we'd been trying to busy ourselves with."

The others are silent for a moment, thinking about that. The flies circle. Pico wipes sweat from his forehead and takes a drink.

Marsilio pats Girolamo's arm. "You rebelled against God because you wanted something for the world that was different from what God wanted, and in Heaven you couldn't imagine wrongdoing or unkindness or malice."

Girolamo stares at him. He can hear the doves cooing in the eaves and smell the wine and the bread and strawberries that are waiting under a cloth on the credenza. He feels the linen of his robe and the sweat on his thighs. He breathes in sweet air, and lets it out, over and over. He has lost Heaven, but this is not Hell.

"Well put together," Pico says, admiringly.

"And because wanting something different from what God wants is wrongdoing, and you were in Heaven, which is a place where there can't be any, you had to be cast out," Marsilio goes on.

"I can't remember," Girolamo says. He can remember the fact of Heaven, the feeling of it, but never the details.

"Can you remember when you're in Hell?" Pico asks.

"I don't— I don't think so but I don't know."

Marsilio nods. "God can do anything, but it seems apparent that God doesn't like to break the laws of the universe. The fall of the angels happened before Earth was made. Perhaps Hell spontaneously came into being as soon as sin did, as a moral necessity."

"And then when Adam sinned his soul wound up there!" Pico says. "Yes. Very clever."

"And all human souls after him, until Christ harrowed it and made a path for us sinners to come back to Heaven," Marsilio says. "And now Girolamo needs to harrow it again."

"If I can find the way," he says. There is a painting in one of the cells in San Marco of the harrowing of Hell. He remembers the faces of Adam and Moses and John the Baptist as they reach for Christ's outstretched hand. Behind them in the darkness are legions more, the unidentified dead, pressing upwards towards the promise of light.

"The other thing I was thinking, now that we're safely past the

French invasion, is that we should tell more people. There are scholars and churchmen all over Europe who need to know what we now
know with certainty. It's selfish of us to keep it to ourselves. And one
of them might have the insight we need to discover how to get the
stone into Hell."

Girolamo doesn't want more people to know about him, but he recognises the force of the argument. He nods.

"Are you suggesting writing letters to everyone personally, or an-
nouncing it generally?" Pico asks. "We could have another Council
of Florence!"

"I had been thinking about the first," Marsilio says. "I'm not sure
about a Council with Girolamo as the chief exhibit."

"The giraffe," Girolamo says. "With everyone staring and poking
at me. It would turn into a trial and condemnation. Lorenzo said to
be very careful who we tell."

"Yes. That's what I was thinking. Slowly expanding the circle of
people who know, through the circles we already move in, telling only
people we trust," Marsilio says.

"Let's talk to Angelo about this," Pico says.

"A Council would expose you to the Pope's hatred even more,"
Girolamo says. "Though if we had a big proper Church Council per-
haps we could depose him, like they did seventy years ago at the
Council of Constance. That would be good for the whole church."

"We should move cautiously," Marsilio says. "And I think if we do
decide to do this, the first person to tell would be Leo. He can help
us much better if he understands about Girolamo. With some others,
especially those further away and less trusted, I don't think we should
reveal Girolamo's identity, just explain the situation."

"That would be a relief," Girolamo says. "The more people know,
the more likely it is that I'll be burned and sent straight back to Hell."

"That's very sad," Marsilio says. "I was thinking what a wonderful
confirmation it would be for everyone."

"But we don't really know anything," he says, leaning back and
moving his bare feet on the cold tiles.

"Yes we do. We know a lot about the nature of Hell, and that you never met any human souls in it. And the more scholars we have working on this, the more chance of finding things in books we don't have access to."

"And the more previously saved souls we potentially endanger," he says.

Pico pokes at the letter from the Pope again, flipping the seal up and down. "It seems as if things want to go the same way whatever we change. And we have the potential to save souls previously lost, as much as endangering ones previously saved."

"Exactly," Marsilio says. "I think we should see what Angelo thinks about telling Leo."

"All right," he says.

Marsilio looks at Pico. "Have you been purifying yourself? Have you reached a higher hypostasis?"

Pico shakes his head. "I try, but I'm too impatient."

Marsilio nods. "You are already living on borrowed time."

"But I have helped so many simple people come to God," Pico objects.

"They are important too," Girolamo says. "Perhaps the most important."

"I must get back for Sext," Pico says, getting up and walking barefoot across the tiles towards where his sandals landed. "I always seem to be hurrying to services. I don't know how you ever managed to fit anything in around the Hours, Girolamo."

Girolamo tries to smile. He misses the Divine Office constantly, the hours of prayer, the feeling of common purpose. He often finds his days empty now without the structure they bring, even without considering the absence of their devotional purpose. He still finds himself unintentionally stopping what he is doing at the hours for prayer, even though he cannot pray. "I suppose I got used to it early," he says. "Older novices do often find it harder."

CHAPTER 23

And forgive us our trespasses.

This is the first joust Girolamo has attended since childhood. There's nothing evil about them, but they are very warlike, and not really suitable for priests and friars. He only came to this one, held in the Piazza of Santa Croce in honour of the occasion of the marriage between Gianni di Pierfrancesco de' Medici and the widow Caterina Sforza, because Isabella persuaded him. Isabella came back to Florence in Lent, hoping to be received into the new tertiary house of Santa Caterina set up by Camilla Rucellai. The Count is dragging his feet. Girolamo both does and does not understand why. Meanwhile, she is in Florence, living in lodgings with a respectable widow on the square of Santa Croce. Girolamo spends time with her. They walk the walls of the city in the early morning and he teaches her how to cast out demons.

It is a beautiful autumn day, just before the Feast of Santa Reparata. The window of Isabella's room looks down onto the square of Santa Croce, where sand has been strewn for the tournament. Girolamo looks down and sees the stand set up in front of the church for the dignitaries, and crowds pressing close all around the other three edges of the space marked out. There are people in all the windows, many of them hanging out cloth in blue, red, white, or green to mark their allegiance to one of the four quarters of the city in whose name the horsemen would compete. Mistress Baccio, whose rooms these are, has hung out a green bedcover for Santa Croce. Her son Zanobi and her daughter Laura are there. Zanobi is apprenticed to a goldsmith and Laura works as a servant to the Tornabuoni family, but they are both free for the holiday. They are both of an age to become wild with excitement, about fifteen and thirteen, Girolamo guesses. They keep jostling each other and leaning far out, though there is nothing to see yet.

"Have you seen a joust before, Messer Savonarola?" Mistress Baccio asks politely, elevating his status a little.

"Oh yes, often, when I was a boy in Ferrara. The Duke of Ferrara was a very enthusiastic jouster when he was younger. There would be jousts and tournaments much more frequently than you have them here in Florence. I remember my father taking me when I was small enough he had to lift me up to see the horses. And my sisters would always complain they wanted to go too. At that age, Chiara loved horses, and Beatrice loved excitement, so you can see a joust would be perfect for both of them. One year, when my grandfather was particularly in favour with the duke, he got seats for all of us at the side of the stand, near the back. I must have been fourteen or fifteen, so they'd have been thirteen and twelve. Both of them were almost bursting with excitement while we waited, like your two here." He remembers that joust so well he can almost smell it, the slightly spicy dust of Ferrara, Beatrice's sickly lilac perfume, and their snack of grilled eel with the Ferrarese scroll-shaped bread. He can also remember the brown horse winning, and the black, and the grey, and the grey mare slipping and the horseman falling, and slipping but managing to keep his seat, and slipping and swaying and almost managing to keep his seat and then falling beneath the mare's hooves, with Chiara crying out and his grandfather running onto the field to set his bone. All of these things, all of these memories, from different iterations of his life, in all of which he had done nothing but sit in the stand next to his family, watching. All these tiny changes, which led to no great changes. Eddies in the river of time.

"But only once?" Isabella asks.

He is brought back to the present, the one and only moment when he stands at Mistress Baccio's window overlooking the square by Santa Croce in a silence that has lasted a little too long. "Yes, we only had seats in the stand that once. The next winter my grandfather died, so we were back to standing in the crowd and my sisters had to stay home. We weren't lucky enough to have a friend with a window like this. Thank you again for inviting me, Mistress Baccio, Cousin Isabella."

They have told people he is her dead husband's cousin. The supposed relationship makes it socially possible for them to be friends. Even for those who knew her before, since she has been away for several years, they can't say for sure that she didn't marry some Ferrarese cousin of his in the meantime. A man who never existed could have whatever relations he wanted. Girolamo squares the lie with himself by asserting in his heart a spiritual cousinship with her.

"There's the cardinal, look," Mistress Baccio says. Girolamo looks where she is pointing, and sees Cardinal de' Medici, known to his family and friends by his childhood nickname of Leo. He is a serious, plump young man of twenty. He walks into the stand specially built in front of the church for the dignitaries. Places there are as closely coveted as they had been in Ferrara long ago. Leo takes his seat close to the centre. In honour of the joust and his cousin's wedding he has chosen to wear the full red robes and special flat tasselled hat of a cardinal. He is escorting his sister Lucrezia Salviati and her children. She has three of them with her, all boys, and very close together in age. They all have big eyes, and the middle boy has his grandfather Lorenzo's recognisable nose. Lucrezia settles the children between her and Leo. She is wearing a festive brocade gown of dark pink. For the first time in Girolamo's memory of her she doesn't appear to be pregnant. Of course, her husband Jacopo Salviati is away, serving as ambassador in Venice.

Girolamo watches Leo scratch his chin. Angelo was opposed to telling the young cardinal about Girolamo's demon nature, though they have all agreed that Ficino can feel out some of his correspondents about the situation in the abstract. Angelo felt Leo was too young yet, and already had enough burdens, between Florence and Rome, without that as well. After the Pope's letter came he travelled to Rome and spoke to Pope Alexander about Pico—Brother Giovanni—and the Pope had thus far allowed the preaching to continue. Although they have met, Leo is still largely a stranger to Girolamo. He watches him sharing a basket of sweet pastries with the children, licking sugar off his fingers and making his eldest nephew laugh. He leans down and offers one to the sculptor Michelangelo Buonarroti, who is sitting in the row below. Michelangelo takes one, with a grin up at Leo. Since he completed his great John the Baptist for the cathedral he has become very popular in the city, and is working on a façade and a new library for San Lorenzo. Girolamo can see from up here that his curly hair has marble dust in it.

The parade of horsemen rides in, sixteen of them, all from the city's best families, the sons of those whose names are put into the purses. You have to be quite rich to be able to afford a horse and the special tournament armour. But in Florence rich and poor live close together and know each other, so sections of the crowd roar enthusiastically as each horseman comes out. These are their bosses, their customers, their rivals for girls. The crowd may be standing while the competitors are riding, but they have rubbed shoulders with these young men as they have gotten drunk at Carnival and taken communion in the cathedral. They have seen them flirting with their daughters and adolescent sons. They know their political opinions and whether they are good credit risks. There are no strangers here. So Florence has turned out enthusiastically to celebrate this wedding.

The occasion marks an alliance, not just with the bride's home city

of Milan, but with the domain Caterina inherited from her first husband, Girolamo Riario, nephew of Pope Sixtus. The small but fortified towns of Imola and Forli properly speaking belong to her young
son Ottaviano Riario. Until he is of age, this wedding makes them part
of Florence's sphere, though they are not in Tuscany but over the
mountains in the Romagna, where they can guard Florence's flank.
Gianni de' Medici, the bridegroom, Leo and Piero's cousin and one
of the Council of Seven, is competing in the joust. He rides in to a
great cheer, in his engraved armour, on a white horse with nodding
red plumes. Caterina, the bride, is not competing today, despite her
warlike reputation. People have been joking about whether she would.
She walks in now with great dignity and takes a seat on the other side
of Leo. She is dressed in blue and violet and wearing enough gold and
jewels to ransom a city. Even from above she glitters, with jewelled
combs pinning up her elaborate hair.

"Her brother's the Duke of Milan," Zanobi says.

"Look at that velvet! Is it true she threatened the Papal Conclave
with a cannon?" Laura asks.

"Yes, after the death of bad old Pope Sixtus," Mistress Baccio says,
craning her neck to look at Caterina over her daughter's shoulder.
"That's when they started to say she was as good as a man. Then she
became really notorious at the siege of Forli of course."

Isabella nods. Everyone has heard the story of how she laughed
from the top of the walls at the soldiers who had her children captive
and threatened to kill them. She exposed her genitals and said she
had the means to make more. Her four boys, who look to be between
about fifteen and ten, follow her in now and sit down at her side,
though the youngest is bouncing up and down with excitement. They
too are richly dressed, and seem to have forgiven their mother for her
indifference to their welfare. Leo offers them his basket, and they take
pastries, though Caterina shakes her head.

"I wouldn't want to be married to her. I'd be afraid she'd eat me in
the night," Zanobi says.

She does have something of the glitter of an insect, Girolamo thinks. She is wearing a dagger in a jewelled sheath. She has about her an air of danger. Then she wipes a crumb from her son's cheek, and seems like any mother.

The last of the horsemen comes onto the field, and Crookback's big black horse rears up on his hind legs before settling back. His shield is a white boar. "I thought it was all to be Florentines," he says. Crookback disconcerts him, as he always does. He is almost sure he is a demon.

"Crookback is part of the bride's family," Mistress Baccio says. "He's married to her daughter."

"There must be a big age difference," Isabella says.

"Bianca's seventeen, and Crookback's forty or so," Mistress Baccio says. "A bit more than usual, perhaps, but it's not May and December. He was a widower, but he has no sons. There she is, look, just taking her place next to her brothers."

Bianca Riario Plantagenet is young and slim and very pregnant. She is wearing gold brocade over white pearl-embroidered silk, and a duchess's coronet. She has more pearls sewn into her sleeves, and diamonds in her hair. She outshines every other woman on the stand, because as Countess of Ravenna and Duchess of Glusta she is not obliged to follow the sumptuary laws of Florence. She is not beautiful, but she holds her head up and makes up for it in dignity and wealth.

"Does she—" Laura begins.

"Hush now, they're starting," Mistress Baccio interrupts.

As the horsemen move ponderously into position, one at each end, Girolamo thinks about the mutability and weight of history. King Charles has gone back to France, as always, but the Imperial invasion, which in every other iteration had been defeated by God sending a storm, has not manifested. They had done nothing directly to prevent it, but some combination of changed events must have headed it off. Pisa has not revolted and so Capponi did not die trying to retake it, and is alive and well sitting in the stand on the row below the bride and the cardinal, throwing his head back laughing at some remark of his wife's. Yet Isabella had come back to Florence with her vocation at just the same time she always had.

In the history he remembers, Gianni de' Medici and his brother had been exiled by their cousin Piero after Lorenzo's death, then come back to the city after Piero fled. They had written to him asking permission, and he had granted it, glad to see the city swelled again by its exiles. They served in his Great Council, discarding the now-hated name of "de Medici" and called themselves "Popolani" "of the people." They were supporters of his. Gianni had been sent to Imola to negotiate with Caterina Sforza, and the pair had fallen in love and married in secret—though Gianni had told Valori, who had passed it on to Girolamo. Now this time they were marrying as a public alliance, a year earlier than their secret marriage. In all the other iterations, Crookback had never come to Florence, nor had his wife, Bianca, but here they were. This tournament would never have happened in Girolamo's Florence, even had Gianni and Caterina married openly. The tournament, and the alliance it represents, relies on the special status of the Medici. He might have condemned it as vanity, but it wouldn't have come to that, no one would have suggested it. What keeps some things the same, while others change? If history is a tide sweeping down a river, and individuals are leaves being swept along on top of the current, what makes Isabella come back and the Emperor stay at home? How much can be changed? Can all of it?

The bridegroom takes his place at the Santa Croce end, under the Baccios' window. Crookback is ready at the far end. They lower their lances. The handkerchief drops. The horsemen thunder together, their lances poised. The young Baccios shriek, along with most of the crowd beneath them. Isabella puts her hand to her mouth. The lances clash, and the bridegroom lands unceremoniously in the dust. Mistress Baccio laughs. "They'll have a hard time handing him the prize after that!"

"Are they bound to hand him the prize?" Isabella asks.

"It's usual," Mistress Baccio says, as Crookback circles his horse. The crowd is booing loudly. "Magnificent Lorenzo won it at his marriage joust, and his poor brother Giuliano at his coming-of-age joust. It doesn't really matter whether they're really the best, when it's in their honour. But being knocked off at the first pass!"

The next two horsemen are taking their places and getting ready to charge.

"At his joust, Magnificent Lorenzo crowned Simonetta the Queen of Love and Beauty," Mistress Baccio goes on.

"Who's Simonetta?" Laura asks.

"Simonetta Vespucci. You must have heard of her, though I suppose she did die before you were born. She was Florence's mascot. Young, beautiful, unmarried. Painted as a goddess by Botticelli. She died very young, and everyone wrote poetry about her," Mistress Baccio says.

"So why was it wrong for Lorenzo to crown her?" Laura asks.

"Because it was supposed to be a tournament to celebrate his marriage to Clarice Orsini," Isabella explains.

"What did she think?" Laura asks.

"Clarice? She was still in Rome when the tournament happened. I don't know what she thought afterwards. Probably wasn't very happy about it, I should guess," Mistress Baccio says. Angelo would know, Girolamo thinks, but asking him probably wouldn't be a good idea.

There is another charge, another moment of almost unbearable excitement as the lances clash. This time neither horseman is unseated, and they ride on to the opposite ends to try again. The horses are beautiful, highly groomed, and in perfect condition. The horsemen too are in the prime of life, young and strong and confident, wearing decorative armour. One of these is wearing red, and the other white, with a dove on his pennant, the sign of the Santo Spirito quarter. This time his lance breaks with a great crack, and the sigh of the crowd rises up to them at the window.

"It's so exciting," he says, caught up in it as he was in childhood.

The others laugh; they have seen jousts before, if not ones quite this splendid. The bridegroom gets a new horse, and unhorses Piero Soderini, to great cheers. Next Lorenzo Tornabuoni faces Crookback.

Laura almost falls out of the window cheering for her employer, but Crookback unseats him easily. The crowd boos him again, though Lorenzo Tornabuoni says something that makes people laugh.

Crookback wins every bout he enters, and is booed loudly every time.

At the end, though Crookback has clearly triumphed by any reasonable measure, Gianni is awarded the prize by Leo. He gives it to Caterina, as everyone expects, and she accepts it graciously. Once she is seated again, Crookback rides up to the stand and takes Bianca up beside him on his crupper, the material of her gorgeous robe stretched across her big belly. She clings to him as they ride out of the square.

"What does that mean?" Laura asks.

"I suppose that he loves his wife," her mother replies, uneasily. "Those mercenary captains are strange folk."

CHAPTER 24

As we forgive.

OCTOBER 5TH, 1496

After the joust, Girolamo walks with Isabella to San Marco, where she is to meet with First Brother Tomasso as part of her preparation for taking Dominican vows. "Have you told him the truth about yourself?" he asks, as they circle around the vast bulk of the cathedral.

"I've told him I'm not really a widow, and that I have confessed my sin," she says. "I haven't told him it was with Giovanni."

They turn by St Zenobius's elm tree column and walk up past San Lorenzo. The market is closed today, for the festival. A one-legged beggar is scratching himself on the steps of the church. He asks half-heartedly for alms, and Girolamo gives him an apple, which he bites into.

"An apple?" Isabella asks.

He blushes. "I like apples."

On the road up to San Marco, he sees a demon skulking in the narrow alleyway between two buildings. It is long-eared and hairy and has hands like a bat's wings. He looks at Isabella. "Can you see it?"

She peers into the alley. "I can see a shadow." She points accurately to where the demon is.

"Very good. Now banish it."

She looks both ways. Two merchants are passing on the other side, and the beggar on the church steps is eating his apple. No one is paying any attention to them. "I don't have any holy water!"

"Holy water always works, but doing it in Jesus's name works too, if you have faith," he says.

Isabella takes a deep breath. "Come out. I banish you in the name of Jesus Christ," she says, and makes a circle of her fingers, as he has taught her.

The demon wails and clings to the stone with his bat hands, but vanishes after a moment, and a smell of spring flowers and rain fills the alley, extinguishing the stink of rot and excrement that had hung in the air. Isabella turns to him with shining eyes, delighted. "You did it," he says. "You did it alone through faith and the name of God." It is all quite different from what happens when he banishes demons.

"I think that is a sign that God wants me," Isabella says, as they move on. "And Sister Camilla wants me to join her. But I need to have First Brother Tomasso's permission."

"She is aware of your powers," Girolamo says. "Brother Tomasso can not see demons, and isn't very interested in prophetesses."

"Will you come in and talk to him?" she asks, hesitantly, not looking at him.

"I don't have any standing now to help you." *This time* he does not add. She is so fierce and forthright and pure in heart. Besides, he strongly believes she should be a Dominican. She made such a good one.

"Even without having a position, First Brother Tomasso listens to you," Isabella says. "He knows God speaks to you. I'm not sure Giovanni is trying as hard for me as he could. He really does think it was a different sin for him and for me."

"It was a much worse sin for him, to seduce a virgin," Girolamo says. "And I know he's read St Jerome."

"You know all these things. Please come in?" she implores, as they come to the square outside San Marco. The trees are turning gold and brown. San Marco itself is white-walled and red-tiled and beautiful. He looks up and sees the Wailer, the bell that he thinks of as his, hanging at the top of the tower. After they arrested him, they arrested the bell too, they dragged it through the streets and flogged it, and afterwards gave it to the Franciscans.

It is laceration for him to go inside San Marco now he has renounced it, to see the courtyard and the cloister that no longer enclose him, to see Brother Angelico's crucifix and the lunette of friars welcoming Christ as a pilgrim, which were once his everyday joy. It is like going home knowing it can never be your home again. It is like his memories of Heaven. He digs his nails into his palms as hard as he can.

"All right," he says.

Isabella smiles at him as she knocks at the postern.

Brother Silvestro greets them and escorts them through the cloister to the parlour. Silvestro avoids his eyes. Silvestro and Domenico have never been able to understand why he had to leave San Marco, and can't forgive him for it. He can't give them any satisfactory explanation without telling them of his nature, and then they'd be obliged to try to exorcise him and tell the Pope. He looks away, and hesitates a moment at the frescoed crucifix, looking at St Dominic's face as he kneels, and Christ's face. He wants so much to believe Marsilio is right and he can be forgiven. He wants to beg, like the thief crucified at Golgotha, "Lord, remember me when thou shalt come into thy kingdom." He longs for forgiveness, but he knows it is impossible. He is a demon. He turns away from the fresco. Salvation is not for him, but he can help others.

First Brother Tomasso is waiting in the parlour, looking very old and frail. His hair is no more than a white wisp around his tonsure, and he can no longer turn his head at all. He is sitting with Pico. The little parlour is the monastery's formal place to meet with outsiders, but it always has a slightly disused air.

242 • JO WALTON

"Thank you for seeing me," Isabella says.

"And Brother—that is, Girolamo Savonarola, yes," Tomasso says, making a flustered gesture. "Have you come to—why have you come?"

"I've come to support Isabella's plea to enter the novitiate," he says. Pico nods at him.

"If she wants to devote herself to God, I've found a proper place for her with the sisters of the Convertite," Tomasso quavers.

"It would be much more appropriate for her to be a Dominican," Girolamo says, looking to Pico for support.

"Is that really what you think God wants?" Tomasso asks.

"She's an educated and spiritual woman, and I believe—" he begins, but the door bursts open and Angelo rushes in, his face as horrified as Girolamo has ever seen it.

"First Bro—" he begins.

"Don't bother, Brother, I can announce myself," says a well-remembered voice with the accent of Bologna. Pushing Angelo out of the way, First Brother Vincenzo sweeps into the room. He looks around at them one by one. Girolamo drops his eyes at once and freezes where he is, leaning forward slightly, his hands on his knees. "Well, well, well."

"Th-thanks be to God, First Brother Vincenzo," Tomasso says. "To what does our humble monastery of San Marco owe the great honour of your visit?"

"Oh, I'm not visiting. I wouldn't stay here. I will stay at Santa Maria Novella, where they have been expecting me and where they have appropriate apartments." Pope Eugenius had stayed at Santa Maria Novella when he came to Florence for the Great Council in 1439, Girolamo remembers. He wonders what excesses of comfort the brothers of Santa Maria Novella will arrange for Vincenzo. "His Holiness suggested that I might need to look into your affairs, but I didn't expect to find all the conspirators together like this. You have been forbidden to preach, Brother Giovanni, and yet you continue to do so. How do you explain this?"

"The Cardinal gave me a dispensation," Pico says.

"Well, I dispense with his dispensation, and you will be silent until further notice. You're a heretic, or the next thing to it, and a Jew-lover. But you haven't been properly trained, so perhaps you should be excused for your breach of the rules of the Order about appropriate preaching. I will take you back to Bologna and make sure that there you have the correct instruction in all these things. And you too," he says, turning to Angelo. "It's ridiculous and inappropriate for a Dominican brother to serve on a political council. We take vows to renounce the world. Remaining involved in politics is inexcusable. His Holiness won't have it. You can both come to Bologna and serve a proper novitiate, none of this slack nonsense."

"The brothers have—" Tomasso begins to protest, but Vincenzo cuts him off and turns on him with a sharp gesture and a swirl of his sleeve.

"They may be excused for ignorance, but what were you thinking, Brother Tomasso? Or were you thinking at all? I suppose I can't blame you either. You are clearly senile. I'll relieve you of your office and let you live your declining years in peace, and we'll hold a new election while I'm here and have a more appropriate First Brother in place."

"Thanks be to God," Tomasso says, the only possible response. He puts his hands to his face to hide his tears, which only makes him look more senile.

Vincenzo turns to Isabella. "You're Brother Giovanni's whore, I take it. I had heard that you were hanging about the monastery. Get out. I'll see he does penance for this."

"I am no one's whore," Isabella says, standing up and meeting Vincenzo's eyes. "Nor am I under your discipline, as these men are, that they have to stand here and take your insults whatever the justice of the matter may be." She turns on her heel, then looks back at where Girolamo is sitting frozen in place. "Are you coming, Girolamo?"

"Yes, go. What are you doing here in the first place, *Girolamo*?" Vincenzo asks. He makes Girolamo's unadorned name sound like an insult. "I thought we'd got rid of you. You failed at Bologna, then you failed here, and you too had a cardinal to dispense you of your vows!

Not even our own Dominican cardinal but a Medici cardinal. Is this a Medici conspiracy?"

"It's no conspiracy at all," he says. He had not remembered that he was no longer under Vincenzo's power until Isabella reminded him. He leans back in his chair and looks up as calmly as he can. Torture broke him, and Hell broke him, and those things taught him there was no need to be afraid of this man any longer. "You're attacking us very cleverly, with injustice in the guise of mercy, but we have done nothing wrong. But maybe you are wrong to remind us that we do have a cardinal in our pocket and the power of the Medici on our side."

"A cardinal is a prince of the Church, true, but His Holiness sits on the throne of Peter and sent me here," Vincenzo says, stroking his wispy beard.

"Popes come and go, the Medici have been in power in Florence for more than seventy years," Angelo says.

"God sits above even popes," Girolamo says, but he knows almost immediately that this is a mistake.

"Who are you to speak for God?" Vincenzo rails. "You failed friar, with your intimate name in a whore's mouth. Who do you think you are, all of you? As she says, you have all taken vows of obedience. You have all broken them, Girolamo with a cardinal's permission, Brother Tomasso out of senility, and you two out of sheer arrogance I suppose. You thought your worldly positions were so important you could keep them even after you went into the cloister."

"That's true to a certain extent," Tomasso quavers. His wrinkled face is tear-stained, but he is sitting up straight. "I gave Brother Angelo permission to keep serving on the Council of Seven because that did seem to me to be important. And he has also kept writing poetry, I don't know if you know about that, but you should read his *On the Road to Damascus*. I may be old, and you may be right that the responsibility of running San Marco may be too much for me, but I'm not senile yet. I may have allowed Brother Giovanni and Brother Angelo too much freedom, but if so that's my fault, and I'll do penance for it if you think so after looking into it. What you don't know is that

Brother Giovanni knows the future. God has shown it to him. He knows what's going to happen."

"Senile old fool. Why didn't he predict that I was coming, then?" Vincenzo asks.

Because you never came before, Girolamo thinks. Because all the other times, he had managed to separate the Tuscan congregation from the Lombard before things came to this pass, so this was an attack they weren't prepared for. After forbidding him to preach, the Pope was supposed to offer to make Pico a cardinal, not send Vincenzo to chastize him.

"I'll soon beat that out of him in Bologna," Vincenzo goes on.

"Why do you want to stop Brother Giovanni preaching, except that what he's saying is truth from God and you don't want people to know it?" Isabella asks. She is still standing in the doorway, in her mended grey gown with her hair neatly covered.

"Because he is spreading lies from the devil and I don't want them to hear that," Vincenzo spits.

"He saved Florence from the French," Tomasso says.

"You're very active in his defence, but I notice he isn't saying a word for himself."

Girolamo too has noticed that Pico hasn't said a word for some time. From the doorway, Isabella is signalling to him that they should leave, but he doesn't want to miss what happens.

"Are you giving me permission to speak?" Pico asks. "You told me to be silent."

"What do you have to say for yourself?"

Pico gets to his feet. He is notably taller than Brother Vincenzo. "Have you read my books, or my published sermons? I'd be happy to give you copies. You can read, I suppose? You don't want to hear about God, so I suppose you don't want to hear about how we've been feeding and clothing the poor, educating their sons, and dowering their daughters. Doubtless you don't care about healing the sick, or visiting prisoners, or casting out demons, or doing any of the other work Christ called us to?"

Vincenzo makes a chopping gesture, and Pico falls silent again, but remains where he is.

Angelo moves forward suddenly. He has been standing against the wall where he was pushed when Vincenzo came in, but now he steps between Vincenzo and Pico, deliberately drawing his attention, though he is so much smaller. "What do you really want?" he asks. "Maybe we can compromise."

"What do you mean?" Vincenzo asks, belligerently, beard wagging.

"You don't really care what we do in Florence, and you don't really want to take me and Giovanni back to Bologna to disturb things for you there. You can talk about beating us into submission, but that's just to frighten us. We're assets to the Dominicani, both of us, we're show dogs with names all Europe knows. You don't really want to have us in your kennel disrupting the others. You certainly don't want us complaining that you've abused us, not just to our friend Cardinal Medici but to all the scholars of Europe. You won't get many novices then, nor scholars, and you want scholars."

To Girolamo's surprise, Vincenzo looks taken aback. "I want the Pope to stop harassing me about you," he says.

"We can give you that," Angelo says. "Brother Giovanni will soften things and slow down."

"That won't be enough. Florence will have to change its policy and ally with Spain."

"Oh, but how could we affect something like that? We're just friars. The Pope might blame us, but Florence's foreign policy isn't under our control. Would you like an introduction to Cardinal de' Medici? Would you like to visit the Medici Palace while you're staying at Santa Maria Novella. And perhaps a donation?"

"You can't buy me," Vincenzo says, uncertainly.

"Then tell me what you do want," Angelo says, his tone very reasonable. "This is Florence. We can do a deal."

"I'm not doing a deal with you. You're under my authority."

"Technically, yes. But Cardinal de' Medici will absolve me of my oath as easily as he did Girolamo, if necessary. I don't want it to be necessary. I like being a Dominican. I don't want to harm the order by sending the news that I left it and why racing across Christendom. You don't want that either."

"Get behind me, Satan!" Vincenzo bellows. "I am taking you both to Bologna! It'll take that to satisfy His Holiness that I've done my duty."

"For how long?" Pico asks. Angelo steps aside smoothly.

"Three years," Vincenzo snaps. "And then a year of mendicant preaching, and then another year at Bologna. Then we'll decide where you belong."

"Impossible," Pico says. "We'll come to Bologna in obedience, and to appease Pope Alexander, but we can't stay that long. I propose a month, and then we return to San Marco."

"Nonsense," Vincenzo says. "Two years, and a year of mendicant preaching."

"A month, then a month of preaching," Pico suggests. "As Brother Angelo said, you can't really want us in your well-ordered kennel, but here we are an asset to the Order."

"Six months, and six months preaching," Vincenzo says.

"Done," Pico says. "And we won't need to bother Cardinal de' Medici beyond letting him know what we're doing, because he does take an interest in us, especially Angelo."

"I'm sure he does," Vincenzo spits. Then he turns to Girolamo. "You can get out of here, and don't ever let me see you here again."

Girolamo gets up and moves to Isabella's side. She looks at him warily. There is no possible salutation they can give that won't make things worse. He just has to trust Angelo and Pico.

"We'll see you tomorrow in your rooms, before we go," Angelo says.

Girolamo can't believe they're really going to Bologna. He stumbles along beside Isabella, passing the little refectory and out into the courtyard, then out of the monastery, in silence, and possibly for the last time. Clouds have covered the sun, and the afternoon is fading into evening.

"Fancy Giovanni haggling like an old fishwife," Isabella says. "Three years. A month! Two years."

"A year won't hurt them," Girolamo says, though he can't imagine how he'll manage without them. "I must tell Marsilio."

"I'll never be a Dominican now," Isabella says, sadly.

"Because you don't want to be under First Brother Vincenzo's authority?"

"Because Tomasso knows about me and Giovanni now, so he'll never let me," she says, and sighs. "God must not want it after all."

"It's not as easy as I used to think to know what God wants," Girolamo says.

CHAPTER 25

Those who trespass against us.

Piero's return reminds him of Gozzoli's painting of the journey of the Magi in the Medici chapel. It isn't one man coming home, it is an entire procession, with laden horses, exotic animals, and a whole train of fancifully dressed retainers. There is a cheetah on a lead, hooded falcons on saddle perches, three huge brown deer with broad antlers, a pair of tiny elegant deer with straight horns, an enormous cow with huge curved horns as big as an elephant's tusks, and right beside it, an elephant. It is no private return, either, but a civic event, the return of the heir. Piero rides a black horse with gold-trimmed saddle, and wears a half cloak made of white fur tossed over his shoulder and held with a great gold clasp shaped like a pair of hands. His boots are high and polished, and he wears padded German-style knee breeches.

"He looks like a lord," Isabella murmurs. She is right. He is making no gesture in the direction of the traditional red guildsman's coat of the Florentine political classes. The crowds don't seem to mind. They are cheering, clearly delighted to see him and thrilled by the animals. He has timed his return for after Easter, and brought baskets of little almond cookies which his retainers toss into the crowds. "Balls, Balls!" they shout, and Piero inclines his head to them graciously. He has the famous Medici balls painted on his shield, and on the livery of his men.

Girolamo, standing with Isabella in the crowd outside the Senatorial Palace, almost wishes he had a fur cloak to wrap himself in. The spring wind is cold, and his scholar's cloak, which wasn't new when he bought it, is wearing very thin.

Piero's wife, Alfonsina Orsini, who has loyally accompanied him in all his travel, rides behind in a jewelled palanquin on top of the elephant. Their son and daughter, aged four and three, sit beside her. Three-year-old Lorenzo is dressed in cloth of gold, with the emblem of the sun on his hat, and his younger sister, Clarice, is dressed in silver with the moon on hers. She sits with her chubby legs sticking straight out in front of her, under her silvery skirts, with her little silver shoes visible.

The crowd is enraptured. Girolamo looks away, to where Marsilio is standing with Leo and the rest of the Medici family and a crowd of others in front of the Senatorial Palace. Girolamo sees Marsilio more often since Pico and Angelo left for Bologna. The older man makes time for him every few days now. Girolamo can't help loving Marsilio, no one could, but he misses the others. They have written to say they are leaving Bologna after Easter to move separately through hill towns, to end up in Florence in the autumn. It seems years, not five months, since they left. He is still walking the walls daily with Isabella in the early mornings, though now she is as good as he is at casting out demons. He takes her with him to Santa Caterina, where he goes twice a week, at Pico's suggestion, to help the women there recognise true prophecies. Isabella still hopes to be received there. He also escorts her to festivals and events like this, as if she were truly his cousin.

First Brother Tomasso died during Lent, at exactly the same time he died in all Girolamo's memories, but the Chapter of San Marco are sure it was of a broken heart. To spite Vincenzo, they have elected

Pico First Brother in his absence, and Silvestro, who is acting for him, has petitioned Bologna and Pope Alexander for his early return. Silvestro and Domenico are preaching the need for purity and reform of abuses. Florence has not changed her policy of alliance with France, but Pope Alexander has made no more moves against them. Girolamo wonders about that. This Florence never became as pure as that of his memories. Pico helped the poor, certainly, but things went on much as they had been under Lorenzo. Florence had taken steps towards being the City of God, but it was not the open affront to the corruption of Rome that it had been in other iterations. He hopes that will be enough. He hopes Piero won't want to change all the good work they have done. He wishes he could pray. He wonders what prayers others in the crowd are sending up for Piero's return.

Flag tossers went ahead to welcome the parade through the streets, and now they are escorting it back, tossing the flags and catching them with great enthusiasm. The crowd surges forward, pushing Isabella against Girolamo. He steadies her, and is uncomfortably aware for a moment of her breasts pressing against his arm. He moves away as much as he can. Sometimes Isabella appears in his dreams in disturbingly sensual guise. He despises his disloyal flesh.

Piero dismounts grandly in front of the Senatorial Palace. One of his men holds his magnificent horse. "Do you think he looks wiser?" Isabella whispers.

Girolamo has to admit that he doesn't. "You can't see wisdom at a distance," he says. A horseman in Piero's livery with a huge falcon has stopped close to them. He looks at the great scaled feet of the bird, firm on their perch, and the huge pinions. Can you use a bird that size for hawking? It could carry off a lamb. "Ask me again when we've had the chance to talk to him."

Leo spreads his ample arms and embraces his brother to his red-draped bosom. Alfonsina and the children are helped down from the elephant, and Piero presents it to Leo. He accepts, laughing, says he is delighted, and beams all over his face. The handlers lead away the leopard, the falcons, the strange cow, and the deer, taking them inside the palace. The city's lions that are quartered downstairs in the Senatorial Palace roar a welcome.

Giuliano and Giulio, Piero's brother and cousin, rush forward now to greet Piero. They are both at the awkward gangly age between boyhood and manhood. Then Lucrezia (pregnant again, and waddling) takes her turn, followed by her husband, Jacopo Salviati, and her boys, then Piero's other sisters with their husbands and children. Alfonsina and the children are lost in the throng by the time Gianni and Caterina come forward, with Gianni's brother Lorenzo and his wife. Piero's uncle Rinaldo Orsini, Archbishop of Florence, goes next. Then follows Brother Mariano, representing Santa Croce, and Brother Silvestro for San Marco, followed by representatives of all the other major monasteries. Then come the Guild leaders, the current Eight First Men, and the Standard-Bearer of Justice. At last Marsilio goes forward. Piero embraces him mechanically. They exchange a few words, then Marsilio retreats, looking thoughtful. He always looks thoughtful, Girolamo can't learn anything from that.

Free wine is being given out in the Loggia. The crowd cheers and pushes forward towards it. "We should go," Girolamo says to Isabella.

She nods. "I don't want to be here if it gets rowdy. And we've seen everything there was to see."

Marsilio has come down from the dais and joins them.

"What did he ask you?" Girolamo can't contain his curiosity.

"Where Angelo was." Marsilio shakes his head gently. "When I told him, he said, 'Good.'"

"That doesn't sound like wisdom," Isabella says.

"He may have spent too much time with lords and kings," Marsilio says. "Perhaps I should have gone with him."

"No you shouldn't, we needed you here. What's he doing now?" Girolamo asks.

"He's arranging for the beasts to be displayed in rooms on the ground floor of the palace, so everyone can see them before he moves them out to Carregi," Marsilio says.

"I expect that will be very popular," Isabella says.

Most of the crowd are gathered around the wine barrels. Shouts of "Balls" are thick in the air. The dignitaries and family are still gathered around Piero on the dais, and starting to move inside, where a feast is waiting. Brother Silvestro notices the three of them and comes over to them and greets them briskly. He is frowning, he doesn't approve of this superficial indulgence any more than Girolamo does. "Animals and frivolity and nonsense," he mutters. "The sooner Brother Giovanni comes back and reminds people what's important the better."

"Yes indeed," Girolamo says. Near him in the square is the spot where, in his memory, the Bonfire of the Vanities had burned.

"We will all welcome his return," Marsilio says.

Silvestro looks at Isabella. "Come and see me."

She brightens. "I will."

"Sister Camilla has been saying good things about you." He looks at Girolamo. "Do you still support her vocation?"

"I always have," Girolamo says, smiling.

Silvestro stumps off. Girolamo looks after him. "That's good," Marsilio says.

Michelangelo Buonarroti comes over, a cup of wine in his hand. He is growing a beard. "I have it!" he says, delightedly.

"What?" Girolamo asks, but Marsilio knows.

"That huge block of marble that's been standing about for so long?"

"Yes. I am going to carve the prophet Amos, to go high up on the cathedral. I thought I'd do him with the face of Brother Giovanni. What do you think?"

Isabella and Girolamo exchange a glance. Marsilio nods gravely. "I think that would be splendid," he says.

Michelangelo looks at the others. "And his body too," he says, with a hint of defiance in his tone.

"Well well," Marsilio says. "I'm cold. Let's all go to my rooms and have some warm wine."

"Shouldn't you be at the banquet?" Isabella asks.

"No one will miss me, and I'd rather be with friends," Marsilio says.

"I've had my wine, now I want to get on with my work," Michelangelo says with a wave as he heads for his workshop down by the river.

The crowd thins out as the three of them walk towards the Medici palace. They walk around the cathedral—both Marsilio and Isabella have become accustomed to Girolamo's refusal to go through the building as a short cut, the way everyone else does. They talk of Piero's return, and what it might mean.

"I was wondering what people in the crowd were praying for," Girolamo says.

"But not praying yourself?" Isabella asks.

"I can't pray," he says.

She looks horrified. "Why not?"

"I can't explain."

"But is it because—"

"He really can't explain," Marsilio says, in a tone meant to discourage enquiry.

"I'll pray for you," she says.

"Thank you," he says, sincerely.

"No, not in the usual way. If you can't pray, I mean you can tell me what you want to say to God and I'll say it for you. I'll pass it on."

Marsilio stops walking. "What a fascinating idea. I could do that too, Girolamo."

"But—" He doesn't know what to say.

"It would be like intercession of the saints," Isabella says.

"Yes, it would, wouldn't it," Marsilio says, beaming at her. "Girolamo, you should write down what you want to say, and we'll pass it on for you."

"But—" The theology is all unknown. "I want to talk to Pico about this."

"He'll be back soon," Marsilio says. "And meanwhile, let's try it."

"And then God will help you! And I'll be accepted into Santa

Caterina!" Isabella skips like a girl. Girolamo isn't looking. He's trying to think what he wants them to say.

Later, back home on his own, as the Pardos sing quietly in Hebrew in the next room, he tries to write down prayers. For Isabella, he writes down the lesser doxology, "Glory be to the Father, and to the Son, and to the Holy Spirit, as it was in the beginning, is now, and ever shall be, world without end." At first, writing it is comfortable and familiar, but as he writes on he remembers the false San Marco he raised in Hell, the absence of Christ from the walls, and the time he preached salvation that could never be for them. Marsilio tells him that God loves him, but he knows that in Hell he has raged against God, reviled him, hated him for condemning them to this. He can write the words "Glory be to God," but the devil can quote scripture. "Gloria," he whispers aloud, in Latin, into a hollow emptiness, a palpable absence.

His pen has torn through the paper, but he gives it to Isabella anyway. To Marsilio he says that he couldn't do it. "Maybe later," Marsilio says. "Keep trying."

CHAPTER 26

Lead us not into temptation.

It is spring again. Rain runs down the big windows of the long room in Camilla Rucellai's Santa Caterina. Sister Camilla and Sister Bartollomea and the new novice, Sister Isabella, have their notebooks neatly in front of them when Sister Elena shows in Girolamo. He takes his seat on the other side of the table. Sister Vaggia is in the Annalena. She needed to be moved from Santa Lucia but she doesn't really have the vision to be here.

"Is it my turn to start?" Bartollomea asks. "Friday, visions of blood and destruction. No dreams. Saturday, a temptation. Sunday, nothing. Monday, nothing. Tuesday a strange foreboding all afternoon that went off at sunset. Wednesday, a dream of flying like a bird over the city."

"Good," says Camilla. "Friday, when praying, the vision of a rose I often have. Saturday, a confusing dream of three friars being burned in the Senatorial Square."

Isabella raises her hand. "Sunday," she says.

"Who were they?" Girolamo asks.

"You and Giovanni and Angelo," Isabella says.

"You and Brother Silvestro and Brother Giovanni," Camilla says at the same moment.

Girolamo shakes his head. "I wish I understood how this works."

"They can't both be true," Camilla says.

"Not in this world," he says.

"Monday, the rose again. Tuesday, nothing. Wednesday a dream of a boar trampling orchids."

"That must be symbolic," Bartollomea says.

They all nod. Isabella hesitates, her hand on her book. "Apart from the dream on Sunday I already told you, I don't have anything except confusing dreams. Nothing clear enough to write down. I went out with Elena and Luisa and did the circuit of the walls every morning except Sunday, and banished two demons every day except Wednesday when I banished four."

"Girolamo?" Camilla asks.

He gives them his demon count.

"Any prophecies?"

"Nothing new," he says, as he always does.

"Girolamo, God tells me you are troubled, and I wish you'd talk to us and let us help," Camilla says. Isabella nods emphatically, and Bartollomea tentatively.

"I wish I could," he says, sincerely. The others, even Marsilio, think it's too dangerous to share with women.

They talk about fasting and how it can help visions, and Camilla talks about the visions of the rose the Virgin sends her when she is saying the rosary. "I can even smell it," she says. "I think we should all try to do this. It's a great gift, it gives me strength to go on when things are hard."

Girolamo leaves them before evening prayer. Pico and Angelo have been home in Florence for six months. Crookback has come to the city to renegotiate his contract.

"We ought to meet with Crookback and test the stone," Angelo says, when he and Girolamo are doing the evening circuit of the walls. Angelo needs holy water to banish demons, he carries a flask of it with him. It is a beautiful evening. Crocuses and anemones are pushing through the new grass under the city walls, and on the trees the leaves are a fresh spring green. There has been no sign of demons yet today, and the circuit is almost complete.

"Shall I invite him to my rooms?" Girolamo asks.

"Why would he accept an invitation to your rooms?" Angelo is dismissive. "He's a duke. It should be Marsilio's rooms in the Medici Palace, and we should all be there. He'll respect Pico's rank at least— his old one and his new one."

"All right," Girolamo says. "How are things with Piero?"

Angelo sighs. "He resents me more than ever. I'm trying to keep out of his way and let Capponi manage him. Capponi's loyal and capable and sensible."

Girolamo nods. "Don't eat with Piero, just in case."

Angelo looks sad. "I don't want to believe that he really did that. But I won't risk it."

"I can still smell that vomit, so I know he did! I want you to live for many more years and write lots more poetry," Girolamo says.

"It's hard to write poetry when I'm mortifying myself, and I need to do it constantly because otherwise lust overcomes me," Angelo says, kicking at a stone.

It adds a new dimension to the secrets of the confessional when the confession was made in another history, Girolamo thinks. This is not the Angelo who confessed to him, and yet he cannot cease to know what it was that he confessed. He does not want to know who Angelo lusts for now, but he knows without asking it would be a grown man and not a woman or a boy.

"Lust is one of the most difficult things," he says. "For all of us." He still has disturbing dreams about Isabella.

"Worse for Pico than any of us. He never tried continence until he took vows. I think it must be why he hesitated the other times," Angelo says. "I suppose he doesn't have time for it now, with the Office and preaching and running San Marco."

"He's been excommunicated again," Girolamo says. Brother Mariano read out the letter from Pope Alexander in the square by Santa Croce. Pico hasn't taken any notice, he hasn't even stopped preaching in the cathedral.

"Ahead of schedule," Angelo agrees. "I don't understand why the Pope can't just leave us alone, we're not bothering him."

"It's the reproach of Florence's purity showing up the corruption in Rome. The Pope is selling offices, marrying his children to royalty, having orgies in the Vatican—while Florence is following the word of God."

"Also I suppose that he wants us to change our alliance from France to Spain and the Empire," Angelo says. "Piero's wavering on that. Maybe if he does change, the Pope will be satisfied in his worldly ambition and leave us alone to work on the spiritual side. No demons at all tonight, we must be getting somewhere."

"Or the nuns of Santa Caterina are getting them all in the mornings. I've never met Pope Alexander," Girolamo says. "Not in any world. So I don't know whether he might be a demon himself, and whether he might not be venal but actively working for evil. Or maybe his son. They say very bad things about Cesare Borgia."

Angelo sighs. "That's a worrying thought. But for now, Leo has set off for Rome to put things right with the Pope again, which doesn't make things any easier with Piero. As for possible demons, I'll invite Crookback and let you know when we're going to meet him."

"Are we going to tell him, or just hand him the stone?" Girolamo asks, turning the stone in his hand, trying to picture himself giving it to Crookback.

"Would preparation be better?" Angelo asks.

"It's very hard to know," Girolamo says. "If God sent the stone, he sent it to me, not to him. Maybe he isn't ready for it. Maybe it would be dangerous. If God didn't send it, if it is demonic, then even more so."

"Let's see how it goes," Angelo says. "Maybe not talking about it, just passing it around might be better. Or if you think it's dangerous, just don't get it out."

He nods, reluctantly.

Marsilio's room in the Medici Palace is tidier than Angelo's was. The bed has blue and violet hangings, and the tapestries too are in shades of blue, showing scenes of young men in classical dress against backgrounds of pillars and porticos. There are two portraits, on either side of the door, of Plato and Lorenzo. There are books and letters, but they are orderly and well kept. The writing slope where Marsilio works stands closed beside an orderly inkpot. The west-facing windows are closed for warmth but the shutters are open for whatever light the early evening affords. The setting sun is helped out by a fire, burning cheerfully in the fireplace, and a lamp, set on the table beside a tray with jugs of wine and water and a plate of apples. The effect of the room is comfortable and calm, an effect that is dissipated at once when Angelo leads Crookback into it.

Crookback never merely walks, he stalks or swaggers or sidles. He follows Angelo in strutting, head cocked and hand on the dagger at his hip, as if half expecting a trap. He smiles sardonically at the three men sitting there, all on one side of the table as if that were any kind of protection. Angelo introduces them, and he bows like a noble, which Girolamo supposes he is. He is wearing buckled leather armour now, not his tournament finery, and he smells of sweat and horses and of the camp. He has fine lines on his face and an old scar on one cheek. Girolamo is more and more sure the man is, like him, no man at all, and less and less confident that getting him to touch the stone is a good idea. He has asked the others to pray about it, and they have assured him that they have, without response. Marsilio keeps telling him that he should pray, or have him pray for him, but he knows he can not, that prayer for him would be howling into a wilderness where God would not hear him, howling into Hell. He longs to, but he knows he can no more pray than he could fly.

"Welcome to my rooms, Your Grace of Glusta," Marsilio says, bowing like a scholar. Pico and Girolamo also rise and bow, then settle back into their chairs.

The mercenary captain takes a chair without being asked and draws it up to the other side of the table and sits with his back to the door. Angelo sits beside him, grimacing at the others. "We say 'Glo-sta.' But Gloucester is a long way away, and Crookback will do, among friends, and I am among friends, am I not?" He smiles around at them, charmingly, disconcertingly. Girolamo looks away.

Pico smiles back. "Of course you are. England's loss is Italy's gain."

Crookback looks assessingly at him. "I left England years ago when the wars were done and my brother was safe on his throne. I am not made for peace, but war, and Italy has served my purpose very well."

"Wine?" Angelo asks, his voice seeming softer and more quiet than usual.

"Wine, no water," Crookback replies. Angelo pours for all of them, neat for the mercenary, and mixing in water for the others. Crookback knocks back the wine in one draft and settles his glass back on the table. Then he looks at them each in turn, and laughs again. "Well, I've drunk with you. Now you can tell me what this conspiracy is about."

"It's not a conspiracy!" Angelo objects at once.

"I'm not blind, man," Crookback interrupts. "I'm just trying to save time and tiptoeing around things. What else could it be? Two schol-ars and two monks, meeting in secret with a mercenary captain? You were on the Council of Seven, until Piero de' Medici came back to take up his inheritance and threw you out of favour? Of course it's a conspiracy, but you needn't fear I'll betray you, not if you pay me well enough. I'm an honest man. I stay bought. And it was the Council who hired me, not the Medici. I don't care who rules Florence, or any Ital-ian city, as long as they make a decent fist of it. It's been profitable but dull enough defending Florence these last years with nothing to do but growl at the French as they pass by. The White Boars will be glad of a proper bit of fighting. It's what we like! And the cardinal humiliated me at the tournament in front of my wife, and I don't care for that. So I'm ready to listen, and you needn't worry I'll take what you say to my employers."

"You have mistaken us, sir," Marsilio says, authoritatively.

At that Crookback sits back, frowning. His deformity is very visible as the leather of his jerkin strains against his shoulders. "Then what do you want with me? What Brother Angelo told me wouldn't deceive a child."

Marsilio looks to Girolamo. They have not discussed what to do if Girolamo thinks it unwise to offer the stone and yet Crookback has seen through the surface of their intentions. He looks at Pico, who nods encouragingly. There seems nothing Girolamo can do now but draw the stone out from the pouch around his neck and hand it reluctantly to Marsilio. He feels the stone doesn't want to leave his hands. He almost grabs it back, but restrains himself. Marsilio turns the stone in his hands. "Do you know what this is?" he asks.

Crookback shakes his head, but he can't take his eyes off it. Marsilio picks up an apple in his other hand and brings it to his nose. He closes his eyes. He reaches out towards Crookback with his right hand, the hand with the stone. Crookback reaches towards him. Just as Crookback touches the stone, Marsilio begins to glow. Crookback screams shrilly, and falls back in his chair. Marsilio opens his eyes, still glowing.

For a moment, Girolamo thinks Crookback is dead, that the stone has killed him. He is lying back in his chair with his eyes open and glazed, staring at nothing. He does not seem to be breathing. Girolamo sits frozen in shock for a moment. Pico reaches out across the table to take back the stone from Crookback's hand. As he touches it, Crookback comes back to life, and more than life, to furious whirling motion. He kicks over the table with a great crash—lamp, bowl, jugs and glasses fall and shatter, apples scatter and roll about the floorboards. Girolamo and Marsilio are knocked backwards, and Pico, who was leaning, falls forwards. Girolamo's chair topples, and he crashes to the floor. He gets up again as quickly as he can. Crookback is on his feet, standing warily, his dagger in his left hand poised to thrust, and his right clutched around the stone. Angelo is lying on the floor, underneath a broken chair, groaning loudly.

"Stop. We are your friends," Pico says, with commendable calm, though his voice is pitched higher than normal. He is lying on his belly on the floor, near Crookback's feet.

"How—" Crookback's voice catches in his throat. "How dare you!" His eyes meet Girolamo's. "How dare *you*?"

"I thought you might rather know," Girolamo says, apologetically. He and Crookback are the only ones standing. Their eyes lock, and he sees anger and fear in the eyes of the other.

"So I might join you in your milk-and-water ways, pretending to be good and holy when you're hanging over the abyss and you know what's waiting?" Crookback laughs derisively, and takes a step away, backing towards the door. "Meddling with little things to help your friends, when you know what's coming in twenty years' time? Oh yes, I'd rather know. I should thank you for that. But I don't think I will."

"Give me back the stone," Girolamo says.

"You don't even know what it is, do you?" Crookback asks.

"It's the stone of Titurel, the Holy Grail," Pico says, gently, from the floor. "Give it to Girolamo. We mean you no harm."

"You can't do me any harm, you mean," Crookback says, still backing towards the door. "This is what Christ gave Peter. It's the key to Heaven. I'm not giving it back to a bunch of soft fools like you. What were you planning to do with it anyway?"

"Harrow Hell and free the trapped souls," Girolamo says. It sounds like a ridiculous plan as he says it.

"What, free all the demons to ravage Earth? Not such a bad plan as I thought," he sneers. "But I think it might be better used to renew our old plan of storming Heaven. This is my one and only chance. You'll never let me have it again. Are you with me Asbiel? You were once. Remember how we wanted to reshape the universe and remake the world without pain?"

Girolamo stares at him, stunned by hearing his old name. He does almost remember, now, the desire if not the details. Raphael's appalled face, Gabriel weeping. Michael wide-eyed with shock, with his hand on his sword.

"It was a noble resolution, brother," Crookback goes on. "And don't pretend it wouldn't have been a better world."

"We didn't know," Girolamo says, forcing the words out. They had wanted a world without pain, when pain was just an intellectual concept. "We didn't know enough. We were proud."

"And why shouldn't we have been proud?"

"You have free will," Marsilio interrupts, conversationally. He has not risen from the floor. The fallen table is between him and Girolamo, so he can't see Marsilio to know who he's addressing.

"Free will," Pico repeats. He has pulled himself into a sitting position. "Which angels and demons lack."

"Free will so you can choose, and you're not bound to repeat the same plan which worked so badly last time," Marsilio goes on, getting up, leaning on the fallen table. He is still glowing blue. "Free will so that you can repent your pride even now and choose God's mercy."

"We're demons. God's mercy isn't an option for us," Crookback snarls, and Girolamo knows he is right.

"Indeed, when you're in Hell, but here you may have it," Marsilio says, walking towards Crookback, unarmed, confident, and glowing, his hand outstretched.

"What are you?" Crookback asks, looking at him.

"You know my name. I'm a teacher and a translator," Marsilio says. "Give me the stone. There is hope. God loves even you, Richard of Glosta."

"Stop there," Crookback says, slashing wildly with his dagger.

Girolamo believes that he means it as a warning, but Marsilio does not stop. He reaches for the stone, even as Crookback's dagger strikes him. There is a wash of blood, too much blood, and Girolamo runs forward, around the table, shouting, as Pico tries to reach for Crookback's legs, to pull him off balance. Marsilio stops glowing and starts to fall. At that moment the door opens, one of the Medici guards has been alerted by the noise and come to investigate. Crookback spins on his feet and leaps, pushing the guard back, so that he staggers and stumbles backwards. Then Crookback runs out past him and takes off down the stairs, with Girolamo pursuing. "Stop him!" he yells, but Crookback is yelling too, in a voice much more used to giving orders to armed men. Nevertheless, the guards at the gate are alerted and draw their swords. Crookback cannot disguise his drawn dagger, dripping blood. "Boars! To me! Treachery!" Crookback bellows. Four mercenaries in White Boar livery come running out of a side room, swords in their hands. The Medici guards hesitate.

"He's gone mad and killed Marsilio Ficino!" It's what Girolamo was about to say, but Crookback gets the accusation out first. Girolamo is still running, but so is Crookback. The Boars open their ranks to let Crookback pass, but Girolamo finds himself facing steel on both sides, as the Medici guards too threaten him. Everyone loves Marsilio, there is no sympathy in their faces. He hesitates. Crookback has the stone, but flinging himself on the blades would be immediate suicide.

"A horse!" Crookback bellows.

"It's Crookback who has killed Marsilio," he pants. It's clear that none of them find him convincing. "Look, he has the dagger. He did it."

"Savonarola has always been mad, and now he has become quite unhinged. He killed Ficino and attacked me. Let me get away from him!" Crookback says, and despite his dripping dagger the Medici guards step aside. Crookback and his men back out of the gate. Someone has brought a horse up in the street outside, and one of his men boosts Crookback up onto the saddle.

"No! Stop him!" he shouts, and behind him he hears Pico echo his command. The gate guards belatedly step forward, and Girolamo follows them out onto the street. It is dusk and Crookback and his horse together cast a demonic shadow.

Behind them, he hears Piero de' Medici asking what the disturbance is.

"To camp!" Crookback orders, and gallops off through the streets, disregarding pedestrians who leap out of his way to avoid being ridden down. His men scurry after him. "Boars, to camp!"

"Well, that went badly," Pico says, staring after them.

CHAPTER 27

But deliver us from evil.

"No," Piero says. "Absolutely not. Florence is not going to war with its own mercenary captain."

The fire upstairs in Marsilio's room, started by the falling lamp, has been extinguished. Marsilio, looking tiny in death, has been carried to the nearby church of San Lorenzo, where the monks are praying over his body. Girolamo can't believe he's dead, even though he saw him fall. He died glowing and is assuredly with God, they do have that comfort.

Angelo has a cut on his forehead, and he says it hurts to breathe. Girolamo thinks he may have broken some ribs. He also keeps coughing, from breathing the smoke. The three of them are standing in front of Piero's desk in his little studio. No one else is present. He has not asked them to sit. Piero's desk is piled with precious objects from his travels, reliquaries, books, a crystal bowl of gems, his white fur cloak, a little statue of a naked goddess. It reminds Girolamo of the Bonfire of Vanities.

"He killed Marsilio," Pico repeats.

"I don't care," Piero says. "I mean, I care, we can't have Crookback behaving that way, killing my father's men and setting fire to the palace. But I'll reprimand Crookback and he'll apologize and that's the end of it. We need the White Boars if we're going to conquer Siena."

It is the first Girolamo has heard of a war with Siena. He looks at Pico, who looks dishevelled, his habit torn and dirty, his hair rumpled and with a huge sooty mark on his cheek.

"Hire another company of mercenaries, get rid of Crookback and then use them for Siena," Angelo says.

Piero shakes his head. "Are you a child? Imagine I offered a great deal of money to Cesare Borgia, or Francesco Gonzaga. They'd come here with their armies, yes, and fight the White Boars. At the end of that, what happens? Does whichever leader is left standing bow to me and take his troops off to fight in Siena? You're not that naïve. He'd be here, and Florence would be in his power. We could trust my wife's Orsini kindred, but they're in exile right now, fleeing from Borgia."

"All right," Pico says, speaking quietly and very precisely. He leans forward and plants both palms on the desk. "It's not all right, and you know it, but all right. Do it that way. Keep him. Forgive him for killing Marsilio. But he has stolen something from us, and we need to have it back. It's a little jade plate, quite valuable, that belongs to Girolamo. You have to make getting it back part of his apology."

Piero looks at Girolamo for the first time. Girolamo fights off the urge to smooth down his clothes. "You had a valuable jade plate?" he asks, in a disbelieving tone.

Girolamo pulls out the pouch where he carried the stone, which feels very empty without it. "I did."

"And this was doubtless part of some mystical nonsense?"

Pico and Girolamo both start to speak at once, and stop. "Crookback may be able to do inestimable damage with it," Girolamo says.

"Magical damage?" Piero asks.

Girolamo nods, though magical damage doesn't seem a strong enough term for renewing the war in heaven.

"You have to get it back, Piero," Angelo says.

"I've had enough of this," Piero says. "Enough of you. I won't take your orders. I don't have to do anything I don't want to. You are also my father's men, not mine."

"That's true, but we will be your men and serve you as we did Lorenzo," Angelo says.

Piero shakes his head. "I know the three of you persuaded him to send me away. I've had long enough to think about it. At first he convinced me it was for my own good and Florence's, but after a while I could see who benefitted, you three, and Capponi, and my cousin Gianni. I was young, he said. Well, I'm older. I was inexperienced. Well, I've spent time with Maximilian, time with Ferdinand, watching and learning how they rule. I'm not putting up with interference from you. You've had it your own way for five years, but you're not in charge now."

Angelo winces. "I know that, and I'm very glad you're ready to be master of the shop now—"

"Master of the shop," Piero says, dismissively. "My father used to say he was that, I know. But Maximilian offered to make me Duke of Florence. Or I can wait, and have the title when Leo is pope."

"Well, good," Angelo says. "I know you're in charge. But—"

"Or Pope Alexander might give it to me now, if I give him something in return," Piero goes on, ignoring him. "After all, how many times are we Medici supposed to save you from your heresy, Pico? I was afraid you were too popular and there would be a riot if we tried to arrest you, but this Crookback affair gives us a perfect excuse. Not very saintly, is it, fighting with a mercenary captain over a magic stone? And it will make Brother Mariano and the Franciscans pleased with me too if I get rid of you."

"You can arrest me, you can send me to the Pope, you can do whatever you want and I'll raise no trouble as long as you get the stone back from Crookback and give it to Girolamo," Pico says, passionately.

There is a silence. Piero looks at Pico's hands splayed out on his desk, and then up at Pico's face. He looks back at his hands. Pico picks them up, one at a time, and folds them. They have left sooty marks. "I can arrest Girolamo too," Piero says.

"Fine," Pico says, not even glancing at him. "Arrest all three of us, execute us, that's all very well as long as Girolamo has the stone. It's more important than any wordly considerations, more important than life or death."

"I see," Piero says. "What on earth is it?"

They do look at each other now. Angelo's face is grim and grey with pain. The others seem to want him to explain. "It's the Holy Grail," Girolamo says.

Piero laughs. "The Holy Grail! You are all quite mad. I'll do my best to get this thing from Crookback, but if he thinks it's the Holy Grail too, then he might not want to give it up. Meanwhile, I'm arresting you. Guard!"

Two of the Medici guards come in. "Take these men—no. Take him and him," he points at Angelo and Girolamo, "To the People's Palace, and you'd better take Brother Giovanni to the cell my great-grandfather was imprisoned in at the top of the Senatorial Palace, the little inn."

Pico starts to laugh. "Well, Fortune is a woman all right," he says.

Girolamo has never spent any time in the People's Palace before. In other times, they brought him here regularly to torture him, as they do Pico now, but then took him back up the many stairs in the Senatorial Palace to the little inn and his solitude. There is no solitude here. All the prisoners share one large room, partially below ground level, so they are surrounded by thieves, sodomites, blackmailers, and drunks. Everyone's friends and enemies call to them through the bars. He has more enemies than he could have imagined, largely because Piero has taken up Crookback's accusation and had him accused of killing Marsilio. Everyone loved Marsilio, and so everyone who believes he did it hates him. Angelo is accused of meddling in politics, which he can't really deny. Girolamo denies murdering Marsilio until they torture him, when he admits it and then denies it again as soon as they stop. Pico, on the other hand, admits nothing, no matter how many times they dislodge his arms from his shoulders and reinsert them. He steadfastly insists he was doing God's work. Girolamo would admit even that he is a demon, if it would get them to stop torturing him, but they don't ask, and so he is able to keep it to himself.

"May twenty-third," Angelo whispers to him late one night, when everyone else is asleep. The two of them are in a back corner, in complete darkness.

"That's right."

"You think it will be the same?"

"I don't see any reason why not."

"I don't see any reason why it is the same, when so many things are so different," Angelo says, emphatically.

"God must want it."

"Must want you to die then. I have lived longer than I normally do. Is there something different about the date of your death and mine?"

"Not that I know about."

There is a silence, and then he feels Angelo's arm around his shoulders. The two men have touched so much in the last few weeks in the cell, huddled together, hugged, trying to offer what comfort they can, that he thinks nothing of it.

"Next time, I'm going to abolish torture very early," he says quietly, as his shoulders send a twinge of agony through him. "If there is a next time. If Crookback doesn't use the stone to storm Heaven."

"If the four of us, with half a dozen other trusted friends of Marsilio's, the best minds in Europe, couldn't work out how to use it, how is he going to?"

"He might remember. He remembered the War in Heaven."

"He did. He called you brother."

"All angels are brothers," Girolamo says, in the darkness.

"But not demons?"

"I suppose so."

"It suggests that he isn't all evil."

"I'd rather cling to the thought that he won't know how to use it," Girolamo says.

"And we will have a lot more time to work on the problem," Angelo says. "Another whole iteration." He slides his arm lower, away from Girolamo's hurt shoulders and around his waist. "Have you ever copulated, Girolamo?"

Girolamo freezes, and knows Angelo can feel that.

"I'm—you know what I am!" he says.

"I know. I just thought—"

"You can't die with that on your conscience!"

"It's all right if you don't want to," Angelo says, and loosens his arm.

"It's not a case of whether I want to, it's a case of what's right." He isn't sure whether or not he wants to. He knows what men do together, he has to know to be able to understand confessions and set penances. It has always been women who have inspired his lust. But no one has ever invited him before, except the solicitations of prostitutes of both sexes, who have only ever inspired him with disgust and pity.

"We're already in prison and they're going to execute us whatever we do. And we don't have the stone, and you're already damned and you know it, and they let Silvestro and Domenico confess to you, so they'll let us confess to Pico, and I can confess fully."

"You won't be truly contrite if you're already planning to confess!" Girolamo says.

"Yes I will. I'm always contrite afterwards."

"It doesn't work that way! Go and find one of the sodomites, there are enough of them in this cell. I'm sure they won't mind being woken up."

But Angelo doesn't go, and he doesn't push him away, but they don't move any closer either, they just sit there, leaning on each other in the darkness until eventually the grey dawn lightens the window and day comes. Jailers bring hard bread, and later take them up to be tortured.

And on the last day the comforters come and take them to the Senatorial Palace, and it is all the same as his death in every iteration, except that Pico and Angelo hang beside him instead of Silvestro and Domenico. They are hung over the fire, and he falls, not forward on his face like good people, but on his back, like the damned.

PART FOUR

RETURNED

CHAPTER 28

He had imagined Hell would not be as bad this time, because he would not have the shock of finding out who he was. He was wrong. As he slams into it suddenly there is no hope, no change, no breath, no friendship, no God. He is tormented by everything he said, everything he tried to do, and the ultimate futility of it all that ends here. He remembers Angelo's arm in the darkness and Marsilio telling him God loves even him, and he writhes with the agony of memory. And he is weak now, without much of his pride, and therefore a prey to the strong, who are all around him with their mockery and scorn.

Even though he knows that it will avail nothing and achieve nothing except to make his own pain worse, he doggedly tries the things they have discussed. He can make the sign of the cross in the dust, but it is only an empty symbol. The spirit of Hell is that very meaninglessness of the cross here. He rubs it out, then draws it again, over and over. He is not crying. There can be no tears. No relief. That God sent his son to save the souls of mortals is a matter for anger and sorrow, because the demons are still here. There is no breath to draw.

He tries to remember the War in Heaven. His memories of Heaven itself are the same as they were on Earth, recollecting God's love only to know how much he has lost. As for the rebellion, he now remembers every painful action, every moment. There is no oblivion. If he were to strike his head on a stone and cut it in two, he would have dealt himself a great wound but he would still be conscious and remember his own pride, his own stupidity, his words and acts and everything that had led down the road to Hell. It was not in ignorance as Marsilio had too kindly suggested. There had been warnings. He had not known what he was doing or understood what the real consequences would be, but he had understood he was acting against God and still gone on. He will have to tell Marsilio, and then even he will despise him.

He travels as far as he can through Hell, searching for mortal souls, and finds nothing but demons. His interactions with them are very unpleasant. He can try to hide, or he can try to appear strong, but because his place has changed in their hierarchy of Hell he is a constant victim of their spite and mockery and attacks. He tries to bear it, but from time to time he grows angry and retaliates, and then hates himself more.

He both craves and fears another iteration. As time goes by, he yearns for one, and as more and more time goes by, although it is not truly time, but mere duration, he comes to know he has lost that chance, wasted it, and it can never come again. That is when he loses the hope he did not know he had, hope of another chance, another life, of the sweetness of Earth, if not the remoter chance of winning Heaven. Even without hope, in utmost despair, in the depths of Hell, marking a meaningless cross in the dust to see its meaninglessness, he no longer curses God. He knows that terrible as this is, it is what he deserves.

Then Crookback finds him. As a demon Crookback is majestic, a prince of Hell, huge, towering up, his great head balanced on a pair of hands the size of a cathedral dome. He walks sideways on his giant fingers. Girolamo stands before him, stripped now even of pride and wrath. Crookback casually tears him in half and eats the halves. He vomits up the remains, and then smears one of his pillar-sized fingers through the pile of vomit. "Next time, leave me alone," he says.

The smear in the itchy gritty mud of Hell re-forms into his demonic body, with its three poisoned breasts and flayed belly. The process of re-forming is even more painful than the excruciation of being torn apart and eaten. Every exposed nerve is agony. But these are the quotidian pains of Hell and he takes no notice. "What did you do with the stone?"

The monstrous form of Crookback glares down at him. "Do you think there's nothing worse I can do to you?"

This is Hell. All possible answers are wrong.

PART FIVE

LENT

CHAPTER 29

Thy kingdom come, thy will be done.

The library is dark, but he can see by the shapes of the windows that it would be well lit in daylight. It is not a proper scriptorium such as they have in San Marco, but it is a good room. It smells of leather and good wax candles. The demons completely fill all the space in the room, and the sound they make is deafening, louder than the streets of Florence at the end of Carnival. Whatever is drawing them, it is here. "Stay back," he says to the others. "And no more water unless I call for it." He takes a step inside. The demons withdraw reluctantly, making a clear space around him. He moves to where they are thickest, holding the lantern high in one hand and searching with the other hand outstretched until he touches it. He finds himself reluctant to grasp it, though it seems to be just an ordinary brown-covered book. He draws it forward, ignoring the howls of the demons. They cannot speak proper words unless they are encased in flesh, but they keep up their endless gibbering and laughter. He turns the book so he can read the title in the lamplight. Pliny. Strange. He was a secular author, a Roman, a no one. Not the kind of book you'd expect demons to be drawn to. He opens the cover, and sees that the pages have been hollowed out in the centre to make the book almost a box. In the gap is a flat green stone, about the length of his palm, and as thick as his thumb, with a shallow depression in the centre.

"Now I have you," he says, conversationally. He sets the lantern down on the writing table and moves the book to his right hand.

As soon as his fingers touch the stone, memory crashes over him like a wave. He screams and falls to the floor, curling up into a ball. First the terrible knowledge that he is a demon, not a man. Then the memories of all the other iterations where he has not known it until finding himself in Hell, and the last one where he had known it on Earth. The demons are howling and screaming all around him. He cries, choking on his sobs, weeping all the tears he cannot weep in Hell. Then Silvestro throws his holy water, soaking Girolamo, damaging the books, and making a clear path through the demon-filled room. The shock of it, of the event that has never happened before, brings him to himself, to this unique moment in the library. He sputters and sits up, clutching the stone tight.

He struggles to get himself under control. He wants to get to the others as soon as he can, but first he needs to get rid of the remaining demons. Weak as he is, he does not know whether he can impose his will on them. He pulls himself slowly to his feet, using the table leg for support. He wets his hands on his robe, and flicks the holy water at the remaining demons. "Begone in the name of Jesus Christ!" He keeps going until they have all fled or been banished back to Hell. The library is empty of them, but very damp. He hopes Matthias Corvinus's bequest to Santa Lucia can be salvaged.

"Are they gone?" Silvestro asks. "It feels as if they might be?"

"Yes, they're gone." He wipes his face on his wet sleeve and draws a long delicious breath of life-giving air. What a miracle breath is!

"What happened?" Silvestro comes into the library and helps him to his feet.

"Sometimes they are too strong, even for me," he says, taking up his lantern again. "That's why I need your help, brothers. And now I must go."

"Thank you, Brother Girolamo," the First Sister says. "Thank you for believing me, thank you for coming here."

"You know you can call on us in San Marco whenever you need assistance," he says. He puts the book into his sleeve. "I must go."

"Are you taking that book?" she asks, sharply.

"I need it," he says.

She frowns. "The king of Hungary sent those books here to us."

"It might draw more demons, and I might not be able to banish them again," he says.

"Oh! In that case take it and be welcome."

He takes a step towards the gate, his loyal brothers at his heels like a pair of mismatched hounds.

"Is it true that Magnificent Lorenzo is dying?" the First Sister asks.

"Yes," he says. "Pray for him. He is one of the best men of our age, and soon to be a saint at God's side."

Her eyes widen in surprise. "It's true then that you foretold it?"

"There is very little in the future we cannot change if we try," he says, and leaves. Domenico bids the nun a good night and God's blessing.

The bridge across the Arno is lined with shops, all closed up now for night. There is the butcher reputed to be a notorious haunt of sodomites, and the barber he used to visit in his last life, not because he gave the best haircut but because he read Cicero and St Jerome. A watchman raises his lantern to see who they are, then lets them go on undisturbed. Silvestro murmurs a blessing as they pass. There is a mist on the water, and a chill air rises with a whiff of the tanneries downstream. Girolamo knows he should go back to San Marco with his brothers. In the morning Pico will come to take him to Careggi, to Lorenzo, and the others. He is too impatient. He has another chance, he has the stone, and he is on Earth! He wants to shout and jump for joy. At the very least there will be food and beauty and friendship and hope. At best, he has the stone again and anything is possible. He does not want to storm Heaven, like Crookback, but he longs to break open the gates of Hell. He cannot bear to waste what remains of the night.

"Go back to San Marco," he says to Domenico and Silvestro. "I have to see the Count."

"Now? Tonight?" Silvestro asks, amazement clear in his voice.

"Yes."

"Does it have to do with what happened in the library?" Domenico asks.

"Yes."

He can feel them looking at him but he doesn't answer their unspoken questions, and they don't ask him anything else. He stops at the corner of the market, silent now, except for rats rustling through the remains of stinking spoiled vegetables.

"I'll see you later," he says.

"But you'll miss Dawn Praise," Domenico ventures.

He has forgotten, under the weight of knowledge. This afternoon feels no closer to him than all the other times he lived through this day. His last time in Hell, and before that, his last iteration, where everything changed, feels much closer. He rubs his fingers over the stone for reassurance. "Because of what happened in Santa Lucia, seeing the Count now is very important. Dawn Praise can manage without me for once."

"Thanks be to God," they murmur, and go on in silence towards the monastery.

Once he is alone he can restrain his impatience no longer. He runs across the empty marketplace and down the Via Porta Rossa. He lived for so many years in the building that he knows the trick of opening the outer door and slips inside easily without needing to disturb anyone. He runs up the two flights of stairs and hesitates on the gallery that runs around, linking all the rooms. Where will Pico be? The little study where Girolamo later lived? Or the room on the end where Angelo died, which became the Pardos' dining room, but which he knows was originally Isabella's bedroom. They have servants, he knows, he doesn't know where they sleep.

He hesitates on the gallery. He could still leave, go back to San Marco, wait for morning. It's well on into the night now, a strange time for visiting. But he couldn't bear it. He could hardly stand the deception with Silvestro and Domenico as they walked together. He can't go to services and pretend, not when he cannot pray. He needs to talk to people who will understand. But he can't be sure Pico is even here. He will be in Florence the next morning and come looking for Girolamo in San Marco. But could be at Careggi now, or at the Medici Palace. In any case Isabella will be here, and she will know where Pico is.

He lifts his lantern and knocks on the door to the study, his door as he thinks of it. It looks cleaner than when he last saw it, less scuffed. He wants to kiss it in its familiarity, run his fingers over the pattern in the wood grain. Everything is wonderful, because it is Earth and not Hell, because it is beautiful, or has the potential to be beautiful, because God's grace is hovering over it. There is no response to his knock. He walks around the corner, the shadows dancing as he walks, and knocks on the bedroom door. "Pico?"

"Who's there?" Pico calls.

He is delighted to hear his voice, and very relieved to find him here. He opens the door. "Pico? It's just me, Girolamo."

Pico and Isabella are both in the bed. Pico snatches the covers and pulls them over Isabella. Girolamo has seen no more than a tangle of limbs and her long dark hair lying spread across the pillow, all immediately smothered in blankets. "Brother Girolamo? What is it? What brings you here?" Pico sits up, swinging his pale hairy legs over the side of the bed. "How did you know to come here? What's happened? Is it Lorenzo?"

Pico looks annoyed to be woken. Yet the expression on his face as he looks at Girolamo mingles friendship and respect. This is not how he looked at him when he knew what he was. There was more intimacy, indeed, but also some contempt. A tiny part of Girolamo wants to retain his respect, although he knows how unworthy of it he is. He knows it will vanish as soon as Pico knows what he is, never to be seen again.

"Lorenzo will live until Sunday, it's not that. How I knew to come here is hard to explain. I have found something you need to see, Pico."

"All right. How exciting. Give me a moment to get dressed and I'll be with you."

"I'll wait in the study," he says, and leaves.

In the study he is almost surprised not to see his little bed and his own small collection of books. He walks around the table and admires Pico's much more extensive collection. He looks up when Pico comes in grinning, tucking his shirt in. "You nearly frightened my little Isabella out of her wits," he says. "I had no idea you knew about this place."

Girolamo pulls the book out of his sleeve. "Look at this," he says. Pico takes the book eagerly, then raises his eyebrows. "Pliny?"

"Open it."

He opens it, and sees the stone. "Oho! What is it?"

"Take it out."

He takes it out, and looks at Girolamo expectantly. Girolamo feels his hopes sink.

"You don't feel anything?"

Pico rubs it. "I'm excited it was hidden in the book. What am I supposed to feel? Feeling things when you touch stones is rather more in Marsilio's line than mine."

"We'll need Marsilio, or Lorenzo." The first time he had the stone, nothing had changed. The second time, he had remembered when touching the stone and Lorenzo at the same time. This time he had only needed the stone. Maybe it would be the same for Pico, whose second time this was. Hoping, being able to have hope, thrilled through him.

"Well they're together at Careggi. We can go there in the morning. I was planning to take you there then, anyway, if you'd come. You've always been so resistant to meeting Lorenzo." Pico yawns. "Where did you find this?"

"At the convent of Santa Lucia. They came to complain to me of an infestation of demons." Pico is still looking at him with friendship, respect, and intelligent curiosity. He is a well-made man, with a face infused with beauty, and more than beauty, Pico's own characteristic self, his familiar expressions. Girolamo can't bear to deceive him any longer. "No, I can't wait, I have to tell you everything right now, though you won't remember until you touch Lorenzo and the stone, if you even do then."

"What? Remember what? Are you all right, Girolamo? You seem very strange."

"I'm not all right." He sits down by the table, in his usual place, facing the door, in one of the wooden chairs made to his own design. He shoves aside Pico's big silver hourglass impatiently and sets the hollow volume of Pliny down in front of him. "It might be better to wait, but I want to tell you now."

"Go on then. I'm very curious." Pico sits down beside him, his face full of curiosity and love and respect. He hands Girolamo back the stone.

"This is the stone of Titurel," Girolamo says, turning it in his fingers.

"What!" Pico looks delighted. "How do you know?"

"I'm a demon. I keep living through successive versions of my mortal life, and ending up back in Hell. Two iterations ago I found this stone, and last time it let me remember, when I touched Lorenzo. You and Angelo and Marsilio and I worked together for years to—"

"You're a demon?" Pico says, recoiling in horror.

"Yes, but I'm not— I mean you well." He can't say he isn't evil, he is, by definition, as he is forever outside God's love because of the nature of his sin. "Marsilio thinks I can use the stone to harrow Hell again."

"Marsilio does?" Pico has one hand on the big hourglass.

"Not this time, last time. I haven't seen him yet this time."

"How does the stone work? Do you stare into it?"

Girolamo automatically looks down at it in his hands when Pico says that, and so barely sees him raise up the hourglass and bring it down hard on the back of his head. It gives him quite a hard blow.

The glass breaks and showers him with sand. He is not unconscious, but sits dazed while Pico ties him to the chair with the sleeves of his shirt. Then Pico, bare-chested, puts his head out of the door and calls for a servant. "Cristoforo. Bring me some rope."

"Don't trust Cristoforo," Girolamo says. "He'll accept money from Piero to poison you."

Isabella comes in as he is saying this. She is dressed and her hair is decently covered. "What!" she says, stopping in the doorway.

"Don't come in here. Girolamo has been possessed by a demon," Pico says.

"Not possessed," Girolamo says.

"But what was he saying about Cristoforo?" Isabella asks.

"He's babbling, it's the demon speaking through him, trying to set us against each other with lies. Wake the servants, if you will. Send Cristoforo in here, and send Reparata to San Marco to find someone who can exorcise him."

Isabella nods and backs out, frowning.

"I'm not possessed. I am a demon. I always have been. I only just remembered, when I touched the stone." He still has the stone clutched in his hand.

"I understand that you feel that. You'll soon feel yourself again when the demon is driven out."

"Get Marsilio," he says.

"Marsilio's out at Careggi with Lorenzo, who is dying," Pico says, impatiently. "He can't be interrupted for this. Your brothers will exorcise you."

"They already poured holy water over me twice tonight. I'm still damp from it," he says, looking down at his habit, which has tidemarks. "And we have to get to Lorenzo before he dies, if he's going to send Piero away in time."

CHAPTER 30

On Earth as it is in Heaven.

Cristoforo comes in, a big sullen serving man from Mirandola. "Fetch rope," Pico says to him.

Cristoforo spreads his hands. "Rope? Where from?"

"Don't we have any?"

"Not that I know of. Why would we? Maybe in the stables?"

"Well go and see!"

Cristoforo goes off. Girolamo wonders idly where Pico stables his horses. Isabella taps at the door and comes in carrying a dark green ruffled shirt, which Pico takes from her and shrugs on impatiently.

"I've sent Reparata to San Marco," she says.

"Stay on the gallery in front of this door, and don't let anyone come in for a little while. I'm going to try exorcising him myself." Pico has picked up a book and is flicking through it.

"Do you know how?" Isabella asks, as she goes back out obediently. "Be careful!"

"I've got several versions written down," Pico says.

Girolamo laughs. Pico spins on him, alarmed. "We just need to wait until Marsilio has time, and then you'll remember and laugh too," Girolamo says.

"If you don't mind, Girolamo, or whoever you are right now, I'd prefer it if you didn't talk, because everything you say is like poison in my mind, taking up space and making me worse, instead of better. You're trying to make me distrust my friends, and I can't tell truth from lies. If you remember this when you're yourself again, forgive me. And if there is anything of my friend in there now, if you care for me at all, if you really came in hope of my help, please be quiet, for my sake."

"But Pico I—"

"If you were yourself, you would know that never in my life have you called me Pico! It was the first sign that you weren't yourself, before I even realised how strange it was that you knew your way around this apartment where you'd never been. Are you going to be quiet or should I gag you?"

"I'll be quiet." Of course, he'd always called him Count, and had found it hard to break the habit. All his lives are the same, except for trivialities, except the last one. It is the last one he wants to build on. In the last one, where they had changed things, where they had made progress, he had learned to call him Pico. He wants so much to explain, but he is quiet. Pico writes something and clutches it in his hand. Then he tries to exorcise Girolamo in Latin, Greek, Hebrew and, finally, stumblingly in what he thinks must be Arabic, or perhaps Aramaic. None of it affects him at all. His hands are starting to cramp by the time Isabella says that Cristoforo is back. Pico lets the servant in, and Cristoforo reties him with rope, much more tightly. The fibres of the rope cut into his wrists. Then Isabella says that two monks are here, and shows in Domenico and Silvestro, each carrying a flagon of holy water. They are both very deferential to Pico.

"Your First Brother has been possessed by a demon," Pico says, after Isabella has gone. He did not look at her in front of the brothers, and she moved submissively, like a servant.

"I knew something had happened to him in the library!" Domenico says. "He was so abrupt, almost rude to the First Sister. It isn't like him."

"He said some demons are too strong even for him," Silvestro said. "But in that case I don't know what we can do, without his aid. We're so much weaker than he is. We may be in danger ourselves."

"I can write you a protection in Hebrew," Pico says.

"Oh thank you, Count, thank you so much," Silvestro says.

Pico sits down again next to Girolamo and cuts two long strips of paper. Then he takes up his quill. Girolamo looks to see what he is writing, and sees it is the biblical verse that begins "Hear, O Israel." What Pico is doing is heretical, and worse, a Jewish superstition. Nor would it work to repel demons, not in that truncated form. He wants to reproach Pico for believing it, but keeps silence. Pico pins the strips around Domenico and Silvestro's upper arms, under their habits, with the text against their skins. They smile at each other, and at Pico, and look much more confident.

Their attempts to exorcise Girolamo would have been funny, in other circumstances. At the end he is so cold his teeth are chattering.

"If it is the stone that has caused him to be possessed, perhaps we should take it away from him?" Domenico suggests.

"I touched it, to no ill effect," Pico says. "But it does seem to be the cause of his possession."

He remembers Pico last time standing before Piero insisting passionately that the stone was more important than their lives. "I need to keep the stone. It's very important." His voice sounds inadequate. "Very very important. Please. More important than you can imagine now."

They are all quiet for a moment, staring at each other. Somewhere far off, outside, a dog howls.

"What if I promise to give it to Marsilio?" Pico asks.

He is tied to a chair. He can't stop them taking it. He nods. "Put it back in the Pliny, and give it to Marsilio as soon as you can." He lets Pico take the stone. As soon as Marsilio touches it he will surely remember, and then everything will be all right. Unless, of course, the stone only restores memory for demons, in which case it would solve nothing. If so, then Girolamo would be very lonely, not just in this iteration but every iteration from now on. But it would be safe with Marsilio in any case.

"I wonder what would happen if I broke it?" Pico asks, turning it in his hands.

"No!" Girolamo says. He struggles against his bonds. "Give it to Marsilio. You promised. It's the Stone of Titurel." He can't imagine what would happen if Pico broke it. Would it always be broken, or would it be whole again next time? Would there be a next time? They had taken it for granted that there would, unless he was successful, but they did not know enough to do that. In Hell, he had been sure this time would never come. "Don't break it. We can't risk it." Different knights had won the jousts, but Brother Vincenzo had always hated him and the French had always invaded. Pico wasn't poisoned, but Isabella came back to become a Dominican in Florence at the same time she always did. He didn't have any idea what would happen next time if Pico broke the stone now, but even if Lorenzo was wrong about it being a harrow, the stone was what made him remember. "Please!"

"You're protesting so much it makes me think it would drive the demon out of you," Pico says.

"I think so too," Domenico says, reaching for it. "I'll do it if you don't want to."

"There is no separate demon! Don't break it!"

Pico sighs, and puts the stone in the book as he had promised. "It doesn't seem as if it would be easy to break. And we can try it later if necessary. After I have given it to Marsilio, and if Marsilio thinks it's a good idea." He looks quellingly at Domenico, who bows his head submissively.

Girolamo feels fairly sure Marsilio will never agree that breaking the stone is a good idea even if it doesn't restore his memories of his last iteration. Marsilio will at the least recognise it as something powerful.

Silvestro begins another exorcism. It is as ineffective as any exorcism is bound to be, since Girolamo has not possessed the flesh of another. All the same, he does not enjoy hearing his friends try to send him back to Hell.

"I hate to suggest it, but should we call Brother Mariano?" Silvestro asks at the end.

"Oh no!" Girolamo says, horrified.

"I think that means yes," Pico says.

Girolamo's heart sinks. "No, think about it," he begs. He is about to say that Brother Mariano is an enemy.

"Be quiet!" Pico says. He sends Cristoforo to Santa Croce for Brother Mariano. It is dawn now, and light is coming in. Pico opens the shutters and stands fiddling with the fringe on the tapestry of Susanna in front of the Elders. Domenico keeps praying over Girolamo, to no avail. He wonders whether he could fake an effective exorcism, quickly, now before Brother Mariano arrives. None of them can see demons. He could pretend to rave, as Sister Vaggia did, and then pretend to faint, and then come round and pretend not to remember anything since the library. But what if they then insisted on taking away the stone, or destroying it?

Before he makes up his mind to risk it, Brother Mariano sails in, full of self-importance and accompanied by two of the guards from the People's Palace. They take up positions on either side of the door. "Brother Girolamo has been taking too much on himself, as always," Mariano says as he bustles in. "This was bound to happen sooner or later because he kept risking himself."

"He was doing God's work against Hell to keep you safe in your soft bed," Domenico says. "If he has fallen this way, it is because he was fighting the demons, not being complacent about the presence of evil."

"I thought you wanted my help," Brother Mariano says. He takes off his thick brown cloak, folds it, and puts it on the table, next to the broken remnants of the hourglass. Underneath he is wearing the inevitable donkey-brown habit of the Franciscans, belted with rope.

He'd never be short of something to tie people up with, Girolamo thinks, irrelevantly.

"We do want your help," Silvestro says, frowning at Domenico. "Thank you for coming. Why did you bring the guardsmen?"

"I didn't know what to think, when the servant of an excommunicated heretic came to the monastery asking for help for a possessed Dominican," Mariano says.

Girolamo realises for the first time that there is a risk to Pico in this. One of the things that keeps Pico safe in Florence, despite being excommunicated, is Girolamo's friendship and reputation. Another is Lorenzo's friendship and patronage. With both of those withdrawn, his life might be much more difficult. But Pico is a Count, and used to other people doing what he tells them to. He is also a brilliant scholar who is primarily interested in scholarship. Even though he has already been excommunicated and imprisoned and forced to recant some opinions, he still doesn't naturally think of himself being an object of other people's power. He can't believe Brother Mariano could really hurt him. But he can. If Mariano found out about the amateur tefillin tied at this moment around Silvestro and Domenico's arms, Pico could be executed at once under the earlier excommunication. His brothers and nephew would no doubt protest, but it would be too late. Girolamo looks at the table, but there is nothing more incriminating than a cut piece of paper and the means of writing, which any scholar might have. But beside it is the open volume of Pliny, with the stone visible.

Mariano walks over to where Girolamo is tied to the chair. He bends over and peers into his face. "Possessed, you say? He doesn't look much different to me. Same fanatical eyes as ever. But no. He's lost his arrogance. What exactly happened?"

Domenico and Silvestro look at each other, and Silvestro begins to explain. "At the First Sister's request, we went to the convent of Santa Lucia. The two of us felt the presence of demons, and First Brother Girolamo confirmed that the place was swarming with them. We walked around, and he cast out a demon that had possessed a nun."

"Did you see this?" Mariano asks.

"Yes, we both saw it clearly. She was raving and prophesying and abusing Brother Girolamo. He cast the demon out in Christ's name. Then we went to the library, which he said was full of demons. He found a book, opened it, and fell to the ground shrieking. He lay there, curled up and weeping. I thought a demon had got him, and threw holy water over him. He then stood, went through a long ceremony of exorcism. He exorcised the demons, using holy water, after he found the book. He thanked me for my help."

"In whose name did he cast them out?"

"In Christ's name," Silvestro says.

Mariano sighs, as if he had been hoping to hear that Girolamo had cast them out in the name of Beelzebub. "What happened then?"

"Nothing. We left."

"He took the book," Domenico adds. "The book that was drawing the demons."

"Where is it now?" Brother Mariano asks, avidly.

"It's here," Pico says, picking it up and closing it quickly.

"Give it to me. It should be under proper supervision."

Pico holds on to it. "I promised Girolamo that I'd give it to Marsilio Ficino."

"It doesn't matter what heretics promise demons," Mariano sneers.

"It'll be safe with Ficino," Pico says firmly, with a noble arrogance Girolamo has never seen him affect before.

"As safe as it was with Brother Girolamo, no doubt," Mariano holds his hand out. "Give it to me, Count, in the name of St Francis and the Church." He puts a heavy stress on Pico's title even as he is giving him orders.

Pico hands the book over, with a guilty look at Girolamo. Mariano finds the stone at once. "What is this?"

"It's the Holy Grail," Girolamo says, to avoid having to listen to Pico stumbling through an explanation.

"Oh, so you're talking now? Tell me then, are you possessed by a demon, Brother Girolamo?" Mariano asks.

"No," he says.

"What, so you were pretending? Playing a late Carnival trick on your friends?" Mariano's voice is heavy with sarcasm.

He shakes his head. "I don't know if I can explain." It's all too clear that Brother Mariano is already licking his lips over the anticipation of seeing his body in the flames.

"He wasn't like himself," Domenico says. "He insisted on seeing the Count immediately instead of going to Dawn Praise. He never misses the Holy Office, never."

"He kept calling me Pico, when he always treats me with respect. He was almost hysterical. And as for coming here in the middle of the night, he's never done anything remotely like that. And he has never been to this apartment, and he not only came here but he knew where the bedroom was, and the study. And he said he was a demon, in so many words, and that he remembered other lives."

"Did you say that?" Mariano asks him, staring into his eyes.

He has a choice. He can admit he said it, and condemn himself, or deny it, which would condemn Pico. Domenico and Silvestro are easily led, and now, before Girolamo has acted against the Franciscans, Mariano would be happier to destroy Pico than him. The most important thing is the stone, which Mariano has and might be convinced to return to him. But although logic suggests denial, Pico's soul is much more important than Girolamo, body or soul. He nods. "I did say it. I do remember other lives, other versions of this life. I know in detail everything that will happen until May of 1498."

Mariano twitches, but doesn't bite at that deliberately offered bait. "And you are a demon?"

He nods again. "But I have not possessed anyone. I am also who I have always been."

To do Brother Mariano justice, the next thing he tries is a simple exorcism. It is the same one Silvestro and Domenico have each tried, the Church's standard formal exorcism.

"We thought about breaking the stone," Domenico says, when it is clear the exorcism has not worked.

"That would be precipitate," says Brother Mariano, patting the book greedily. "Whether or not it is the Holy Grail, it is clearly a thing of power."

"Marsilio," Girolamo mouths to Pico, who looks away.

The two guards drag Girolamo to the prison in the People's Palace. "Is being a demon an offence?" he asks on the way.

"Trafficking with demons is," Brother Mariano says, precisely. "Being possessed by one is an affliction, but you say you're not possessed. But there's no need to worry about the theological niceties, since being a heretic certainly is an offence, and what you've been saying about other lives and knowing the future is certainly heresy."

"I'll say anything you want under torture. I always do," he says. "It's useless, really. It should be abolished. It doesn't bring out the truth at all, just what they want you to say. It reminds me of Hell. You'd think the pain would be constant, in Hell, wouldn't you, but how could it be when it's the anticipation that's the worst? You'll find out."

Brother Mariano crosses himself and looks at him uncomfortably. "You are a madman."

CHAPTER 31

Give us this day our daily bread.

APRIL 13–20TH, 1492

After a week in which he is given the drop every day except Sunday, and each time had his arms put back into their sockets, Marsilio finally comes to see him. He comes into the common cell where Girolamo has been put, and the sodomites, debtors, and thieves clustered there make way for him. He has a kind word for many of them as he comes through to the dark back corner where Girolamo sat with Angelo last time, and is now sitting alone. He has caught a fever in the prison and keeps coughing and shivering.

"Oh, Marsilio, I am so glad you came," he says.

"I don't know you very well, but Count Pico said you were pleading to see me, and so did Brother Mariano of Santa Croce, and Brother Domenico of San Marco, and a man who had been imprisoned here and was released," Marsilio says. There is no more than common recognition in his eyes as he looks at Girolamo. "Of course I came."

"You'd do as much for any dog that begged to see you," Girolamo says. "Have you touched the stone?" He is hoping against hope that Marsilio has not, that there is still a chance he will remember.

"The green stone you found in Santa Lucia and say is the Stone of Titurel? Yes. Pico told me that was very important to you, and so I asked Brother Mariano and he let me examine it, and hold it for a moment."

Girolamo feels hot tears burning at the back of his eyes. He does not have companionship, not across lives, he never will have, memory is for him alone. He will have to start again afresh and alone in every iteration, and that is if he is even granted more iterations after this. He takes a deep breath, coughs, recovers, and starts again. "All right, listen. It's the stone of Titurel, and I am a demon. I remember many iterations of this same life."

"Metempsychosis of a demon?"

Girolamo smiles through his tears. "Yes. That's what Pico said last time. I am a demon, but I mean nothing but good. It's not possible to save my own soul, but I want to save the souls of others, as many as possible. When Lorenzo touched me with the stone, he knew what I was."

"Lorenzo? When? Pico said you only found it a week ago." Marsilio sounds puzzled.

He is overcome with a coughing fit when he tries to speak. "Last time," he croaks. "Last time Pico took me out to Careggi to see if I could tell if Lorenzo's glow came from Heaven or Hell. And Lorenzo was glowing when he touched the stone. Were you—" A last hope rises in him.

Marsilio looks around the cell. The other prisoners have left them a clear space, but there is nowhere they can be out of earshot. "You're raving," he says gently. "It's wrong for a madman to be in here. And you're sick. I'll try to speak to the jailers on your behalf."

"I'm not mad," he says, hopelessly. Marsilio wouldn't need to be glowing, of course. His soul was always in his higher hypostasis.

"You are, my dear," Marsilio says.

Astonishingly, the jailers believe him. (Every Florentine loves Marsilio, in all times.) The torture stops. Three days later Girolamo is escorted to the hospital of Santa Maria Nueva, where he is given a tiny white-painted cell to himself off the new courtyard. The door is kept locked, and the window is small and very high. He watches the square of sunlight move across the room. He listens to the swallows in the eaves. A doctor listens to his chest and bleeds him. He is brought good Lenten food, barley broth, and wrinkled apples, and fresh bread, all of which he savours. The second day he is there, Marsilio comes to see him again.

"Are you sure you don't want one of us in there with you?" a Medici guard asks. "He's much bigger than you are, and a lunatic."

"Brother Girolamo won't hurt me," Marsilio says, confidently. He comes into the cell, and the door is locked on both of them.

"I'm sorry to offer you such poor hospitality, but it's better than last time," Girolamo says.

"Clean, and light, and much warmer, and private," Marsilio says. "You see why you had to be mad?"

"Let's sit on the bed, as there is nowhere else to sit," Girolamo says. They sit down.

"Now," Marsilio says. "Lorenzo died in the higher hypostasis, glowing. You cannot have known that—I made sure our Pico didn't tell you. So I believe you. Also you say that you are a demon, but I do not sense evil in you. Rather you seem to me like a soul in torment. I have been reading about fallen angels. Origen perhaps, and Gregory of Nyssa certainly seem to consider that they may be redeemable. It does not seem to me impossible."

Girolamo smiles. "You are wonderful. You always are."

"Am I saying what you have heard me say before?"

"You said God could love even me."

"Aha! Did I? But you didn't believe me. What else did I say? Tell me everything!"

"First, were you in the higher hypostasis when you touched the stone?" Girolamo asks.

Marsilio nods.

"Then you won't remember from life to life, and only I will," Girolamo says, and sighs, but he has had time to come to terms with it.

"Well. Let me tell you the most important things." Girolamo can hardly stop it all tumbling out at once, even though he can hardly speak for coughing. "You and Lorenzo thought I could use the stone to harrow Hell, and find a way for contrite demons to be forgiven. Only I have to have a way to get it into Hell. And we never thought of one. But before I died again, Crookback got the stone. Don't let Crookback have it!"

"Brother Mariano has it, and I can't stop him doing whatever he wants with it. He talks about sending it to Rome, to Pope Innocent, but I hear the Pope is sick. But who is this unfortunate Crookback?"

"He's a mercenary captain. The Duke of Glosta?"

Marsilio shakes his head. "I never heard of him. But I don't know mercenaries."

"Ask Angelo. He knows about him. Crookback's another demon. But when we tried him with the stone and he remembered who he was, he said it was what Christ gave Peter, the keys of Heaven." Girolamo spits blood and phlegm onto the floor and wipes his mouth on the sleeve of his habit, which is dirtier and more ragged than usual, from too much hard use. "Then he killed you, so we never had the chance to talk about that."

"Killed me! Why?" Marsilio's eyes are round with astonishment.

"You were trying to get the stone back from him. He had a dagger, but I think you didn't think he'd use it against you."

Marsilio sighs. "How foolish of me. When was this?"

"April of 1498. So you didn't make it to sixty-six and 1499."

"Now you really have no other way to have known of that conceit! But walking onto a mercenary's dagger seems like a dangerous and ignominious end."

"You were glowing. Your soul would have gone straight to God."

"Yet here I am. How does that work, the lasting refuge of our souls if we have repeated metempsychosis in the same lives, with different fates?"

Girolamo shifts on the straw mattress, trying to lean against the whitewashed wall and cough less. "We talked about that a lot, but we couldn't really know. You thought God wanted our souls and we would all end up with him. I never interacted with any human souls in Hell, and this time I went looking as we'd agreed, and I searched through Hell for a long long time but I still couldn't find any."

"That might mean apocatastasis, the salvation of all souls, or it might mean they're sleeping until Judgement Day and then they'll be sent to Hell," Marsilio says.

He nods. "I don't know which. Oh, and I drew the cross in the dust, in Hell, but it meant nothing, nothing at all. You can't imagine the desolation of that."

Marsilio puts a hand on his knee. "But here it means something," he says. "It means something to you. Pray for redemption, Brother."

"I cannot pray," he says, choking on the words.

"Have you tried?"

He has not tried in this iteration. He tries now, and once again the words of prayer are empty, hollow. He falls into another coughing fit. There is a knock on the door. "Time's up!"

Marsilio stands. "I will try to get the stone from Brother Mariano and bring it to you. Piero ought to help me there, and Leo when he gets home. You have a bad cough. But you're in the right place, they'll take care of you here."

"Before you go let me tell you the other important things."

"I'll come back," Marsilio assures him.

"But quickly, in case!"

"All right. But be quick. They won't stand for much delay, and I want to be allowed in to see you again," Marsilio says.

"The next important thing is that Pico and Angelo must not eat with Piero in the autumn of 1494, because he'll try to poison them. And when Piero goes out to treat with Charles, I have to go with him, or he'll give everything away, lose Pisa. Or if they've killed me already, which seems likely, then Pico can go, if he's a Dominican by then. You'll have to tell him what to say, which is to tell Charles he's God's instrument, the Sword of the Lord, and that he and Florence are on God's side, so of course he'll spare Florence. Then he will.

Otherwise, after Piero runs away I expect the French will sack Florence, and that would be very bad."

"Very bad, yes, I can see that." Marsilio looks overwhelmed and bemused. "I'll write it down so I don't forget. Is that the worst?"

"Yes. There's usually an Imperial invasion too, but God will destroy their ships if we use the Madonna of Impruneta. That didn't happen last time, for some reason. I mean Maximilian didn't invade. I don't know what we did to change that. But Piero poisoning Pico and Angelo and then giving away Pisa and running away is the worst, and that happens in two and a half years."

The guard opens the door. "I will see you again, and meanwhile I will pray for you," Marsilio says, and leaves.

He doesn't come back. Doctors come, shake their heads over his cough, and give him foul boluses for his fever. He is given fresh soft bread, a rich mushroom soup, and warm wine with honey, which helps his cough. Brother Mariano comes and questions him about the future. A guard comes in with him.

"You said you'd say anything under torture," Mariano begins. Girolamo is sitting on the bed. He has not asked Brother Mariano to sit down, so he is standing under the window, leaning on the wall. The guard is standing in front of the door. He is a young man Girolamo remembers seeing as a regular at his sermons, in memories of other iterations.

"Anyone would." Mariano had been present at several of the torture sessions. "Didn't you see what they did?"

"Then you weren't telling the truth?"

"About what?" Girolamo asks warily.

"About the French invasion?"

"Oh that. That's the truth."

"And that Piero de' Medici will run away?"

Girolamo sighs. "I don't know why no one will believe me about that."

Mariano glances at the guard, and then looks back to Girolamo. Girolamo coughs, and wipes his mouth.

"If that cough doesn't kill you first, they'll hang you," Mariano says.

Girolamo nods wearily. "I know. Over a fire. But at least it'll be just me this time."

"He's mad," Mariano says to the guard.

"We all know that here," the guard says.

"But he does know something of the future if it can be sifted from his ravings."

"He always has," the guard agrees. "Did you ever hear him preach, before the demon got into him? Make the hairs stand up on your neck sometimes."

"What he said about Piero de' Medici is treason."

"Right enough. Doesn't mean he's wrong, though."

Girolamo can't help laughing, though it makes him cough. They both look at him, the guard with a smile and Mariano in annoyance.

"What do you want to know, Brother Mariano?" Girolamo says, wheezing. "I'll tell you what I know. But all I know is what happened in other futures, and this future will be different so my knowledge is of limited application."

"Who will be pope when Innocent dies?" Mariano asks.

"Cardinal Borgia," he replies immediately.

"The Chancellor? But he's a Spaniard, and some people say he's secretly a Jew!"

"Nevertheless, he'll be pope whatever he is. Some people say he's the Antichrist, or his son Cesare is. He'll make Cesare a cardinal and marry his other sons and daughters into Spain and Naples. He'll be a terrible pope, even worse than Sixtus. If you can do anything to affect the conclave and get someone else elected, that would be very good."

Mariano sniffs. "And when will Pope Innocent die?"

"Middle of July," Girolamo says. "I don't remember the exact date. News comes on the regular weekly courier one Friday that he's much sicker, and likely to die, and Leo leaves, but he doesn't make it to Rome before Innocent is dead. He's there for the conclave though."

"And when will I die?" Mariano tries to ask it as if he doesn't care, but his voice cracks and gives him away.

Girolamo looks at the guard, who he likes much better than Mariano. "Both of you were alive in May of 1498, that's all I know."

"I'll be going now," Mariano says.

"Wait!" Girolamo gets up. The guard takes a step forward and raises a hand, ready to stop him if necessary. Girolamo keeps still, standing by the bed, trying to look harmless. With this cough he really is harmless, he'd be out of breath and doubled over almost at once if he tried to attack. "Do you still have the stone?"

"I do, though a number of people have been trying to get it away from me."

"Who has been trying to get it?"

"Ficino, and Pico, and Brother Silvestro, and the Archbishop." Mariano sighs. "Who would have thought you had so many friends?"

"Not Crookback?"

"Who's Crookback?" Mariano sounds genuinely puzzled.

"A mercenary captain?"

"I never heard of him. The only person I ever heard of by that name was the usurping king of England. Not this one, the last one, Riccardo, the one who killed his nephews."

"Oh," Girolamo says, and sits back down. Had he caused that change? Did Crookback remember without touching the stone? What had he done with it? "Is he dead? When did he die?"

"Five or six years back." Mariano knots his brows. "What does he have to do with anything?"

"I don't know," Girolamo says, honestly. Is Crookback on his own trajectory into and out of Hell? Does he remember, and change things too? "If he's dead it doesn't matter."

Mariano shakes his head.

"He's been driven mad by the demon," the guard says, smiling at Girolamo as if he were an imbecile. "You can't expect him to make sense."

"Pico and the monks of San Marco want to break the stone, they think that will free you of your demonic possession," Mariano says, crisply.

"They're wrong," Girolamo says at once.

"I won't let them have it. It's safe in Santa Croce."

"You wouldn't let me have it? Just until I'm dead, and then you could have it back for whatever you want it for?" He moves forward, and the guard makes a little warning grunt. He moves back again, and sits down, looking up at them, his hands together supplicatingly.

"I don't trust you with it," Mariano says, and leaves. Since Girolamo means to take it into Hell with him, he supposes Mariano is right not to trust him. He sits on the bed and tries to think about Crookback. He was always the king's uncle. But this time he killed his nephews and made himself king.

Brother Mariano gives orders that have Girolamo moved back from the hospital to the prison under the People's Palace. He has him scourged to drive out the demon. His cough, which had been getting better, gets worse again.

Pico comes to see him. He looks distinctly uncomfortable in the prison cell. The other prisoners all beg him to intercede for them, or for money to pay their debts. He shares his purse with them, then stands over Girolamo. "I'm here on behalf of Marsilio. He said to tell you they won't let him visit you. He believes you, though no one else does. He can't get you the stone. But he says to tell you he's still trying," Pico says. "This is a horrible place. I blame myself for involving Mariano. He's investigating me too, you know."

"I didn't know, but it doesn't surprise me," Girolamo says. "Don't let him find out about the tefillin. Warn—"

"I still don't want to hear any demonic messages," Pico says. "Sorry." He shrugs uncomfortably, and leaves.

His next visitor surprises him. It is Lucrezia Salviati. She arrives when he is gnawing the last of a crust of bread old Tomasso dropped in to him. They are not fed in the prison, and have to make do with what their friends bring them. Lucrezia is pregnant, as so often in his memory, and wearing a blue velvet mantle over a cream underdress. She has come to see, and to free, one of the drunks, who is a servant. She has a bodyguard and an older female servant with her. He vaguely recognises them from the time he ran into her coming out of the Medici Palace in his last iteration. The drunk she is releasing is very grateful, and plays out a scene that could be straight from a morality play, thanking her and swearing never to drink too much again and get into a brawl again.

"You were my mother's man, and now you're mine. I had to come myself, I was afraid my husband would dismiss you if he had to come here after you again!" she says. "This is the last time I will do this for you!"

"You'll never need to do it again, mistress, I'll never touch a second cup of wine!"

As she is leaving she affects to notice Girolamo and comes over to greet him. "Marsilio told me you were here. I am very sorry for it, Brother Girolamo, and I hope you are restored to your senses and your monastery soon," she says. "Here." He thinks she is giving him a coin, and is about to refuse, when he sees the green glint between her fingers.

"Thank you, my lady," he says, and takes the stone, hiding it in both hands. She turns and sweeps out with her servants, including the grateful drunk. No one presses her for coins as they did Pico, she is part of the Florentine family, she has her friends and obligations and she fulfils them. Everyone here has their own patron to appeal to, and their confraternity brothers, and their guild. Lucrezia came for her own man, or if she secretly came for Girolamo she carefully arranged it to seem that she was performing a usual act of patronage. Was the drunken brawl fortuitous, or deliberately set up? She is very clever. He remembers her coming to him to ask if she was safe, and finding out how his powers of prediction worked to know how far she could plot with Piero. She should have been a man, he thinks, as he has

CHAPTER 32

*And forgive us our trespasses, as we
forgive those who trespass against us.*

1492–98

Brother Vincenzo sweeps in from Bologna. He is, as always, furious
with Girolamo. "You're not faking, are you? Or are you? No, you can't
be, you look positively humble for a change. Did you deliberately get
infested with a demon to waste my time? Are you expecting me to
save your life just so the Franciscans don't undermine my authority?
It's more than you're worth."

He doesn't seem to want answers to his rhetorical questions, so Girolamo says nothing. Vincenzo has the guards take Girolamo across
the city to the rival Dominican monastery of Santa Maria Novella and
has him locked up in a monk's cell there. The cell has a bed, a chased
gold crucifix on one wall, and a peeling fresco of St Peter Martyr writing "Credo" in his own blood. There is a grey, white, and black rag
rug on the stone floor. Even though it is comparatively luxurious,
which he would usually disapprove in a monk's cell, he finds it a balm
after the prison. A novice from Santa Maria Novella brings him a bowl
of warm water to wash in, and though he has to come right into the
cell to put down the steaming bowl, he won't talk to Girolamo and

seems to be terrified of him. After the time in the prison, Girolamo is very glad of the chance to get clean. The water is black when he is done. He puts on a clean white habit the novice brought. By this time his own is barely good enough for rags. The borrowed habit is too short for his arms and the hood hangs forward over his face. Vincenzo comes and peers at him, strokes his beard, then goes away in evident disgust without saying anything.

Later old Brother Tomasso brings Girolamo a clean and mended summer habit of his own from San Marco.

"What's going to happen to me?" he asks. "Are they going to burn me?"

"Pah. Except for Jews in Spain, only a couple of dozen people have ever been burned for heresy. It's a hundred and fifty years since we burned a heretic in Florence," Tomasso says. "Brother Mariano was just trying to frighten you. As long as the threat's there, they hardly ever have to actually do it."

"They burned me—" He stops. "How about Jan Hus? And Joan of Arc?"

"That wasn't in Italy. And they were meddling in politics, both of them," Tomasso says. "I remember the English burning Joan in France, when I was a young monk. Don't worry. They're just going to exorcise you."

"They've already exorcised me until I'm half dead of it, to no effect," Girolamo says.

"First Brother Vincenzo says they were amateurs, and he's going to do it right. He seems to know what he's talking about." Tomasso smiles and bobs his jutting head. "It'll be good to have you back. We've missed you at San Marco."

The next morning, they lead him into the great high-arched basilica, with its grey stone pillars, black-and-white arches, and walls that are white where they are not decorated. The monks of Santa Maria Novella lead the way in full black-and-white Dominican robes, chanting. Next comes a priest with an incense-filled censer, swinging it to and fro, scenting the air with the heavy musk. Girolamo follows in his plain white summer habit. Behind him come the monks of San Marco, followed by the Dominican monks of Fiesole, and last the nuns of Santa Lucia, led by the First Sister, who looks chastened. The church of Santa Maria Novella is three times the size of their church at San Marco, almost as big as the cathedral. It is packed for this ceremony with monks of all denominations, and townsmen, some in the red cloaks of guildmasters, but more of them humble men in work clothes. He does not see Pico or Marsilio, but Angelo is visible, in his scholar's robe, looking lost among the crowd. There are no women present except the nuns of Santa Lucia.

First Brother Vincenzo is standing before the huge hanging crucifix of Giotto. The monks of Santa Maria Novella move smoothly to the left and take up their ranks before the great frescoed crucifixion of Massacio, so skillfully painted that it looks almost like another chapel. The monks of San Marco and Fiesole move to the right, under the crucifix of Brunelleschi. The two groups, in their matching black-and-white habits, would have seemed indistinguishable to anyone who did not know them, just blocks of monks. To Girolamo they are all individuals. He tries not to meet any eyes when he is is left standing alone in a circle of grey-and-white tiled floor. Giotto's painted Christ looks down at him sorrowfully, and looking up at it he misses God so much that he starts to cry spontaneously.

Girolamo has realised that this is his last chance, and also that he has to make it convincing. The awe-inspiring surroundings help. As Vincenzo comes forward and begins the exorcism, Girolamo begins to babble in Hebrew. He has decided that the most convincing babbling, in the unlikely event that anyone understands it, would be fragments of psalms. They sound empty in his mouth, which makes him cry harder. It helps that he knows the ceremony so well, from having it performed over him so many times in the last weeks—he is never so formal when he banishes demons himself. When Vincenzo tips the holy water over him, he is ready, he falls to the floor as he did in Santa Lucia, curls up, and begins to repeat a psalm loudly in Latin "Have mercy upon me, Lord!"

The words are still empty, to Girolamo's ears, still spoken to a closed ear. God has withdrawn himself from Girolamo and all his kind. If he is to play this masquerade through, he will have to get used to it. People in the crowd are convinced, they start to call out hosannas. First Brother Vincenzo lifts him up from the ground. "It would be better if you've forgotten everything since you touched the stone at Santa Lucia," he whispers in benediction in Girolamo's ear as he gives him the kiss of peace.

"Brother Vincenzo!" he says. Santa Maria Novella is so memorable and distinguished that he thinks asking where he is would be unconvincing, so he settles for "How did I get here?"

"You tried to banish a demon that was too strong for you, and were possessed," Vincenzo says. "It was too strong for your brothers here, so I had to come from Bologna especially to save you."

"Thank you, First Brother Vincenzo," he says, and coughs. "I am not worthy."

"You're right about that," Brother Vincenzo murmurs, while making the sign of the cross.

Later, after a long ceremony of thanksgiving in Santa Maria Novella followed by a long scolding by Vincenzo, on the theme of his unworthiness, he goes back to San Marco with his brothers. He claims he knows nothing since he touched the stone. He goes to the hours of the divine office and takes his part in the service. It is painful, but not as painful as the the memory of drawing the cross in Hell. Here it is as if God has turned away, in Hell it is as if God no longer exists.

He has decided to go through with this life as best he can, as he remembers it, saving Florence from the French, making God's pure Ark and saving as many souls as he can. In addition, he will keep researching ways to take the stone to Hell, if he can, more effective ones than cutting a slit in his belly. It is going to be long and grim, and he is determined to make some small changes—like having Valori ban torture at the same time he brings in the right of appeal.

He can't think how to see Marsilio and what he should say to him.

He runs into him in the street outside San Lorenzo before he has decided. "Better if we don't meet for now, my dear," Marsilio says, quietly. "I'll come and see you when it's time." He moves on, leaving Girolamo staring after him. He knows, and he must know the exorcism did nothing. Girolamo waits for him to come.

His cough gets better. He stops wearing the hair belt, and carries the stone bound against his belly inside a plain linen band. He thanks Pico for detecting his possession, and Pico says it was nothing. But there is a constraint between them. Pico is neither respectfully friendly nor intimately contemptuous, but seems a little afraid. He sees Pico's servant Cristoforo running errands at the Medici Palace, and on making discreet inquiries learns that Pico has passed him on to Piero, on the insistence of Isabella. Her instincts for these things have always been good. He does not see her again. Pico continues to live with her. He trusts Marsilio to prevent the poisoning, and as far as Girolamo knows, Piero does not attempt to poison either Pico or Angelo. They both come to his sermons from time to time. Marsilio does not, but then he never did. Girolamo does not seek him out, although he misses him so much. He misses them all. So much of his life now is going through empty motions, saying what he remembers saying before.

Charles invades, as he always does. Capponi comes and asks him to go with Piero. He says Marsilio suggested it, and that Marsilio is a wise old bird. His conversation with Charles goes as well as it usually does. To his surprise, Piero flees anyway when he doesn't get any credit for the negotiations and the Greys start asking for more share of power.

No one asks about the disappearance of the stone. The volume of Pliny is still in Santa Croce, and he wonders how many people know it is empty. He does not ask Lucrezia Salviati about it. When she comes to see him, as she always does, after her brother flees, to ask whether she is safe, she does not ask in the name of their friends, but in the name of a favour she once did him, which she does not name. He tells her that he knows everything in detail, including her plots with Piero, but that she is safe to continue them, that she can do whatever she

314 • JO WALTON

wants and he will never move against her or her children, though he will not countenance any return of her brothers. He asks if there are any books at San Marco she wants to borrow. They become friends, of a kind, though they seldom meet. They send each other books, and letters about books, regularly. "I am working on a biography of Alexander the Great," she writes. "Do you have the writings of Quintus Curtius?" he responds, and she writes back "I do. But you are the first person to offer them to me instead of telling me Alexander is no fit subject for a woman." He has San Marco's copy of Plutarch's *Life of Alexander* copied for her.

Camilla Rucellai comes to him alone on a cold day in Advent in 1495. In his memories, she came with her husband, Ridolfo, earlier in the year, both of them asking to dissolve their marriage and take vows. Now she comes alone, and he sees her in the parlour. The wind has stripped the leaves from the trees and is blowing down the narrow streets of Florence howling like a wolf. The sunlight through the window casts a pale square on the floor, which seems to shine cold. Girolamo is shivering in his black wool winter habit. His feet are icy. Camilla is wearing a modest matronly grey-and-white dress, with a dark blue wool cloak. She has her hair entirely covered. She wears no jewels, and her thick spectacles are plain. But even dressed as simply as this she seems far more worldly than he is used to, because he is used to seeing her as a nun. She puts her hands into her sleeves for warmth after they sit down. "I want to enter a life of religion," she says. "I always did. My father named me after Virgil's Amazon, Camilla, and educated me in Latin and Greek, but then expected me to marry tamely and make alliances for him, to unite the Bartolini and the Rucellai. My whole desire has always been to dedicate my life to God."

"But you are a married woman. Your vows would have to be dissolved."

"You can do that," she says.

It's true that he can, but it's very rare to be asked. "Does your husband also want to enter a house of religion?"

She blushes fiercely. "I've tried and tried but I can't persuade him. He wants children. He wants worldly success. I know I am meant to be a nun, a First Sister, leading a community of sisters into the light, in your pure Florence." She looks directly at him, her pale eyes magnified by the lenses. "God shows me things," she declares boldly.

He nods, taking that for granted. "But you must be careful with such revelation."

"He shows you things too, doesn't he?"

"For me it is complicated now," he says.

"And have you seen me as a nun, as a Dominican nun, in a house of learning and art and prophecy?" she asks, eagerly.

"I have, many times," he says. "I will speak to Ridolfo and have him release you, with your dowry."

"I don't know that he will listen to you," she says. Outside the wind howls, rattling the pane in the window. "He says you were possessed by a demon, and who knows whether you might still be."

Girolamo raises his eyebrows. He is about to reply when God speaks to Camilla. She closes her weak eyes and leans forward, as if listening to something he cannot hear.

"Oh!" she says, staring at him. "It's true! You were not possessed, were you?"

He looks at her warily. "No," he admits. "I was not possessed."

"So what you said was true. You are a demon. And that is how you know the future. Yes . . . and you mean well, and you are making Florence His city."

"That's true," he says.

"But if you're a demon, you're damned!" she blurts out.

"Eternally shut out from the love of God," he agrees. "But though I am bound for Hell, I do what I can to help others avoid that fate."

She starts to cry, tears slipping down her cheeks under her glasses. She takes them off and wipes her eyes. "Sorry," she says, sniffing, and wiping her nose with a square of linen from her pocket. "Sorry, but it's the saddest thing I ever heard. And you know you'll be martyred?"

"Yes," he says, not surprised she has seen it, as she saw it so many times before. "I will speak to your husband. I will put the fear of God into him. You will have your Santa Caterina."

"And I will do what I can to help you bear your burden," she says.

From that time he has an ally and a friend who tries to understand, which is a blessing. He tries not to lean too hard on her support as she is gathering her little community. Everything else goes on as it did before.

He shouts down Tomasso's suggestion of a Bonfire of Vanities, and they have all-day rival hymn singing, with prizes, instead. Benevieni's clean words to dirty songs are very popular, and if some of the boys sometimes sing the old words quietly, it's not surprising.

He sees the Pardo family in the streets one day, with a group of other Jews, and is glad they are safe in Florence. He preaches a sermon on St Paul's words about a converted Jew being the truest kind of Christian, to try to encourage sincere conversion. He has heard that in Spain, where conversions have been forced, the converts are called "New Christians" and treated badly. He denounces this from the pulpit. No one appreciates this sermon, least of all Pope Alexander. Opposition to him grows, as usual.

His shoulders ache from the old torture, and sometimes his throat rasps from all the prison coughing. He is lonely. But there is breath and beauty and food and flowers and birdsong and art. He tries through reading, and Sister Camilla tries through prayer, to discover how anyone could take an object into Hell, but they find nothing. Life goes on.

Until the day Domenico accepts Mariano's challenge to walk through fire, and it all spins out of control, and Girolamo is arrested again, and taken to the cell in the tower they call the little inn. He is not tortured, this time, because torture has been abolished as barbaric and also useless, but he admits to meddling in politics.

And then at last Marsilio comes.

CHAPTER 33

Lead us not into temptation,
but deliver us from evil.

Marsilio is sixty-five years old, but he is not out of breath when the guards let him into the cell they call the little inn, despite all the steps up between the Senatorial Square and the tower. He goes immediately to the window. "What a wonderful view," he says. "The river, and the hills behind. Though it might be more interesting to look the other way and see the cathedral."

Girolamo nods. There are wisps of cloud down low above the hills, but the rest of the sky is clear and blue. The sun is beginning its descent towards the horizon, and the last sunset he will ever see in this life, perhaps his last ever. "I wasn't expecting you."

Marsilio turns from the window. "I said I'd come when it was time."

"Why didn't you come before?"

Marsilio gives him one of his gentle smiles. "Because we need to be honest with each other, and I don't think we could have been, before. You told me what you are. I don't recall any previous versions of my life, but I believed you and I still do. Lying to each other would have been bad for both of our souls. Now, however, we can be honest with each other. I've been researching how you might get the stone into Hell, though it's very strange to do research thinking I might be retracing steps I took before but don't remember taking."

"We could have been honest," Girolamo protests.

"But you went through with that false exorcism," Marsilio says.

Girolamo sighs, and gestures towards the window. "That view, or a painting by Brother Angelico, the taste of a grape, the twittering of swallows in the eaves, plainsong, or the sound of a girl singing a ballad drifting from a window, fresh new cheese on chewy bread, books I haven't read, and ones I've read a dozen times— Earth is very sweet compared to Hell, and there was valuable work I could do in Florence."

"You've helped a lot of simple souls find God," Marsilio agrees. "But have you prayed?"

"Only into emptiness," he admits.

"Have you tried praying to saints to intercede for you?"

He nods.

"I have thought that perhaps you could write down a prayer and I could speak it for you," Marsilio says.

"We tried that last time," he says. "I couldn't do it."

"Try now."

He takes up a sheet of paper left over from his meditation on the psalms, which he delivered to his brothers that afternoon. He begins to write. Unlike last time he manages to say something, though he knows God will not hear, and as he writes he pours out his confusion and anger and bitterness and gratitude and hope, filling the page with a desperate scrawl. He gives it to Marsilio, ashamed to have him see it. This is and is not the Marsilio who was his friend. He is the same essential man, but different in the detail of his memory and experience. He does not know Girolamo as his other self did. Marsilio glances at the paper, and puts it inside his robes without reading it. "I will pray for you, now and at the hour of your death," Marsilio says.

"Have they built the pyre already?" he asks.

"Yes." Marsilio smiles. "People said the stake looked too much like a cross, as if they were going to crucify you. So they sent Battista up to saw off the crosspieces very short. Now it's narrow and long necked, and with the ladder leaning against it, it looks more like a giraffe."

Girolamo laughs. "I never saw it that way. Thank you."

Marsilio nods, then looks serious. "Now. You have the stone?"

"Yes. Lucrezia Salviati brought it. I've had it safe ever since."

Marsilio nods. "I asked her to steal it from Santa Croce and deliver it to you, and no one ever suspected her."

"She's very clever," Girolamo agrees.

"The best of all Lorenzo's children. She likes you, too. She even asked her friends in the Ballsy faction not to vote to condemn you. How do you plan to take the harrow into Hell?"

"I thought I might cut a slit in my belly and put it inside," he says. "Except I am worried about that killing me."

"What, hours before the fire?" Marsilio teases gently. "Or are you afraid of suicide?"

"Last time, even though we did so much that was so different, I still ended up dying above the fire on the same day," he says. "I can't help thinking it might be what God wants, and if so, I don't want to interfere with that."

Marsilio nods. "So you want to cut the slit immediately before?"

"Yes. But they'd see, and I don't have a dagger in any case."

"And what makes you think it would work?"

"Sheer desperation," he says.

Marsilio laughs. "Well, it's worth trying. It doesn't have to be your belly. And I thought of that too, so I brought a scalpel and some silk thread to sew you up again."

"Wonderful!"

"I think the best place would be in your chest to be close to your heart," Marsilio says.

Girolamo gasps. "And that won't kill me immediately?"

"Certainly not. Infection might kill you later, but there won't be a later, will there? It'll hurt, and you'll have to keep still while I cut into you. Take your clothes right off, there's going to be a lot of blood."

He takes off his clothes and piles them on the stool, as Marsilio pulls the mattress under the window, to have better light. "It will be practice for Hell," he says,

"Really?" Marsilio asks.

Girolamo lies down on his back and sets the stone on his belly. It doesn't feel warm or cold, as it had been against his skin before. "No. Suffering under a friend's knife, for a good purpose, is nothing like Hell, no matter how much it hurts. There's neither hope nor friendship possible in Hell."

Marsilio has the scalpel in one hand, and a mass of cloth in the other. He is frowning a little as he looks at Girolamo's bare chest. Girolamo remembers that Marsilio is a doctor of souls, and though his father was a doctor, surgical skill is not inherited. Girolamo himself studied medicine at Padua, in his youth, when Marsilio had been studying Greek. But perhaps his father taught him some things. He hopes so.

"Don't cry out," Marsilio says. "The guards would be in here in a moment, and then I'd be burning beside you in the morning."

"Are you sure you want to take the risk?"

"The possible salvation of all the fallen angels may rest on this," Marsilio says. "St Luke guide my hand, St Cosmas and St Damian lend me skill."

With no more hesitation, he slices into Girolamo's skin. He blots the blood at once with the cloth. Girolamo shuts his eyes and grits his teeth and endures the pain in silence, even when the stone grinds against his ribs, agonisingly.

"There, sit up," Marsilio says, after a surprisingly short time. "I have to sew you up again, but that will be easier if you lean against the wall."

He sits up. The wound is bloody but not very large. He can feel the pressure of the stone in his chest, but it doesn't hurt. "Much less bad than being tortured," he says.

Marsilio takes up a needle threaded with a length of strong silk. "Glad to hear it. I hope it works."

"I know my body won't go to Hell."

"How do you know that?" Marsilio starts to sew Girolamo's flesh together.

"I have a different body there. But I think this may work, when my flesh is transformed."

"What are you going to do next time, if this doesn't work?" Marsilio asks, continuing to sew, his eyes on the flaps of skin.

Girolamo has been thinking about this. He knows he won't be able to think about it properly in Hell. "This time I tried to do everything as closely as possible to what feels like right. If it doesn't work, and if I am granted another chance, I'm going to try doing different things."

"That seems sensible. What?"

"There seem to be three other paths, if this doesn't work. My first thought is to try this again, only this time to walk into the fire, with the stone. Maybe dying then would take it into Hell with me."

"It's tempting God," Marsilio says.

Girolamo nods. "Yes, but God sends the rain to put the fire out. It might be what he wants. Dying that way, perhaps the stone would come with me."

"Mmm. What are the others?"

"The second is that if what Crookback said is true, if it's the key that Christ gave Peter, then perhaps it needs to be used by the Pope, from Peter's throne."

"You think you could make yourself pope?" Marsilio asks, stitching away neatly.

"Maybe. In 1495, or early in 1496, Pope Alexander offers to make me a cardinal. I could accept that, and do my best with politics in Rome to make myself pope. Alexander's so corrupt, when he dies the college of cardinals might well want to vote for someone more devout. If not me, maybe someone I could trust to use the stone for me. And if I were pope I could at least try to make the whole world pure, as I've tried to do here." Girolamo winces at the pain of the stabbing needle, and tries to hold still.

Marsilio's face doesn't show any reaction. "What's the third?"

"Well, why do I have the stone? Why me, why now?"

"I've wondered about that. You might be the first demon to be contrite." Marsilio ties off his thread and bites the end, neat as a master of the linen guild.

"If that kind of thing is the case, maybe I need to improve my soul."

"Oh yes! Splendid," Marsilio says. He wipes Girolamo's chest and passes him his clothes. The wound burns and throbs, and the thread tugs as Girolamo pulls his habit over his head.

"You think that's more likely to work?"

"I don't know, but it seems better for you. How would you do it?" Marsilio wipes his hands on the cloth, and puts the scalpel and needle case back inside his clothes.

"I thought I'd leave Florence, travel, read, try to learn something different. At the very least I'd be having conversations I hadn't had before and meeting people I don't already know."

"I have some friends in other cities I might suggest you look up." Marsilio smiles. "I can't write down their names and addresses for you, but you might remember."

"Oh, thank you!" Girolamo is absurdly touched that Marsilio, knowing what he is, trusts him with his friends.

"I don't want to burden you with too many. Let me see. There's Carlo Valugi in Brescia, Oliviero di Tadduo Arduini in Pisa; he died this year, but that shouldn't stop you! Marco Aurelio in Venice—and another Venetian, Bernardo Bembo, the poet. He might not be in Venice though, he's an ambassador. His young son is very promising too, Pietro. In Rome there's Domenico Galletti, he's an Apostolic secretary, and a Platonist."

"And should I tell you what I really am?" he asks.

"Of course you should!" Marsilio looks mildly astonished at the thought. "Knowing you are a demon, that there are no human souls in Hell now, that you have the stone of Titurel and are seeking for a way to harrow Hell, that demon souls may be redeemable—even if I can't help, and I might be able to, how could I want to be ignorant of these things, in any world, when they are so important?"

It hurts to say, but it's true. "Pico didn't want to know."

"You startled him and frightened him, this time," Marsilio says. "Tell him more gently, if you're going to tell him. If you march into a man's bedroom in the middle of the night and declare that you're a demon, it's going to be hard for him to take it in. Very few of us can be sure of telling good from evil."

"And Angelo?"

Marsilio looks sad. "Dear Angelo quarrelled with me when I warned him not to eat with Piero. He didn't go, but he hasn't been warm towards me since. I should count it a triumph, because he's still alive, but it's sad to lose a friend."

Girolamo nods. "I know. I shouldn't tell them."

"I would say rather you should be careful how you tell them. Or anyone you want to tell. Even I have doubted you, sometimes, as you seemed to rise so high in the state and gained power, and when you wanted to take the host into the flames."

"But that might be what God wants," he says. "It's so hard to know."

"How many times have you tried to take the stone into Hell?" Marsilio asks.

"This is the second time I've tried knowingly," he says.

"Maybe it will work the next time, the third. Or the seventh."

"I only have three plans: taking the stone into the fire, becoming pope, and improving my soul. That would make it five times." Girolamo feels exhausted at the thought.

"Maybe we will have other ideas, if those don't work," Marsilio says. He pats Girolamo's shoulder gently. "I'll do everything I can to help, in any life."

"Could you teach me to raise my soul to the higher hypostasis?" Girolamo asks, tentatively.

"I don't know." Marsilio looks intrigued. "Didn't I try last time? I wonder why not? Perhaps because prayer is a good part of it."

"Of course," he says, crushed. The wound throbs. "Which do you think I should try first?"

"Perhaps being pope?" Marsilio suggests, cautiously. "We know it's a harrow because Lorenzo recognised it. Crookback recognised it as St Peter's key, for binding and loosing. It seems promising."

"I'll try that first then," Girolamo says. "If this doesn't work."

"Do you want to confess to me?" Marsilio asks.

"I'm a demon!"

"Yes, but you have the stone, and you are contrite. I am a priest. I can absolve you. If you want that."

He doesn't know what he wants. He would love to confess. "I'm not worthy."

"None of us is worthy but by God's special grace," Marsilio says. "Come on now, the sun is sinking, and time is getting short."

Girolamo hesitates for a moment, staring at his bare feet on the red tiles. "I was an angel in Heaven, and I opposed God's will, knowing that I was doing that. I wanted to make a world without pain, before I knew what pain was, or free will. God is both greater and more glorious than even you imagine. How could I have turned away? How could we have imagined we knew better? We wanted a world without pain, before we knew what pain was, and instead we created pain. I thought I knew better than God. That is the sin of pride. And wrath. And more pride, always pride."

"God cannot want empty thrones in Heaven," Marsilio says.

"He sent his son to save humanity," Girolamo says.

"How many times, I wonder?" Marsilio asks.

Girolamo looks at him, startled.

"Go on with your confession," Marsilio says. "You opposed God's will. And you are sorry?"

"Endlessly sorry. I understand now how wrong I was." He shakes his head.

"What else?"

"It's complicated. I have offered communion, as a demon, and heard confessions, and acted as a priest, all the time knowing I was a demon. I knew it was wrong, but I can't see what else I could have done, if it was God's will for me to help Florence. I want to confess it, but I don't know if I am properly contrite. And if I am to try to become pope, or at least a cardinal, or if I am to try this life again and go into the fire, I can't even promise not to repeat my sin."

Marsilio nods. "Go on."

"Cowardice. Gluttony."

"Gluttony?" Marsilio raises his eyebrows.

"You were surprised last time too. I enjoy the taste of food, more than is right. I don't just use it for sustenance. I savour it. That's gluttony."

"I'm not sure it is, but I will absolve you of it if you feel it is. And the rest. I absolve you of pride and opposing God and gluttony, and as for the false priesthood, if it was God's will, it is no sin. If not, then you will know when this works, or doesn't. Give it up if you can, and do as little of it as you can, unless it is God's will. If only we could know." Marsilio sighs. "From what I hear of the cardinals in Rome, it will be easy not to perform the sacraments there."

Girolamo bows his head and Marsilio signs him with the cross. They sit in silence for a few breaths, looking out of the window. The western sky is crimson, the sun is a ball of fire, and the wisps of clouds are like wings of flame.

There is a knock at the door.

"That will be the guards to take me back down all those stairs," Marsilio says. "Well, climbing them is the price for the view, I suppose. I'd like to go to the top of this tower sometime, on a clear day."

"I've done that a few times in this life. It's wonderful. You can see the whole city, like a toy spread out on a table." Girolamo embraces Marsilio, as always amazed at how tiny the great man is. The guard has opened the door and is watching them.

"Well, good luck. Don't forget I'll be praying for you," Marsilio says.

The guard locks the door again. Girolamo hears the bolt shooting into place as he sits down. The sound is like doom, and he struggles against a sudden crash in his spirits. He doesn't feel blessed, or absolved. The stone, inside him, twinges, and the stitches feel red hot. The sun has slipped beneath the horizon and the sky is fading to purple. He tries to console himself remembering the names Marsilio told him. Friends he hasn't met yet, friends for another life, maybe. If there is a next time. Hell yawns huge and terrible between now and then. At the thought of Hell, he notices a demon lurking in the corner of the cell. It is a head scuttling sideways, crablike, on a pair of hands. Could it be Crookback? He throws his shoe at it.

PART SIX

RETURNED

CHAPTER 34

The stone is there inside him when he falls into the fire, not onto his face like good people, but on his back like the damned. It isn't there when he slams into Hell, though he scrabbles at his chest, ripping himself to shreds to try to find it, but of course discovering only a huge gaping absence. There is no stone, and there is no hope, and there never was hope, and even the memory of hope hurts. He has to face his stupidity and naïvety of thinking such a thing might work. He can neither breathe nor pray, and the full reality of Hell, when he had thought he was braced for it, expecting it, is even worse than having it come as a shock.

He knows he will be here for a long, long span, a duration, a term, like a prison term, and at the end of it there will be another iteration. He even knows there will not be another iteration until he gives up hope, but hope is all he has to cling to now, even if it is utterly vain.

There is no purpose in Hell. Everything is futile, everything is painful, and there is never anything new. Anything he does will make things worse, but the same goes for inaction. He goes looking for

Crookback, and finds him at last in a half-ruined fortified town on a hill. "We can't talk here," he says.

Crookback stares at him. His eyes are huge. "You couldn't bring it here. You have to give it to me," he says.

"I'm never giving it to you. But we have to talk on Earth."

"Unless you give me the stone, it's impossible for us to talk on Earth." Crookback laughs, jeeringly.

"You weren't even in Italy. You were already dead."

Crookback bares his teeth and advances. He flees from him, and hides himself in the sharp rocks and clammy mud where he is too hot and too cold and cannot breathe, or cry, or pray.

Later he goes back. Crookback, the great hands with a head on top, is still in the town, which now seems like a great castle. "We were brothers, once," he says.

Crookback tears him to shreds and scatters the shreds. They have to crawl back to each other from the pits of fire and tar and grinding glass shards where they were scattered. Crookback seems to have devoted a great deal of imagination to this.

When he eventually seeks out Crookback's castle a third time there is a portcullis barring the gateway and words written above the door, a quotation from Dante: ABANDON HOPE.

"I'm trying," he growls, and walks on. He does still have some pride.

He sits alone in Hell, trying to pray, mumbling the empty words of prayer, making the hollow shape of the cross, over and over, for long ages after he has lost even the memory of hope.

PART SEVEN

LENT AND RETURNED AND LENT AND RETURNED AND . . .

CHAPTER 35

On.

"Holy Father, Cardinal Pico is here," the servant says. He is new, little
more than a boy. Girolamo doesn't remember his name.

"Send him in," he says. "Always send him straight in, he doesn't
have to wait. And open the window." The room is stale and smells of
smoke and sickness and the herbs and wine they give him for pain. The
servant opens the window, bows and goes out, and Pico comes in.

They say all young girls try the family names of men they might
marry. Lucrezia de' Medici, as a girl, might have considered how it
would suit her to be Mistress Salviati, or Capponi or Tornabuoni. He
remembers his sisters doing it, with likely and unlikely family names,
and teasing each other by using them. Similarly, all clerics, however
much they might deny it, fondle a papal name, just in case. He remembers nights in the dormitory in Ferrara when he was a novice, when
they'd tried to prod him into playing as they'd offered up all the expected names: Benedict, Gregory, Clement. "Sixtus," they'd teased,
because Sixtus was still pope at that time, and everyone hated him.
"Girolamo would be Sixtus the Fifth!"

When it really came to it, he chose the name Felix, which caused a little consternation at first, as there had been an antipope Felix during the Great Schism, and so there was a question about numbering. He was Felix the Sixth, which tacitly acknowledged the existence of the antipope. He chose Felix for its meaning—happy, fortunate, lucky. It is a name of hope, and he is hopeful that this third time he will succeed at last. The stone is a harrow, to harrow Hell, it is St Peter's key, and he sits on St Peter's throne.

Pico sits down on the chair beside the bed. He is, as so often, carrying a pile of books and papers. He is silver haired around his tonsure now, and wears his Dominican habit under his cardinal's red robe. Pico is beloved by many for his books of philosophical theology. Girolamo hopes Pico will succeed him as pope when he dies, which won't be long now. Girolamo has a growth gnawing at his belly. His doctors look grave, and won't tell him anything, but he thinks he has days rather than weeks.

"I brought you Marsilio's letters," Pico says, putting down a box beside Girolamo's hand. Marsilio died in 1499, at the age of sixty-six, exactly as he had wanted. Girolamo misses him constantly, even after twenty years. He was the only person to whom he had told the whole truth, this time, though Pico and Angelo and Camilla knew some of it. He has told them about the stone, and about what he plans to do with it, and they have helped him tirelessly, quartering the Vatican library, and reading books from all over Europe. He has performed various mysterious rituals with the stone that he hopes may invoke St Peter's power to bind and loose. Angelo is dead now too, carried off three years ago by one of Rome's sudden summer fevers. Camilla is in Florence, thriving in her new dedicated building of Santa Caterina beside San Marco, with Isabella and her other sisters.

"Reading them will be a comfort," he says, putting his hand on the box of letters. He is very weak, moving his hand exhausts him. He can't seem to eat properly, and food does him no good. They bring him chicken broth and beef broth, as if he can't tell the difference between that and his usual Lenten fare. He swallows it obediently, but it doesn't strengthen him. Now he is cold again. He can see the fire burning brightly, and he is covered with warm blankets and has a warming pan at his feet, but he shivers in the draft. "Can you shut the window?"

"Reading Marsilio's letters again now made me think of something," Pico says, as he crosses to the window. He has lost none of his enthusiasm in aging. "Remember how he found things in the Hermetic corpus he thought might be relevant?"

Girolamo nods. "We tried them."

"Yes! But we never combined them with the illustrations in the Virgil, and I think perhaps they're meant to work together." Pico comes back to the chair by the bed and sits down.

"How?"

Pico begins to explain. Girolamo is distracted by the pain. "We'll try it," he says, as he has said to everything Pico and Angelo have suggested. Pico left San Marco in Silvestro's hands and came to Rome on the promise of books he hadn't read. While he winged his way through the Church Fathers, Angelo plodded through the vast number of Vatican documents that were mouldering in boxes—letters from kings dead for centuries asking for annulments for marriage beds long since cold, or begging for support for long-lost wars. Sometimes he came across instructions for a ritual, mixed in with the rest. There was nothing, as Girolamo had hoped there would be, in the ceremony of consecration. Angelo had already been in Rome as his secretary while he was a cardinal, and it was largely Angelo's promises and arrangements that had led to his election.

His mind drifts, going back to that election, years before. He is eating breakfast when Angelo bursts in, interrupting him.

"The Holy Father's dead," Angelo says from the doorway. Girolamo puts down the half-eaten golden plum from his hand, and swallows what is in his mouth. It is a warm June morning in 1497.

"Dead? Pope Alexander? How?" Girolamo is so surprised it takes him a moment to remember to add "God rest his soul."

"Stabbed several times and his body thrown in the river," Angelo says, speaking crisply and concisely. He comes in and puts a loaf of bread down on the table.

"What!" Girolamo starts up from his breakfast, astonished as he so seldom is. "Who did it? Are you sure it's His Holiness, and not his son?" He hadn't liked the Borgia pope at all, but he is shocked at this violence. It never happened before. It was always Juan Borgia, the leader of the armies of the Church, who was found dead in the river. No one ever found out who did it. Girolamo had written Pope Alexander a letter of condolence on the loss of his son, in other lives. In all the other times he remembers, Pope Alexander was still alive when Girolamo burned. He should have had another year, at least.

"I'm sure," Angelo says, tearing the end off the loaf and spreading butter on it. "Everyone was saying it in the streets. They say his face has turned black, but he's perfectly recognisable. Juan and Cesare are swearing revenge on whoever did it, but rumour says it was them. They were certainly the last people to see him alive. They say they all had dinner at Vanozza's, and that he left them part way back to the Vatican, saying he had business. The boys thought he must be visiting a mistress. Some boatman saw his body being thrown into the river."

"I should go to the Sistine," Girolamo says. A bee has come in through the window and is buzzing over the plum on his plate.

"You should finish your breakfast and contact your allies," Angelo says. He hands the buttered bread to Girolamo, who takes it and sits down again. "This is going to be a long struggle. Cesare's bound to try for it, but he's very young, and so is Leo. Della Rovere's likely, but he's tainted by the French alliance, and he'll have to get back from France. The conclave probably won't start until then. Eat!"

"What if the conclave starts before Della Rovere gets here?" Girolamo takes a bite of the bread. It's good, yeasty and chewy and full of tasty grains, not the over-milled stuff he is always being served in Rome. Angelo must have gone down to the bakehouse in the Theatre of Pompey for it. The butter is good too, fresh and creamy.

"That would be bad for the French and good for the Spanish and the Empire. You might stand a better chance. You're Italian, you're known for being opposed to simony and nepotism, and for having God's ear."

"God hasn't told me anything about this," Girolamo says.

"God doesn't show you everything, you know that," Angelo says. "But everyone knows you are a prophet. Everyone knows you want good government, purity, to build the ark. All of this bargaining and offering bribes and making alliances might seem sordid, but it really is more important than anything that you or someone you can trust with the stone becomes pope. This isn't our only chance, but it might be our last chance for a long time, depending on who is elected. I wish I could come in with you."

"I wish you could go in instead of me," he says. "You're so much better at this than I am."

Angelo tears off another piece of bread and divides it in half. One half he drops to his little lapdog under the table, the other half he starts to butter. The dog's feathery tail thumps hard on the marble floor. "There will be bribes. Lots of money, lots of promises. They say last time Borgia promised everything he had. You can do that. Don't keep anything back."

"I don't want to bribe people."

"I know. But you can't win a papal election with righteousness alone." He bites into his bread.

Girolamo sighs. "I thought he'd fall ill, and we'd have time." He can hear excited voices from the kitchen and from the street. Rome becomes like a kicked anthill when the pope dies, even when it isn't a violent death. The situation in Rome is unique. Because of the Donation of Constantine (still in force despite Lorenzo Valla's masterful literary denunciation fifty years ago) the pope is the secular lord of Rome in addition to the religious leader of the whole world. The papacy is not hereditary, much as Cesare Borgia might wish at this moment that it was. But it also isn't elective in the way that offices in a republic are elective. The closest parallel is Venice, where the Doge is elected for life but can't be the son or grandson of an earlier Doge.

But the Doge is elected from a closed group of Venetians. In theory, any man can become pope, anyone at all. Rome's alliances and connections all change with the pope. When Sixtus was in power, Genoa was favoured, and his Della Rovere and Riario cousins and nephews were powerful. When Innocent took over, they were thrown out. When Alexander was elected, suddenly Rome found itself allied with Spain and Naples. The people of Rome have no influence over who will be elected, but it will have a huge effect on their lives, and at times of election they make their voice heard.

"Well, this is sudden, and we have to make the best of it," Angelo says.

"I know," Girolamo says. He feels a wet nose pressing against his knee, and puts his hand down to move the dog aside. "Lie down, Achates!"

"Would you be prepared to compromise?"

"On what?" Girolamo asks, cautiously. The dog flops down on his feet.

"Too many cardinals might be afraid you'd clamp down so hard on sinful living that they'd be in trouble. They'd oppose you if they thought you'd insist on clerical celibacy and getting rid of simony."

Girolamo shakes his head. "Then let them. You know what the church has become. If I am to be pope, to be First Brother of the Christian Church, it will be to build the Ark, to sweep the house clean. Simony, and the sale of indulgences, and all this nepotism, has to stop. As for clerical celibacy, the Greek church allows married priests, and look what happened to Greece! But we are worse than they are, refusing to allow marriage but turning a blind eye to concubines and sodomy!"

"All right," Angelo says, putting up a hand to stop him. "How about stacking benefices?"

"It's wrong, but I'd be prepared to phase it out gradually, so that in particular cases it could carry on for now," Girolamo says. "In any case, I want to redistribute revenues so that priests can live on one benefice; there's no point saying they have to when some of them are so small the bishop would starve. They're supposed to be shepherds, but even shepherds have more to live on. The system needs to be reorganized, not just in Italy but everywhere."

"Good," Angelo says. "Now, if you can't get elected, then you need to support someone who you can trust to use the stone when he's on the throne, after we've worked out how. There has to be documentation at the Vatican somewhere. We'll find it."

"Maybe Piccolomini?"

Angelo nods. "He's a humanist and a good man. But to do anything at the conclave, to be effective at all, you need an alliance, a group of cardinals who will back you and whose votes you can trust. Otherwise you'll become part of someone else's faction. We're unprepared here." He hesitates, looking across the table at Girolamo. "Shall I visit Leo? See if I can reconcile you? You don't know Leo, but he was my pupil and you're both my friends."

"He fled Florence with Piero when the French were coming, disguised as a Franciscan. He must blame me for his family losing control of the city. Piero and Alfonsina won't attend a gathering if they know I'm going to be there." But in another life, Leo had been an ally.

"Yes," Angelo says. "Piero's never going to forgive you. He's still scheming to get Florence back. But Leo is different. He has spent two years travelling beyond the Alps, walking with a group of friends, each taking turns to lead and decide where to go each day. He's never had the sense of privilege Piero had, and I think he has learned from his travels. Now he's back in Rome, and he is sure to want allies at the conclave. If Leo's with you, then Cardinal Orsini would be too. Otherwise he'll be an enemy. Hmmm. Cardinal Carafa is a Dominican. . . ." Angelo takes a plum from the dish but just stares at it, as if doing calculations in his head. "If we can persuade Leo, we have a chance."

"All right," Girolamo says. "His father was a good man. And I like his sister."

Angelo nods. He is accustomed to Girolamo sending Lucrezia

books from time to time. "Good. Why don't you go to the Vatican now, see Piccolomini, see whoever else is there—you probably won't be able to avoid seeing Cesare, and I'll see what I can do."

He shivers, and comes back to himself. That breakfast was long ago. Angelo is dead, they were victorious in the election, he has been pope for twenty years and tried hard to purify the church and the whole world. Simony and nepotism have decreased, clerical incomes have been rationalised, and the sale of indulgences has ceased. Della Rovere is dead, and Cesare Borgia gave up being a cardinal and became a mercenary captain, and died in a duel with Crookback in Naples.

Pico is looking at him reproachfully.

"What do I need to do?" he asks.

"Weren't you listening at all?" Pico asks.

"Sorry."

"Let's go to the Sistine and try it."

They have done rituals in the old crumbling church of St Peter's, where Peter himself is buried; and in St John Lateran, the cathedral of Rome, where he has had the Florentine sculptor Michelangelo make a crucifix, and a series of marble saints, each better than the last. They have done other rituals in various corners of the Vatican, including in the splendid chapel built by Sixtus, and called the Sistine, after him. Now they will go there again and try Pico's new ritual under the star-spangled celestial blue of the ceiling, watched by the huge frieze of paintings around the walls done forty years before by great Florentine artists to mark the reconciliation of Sixtus with Florence. One of them shows Christ handing the keys to Peter. They look like keys, in the painting, not like a small green plate. He touches the stone for reassurance, and looks at Pico. He sees beyond him a small demon in the corner of the room. It is nothing but a head on a pair of hands, scuttling out of the shadows crablike. "It's Crookback!" he says.

"What? Where?" Pico starts to his feet. "I thought he was dead!"

"He is dead, ten years ago, fighting for Venice against the Emperor in the war for Milan." In Hell, Crookback is vast, but here he is tiny, hardly bigger than Angelo's long dead brown-and-white dog Achates. He cannot speak, and he is not shrieking or howling. "What do you want?" he asks, cautiously.

"You know, if you're going to talk to people who have been dead for years, there are much more interesting people than that old mercenary," Pico says.

"But he's the one who's here," Girolamo says. He takes a deep breath, savouring the ability to breathe while he can.

"But why is his ghost here?"

"It's not exactly a ghost, and I think he's here because we can't talk in Hell," Girolamo says, absently. "But we can't talk here either, not like this. I wish Marsilio were here!"

Crookback comes nearer, sidling along the wall.

"Are you sure you want to talk to him?" Pico asks. "Are you even sure he's here? I can't see anything."

"I don't know whether to talk to him or banish him," Girolamo admits. "But he's definitely here. I can see him as clearly as I can see you. He's right there, under Raphael's fresco of St Jerome."

"Can't you ask Marsilio? If you're close enough to death that you're talking to dead people?"

"Marsilio's in Heaven, that's one thing I am sure of."

"You're not glowing. Marsilio and Lorenzo were glowing when they died."

"They're saints. I'm not." He tries to pray to Marsilio in Heaven, but as always for him, prayer feels hollow, empty, pointless.

Crookback scuttles away from the wall, approaches the bed. "What do you want?" Girolamo asks him. "What did you do with the stone?" He remembers Hell, remembers what Crookback did to him there, remembers the castle with ABANDON HOPE written above the entrance.

Crookback bounces on his fingertips and then, with no warning, springs at Pico, who stands unalarmed, unable to see the monstrous form clutching his chest, trying to push into his mouth.

Girolamo opens his fingers and speaks the words of banishment as fast as he can, before the demon can possess his friend. He sinks back on the bed exhausted.

"Is it gone?" Pico asks, tentatively.

"Back to Hell, whatever he came here for," Girolamo says. "Let's do your Virgilian ritual. There isn't much time left."

"You told me I'd die before the French came, and then told me I'd be safe from that fate as long as I never ate with Piero de' Medici," Pico says, as he helps Girolamo out of bed.

"I don't know when you'll die now," he says, as they walk down the long cold corridor. He is shivering. They pass the portrait of him in his habit that Raphael did, next to the one of Pico. "We're beyond everything I have seen, except the Sack of Rome, and the ruin of Italy, and I think I may have averted that too. Pray that I have."

"I will," Pico says, fervently. "And here we are, working for apocatastasis. I had to lie and say I didn't believe in it and neither did Origen when the Inquisition asked me about it. I never thought I'd give half my life to trying to make universal salvation work."

"We've done a lot of other things too," Girolamo says. "We've made a good start on purifying the Church, or at least getting rid of the worst abuses. And your Christian humanist schools will make a huge difference over time, as they spread and each generation educates more children. And I've made them treat the New Christians properly in Spain."

They go to the Sistine and perform the ritual. Girolamo collapses afterwards and has to be carried back to bed. "It's time for your last confession," Pico says.

"Call Brother Ambrose," he says. Pico looks hurt, but nods and does it. Brother Ambrose is Girolamo's confessor, an Augustinian monk. Girolamo wants to make a good confession and die as well as he can, in case it makes a difference to the stone. He can't reveal to Pico now that he is a demon, not after all this time. "After all, you hit me over the head with the hourglass," he says.

"I did nothing of the sort!" Pico objects, astonished.

"No, of course not. I don't know what I was thinking." Brother Ambrose can cope. While Marsilio was alive, he was his confessor. He also prayed for him, conveying Girolamo's empty prayers to God. Since his death he has tried to pray himself, but never feels that he is heard. "After I've confessed, come back and read to me," he says. Pico nods, and Girolamo sees that he is near tears.

So it is that this time he dies with his hands folded over the stone on his breast, with Pico reading to him from Plato's *Phaedo*.

CHAPTER 36

And he falls, not forward onto his face like good people, but on his back, like the damned. Returned to Hell again, bereft, to wait without hope.

CHAPTER 37

On Earth.

APRIL 7TH, 1498

The trial is set to begin at noon. The brothers of San Marco, led by the Angels in their white shirts, process from the monastery to the square in front of the Senatorial Palace. The fragrance of cut boughs fills the square. Half the Senate seems to be gathered in the Loggia, and more than half the city in the square itself. A walkway has been set up and filled with brushwood, green and full of sap. When it is lit, the two monks will walk over fire through the crowd. Girolamo sneezes, and blows his nose on his sleeve. Half the brothers of San Marco have spring colds, and now he seems to have caught one too.

The women and the Angels are stopped at the entrance to the square, where the company of mercenaries Silvestro has hired for San Marco are waiting. They are an eclectic bunch from all across Europe, led by a kilted Scottish captain, Ian Monroe. He nods to Girolamo, and his men close in around the procession of monks, leading them across the square. The sky is still clear, there's no sign of the clouds that will close in with the spring storm later.

The Franciscans of Santa Croce process in from the other side as they come. The square is packed with men, supporters and adversaries alike. Women and children have been kept out, but he can see them packing the windows of all the buildings around, ready to watch the trial by fire as he and Isabella watched the joust. It is a rare entertainment, he supposes. He shakes his head. "Are you all right, Girolamo?" Pico asks.

He turns and sees him at his side, in his Dominican habit. He nods. "Just look how many people are gathered. Friends and enemies and those for whom it's just a spectacle."

"They've soaked the brushwood with oil and pitch and put gunpowder in it, to make it burn faster," Domenico says, at his other side. "Are you sure you don't want me to go into the fire? I'm ready."

"I am also ready," Girolamo says. Ready for martyrdom, or for Hell, or for whatever is coming next. He is ready to die. He has died in this square so many times, what can one more death mean? The fire will hurt, but it is nothing to Hell. It feels to him as if this avowal of faith might really be what is needed to get the stone into Hell.

"I'm sure this will bring down Pope Alexander and heal the Church," Pico says.

Girolamo remembers the irritations and delays, and is prepared for them. He times it as well as he can, half an eye on the clouds. At the last minute, Brother Mariano contrives another delay, and Girolamo shrugs him off. "I'll go alone," he says. "I'm not afraid." At last, dressed in the plain white habit Brother Mariano insisted on, stripped of the host and the crucifix but with the stone safely around his neck, he walks out confidently from the Loggia into the roaring fire. He is trying to pray, and behind him he can hear Domenico, Silvestro, and Pico praying fervently, chanting the "Our Father" as he has asked. The crowd gasps.

The fire is very hot under his feet, but he remembers Hell, where he expects to be very soon. If he manages to take the stone, then this will all be worthwhile. He feels his robe start to smoulder and walks on, smiling, one hand raised in benediction.

Girolamo makes it a quarter of the way across and is still alive and walking, though badly burned, when the rain comes, the sudden torrential downpour he remembers, that quenches the fires at once. "A miracle!" Domenico shouts, and he hears others take up the cry. The hot steam chokes him, and he feels himself falling onto the still smouldering coals. He clutches at the stone around his neck, afraid of dropping it. Men out of the crowd lift him up. He sees them, ordinary working men, Wailers, with tears on their faces, and among them the Scottish mercenary, Monroe, looking utterly amazed. "A miracle!" everyone is shouting, as Girolamo falls into darkness.

He expects to slam into Hell, so when he wakes to a cool breeze, breathing, with an arc of sunlight illuminating his crucifix, he thinks for a moment that he is in Heaven. Then he realises it is his cell in San Marco. A doctor is trying to make him drink something; he pushes the cup away impatiently. He had been sure he would die in the flames, and is confused to be alive. He clutches for the stone. It's still safe around his neck, though he is naked under the blanket. What went wrong? Pico is there, bending over him. He tries to speak to him, but nothing comes out but a hiss.

"Drink this," the doctor says, authoritatively. "It will ease your throat." He drinks it, and the searing pain of swallowing makes him pass out.

Girolamo is woken again by pain, radiating out from his feet. It is dark, and he knows where he is. Had he felt God's presence when he woke before? He almost persuades himself he did, so he tries to pray now before he opens his eyes. He finds the same emptiness as ever. The disappointment echoes through him and hurts much more than the pain of his burned flesh. He looks up. Pico is nodding in a chair, and a tallow candle is sputtering down in a saucer beside him, filling the cell with its greasy scent. Girolamo tries to speak, and again he cannot. He puts out his hand to Pico, who jerks awake at once.

"How are you?" Pico asks.

He shrugs, and gestures to his throat.

"The doctor says you have severe burns on your feet, which he has treated, and minor burns elsewhere. He says you should drink water with lemon juice and not try to eat yet."

Girolamo would like to say that the last time he tried to drink it didn't go well, but he accepts the cup and sips cautiously. This time the pain of swallowing is terrible, but bearable to his mortal flesh. He tries to speak again, and still can do nothing but make a scraping "Hhhh" of breath going out, or a hiss of drawing it in.

"I'll get paper," Pico says, and leaves, but comes back a moment later with the wax tablet and stylus from Girolamo's desk. He uses them all the time for making notes for sermons. "This seems quicker," Pico says.

"Thank you. Safer too," he scrawls.

Pico bends over to read it, and grins. "No record."

"What happened?" Girolamo writes.

"After? Everyone proclaimed it a miracle, even, at last, Brother Mariano. Your prestige is enormous. We've had half the city here asking after you, friends, enemies, the Lukewarm, ambassadors, and spies. You're suddenly everyone's well-beloved brother." Pico stops smiling. "It was a true miracle, everyone agrees. Did you know God would send the rain?"

He nods.

"So what now?" Pico asks.

He shrugs again. "Council?" he writes.

"A meeting of the Chapter?" Pico asks, frowning.

He shakes his head.

"A Senate meeting?" Pico is holding on to the tablet, so Girolamo can't expand his meaning. He hisses. It's infuriating.

"Oh, you mean a Church Council? To depose the pope? And debate my Nine Hundred Theses? And reform the Church?"

Girolamo nods, although Pico's Nine Hundred Theses had not been on the agenda in his mind. Pico hands back the tablet. "Get Angelo to write to everyone," Girolamo writes. He underlines *everyone,* and adds, "Charles of France is dead, write to Louis. All kings. All cardinals. All."

"Charles dead?" Pico asks, astonished.

Girolamo nods and waves away the distraction.

It takes nearly a year to convene the Council, a year in which Pope Alexander attacks him constantly, to no avail. His standing in Florence is too strong, since coming through the fire. The city will not accept even his excommunication or the interdict Pope Alexander tries to impose in desperation. Valori is unassailable in the Senate. His enemies in Florence are abashed. The cardinals start arriving. Emperor Maximilian comes, so do Stanislaus of Hungary and Isabella of Castille. Louis, the new king of France, does not. Pope Alexander's price for giving him a divorce from his deformed wife so he could marry Charles's widow, Anne, is that he shun the Council. He sends some cardinals along though, and England sends its one solitary cardinal. Girolamo still cannot speak to welcome them, and though it is a constant frustration, he writes speeches and sermons for others to give. His voice seems a small price to pay for this triumph. Pope Alexander writes to him conciliatingly, and he detects superstitious fear behind the words. At first, Girolamo had thought his survival was a failure, but now he battles pride constantly.

"When I was pope, it felt like someone else's agenda. This Council is mine, mine and Pico's," he writes on the wax to Marsilio, who shakes his head. Marsilio is, again, the only one who truly knows what he is.

"I wish I was as sure as you are of what you're doing," he says. "It feels demonic. It feels like tempting God."

Girolamo still can't speak when it's time to open what they are calling the Second Council of Florence. Pico is going to give the opening oration. He's very excited about it all. Girolamo has agreed to give a silent blessing. He is a little worried that things will get out of his control, that they already are. Pico and Domenico are both bubbling with enthusiasm, and without a voice he can't rein them in. He keeps the mercenary escort under Monroe to protect them when they go about in the city, though he has no open enemies now.

Pope Alexander remains in Rome. There wouldn't be room for him anyway, Domenico jokes. Florence is full, as full as it was for the Council of 1439. People have come from every nation in Europe, bearded representatives of the Greek church, monks of every order, bishops, archbishops, cardinals. Even the king of distant Norway has sent a bishop. Every bed in the city is taken. The procession winds from San Marco to the Duomo for the service that will mark the formal beginning of the conference. The streets are lined with enthusiastic spectators, Florentines and curious visitors. It is almost sure that they will depose Pope Alexander. Everyone sees the triumph in the fire as proof of God's support. Girolamo's other wounds have healed, though his feet are still tender. He wishes he could speak.

As they turn the corner by the Baptistery, Girolamo is surprised to see Cesare Borgia in the crowd. He recognises him from his previous life, where they sat on the council of cardinals together. Cesare is a cardinal now, and if he's here he should be in the procession. But he hasn't announced his arrival, and is dressed as a student, not a cardinal. Girolamo frowns and hisses, but no one pays any attention to him. Monroe and his other mercenary bodyguards step aside as arranged as they come to the steps of the cathedral. Is Cesare here as a spy? He wouldn't know that Girolamo would recognise him. Their eyes meet. What Girolamo sees there alarms him, and he hisses again in shock and alarm, trying to call back Monroe to help him, but it is too late. Cesare takes a swift step forward, and before anyone can stop him the knife he had concealed in his hand is sticking out of Girolamo's chest.

CHAPTER 39

On Earth as.

"Then could you lead Jerusalem to righteousness?" Pico asks. They are walking through the woods, near Careggi, leading their horses. Since the night before, when he touched the stone and came back to the realization of what he is, Girolamo has said nothing, done nothing, that is not the echo of what he always says and does in all the lives he lived through unaware.

Girolamo laughs aloud. "You always have the most extravagant ideas!"

"It's a real place in the world. Our crusading ancestors went there. You and I could go to Venice and take ship. I have the money, and I can't imagine a better use for it. We'd be in the city of Jerusalem less than a month from now. You could lead it to righteousness, and the whole world would follow." Pico is so enthusiastic he is almost bouncing on the soles of his feet, scattering dead leaves and bruising the wild-flowers, sending up gusts of their powerful scent. His face as he turns to Girolamo is full of friendship, and respect, and even a little awe.

"All right," Girolamo says. "Let's try that this time."

CHAPTER 40

And the Saracen's sword cuts through his throat, and he falls, not forward onto his face, like good people, but on his back, like the damned. He slams into Hell once more without any moment of respite, into the full and immediate weight of futility and despair.

CHAPTER 41

On Earth as it.

APRIL 6TH, 1492

Lorenzo de' Medici is such a strange mixture: saint, merchant prince, humanist, poet. "I wish I had known you," Girolamo says.

"Too late, Brother," Lorenzo says, glowing, shaking his head a little on the pillow.

Girolamo leans forward, feeling his back twinge at the motion. He moves the volume of Plato that Marsilio has left lying on the bed.

"Marsilio read that at Cosimo's deathbed too," Pico says, taking it up gently.

"It's good to give comfort," Lorenzo says, and Girolamo does not know whether he means that hearing Plato was a comfort to him or that reading it was a comfort to Marsilio.

"Plato saw as much of the truth as anyone could by the light of human reason, and it is good to have independent confirmation of these things," Girolamo says, as he always says, looking from Lorenzo to Pico. "But it is only through divine revelation and the sacrifice of our Lord that we can be saved."

"There is no contradiction," Pico says, very confidently.

Girolamo doesn't want to touch Lorenzo and have him learn what he is. He is so near death, and content in what God has chosen to have him know. He wants to spare him to die in peace this time. He is so lucky to have another chance, he doesn't want to mess it up again, after so many failures, and least of all to risk anyone else. He sighs and makes the sign of the cross in the air above Lorenzo's forehead and gives the blessing. The book with the stone feels heavy in his pocket.

"You should speak to your daughter," he says to Lorenzo as they begin to make farewells.

"Lucrezia?" Lorenzo says. "But what if she sees?"

"She was a pupil of Marsilio and Angelo; if she sees it she can understand why you're glowing," Girolamo says.

"I still think we should show everyone in the city and see who can see it," Angelo says. "If only Leo were here."

"She's waiting inside," Girolamo says.

"Bring her to me," Lorenzo says. "Then later I'll speak to Piero."

As Girolamo and Pico go to the inner room, Angelo asks Lucrezia to go out to her father. Her face opens out with delight, and Piero's darkens with fury.

Girolamo pauses for a moment by Marsilio. "Can I come and speak to you when this is over?" he asks. This time he plans to travel to Hungary to see if he can discover more about the stone from those who might know why Corvinus sent it to Florence. After that, if it doesn't give him direction, he will visit the pilgrim sites of Europe, to the homes and bones of saints who might have pity on him. He will tell Marsilio how to save Pico and Angelo and Florence, and hopes he will send him letters as he travels. He will visit Marsilio's friends, and try to have different conversations and do his best to improve his soul.

CHAPTER 42

There is a shadow by a rock, and he looks up to see an arrow, which lodges itself in his chest, and he falls, not forward onto his face, like good people, but on his back, like the damned. He is returned to Hell, as familiar as a dog's vomit, as strange as dancing marshlights in a bog, as real and immediate and empty and wretched as itself. He could pull out his guts in loops and string them about the landscape, but it would afford him no relief.

Crookback is there. "Curse God," he suggests.

He refuses, and is proud of his refusal.

"Curse God and give me the stone and you can get out of Hell," Crookback says. "That's all you have to do."

"Why are you tempting me?" he asks. "Do you remember, on Earth? Are you trying different things?"

Crookback tears him to pieces and scatters the pieces in distant pits.

CHAPTER 43

On Earth as it is.

He is sitting on the step in front of the Loggia, looking up at the Senatorial Palace as the light fades from the sky behind it. If he turns his head he can see the spire of the monastery of the Badia, and the tower that tops the People's Palace. Here he can see the window of the little inn, high above, in the tower that seems so light and airy, lifting effortlessly and off centre above the battlements. He is counting on his fingers, wondering how many chances God will give him. He has had many lives, uncountable lives, where he did the same thing, unknowing. Then he had a life where he came to himself, where the truth about him was known by Lorenzo, Marsilio, Pico, and Angelo, where the stone was lost to Crookback. The life after that, he discovered none of them remembered, even with the aid of the stone, and he had to be exorcized by Brother Vincenzo to avoid an early death. Then there was the life where he became pope. The life after that, he took the stone into the fire, and died by the hand of Cesare Borgia on the steps of the cathedral. The next time, he went with Pico to Jerusalem, where they were both killed by the Saracens. The time after, he travelled alone to Hungary, where he had been able to learn nothing of where Mattias Corvinus might have come by the stone, and then throughout Europe, meeting Ficino's humanist friends, reading, trying to pray, visiting pilgrim shrines, improving his soul as best he could. He was killed by bandits in Spain. This seventh time, in three weeks of knowing what he is, he has done nothing, told no one, not even Marsilio. Marsilio said seven might be a significant number, if three was not.

Is this torment? Or is this purgatorial, with even Hell being part of it? Can he get the stone into Hell and make a way out, a possible path towards universal salvation? He should tell Marsilio, and then he'd have someone to confide in. But starting the relationship again is difficult. He doesn't want the Marsilio of today, the Marsilio to whom the whole idea is new. But the only way to have his old friend who has thought about it a great deal is to start again every time. Maybe he'll tell Pico and Angelo this time too. He doesn't know what he'll do. He has come to the end of ideas. He feels directionless, rudderless, drifting. He prays for help, but God's ear feels closed to him, as it always does.

The Senatorial Palace is unbearably beautiful. All of Florence is, this whole world God made for humanity. He can breathe and eat and look at beautiful things. He can almost pray, and he can listen to others pray. He does not know how to make his soul greater, or how to purge it. St Gregory of Nyssa writes about the pains of purgatory as being like a refiner's fire driving the dross from the gold, or like cleaning mud off a rope. He remembers Heaven, remembers opposing God's will. He knows he is unworthy of forgiveness. He fears he is no longer anything but mud, with no rope under there at all. He looks over at the spot where they build bonfires in this square, whether to burn vanities or to burn him. "Thy will be done," he says, and tears spill over and he wipes them away. "Let me be seared." A boy is staring at him. Dominican brothers should not sit weeping in public squares. The first star is just visible, glimmering above the crenellations.

He stands up and begins to cross the square. He sees Isabella coming from the direction of Santa Croce. She must be going home, but he wonders where she has been. She is carrying a basket. Her head is covered and she is wearing a plain blue dress, though a respectable woman would not be walking alone at this time of day. He smiles before he remembers that he does not know her yet. She slows her steps. "Brother Girolamo? Did you want me?"

"Isabella," he says.

She starts with surprise. "How do you know my name?"

"I know many things," he says. He wants to talk to her, he wants to tell her everything, confide in her. He wants her sympathetic intelligent friendship. He knows her well enough to trust her, and he has never told her before, so it will not be a repetition, the way it would be with the others.

She is still staring at him in consternation. "Did God tell you about me?"

"It's very complicated," he says. "I know you can see demons."

Her eyes widen even more. "Not exactly see, more that I sort of know when they're there," she admits.

"We shouldn't stand here, it's getting dark," he says. Some houses already have torches thrust into sconces outside, and the taverns have two, one on each side of the door. "Can I escort you home?"

She is flustered. "No, I'm perfectly all right alone. I'm used to it."

"Pico shouldn't leave you alone so much," he says, without thinking.

"How do you know about that?" she asks, sharply. "Did Giovanni tell you about me? Did he point me out to you?"

"No, nothing like that. The way I know this is from God, or—at least not mortal. Let me walk with you."

"Will you explain?"

"I'd like to. But it's a long complicated story and I'm not sure you'd believe me. Let me walk with you in any case."

She nods, reluctantly. She has been to his sermons, and they are in public streets. Other people pass them, men going home from work, groups of young men going to taverns and brothels, a few little clusters of women hurrying home. They walk in silence for a few paces, as he considers where to start. "I remember other lives," he begins, as they walk towards the guild church of Orsanmichele. "But they're not different lives as Plato writes, they're all this life."

She thinks about that for a few minutes. They pass Verrocchio's statue of Doubting Thomas and turn down a side street. He knows the way as well as she does, of course. "So you knew me in other versions of your life?" she asks.

"Yes. In some, I helped you become a Dominican nun."

Isabella gasps. "Not at the Convertite, the convent for reformed prostitutes and fallen women?"

"You said you'd done nothing Pico hadn't done, and I'd heard his confession and accepted him at San Marco," he says.

She laughs, a comfortable sound. They are by the old market, where the last of the stalls are shutting down now. "He always says he wants to take orders one day. It's why he hasn't got married. But—it's uncanny, what you know."

"It's uncomfortable," he says.

"Come up and tell me," she says. "It's only just down here."

He knows, but he doesn't say he does. He follows her across the market and in through the familiar door. Inside the apartment, she doesn't take him to the little study this time, but into a room on the other side, where the walls are painted in red and green lozenges, with motifs of fanciful parrots. The wall hangings too feature parrots. It's a big room, but sparsely furnished. It had belonged to the Pardos when he lived here. He wonders what they thought of the birds. "Did you know Cardinal Sforza has a parrot that can recite the creed?" he asks.

"Really?" Isabella shakes her head, smiling. "Does it understand what it professes?" She lights the lamp and sets it on the table. He sees a sewing basket and two chairs of his design.

"No," he says. "It just squawks it out, without any comprehension."

"Wine?" she asks. He shakes his head. "Oh, of course, it's Lent." She gestures him to a chair. He sits. The room smells of lavender and oranges. There is a bowl of oranges and lemons on the table. She takes up her mending and bends her head over it as they talk.

It's difficult to know where to begin, but once he begins to tell her it all pours out, and it's difficult to stop. She asks intelligent sympathetic questions that keep him talking. "So there are two kinds of demons, are there?" she asks.

"What do you mean?"

"The kind I can almost see, the insubstantial kind that can't talk and can be banished with holy water, and the kind like you, the embodied kind. Is that right?"

"We're all the same in Hell," he says, sadly.

"Maybe. But on Earth, there are two kinds?"

"Yes."

"What's the difference? I mean you know how you get out, to repeat your life. How do they get out in that form? Is there already a gate? It can't be the one Jesus opened, because the world was full of demons when he was alive, swarming with them, two thousand in one poor man, the ones that went into the Gadarene swine."

"I have no idea how they get out in their insubstantial form. I've never done that when I'm in Hell," he says, intrigued. He has never thought about it before.

"Have you seen the same demons here and there?" she asks.

"There's Crookback," he says. "I've seen him here embodied as a man, and here as a demon, and also there as a demon. He— I need to talk to him, but I can't see how. We can't talk in Hell, and the times I saw him here as a demon of course we couldn't talk."

"Can you talk to him when he's embodied?"

"I don't even know whether he's an Italian mercenary or the King of England this time. And the one time we tried with him and the stone it was a disaster," he says, and tells her about it, which leads to telling her more about his other lives and failed attempts to get the stone into Hell.

"But in all those lives you've never earned your living," she says at last.

It hadn't even occurred to him that he hasn't. "No. I never have."

"But you could," she says, assessingly. "You could work as a copyist, or a secretary, or a translator."

"I suppose I could. If I leave San Marco."

"I think you should. You don't think it's right to stay a priest, knowing you're a demon. And since you've come to me for advice, I think you should try to lead a normal life. An ordinary life, I mean, one where you're not a prophet or a pope or anything. That might be good for your soul. It seems to me you've read every book that might help, in all those lives."

"Either that or Pico or one of the others read it for me," he agrees. "But what about Florence? What about the world?"

"Leave it to look after itself. When you were pope you saved a lot more people, but you don't think you should be doing that every time," Isabella says.

"No, but my life in San Marco is the one that feels right, that I repeated every time I didn't know what I was."

"And if you're not here, Florence won't be spared by the Sword of the Lord?"

"If I'm not here and I don't explain to someone else how to do it," he says.

"But maybe that's what God wants, for Florence to be sacked then. Maybe it would avert something worse later," she says. "Or maybe Giovanni will think of it for himself, or think of something even better for Florence, if you don't interfere."

"I don't know. It's so hard to know what God wants!"

"Yes, isn't it?" she agrees. "But you're not God, and you *don't* know what God wants. You say you're trying to make your soul better. Leaving the world to get on with it without your demonic prophecies and living an ordinary life like ordinary people is something you haven't ever tried."

"Yes, maybe I should try that. But I wouldn't know where to start."

"You'd want to be somewhere they don't know you, and out of the way of all the armies, and somewhere big enough they want books copied," she says. "If I were you, I'd try Venice. You've never been there, have you?"

"I've passed through it, but never stopped for long," he says. He feels a little of the same exhilaration he felt telling Pico he'd go to Jerusalem. He thinks of the canals, and the tall palaces with their air of looking East to Greece and the Ottomans, not West to Europe.

She bites off a thread. "You'd be as helpless as a baby," she says. "It seems to me I'd better come with you."

"You! But—" He remembers the sensual beauty of her loose hair, on the road to Genoa, and the time he had burst into the bedroom.

"I know how to do all the practical things you don't, how to find somewhere to live and make sure there's food on the table. And I could pray for you, offer up your prayers the way you said I thought of before, and that Marsilio Ficino did for you. From what you're saying, it seems I have another two years of Giovanni before either Piero kills him or he takes vows. It's hard to give that up, but—it's only this time, isn't it? I know that now. And if he takes vows, then at least he'll be alive, even if I never see him. I love him, but I'm lucky to have had as much of him as I have, a man like him, and a girl like me. I could barely read when we met. I'm a bean seller's daughter."

"I will have to get released from my vows, the solemn release, so that I can marry," Girolamo says.

"Marry!"

Girolamo blushes; he feels his cheeks burning hot. "I'm sorry. Were you thinking to come as my housekeeper?"

"I'm soiled goods," she says.

He shrugs, still blushing fiercely. "That doesn't matter. I've virginity enough for both of us."

Isabella laughs, and puts her hand over her mouth to stifle it.

"And I'm not even human," he goes on. "You'd be honouring me. But you said a normal life, an ordinary life, so I thought you meant—"

"I don't know what I meant," she says, looking down.

"You love Pico."

"I do," she says. "And he's fond of me too. But I can't stand in his way of going to God."

"I wouldn't want to stand in yours," Girolamo says.

"Christian marriage serves God too," she says, though she is still not looking at him. "And I really could help you, and if it did help with the big thing, with the stone, with apocatastasis."

He is surprised she remembers the word, and then not surprised. Pico had been made to recant on that point by the Inquisition, though it wasn't truly heretical. He had probably talked to her about it. Or she might have read about it on her own. He has a lot to learn about her. He consistently underestimates her. "Yes. You can help with my soul."

"And it won't do any harm to my own," she says, with a little smile.

"And maybe we could have a dog," he says.

She laughs. He likes her laugh. "A dog?"

"Angelo had a little brown-and-white dog with a feathery tail when we lived in Rome. He was called Achates. I've never had a dog. It seems the kind of thing ordinary people have."

"Then we'll have a dog, and a cat, and maybe later a baby," Isabella says.

"I must inquire about giving up my vows. It'll take months, and it'll take months at least for Pico to be ready to go into San Marco. And I should tell Marsilio."

"I don't know. He'd want to try things, wouldn't he, Platonic things, things that would get in the way of you leading an ordinary life. Having a friend like that who knew would make it too special."

"But—he said he always wants to know, to know for sure the things he only guesses," he explains.

"Then tell him, but tell him you're going to try an ordinary life without any meddling," she says, licking the thread to rethread her needle. "And when we go to Venice, we needn't give him our address."

"I suppose you're right," Girolamo says, and as he says it the door bursts open, and there is Pico.

"Did you—" he begins, and stops. "Girolamo! What are you doing here?"

"Girolamo tells me you're going to become a Dominican," Isabella says, setting her needle carefully into the hood she is mending.

"I was intending to tell you," he says. He comes into the room properly and closes the door.

"That's all right. Because just as you're taking your vows, which you need to do quickly to avoid the death Girolamo saw for you, Girolamo's going to be getting a dispensation to lay his down, and we're going to get married."

Pico's face goes through a number of expressions very rapidly, passing through surprise, chagrin, and anger, before settling on delight. "I don't quite understand, but I'm very happy for both of you," he says. "I hope you'll allow me to dower you properly, Isabella."

CHAPTER 44

And once more he falls, not forward onto his face like good people, but on his back, like the damned. He slams into Hell and lies there, looking up into murky suffocating darkness. He cannot bear to think of Isabella, or their children, or the agonising death of their grandson, or the prayers she has faithfully passed on to God for him every day for thirty years. Because he cannot bear it, he cannot think of anything else. His children and grandchildren are gone, erased as if they had never been. He will never see them again, even if he is granted another iteration, and he cannot believe that he will be. He died in his little house on the edge of the canal beside his printshop, with the smell of the brackish water in his nostrils and the stone in his hands. He was praying, with Isabella echoing his prayer. He imagined in his last moments that God did hear, that his ear was opened at last. But it was a false hope, because here he is in Hell with all of it snatched away, impossible, forever out of reach. He knows that must have been his last chance, that this time he will stay in Hell forever, without Isabella, or his children, or the stone, forever without God.

And the torment of having all of it snatched away is Hell. This is what it means to be damned.

CHAPTER 45

On Earth as it is in.

The ropes sing and the sails crack, and the *Santa Maria* makes her way out of the harbour of Palos de la Frontera. Girolamo tastes salt spray on his lips as the ship comes about.

They say Columbus is mad, that Asia is twice as far away as he believes, but Girolamo knows he will find new lands, lands where he will know no one and no one will know him, where even the name of God is strange. When he was pope they asked him to bless the conquests made in the new lands, and to send priests to convert the heathens that they found, and after he read the book of his fellow Dominican Las Casas, he tried to regulate their interactions. He can't bear to repeat his life anymore, to start again with his friends, to speak to Isabella and have her reply as a stranger, to go through the explanations, to fail and fail and fail again. Anywhere in Europe he will meet people he knows, not every day but from time to time. Here there will be no one he knows.

The men on the ships are mostly Spaniards, though he is not the only Italian. They are all strangers. It was not easy to persuade Columbus to take him. He says he has no need for a chaplain, and he can keep records himself. It is Girolamo's total belief that sways him, reinforcing his own belief that if he sails West into the open ocean he will find *something*.

Girolamo does not know what will happen to him in the New World. He does not know very much about the people or cultures he will encounter, whether they will be friendly or unfriendly. He prays as he stands at the rail to God and the Holy Virgin and all the saints, and does not know whether they hear him or not. He stands there for hours, though the spray soaks his face as they sail out into the open ocean. He prays to Lorenzo to intercede for him in Heaven, and he cannot tell whether the salt water on his face is the sea or his tears.

CHAPTER 46

And falling, not forward onto his face like good people, but on his back, like the damned, he slams into Hell once more. Crookback is waiting for him. "Where were you?" he taunts.

"La Navidad," he says. It is the name of the settlement in Hispaniola where he died of fever among bloodthirsty Spanish soldiers and bewildered and brutalized locals, after a mere year on Earth this time. The name means the Nativity, and saying it here fills him with anguish. "Just do your worst," he says, and closes his eyes. Nothing happens. He opens them again. Crookback is still there, a huge head on a giant pair of hands, like a monstrous spider. He has raised a room around them, an immense parody of Marsilio's room in the Medici Palace, but the size of a cathedral. The books are the size of great church Bibles, and the lamp, which set the place on fire the time when Crookback visited, is the size of a fishing boat.

"Are you going to give me the stone?" Crookback asks, peering down at him.

Girolamo stays where he is on the floor. "No. I gave it to you once and you got us all killed." Defiance is pointless, but so is everything else.

"What's the point of haring off to the ends of the world, or hiding in Venice with your . . . woman, when you have the one thing that can change everything?" Crookback makes a sound of frustration and rips Girolamo in half. Girolamo waits for a moment, to see whether Crookback will dissect him further, but when he does not, he drags his two severed halves together and completes himself again.

"We need to talk on Earth," he says, when he can speak.

"I went to talk to you, but you weren't even there," Crookback snarls.

"I won't give you the stone. But I'll be there. I'll talk to you if I can."

"You don't bloody have to do everything yourself. Who do you think you are, so puffed up with pride?" Crookback says. "Stop trying to control everything as if you're king of the world."

Although he has been in Hell for only moments, he feels himself already being drawn out of it, out and up to another iteration.

CHAPTER 47

On Earth as it is in Heaven.

MAY 22ND, 1498

This whole life has been an echo, where everything he says has the weight of all the times he said it before. He has changed very little. He even went to Bologna to give the Lenten sermons, which he has never done since he remembered what he was. Two weeks before Piero poisoned Pico and Angelo, he gave a sermon on the text from Exodus, "Thou shalt not suffer a poisoner to live," in which he not only condemned poisoning but talked about different poisons in detail and the symptoms of arsenical poisoning. He wasn't sure it would work to stop Piero, but he only had to delay him. He didn't think Piero was stupid enough to poison his friends while everyone was talking about poison, but it was still taking a risk. He was very glad to be right. He also tried to stop Capponi leading the army to Pisa, but with no success. Capponi went, and died, as always. He did manage to abolish torture, but they tortured him anyway.

The other difference, this time, is that he has prayed. He does not know whether God hears him, or the saints he names, but he no longer feels that God's ear is infallibly blocked. He prays to Lorenzo daily. He thinks, he hopes, there may have been a miracle.

He is sitting in the cell they call the little inn, high in the tower of the Senatorial Palace, waiting. His last book has been written, the meditation on the psalms, and if he wrote it from memory it was none the worse for that. His shoulders ache fiercely from where the torture dislocated them, but he almost welcomes the natural, Earthly pain. He takes a deep breath, and lets it out again slowly. The next morning they will hang him over the fire, and he will fall back into Hell. He strokes the stone with his fingers. He knows no way to take it with him. He never has. He looks over to where Crookback is lurking in the corner of the cell.

The comforters come and pray with him. He has not forgotten how sententious they are. He thinks of the night he spent with Angelo in the dungeon of the People's Palace, the night Pico read to him in Rome, the night in Venice with Isabella and his children and grandchildren clustered around the bed, the surprise of Cesare's dagger blossoming in his chest. He seems to be always dying and falling hard into Hell.

The comforters explain about Domenico and Silvestro, and he asks to see them. "When you inquire," he says, "tell them that if they want an orderly execution, it would be better for me to have the chance to restrain my brothers. Otherwise, either of them might take the opportunity to make a speech and stir up the people, doing their best to start a riot and rob the occasion of all its dignity."

The eyes of the comforters meet beneath their hoods.

"I'll tell them," the taller one says, and goes out, leaving him alone with the shorter one.

At once, Crookback comes scuttling out of the shadows, sideways like a crab. The comforter has his back to the demon, but he wouldn't have seen him anyway. Girolamo is kneeling, reciting a psalm, but he stops praying as Crookback comes out. He could stop him and banish him even now, but he holds back. He understands this time that he wants to possess somebody so they can talk. Crookback leaps for the comforter and dives down his throat.

"Give me the stone," he says, through the comforter's mouth.

"What are you going to do with it?" he asks.

"I'm going to take it into Hell and make a gateway out, of course, you ninny."

"We were brothers," he says, as he said once in Hell, as Crookback said once to him in Ficino's room. He remembers Michael's face, and Raphael's, angels experiencing pain for the first time as pain came into being because of what he had done.

"Yes. And there isn't much time." The comforter's arms move awkwardly and his eyes have rolled up, showing the whites.

"Do you remember Heaven?"

"Yes! And if you get a move on and give me the stone there's a chance we can get back there someday, when we're purified enough. You can't do this alone, Asbiel, and I can't either. You have to trust me. Hell is always divided against itself. If we can do this together—that's what it's impossible to say in Hell!"

"The house divided against itself cannot stand, that means Hell cannot stand," Girolamo says.

"Let's bring it down, brother."

"You said you were going to storm Heaven," Girolamo says, still hesitating, though he hears the feet of the other comforter on the stairs, returning.

"Do you belive you are the only one who can learn from lifetimes here and in Hell?" Crookback slithers out from between the comforter's lips. The man slumps to his knees. The demon scurries forward to where Girolamo kneels. As he hears the key in the lock, he reaches into his clothes and pulls out the stone. Crookback takes it between two of his demonic finger-legs, and vanishes.

The short comforter staggers to his feet as his companion comes in. Girolamo doesn't know what he saw or what he remembers. He says nothing, as Girolamo goes through the usual words, and they take him down the long twisting stairs in the dark, to the chapel where Silvestro and Domenico are waiting. This time when he celebrates the mass, when he performs the miracle of the eucharist, he does not feel it is a blasphemy. He has tears on his cheeks, but then he always did.

In the morning light, outside in the Senatorial Square, they strip him of his habit, piece by piece. Brother Benedetto, the bishop of Vasona in full bishop's regalia with his mitre, cope, and crook, formally excommunicates him. "I cast you out of the Church Militant and the Church Triumphant!" he says.

"You can do the first," he says, as he always says. The Church Militant is the congregation of the faithful on Earth. The Church Triumphant is the congregation of saints in Heaven. "You don't have the power to do the second."

"Oh, sorry," murmurs Benedetto, flushing, as if he were still one of Girolamo's monks in San Marco. Girolamo wishes he had taught him better when he was. He hates sloppy theology. Girolamo is proclaimed a heretic, and handed over to the civil authorities, the Eight, who are standing in line, in their red robes. He is sentenced to death by hanging. They will be hanged over the fire, and afterwards their bodies will be burned, to make sure there are no remains that the poor Wailers can use for relics.

They are marched out individually, each of them in white, with a comforter in black close on either side. Silvestro is first, then Domenico. Girolamo goes last. The stake, with its crosspieces cut short and the ladder leaning against it from the circle of the piled-up pyre, doesn't really look like a giraffe, but Girolamo smiles to himself thinking of it.

Every time he walked out unknowing from the palace, over the built-up trestles, towards the fire, he had thought he was going to martyrdom, that he would die for one moment and then live forever at God's side. Now he knows what he is, that he is a demon, and that Heaven is still very far away, but possible, perhaps, if he was right to trust Crookback. Silvestro goes up. He calls on Jesus as he falls, but does not make a speech. The square is full of people, both supporters and enemies. Girolamo was right to do his best to prevent a riot. Domenico also calls on Jesus, once, loudly. Then it is Girolamo's turn. The comforters release his arms, and he climbs. From the top of the ladder that leans on the stake, with the noose around his neck, he sees his shadow falling on the upturned faces crowding below. He looks up. He can see Brunelleschi's dome for the last time in this life, huge but elegant, lifting his heart every time he sees it, even now. He tries to keep his eyes fixed on it, but the rope twists as he falls, and he sees the tower of the People's Palace, with the red-tiled roofs of homes of ordinary Florentines in between.

CHAPTER 48

Our Father, Who Art in Heaven.

Girolamo falls forward, onto his face, like good people. The Gates of Hell have been opened.

ACKNOWLEDGEMENTS, THANKS, AND NOTES

There is a painting in San Marco in Florence, done in 1500, two years after the events it depicts. It shows the death by burning of Savonarola, in the square of the Palazzo Vecchio, on the very spot where he held the Bonfire of the Vanities. It wasn't that that caught my attention the first time I saw it. It was the fact that above the painting is a scroll, supported on either end by an angel. This is the kind of scroll you often see, bearing the title of the painting. This scroll is blank. It doesn't say "The Martyrdom of St Girolamo Savonarola" or alternatively "The burning of the heretic Girolamo Savonarola" it was more like the angels were hovering over Florence with a scroll proclaiming "Nope, I've got nothing." The two real starting points for this book are Fra Angelico's *Harrowing of Hell* and Ficino's 1498 letter about Savonarola, in which Ficino explains to the Inquisition that Savonarola was a demon but didn't know. But it was that empty scroll that really started me thinking about him.

I have chosen to use English words when I can, to give the kind of clarity lost by keeping terms in Italian—thus Senatorial Palace,

Mercenary Captain, First Brother, instead of Palazzo della Signoria, condottiore, Prior. Similarly I am using Florence rather than Firenze. The reason for this is that unknown words lend distancing and exoticising. Sometimes you want that, here I wanted to minimize it as much as possible. The Signoria isn't precisely a senate, but it's not some weird unique thing either. They thought of themselves as being just like the senate of Ancient Rome. Maya Chhabra helped with getting Italian names right.

I have also simplified things—Fra Angelico's name was Guido di Piero, Angelico was a nickname. Similarly, Leo's name was Giovanni. Leo was a nickname before he chose it as his papal name. Ten percent of men in Florence in the period were called Giovanni, because John the Baptist was Florence's patron saint. I have tried to simplify this by using Gianni for Giovanni di Pierfrancesco de' Medici, Gio for Lucrezia Salviati's son, Johannes for Bentivoglio, and sticking with surnames as much as possible. If you see "Giovanni" generally you know it means Pico. I have left out tons of people to keep the cast of characters possible to manage. I have also simplified the description of how the government of Florence worked before Savonarola's reforms—the senate wasn't always seventy, it was of different sizes at different times, and there were other councils, and it's all more complex than you can possibly imagine. The utterly strange system of drawing eight names from a purse and shutting the chosen men into the palace for two months where they rule the state from splendid isolation is what they really did. It's no weirder than other procedures republics have chosen to attempt to prevent tyranny. Savonarola's sermons on political reform survive.

If you want to know more about the historical Savonarola, much of his writing is in print. I recommend the biographies by Donald Weinstein and Lauro Martines. Many biographies tend to take sides very strongly, and try to set up a situation with heroes and villains. I think this is a problem with general knowledge of Savonarola too. It's very odd. Many people who think he's a "mad monk" who burned books are astonished to learn that he was a close friend of Pico's. The

Bonfire of the Vanities is the one thing most people know about Savonarola. It really was more like Burning Man than book burning—a joyful celebration with art set on fire. The goal was never to destroy knowledge—there were books on the pyre, but they were not unique copies of anything, and the vast majority of them were put there by their owners. The way I describe it in the first iteration is directly from firsthand accounts of diarists who were there.

The historical Savonarola is not officially a saint, partly because he has been erroneously claimed as a predecessor of Protestantism (a thing that would have appalled him, he'd have been horrified at the thought of salvation through faith alone), partly because the Church doesn't like to admit it was wrong, and partly because the last attempt to clear his name took place in the 1930s under Mussolini. If he were a saint, he'd be a great patron saint of people who finish writing their books in time for deadlines despite hand pain, because he wrote his meditation on the psalms on top of the Palazzo Vecchio after he'd been tortured. Raphael painted him in Heaven in the *Disputa,* and Raphael ought to know.

In the universe of this novel, our history is the iteration before the one in which Girolamo first found the stone.

There are photo essays and bibliography for this book on my website, www.jowaltonbooks.com.

Mary Lace read the book and was appreciative while it was being written. After it was done, I had helpful feedback from Suzanna Hersey, Susan Palwick, Hannah Dorsey, Marissa Lingen, Elaine Blank, Brother Guy Consolmagno, Sherwood Smith, Ada Palmer, Doug Palmer, Patrick and Teresa Nielsen Hayden, and Emmet O'Brien. I want to thank everyone at Tor for working so hard to bring my very different books to the people who will enjoy them, and especially Edwin Chapman for an excellent copy edit. I also want to thank my readers, whose enthusiasm makes it all worthwhile, and especially my Patreon backers, whose help allowed me to spend June of 2017 in Florence working on this book.

Ada Palmer first invited me to Florence and introduced me to its history; she continued to be helpful when I became fascinated and fell down the rabbit hole of research. All errors are of course my own. Carter Hall came all the way up to the top of the Palazzo Vecchio and graciously hung out for longer than he might have wanted in Savonarola's cell. Niall Atkinson's *The Noisy Renaissance* was invaluable, and I'd like to thank Niall also for graciously including me on some expeditions around Florence. Thanks especially to Perché No! for all the wonderful gelato.